The Br

Book Two

Templar Stone

By

K. M. Ashman

Copyright K M Ashman 2019

All rights are reserved. No part of this publication may be reproduced, stored or transmitted in any form, or by any means, without prior written permission of the copyright owner.

All characters depicted within this publication are fictitious and any resemblance to any real persons living or dead is entirely coincidental.

More books by K M Ashman

The India Sommers Mysteries
The Dead Virgins
The Treasures of Suleiman
The Mummies of the Reich
The Tomb Builders

The Roman Chronicles
The Fall of Britannia
The Rise of Caratacus
The Wrath of Boudicca

The Medieval Sagas
Blood of the Cross
In Shadows of Kings
Sword of Liberty
Ring of Steel

The Blood of Kings
A Land Divided
A Wounded Realm
Rebellion's Forge
Warrior Princess
The Blade Bearer

The Brotherhood
Templar Steel – The Battle of Montgisard
Templar Stone – The Siege of Jacob's Ford

(Coming Soon)
Templar Blood – The Battle of Hattin
Templar Fury – The Siege of Acre
Templar Glory – The Road to Jerusalem

Standalone Novels
Savage Eden
The Last Citadel
Vampire

Audio Books
Blood of the Cross
The Last Citadel
A Land Divided
A Wounded Realm
Rebellion's Forge
The Warrior Princess

MAP OF THE HOLY LAND

(Circa AD 1179)

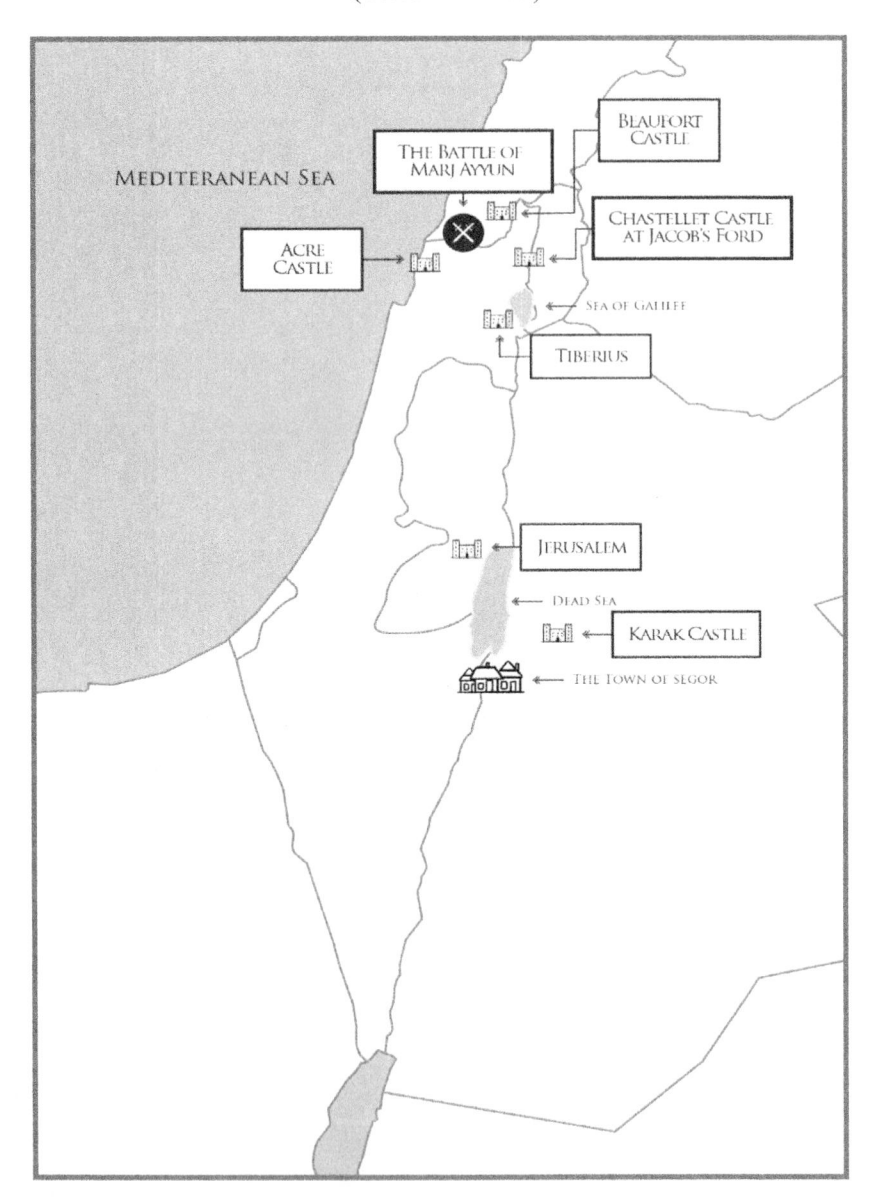

CHARACTER LIST

Aristocracy
Baldwin IV - King of Jerusalem
Humphrey II – Lord of Toron
Raymond III – Count of Tripoli
Raynald of Chatillon – Regent of Jerusalem
Reginald of Sidon – Lord of Sidon

Clergy
William of Tyre – Catholic prelate – King Baldwin's advisor

Christian Forces
Eudes de St. Amand – 8th Grand Master of the Knights Templar
Brother Tristan - Marshal of the Templar Order
Brother Valmont of Lyon - Seneschal of the Templar Order
Jakelin de Mailly - French Templar Knight
Sir Simon of Syracuse – Templar Knight – Castellan of Castle Chastellet
Rénier de Maron – Under-Marshal of Castle Chastellet
Thomas Cronin - Sergeant at Arms
James Hunter - Scout
Hassan Malouf - Bedouin Squire
Arturas – Mercenary Leader

Muslim Forces
Salah ad-Din (Saladin) – Sultan of Egypt and Syria
Farrukh-Shah – Saladin's nephew
Shirkuh ad-Din - Saladin's General
Sabek ad-Din – Saladin's General
Bakir-Shah – Mamluk Commander

Templar Stone

Prologue

In November AD 1177, the Ayyubid sultan, Salah ad-Din, led an invasion force of over twenty-five thousand men from Egypt into the kingdom of Jerusalem. His target was to take the city and return it to Muslim hands after seventy-seven years of Christian occupation.

Following the collapse of an alliance between Phillip of Alsace and the Byzantine Empire, and realising that the main Christian army was campaigning far to the north, Saladin seized his chance and rode northward from Egypt, besieging the city of Gaza on the way and laying waste to the Christian lands along the coast of the Mediterranean.

In Jerusalem city, the young King Baldwin, a sixteen-year-old boy plagued with leprosy, gathered the remains of his forces and rode south to meet Saladin to stop his advance. With his main army unavailable, Baldwin issued an Arriere Ban, a general call to arms to all Christians in the area.

Eventually, Baldwin mustered his forces in Ashkelon, but the Sultan had eyes on the greater prize, and while part of his forces kept Baldwin penned inside the city, his main army headed for Jerusalem itself.

When Baldwin realised what was happening, he and his army, supported by the Knights Templar from Gaza, broke the siege and headed north to cut off Saladin's advance.

They finally met in battle at a place called Montgisard and despite being vastly outnumbered, the Christian forces emerged victorious after being led into battle by the eighty Templar knights.

Saladin barely escaped with his life and had to flee back to Egypt on a racing camel. Most of his army either died at Montgisard or were hunted down and killed on their way back to Egypt by Baldwin's men and Bedouin tribesmen.

Very few survived yet Saladin managed to reach Egypt alive and proceeded to rebuild, not just his reputation but his vast army. The defeat at Montgisard had been devastating, and he wanted revenge.

Chapter One

The Dead Sea Coast

December - AD 1177

The cave wasn't very big, perhaps enough for ten men to lie side by side if needs be, and the low ceiling meant nobody could stand upright without causing injury to their head, but it was dry, and afforded shelter from the oncoming storm. At the back sat a lone man leaning against the sandstone wall, his eyes closed as he rested from the arduous ride of the day. His name was Thomas Cronin, a Templar sergeant of Irish descent.

Elsewhere in the cave lay three more blankets, each belonging to one of his comrades, the two men and one boy who had accompanied him on his unlikely quest. The darkness was occasionally lit up by the flash of distant lightning far above the Outremer, but it disappeared as quickly as it came, to be replaced by the rumbling threats of thunder as a distant storm crept ever closer.

At the entrance of the cave, another man, James Hunter, chewed thoughtfully on a piece of dry bread before washing it down with a mouthful of brackish water from his leather water bottle.

'It's getting closer,' he said eventually, leaning forward to carve a piece of meat from the goat carcass roasting above the fire embers, 'I think we may be getting some heavy rain soon.'

'Good,' replied Cronin without opening his eyes, 'we need to refill our water skins. Only God himself knows why we are all not dead from drinking from that last wadi. I think a herd of camels must have bathed in it; such WAS its flavour.'

Hunter looked over at the sergeant. Cronin hadn't been in the Holy Land long but had already proved his worth a few weeks earlier by managing to locate Saladin's army and informing the king prior to the battle of Montgisard. Now he was leading the small party on an impossible mission to retrieve a relic he was responsible for losing in the first place.

'You have spent too much time campaigning under the rainclouds of England, my friend,' said Hunter, 'and like all such men, take water for granted. Out here, every drop is precious.'

'It tastes of Camel piss,' replied Cronin.

'As long as it keeps you alive,' said Hunter, 'all water is good.' He continued eating in silence. Hunter had been a scout in the King Baldwin's army in Jerusalem for several years, and Henry's army before that back in England so was no stranger to the Holy Land but this was different. He was in the middle of enemy territory on an impossible mission alongside an English Templar sergeant with a penchant for breaking the rules, a Bedouin boy of only fourteen years of age who claimed he was Christian and wanted to be a squire, and a disgraced Templar knight who had hardly spoken a word since leaving Montgisard. In all, it was a strange troupe, yet one totally committed to retrieve the cross lost by Thomas Cronin several weeks earlier.

'Where's Hassan?' asked Cronin opening his eyes, 'he should be back by now.'

'He went to take the horses further amongst the rocks,' said Hunter, 'he's worried about the storm.'

'I'll go and help,' said Cronin getting to his feet and heading to the cave entrance.

'Here,' said Hunter, handing him a bowl full of goat meat as he passed, 'give this to your friend on the way.'

'His name is Jakelin.'

'Yes, him. I don't recall the last time he ate.'

'Yesterday was a fasting day for Sir Jakelin,' said Cronin. 'Today he is allowed to eat. I'm sure he will be grateful.'

'You Templars are a strange lot,' said Hunter carving himself another slice of goat, 'what sort of governance bids you hold from eating, yet expects you to fight in God's name?'

'Fasting is a personal choice, not a requirement,' said Cronin, taking the bowl, 'it clears the mind and allows true prayer.'

'Yet is it true that you can only eat meat on three days during any one week?'

'For the knights, that is the case,' said Cronin, 'but us lowly sergeants adhere to no such directives.'

'Then I think it is you who have the better part of the deal,' said Hunter.

Cronin grunted and headed out into the desert night. He paused for a moment, waiting for his eyes to become acquainted with the darkness before making his way over to where Sir Jakelin sat on top of a boulder, staring out over the dark desert plains below.

'I have food, my lord,' said Cronin, 'you should eat.'
Jakelin looked at the sergeant before taking the bowl and placing it on the boulder beside him.
'Thank you,' he said. 'Have you also eaten?'
'I have,' said Cronin, looking up at the heavens. In the distance, the dark shapes of heavy rainclouds rolled slowly towards them, extinguishing the stars as they came. 'With luck, the rain will only last the night,' he continued, 'and tomorrow we can be on our way.'
'Do you realise where we are, sergeant?' asked Jakelin suddenly, cutting Cronin short, 'I mean, where we actually are?'
'I know the salt sea is to the east of us,' said Cronin, 'and we are headed south to a place I have never heard of called Segor. More than that, I do not know.'
'This place,' said Jakelin quietly, sweeping his arm out towards the hidden desert plains, 'this whole land, from the coast to as far inland as we can imagine is where our Lord Jesus Christ made his home. He lived and died here, and even walked these same hills, seeing the same things that we see. He may even have sat on this very rock. Does that not create awe in your heart difficult to fathom?'
'I know of the stories,' said Cronin, 'and hope that one day I will be able to visit Jerusalem, but I am no scholar of the Holy book and the tales I know are only those recounted by my fellow soldiers and the priests of the church.'
'It is a wondrous place,' continued Jakelin, 'and the tales that whisper on the breeze between these rocks are greater than the most fanciful told by any storyteller. They recount the truth of our Lord who walked amongst men, mortal yet everlasting. A tangible link to the past that I find uplifting and to be here is a privilege granted to few men.'
'Have you been here before?'
'I served as a knight for many years in Jerusalem before I joined the Templars but never came this far south or travelled east of the salt sea. These paths are new to me and I am intrigued to see what awaits us in Zoar.'
'Zoar? Surely we are headed for Segor?'
'They are one and the same place,' said Jakelin. 'Segor was so named by our fellow Christians less than a hundred years ago but the biblical name is Zoar, and it is mentioned in the bible itself. Even Moses travelled there to gaze at its beauty.'

Cronin fell silent and stared at the knight. It was the most he had heard him speak since leaving Montgisard and it was obvious he was indeed a pious man.

'Here,' he said eventually, picking up the bowl and offering it to the knight again, 'you should eat.'

Without turning to face the sergeant, Jakelin took the bowl and slipped a piece of meat into his mouth, his gaze still fixed on the approaching storm as Cronin left to find Hassan.

'My Lord,' said Hassan recognising the sergeant heading down the path, 'you should return to the shelter for rain such as you have never seen will be upon us within moments.'

'I came to help with the horses,' said Cronin, 'where are they?'

'They are safe,' said Hassan. 'There is an overhang against the cliff that will protect them from the storm. I have tethered them there with fodder and water.'

'You are a good lad,' said Cronin, 'come there is food to be had.'

'I know,' said Hassan following the sergeant back up the path, 'I smelled it on the wind and my mouth waters like the heaviest torrent. Tonight, we will feast like Sultans, yes?'

Cronin smiled. The single dinar paid to the goat herder earlier that day had been money well spent and the prospect of fresh meat had raised the spirits of everyone, especially Hassan.

The Bedouin boy had been in Cronin's company for only a few weeks, yet they already shared a special bond, for after saving Hassan from the hangman in Acre, the boy had helped the sergeant find Saladin's army hidden in the mountains of the Negev desert and had played an important role in getting them both back safely to warn the king. Since then they had shared a range of adversities including fighting alongside each other at the bloody battle of Montgisard.

Their undertaking now was much different, and they had been tasked by the Templar Grand Master to find the brigand called Mehedi to retrieve the missing Cross of Courtney. Succeed and they would both be rewarded beyond their dreams but to fail meant they would be declared outside the law and probably be dead within the year, executed as brigands.

As they neared the cave entrance, Sir Jakelin climbed down from his perch higher on the rocks.

'My Lord,' said Hassan, with a nod of deference, 'your horse is secure and well-fed. He will be safe until morning.'

Jakelin didn't reply but nodded in acknowledgement before ducking into the cave and heading towards his blanket rolled out against the rear wall.

'I think the knight does not like me,' whispered Hassan as he disappeared. 'He does not speak to me.'

'He hardly talks to any of us, Hassan,' said Cronin, 'so I wouldn't worry yourself too much.' He looked up as the first heavy raindrops started to fall. 'Come,' he continued, 'there's a shoulder of goat that needs your attention and if nothing else, at least we will be dry when we wake tomorrow morning.'

Chapter Two

The City of Ashkelon

December - AD 1177

King Baldwin IV lay in his bed in the citadel at the heart of Ashkelon city. Servants busied themselves around the room, setting out chairs for the imminent audience with his army commanders while two physicians finished placing clean bandages on the open sores that covered his arms. To one side stood William of Tyre, the catholic prelate who had been his teacher for many years and was now one of his most trusted advisors.

'Are you sure about this?' asked the prelate, a look of concern upon his face. 'You have still not regained your strength.'

'I cannot wait any longer,' said the king, 'there are decisions to make and the Grand Master insists on an audience.'

'Eudes de St. Amand often has ideas above his station,' replied William, 'and should be made to wait until you have fully recovered. These Templars believe they answer to God only and forget you are the King of Jerusalem.'

'Do not be too hard on the brothers,' said Baldwin, easing himself further up the bed, 'remember it was their attack that caused Saladin's ranks to split like a melon, not four weeks since.'

'Can I suggest it was a tactic that could have been carried out by any of our knights?' said William.

'Perhaps, yet it was Amand who suggested it and carried it out to perfection. Their influence should not be underestimated.' He paused and accepted a drink from one of the servants, the coolness of the goat's milk easing the pain from the sores within his mouth. 'So,' he continued eventually after pushing the half-empty goblet away, 'who else should I expect?'

'Raynald of Chatillon,' said William, 'and Reginald of Sidon. Apparently, Eudes de St. Amand will be accompanied by Humphrey of Toron, though I know not why.'

'Well, we will find out soon enough,' said the king. 'As soon as my people have finished, send for our guests.'

'Of course, Your Grace,' said the prelate and bowed his head slightly before stepping back to allow the physicians to finish their work.

Outside the king's chambers, several men waited patiently for the summons. In amongst them, the Templar Grand Master stood head and shoulders above them all, his imposing frame dominating the antechamber. His black beard was full, and despite the fire in the hearth making the room uncomfortably warm, he kept the cloak of his order upon his shoulders, a heavy wool garment of pure white adorned with the blood-red cross of St George. Beneath the cloak, a similarly designed surcoat hung from his shoulders, secured around his waist by his belt and the scabbard that sheathed his huge sword.

Opposite the Grand Master, Reginald of Sidon sat in a chair, his left leg bandaged heavily from a wound received at Montgisard. Unlike Amand, he kept his beard short and though it had been only weeks since the battle, his appearance suggested he had been well looked after by his servants while in Ashkelon.

Beside the Grand Master stood a third man, the dust of the road still patchy upon his cloak. His beard was ginger, and as unkempt as his shoulder-length hair. His face was troubled and his manner quiet.

The strained quiet in the corridor was soon disrupted when a door crashed open and the king's regent, Raynald of Chatillon strode in, acknowledging the others with a nod and a grunt as he approached the guards at the king's door.

'Sir Raynald,' said Amand as he neared, 'I'm glad you could make it.'

'This had better be worth it,' said Raynald, 'I have things to take care of and could do without chattering like kitchen women around a table.'

'I like to think of it as strategic planning,' said Amand, 'as you will soon find out.'

The two men stared at each other for a few moments. Both were formidable warriors but though each had a respect for the other's leadership qualities, there had always been an undercurrent of dislike between them. Raynald was often frustrated by the way Amand commanded the Knights Templar, often ignoring the needs of the kingdom to further his own agenda, while the Grand Master disliked the Regent's propensity to violence at the slightest provocation. Despite this, they each knew that the other had played a huge part in the battle of Montgisard only a few days earlier and both carried wounds from the encounter.

Raynald turned his attention to the ginger-haired man and was about to engage him in conversation when the doors opened and the two guards stepped aside.

'The king will see you now,' announced a servant and all four men trooped inside to take their seats at the foot of the king's bed.

The air was heavy with incense, as was usual in the king's quarters, yet the windows lay slightly ajar to ensure the ingress of fresh air. William of Tyre watched as the four nobles settled, acutely aware of the immense military power each held in their own regions of the Outremer.

'My Lords,' he said eventually, 'thank you for coming. We know that to drag you from your duties, especially so soon after such a momentous battle, is an inconvenience you could do without. Nevertheless, there are still matters of state to attend and business has to continue.' He turned to face the king. 'His Grace, King Baldwin of Jerusalem has been considerably weakened by his exploits in leading the army at Montgisard, yet now feels strong enough to conduct this audience.' He nodded toward the king and stepped back to stand behind the four visitors.

'My Lords,' said the king, 'I echo the prelate's welcome and will keep you as short a time as possible. However, before I begin, please could you update me about the situation in your own spheres of responsibility. Lord Raynald, perhaps you could start.'

'Your Grace,' said Raynald, getting to his feet. 'I am pleased to report the complete rout of Saladin's army. Even as we speak, they scatter like frightened birds and our forces are chasing them down. In addition, our Bedouin allies give them little respite and are rounding up as many as they can to sell in the slave markets.'

'Any news of Saladin?'

'Not yet, but we are hopeful we can catch him before he reaches Egypt.'

'What about our own forces in the north?'

'The army has reached Jerusalem and I have sent word for them to hold there. Most of those summoned by the Arriere Ban have been recompensed and have dispersed back whence they came. The remainder are in fine fettle and bask in the glory the battle has brought upon them.'

'Good,' said the king and turned to the lord of Sidon.

'Sir Reginald, I understand that you are to remain in Ashkelon?'

'For the time being, my lord,' said Reginald. 'At the behest of the Regent, my men will stay until we are sure there is no more threat from any Ayyubid still lurking in the hills. We will garrison Ashkelon and Gaza for the next month and if everything remains quiet, return home when we are content that there is no more risk.'

'We appreciate your continued support,' said the king and turned to the Templar commander.

'Grand Master Amand,' he said eventually, 'it is good to see you again though if truth be told, I am still in awe of your order's charge at the head of the vanguard. It will go down in history as one of the moments that enabled our victory.'

'We were blessed to be involved,' said the Grand Master.

'So, what of your command?'

'With Lord Sidon taking over the garrison at Gaza,' said Amand, 'we have mustered in Blancheguarde Castle to lick our wounds.'

'How many men did you lose?'

'Thirty-three dead, with one more unlikely to survive. The rest all carry wounds of some sort but will live.'

'A heavy toll,' said the king.

'Yet one gladly paid. Jerusalem is safe again and that is what is important.'

'Yes, but for how long?'

'That is why I requested this briefing,' said Amand. 'I still have concerns and have brought Lord Humphrey of Toron who has similar thoughts.'

The ginger man got to his feet and nodded his head toward the king.

'Your Grace,' he said, 'I am honoured to be in your presence.'

'I have heard much about you, lord Humphrey,' said the king, 'and am grateful for all you do to keep our northern borders safe.'

'It is my honour, as well as my duty,' said Humphrey.

'Was it not also your duty to answer the Arriere Ban?' asked Raynald coldly. 'Your forces would have been more than welcomed.'

Humphrey ignored the barbed comment and turned back to the king.

'Your Grace, I have a thousand men camped near Montgisard. We came as soon as we could, but alas were too late and I can only thank God that you emerged the victor. From what I have heard, you faced a formidable foe and you have my highest admiration.'

'Thank God and cold steel,' said Sir Reginald.

'Can we get on with it,' snapped Raynald, 'I have things to do and we waste time?'

'You deem to rush the king's audience?' asked William from behind. 'What a novel approach.'

'With respect, Father William,' responded Raynald, 'it is the king himself that has entrusted me to act in his name and it is his business that needs my attention. Can we get to the reason why we have been summoned?'

The prelate was about to respond when the king raised his hand to stop the impending argument.

'Please,' he said, 'the regent is right. You must all have important business to attend so I will ask the Grand Master to state the reason why he asked for this audience.'

Raynald and Reginald both turned to stare at the Templar knight. They had thought it was Baldwin himself that had issued the summons and were surprised that Amand was the source.

'Your Grace,' said Amand, getting back to his feet, 'thank you.' He looked around the room and took a deep breath before continuing. 'There is no denying that we enjoyed a historic victory at Montgisard. Saladin is in hiding and his army has been devastated. However, our task is not over, nor is it even half done. It is my belief that what happened a few weeks ago was only the opening skirmish of a much greater war, one that is in danger of overwhelming us like a breached dam.'

'Did you not just say that Saladin's army has been devastated?' asked Raynald.

'Indeed I did. However, let us not forget that the tribes we faced at Montgisard came from the southern borders, with most originating in Egypt. There are far more Saracens to the east and to the north able to fall upon Jerusalem should they decide to join forces, numbers so great, they make those we faced just a few days ago look like nothing more than a raiding party.'

'Jerusalem has never been threatened by the northern or eastern tribes,' said Raynald 'I think you overestimate the threat.'

'If that is the case,' said Amand, 'why does Phillip of Alsace lay siege to Hama even as we speak? Jerusalem's army has only just returned from besieging Harim without success and don't forget, Damascus and its territories are already governed by the Ayyubid. If the Saracens in the north are no threat, then I suggest we are wasting valuable resources in our campaigns there.'

'We have them under control,' said Raynald.

'For now perhaps, but we have seen for ourselves how good the Sultan is at rallying tribes to his banner and I suspect that with the bitter taste of humiliation still in his mouth, he will seek retribution, sooner rather than later.'

'Grand Master Amand,' interjected the king. 'You obviously have something specific on your mind. Please elaborate.'

Amand turned to face Sir Humphrey.

'My friend, please share what you have made clear to me.'

The ginger-haired knight got to his feet again.

'Your Grace,' he said, 'as you know my men are based in the castles of Toron and Beaufort north of Galilee. I also garrison the fortress in Tiberius and from there we maintain a secure border between Jerusalem and the lands of the Ayyubid.'

'Your role is well known to us,' said the king, 'and you have our gratitude.'

'Your Grace,' continued Sir Humphrey, 'recently the tribes further to the east have begun to cross into our lands, using the pastures to feed their own flocks while those loyal to Jerusalem find it harder to find good fodder.'

'Problems for shepherds,' said Raynald, 'not knights.'

'Usually, I would agree,' said Humphrey, 'but recently there have been more and more Saracen warriors seen upon the plains, men who think nothing of killing anyone who questions their right to be there. Already many villages have been burned and the inhabitants slaughtered. Of course, we have given chase but by the time we have received the notifications, they have long gone.'

'And why is that a perceived risk to Jerusalem exactly?' asked Reginald.

'Because I have to do something about it. If we allow it to continue unchallenged, soon we will have nobody left under our control to pay the tithe and our coffers will suffer. The farms and villages pay to be protected but our forces are busy chasing shadows. I need to increase patrols throughout Toron and reinforce our influence there, but if I do, there will be fewer men available to patrol the lands between Damascus and Galilee.'

'So you come to us seeking reinforcements,' said Raynald, 'only days after we have lost thousands of men in the defence of Jerusalem.'

'Either that or risk the holy city being attacked again in the near future.'

The regent turned to face the Grand Master.

'And do you support this petition?'

'I support the request for aid,' said Amand, 'however, there is another option, one that has oft been discussed but never actioned.'

'And that is?'

Amand turned to face the king.

'Your Grace,' he said, 'forgive me if I underestimate your knowledge, but please allow me to elaborate.'

'Continue,' said the king.

'Thank you, Your Grace. As you may know, there is only one worthy road from the coastal ports to the eastern plains. It passes north of the sea of Galilee and crosses the river Jordan at a place called Jacob's Ford.'

'I know of it,' said Baldwin, 'my uncle was ambushed there twenty years ago by an army from Damascus.'

'Indeed he was,' said Amand, 'for it has always been a place of contention between many men. To the north, it is protected by swampland while downstream, the river is difficult to cross because of rapids. This makes Jacob's Ford one of the most vital crossings in the land.'

'What of it?' asked Raynald.

Amand ignored the regent and continued talking directly to the king.

'Your Grace, there is no argument that this river crossing is of critical importance. It is the gateway through which all armies have to pass whether it is to campaign against Damascus or to defend Jerusalem from the eastern Saracens.'

'The importance is known to me,' said the king.

'In that case,' said Amand, 'what is to stop us from securing the crossing permanently, controlling all who pass?'

'Do we not already do this?'

'We have no permanent position there, Your Grace,' said Humphrey, 'my patrols go when they can, but the ground is unforgiving and my men have many duties.'

'Your Grace,' said Amand, 'the location is of utmost strategic importance and needs a permanent position. To that end I suggest we build a fortification there, dominating the road and controlling the ford. Once done, any garrison stationed there can protect the south from the eastern Saracens or indeed from Damascus itself.'

'A castle?'

'Yes, Your Grace.'

'And how would we pay for such a thing?'

'Initially, it would have to come from the royal coffers but as we could extract a toll from anyone crossing the ford, it would be repaid very quickly, and your treasuries would profit from further use.'

'We have just fought a war, Grand Master,' said the king, 'my treasury is not as full as I would like.'

'Your Grace,' said Amand, 'our order would be willing to extend the necessary credit to Jerusalem at minimal interest and over a prolonged period of time. In addition, we would garrison the fortress at no cost to you apart from a small percentage of every toll taken.'

'Is this a security meeting or simply another opportunity for the Templars to enrich themselves further?' asked Sir Raynald with a sneer.

'A garrison at Jacob's Ford is long overdue,' said Amand, 'and I see nobody else offering to pay for its construction. It is no sin to seek a small profit, especially if Jerusalem itself could be at risk.'

'Says the man who stands to gain the most from such a venture.'

'I will personally see no benefit,' said Amand, 'except for the knowledge that the holy city's safety is further enhanced. Any monetary benefit will be used by the order to further God's will.'

'Your Grace,' said Raynald turning to the king, 'with respect, there are far more important things that need our military attention, not least, the pursuit and capture of Saladin. Surely, we would be better pressed in campaigning against Egypt while their forces are at such a disadvantage. If we can capture, or even kill

Saladin, then the threat from the Ayyubid would be hamstrung for a generation.'

'I disagree,' said Sir Humphrey, 'there are many Ayyubid commanders just as able as Saladin to pick up the banner in the event his death. At the moment they live in his shadow but make no mistake, this so-called holy war against us is more than one man's whim and we should make as many preparations as we can to defend Jerusalem, including a fortress at Jacob's Ford.'

'What say you, Sir Reginald?' asked the king. 'So far you have remained silent on the matter.'

'Like you, I have had little time to consider the proposals, Your Grace,' said Reginald, 'and am tempted to support the regent's plan about Egypt, but I have to say I concur with Sir Humphrey's account of the threat of the northern and eastern Ayyubid tribes. Sidon is far nearer Damascus than Jerusalem and not a day goes by that I do not receive a complaint from tenants nearer Galilee. Damascus has always been, and always will be a symbol of Ayyubid resistance and is a nest of vipers waiting to be agitated. Until such time that we can wrest that city from Saladin's hands, I think that a fortress at Jacob's Ford an interesting proposition. However, I will suggest caution.'

'In what way?'

'Jacob's Ford holds such importance to both sides, that I suggest that Saladin will not let its construction go unchallenged. If you choose this route, then I suggest that it is done as soon as possible whilst he and his armies are disrupted. To wait too long will invite an attack and further loss of life before the walls are ready to defend.'

'Your Grace,' said Raynald, 'I must protest...' but the king held up his hand and all the men fell silent.

Baldwin closed his eyes to consider what he had heard, as was his habit in such circumstances. For a few minutes, he just lay there, breathing gently and Humphrey turned to Amand, thinking the monarch asleep, but Amand knew differently and held up his own hand to the knight, indicating he should stay silent and wait.

Eventually, Baldwin took a deep breath and opened his eyes again to look amongst the four men.

'My Lords,' he said,' these are worrying times and you have all made valid points. Like Sir Reginald, I am torn between the advice from my Regent and the worries of the Grand Master. Both recommendations have merit and I accept we cannot sit back and do nothing, but we have not yet recovered from Montgisard so the decision cannot be rushed. Leave me to my thoughts and reconvene here at dusk tomorrow where I will share my conclusions. In the meantime, my stewards will ensure you enjoy the best of hospitality.' He waved his hand in dismissal and the four knights left the king's chambers, leaving the monarch alone with William of Tyre.

'And what of you, William?' asked the king when the servants had closed the doors. 'I assume you have your own thoughts on the matter.'

'I do, Your Grace,' said William, 'and you are well aware that I am no admirer of either the regent or the Grand Master. I always detect an undercurrent of self-serving in both men.'

'Yet both are brilliant strategists when it comes to the tactics of warfare.'

'That may be, and I will always bow to their superior knowledge in that field, yet in this case, I have to voice my own thoughts and not be influenced by men of violence, whether they act according to self-interest or God's service.'

'Go on.'

'Your Grace, when you consider your actions, I would bid you remember the following. You are the King of Jerusalem by God's grace alone and as such, are the custodian of the holy city and Jesus' legacy. Your one and only concern should always be, how do you better ensure that Jerusalem is as safe as it can be whilst you have its responsibility in your hands. Keep that in mind and if your heart is pure, then God will support you whichever way you choose.'

'As usual, your advice is ambiguous yet wise,' responded the king, 'and I will lean heavily upon it when I make my decision. But for now, I will get dressed for I will take the evening air.'

'As you wish, Your Grace,' said the prelate with a nod, and stepped aside as two of the king's servants ran to bring Baldwin's clothes.

'One more thing,' said the king, 'what do you know of Sir Humphrey?'

'I hear he is a great warrior,' said William, 'and loyal to the crown of Jerusalem. You would do well to heed his words.'

'Thank you,' said the king, 'you may leave.'

William of Tyre left the room and made his way back to his own quarters. Something inside made him feel uneasy and he knew that whichever way the king chose, men would probably die. It was unfortunate, but that was the way of the world and whatever happened, he had no doubt that it would be the will of God.

Chapter Three

The Dead Sea Coast

December - AD 1177

'Here it comes,' said Cronin as the first heavy droplets of rain landed on the rocks outside the cave.

Hassan joined him and stared out.

'The desert will give great thanks for this,' he said as the downpour got heavier. 'Tomorrow the wadis and the wells will be full of fresh water.'

Up above, sheets of lightning lit up the night sky, closely followed by peals of deafening thunder.

'I'm just glad we found this place,' said Cronin, 'and are not out there.' He turned and walked over to his blanket. 'Let's just hope it's over by the morning and we can be on our way.' He settled down and took a swig from his water bottle before glancing over to where Sir Jakelin was already fast asleep at the back of the cave, his breathing deep and rhythmical.

'He doesn't waste any time, does he?' said Hunter from the opposite wall. 'He laid down and went out like a snuffed candle.'

'Men of his ilk sleep when and where they can,' said Cronin. 'I suspect he will be awake a long time before us to pray.'

'As long as he is bloody quiet about it,' said Hunter and thumped one end of his blanket into a makeshift pillow.

'I will tend the fire while you sleep,' said Hassan.

'No need for that,' said Cronin. 'Just bank it up and get some rest. We have a long ride ahead of us tomorrow.'

Several hours later, Sir Jakelin woke from his deep sleep, his dreams disturbed by something uncomfortable but still out of reach. Slowly he opened his eyes and stared around the cave. The darkness was softened by the still smouldering fire and two burning candles on one of the rocky shelves. Everything was still, the silence only broken by the sound of deeply sleeping men.

He placed his hand flat on the floor of the cave to push himself up into a sitting position and was surprised when it landed in a puddle of water. Quickly he sat up and patted his hand around his bed space. The ground that was so dry and dusty only hours earlier was now a layer of thin mud and he cursed silently as he realised his blanket was damp.

Getting to his feet he picked up his things and walked carefully to another part of the cave before throwing his equipment to the floor and taking his blanket over to the fire to dry.

'My Lord,' said a voice nervously in the dark, 'is there a problem?'

'Nothing serious, Hassan,' replied Jakelin, 'I'm just trying to dry my blanket.'

'Is it wet?'

'It is. I suppose some of the water from the storm seeped down through the roof to my bed space. Nothing to worry about.'

'There is water coming in at the back of the cave?'

'There is, but like I said, nothing to worry about.'

'My Lord,' said Hassan getting to his feet, 'the back of this cave is sand, not rock. If there is water, we are in danger.' He walked over and retrieved one of the candles before ducking low and heading deeper into the cave. He held up the candle and saw a rivulet of water cutting a path through the compacted sand and earth. He placed his head against the wall to listen and frowned in concern at the sound of rushing water so close.

'My Lord,' he said again, this time more loudly, 'I think we should wake the others.'

'What's going on?' asked Cronin, woken by the noise.

'My Lord,' said Hassan, but before he could continue, an almighty crash echoed around the cave and an overwhelming torrent of water burst through the rear wall, engulfing Hassan and sweeping him away in its path. Nobody had time to do anything and within seconds, the flood filled the cavern, smashing their bodies against the walls and out onto the hillside. Cronin landed against a boulder with the wind knocked out of him and he clung on for dear life as the worst of the deluge threw itself out onto the wide mountain slope. Jakelin managed to launch himself to one side before the onslaught and now stood pinned against a tree as the angry waters swept past. Within moments the torrent subsided and though it still flowed, the energy that had built up behind the natural dam was spent and the water subsided to little more than a fast-moving stream.

'Cronin,' shouted Jakelin, 'are you hurt?'

'I just need my breath,' responded Cronin, getting to his feet. 'What about the others?'

As if in answer, Hunter crawled from the cave entrance, coughing and spluttering. He was obviously battered and bruised but seemed to have no serious injuries.

'What happened?' he gasped.

'An underground stream must have burst into the cave,' said Jakelin. 'We are lucky to escape with our lives.'

'Where's Hassan?' asked Cronin, 'he took the brunt of it.'

Everyone looked around before Cronin ran up the slope and disappeared back into the cave. Within moments he reappeared with a look of concern on his face.

'He's not there,' he said, 'he must be out here somewhere.'

All three men turned to check the banks of the newly formed stream without success.

'It's still too dark,' said Jakelin, 'we need candles or we will have to wait until dawn.'

'Our tinder is soaking,' said Cronin, 'and he may be injured. We have to find him.'

All three continued the search until suddenly Cronin called out.

'Down here. I need help.'

Jakelin and Hunter ran down to where the stream had already formed a small pool. Cronin was waist-deep, frantically pulling broken branches and foliage from around Hassan's body.

'Quickly,' he gasped, 'the water's rising, we have to get him out. '

Desperately the three men pulled away the tangle of debris until it seemed the boy was free.

'I still can't move him,' shouted Cronin over the wind and rain, 'he must be stuck beneath the water. '

Hunter reached down as far as he could and felt along Hassan's leg.

'His leg is stuck under a boulder,' he shouted, 'but it's too big to move. We will need to make a lever.'

'There's no time,' said Cronin. 'We have to do something now or he is going to drown in the next few minutes.'

Without a word, Jakelin waded over and crouching down until only his head was above the water, reached down to feel the size of the rock.

'I think I can move it,' he shouted, 'but we may only have one chance. Be ready to pull him out.'

'What are you going to do?' asked Hunter.

'Just take the strain,' said Jakelin, 'and be ready to pull.'

Both men took one of Hassan's arms in readiness as Jakelin took several deep breaths.

'Ready?' he shouted.

'Aye,' they shouted back.

Jakelin took a deep breath and ducked beneath the surface of the pool. His feet frantically sought purchase and when he found solid ground, he placed his shoulder under the rock and pushed upward. Up above, Cronin and Hunter felt the movement and pulled gently to release him.

'It's not enough,' shouted Cronin as Jakelin came up for air. 'He's still stuck.'

'I'll try again,' shouted Jakelin, 'this time pull harder. You may hurt him but it's better than being dead.' He took another few breaths and submerged again. This time he knew where to put his feet and found a much better position with his back. His face grimaced and as he put every ounce of his strength into the effort, the air escaped from his lungs. Still he pushed until suddenly, with the aid of the pressure from the still flowing water, the rock lifted.

'Pull,' shouted Cronin up above and with a sudden rush, Hassan's body flew backwards, into their arms.

'Get him onto the bank,' shouted Hunter, 'I'll help Jakelin.'

Beneath the surface, the knight fell backwards as the rock resettled and he became caught in the current. His body tumbled in the swirl and though he was desperate to breathe, he didn't know which way was up as he was swept downstream.

'He's not here,' shouted Hunter, feeling for the knight beneath the water.

'He must be,' shouted Cronin, 'keep looking.'

Hunter searched desperately, fearing that Jakelin had now become trapped, but with a flourish and gasp for air, the knight finally burst from the surface to hurl himself at the bank a few paces downstream.

'There he is,' shouted Cronin, 'he's alive.'

Jakelin crawled onto the bank and got to his feet before walking back to join the others.

'Do you have him?' he gasped.

'We do,' said Cronin, 'but it looks like his leg is badly broken. We need to get him into shelter for a closer look.'

'The only place is back in the cave.'

'It'll be washed out,' said Hunter.

'It's the only option,' said Jakelin, 'it may be wet but the worst has gone and we have to get out of this storm.' He leant down and picked up Hassan's unconscious body, placing it over his shoulders before heading back up the hill. Hassan let out a muted cry of pain but there was nothing any of them could do. They needed shelter, and they needed it fast.

Twenty minutes later, Hassan opened his eyes to see Cronin staring down at him with concern. Hunter had managed to light one of the candles and now held it close so the boy could see his friend's face.

'What happened, said Hassan weakly, 'where are we?'

'You were washed away by the water,' said Cronin. 'You are lucky to be alive, my friend, we all are.'

'The horses,' gasped Hassan, 'they will be frightened of the storm.'

'The horses are fine,' said Cronin, 'Hunter has already checked. What's important now is you rest until we decide what to do.'

'I can't feel my leg,' said Hassan, 'what's happened?'

'There is no pain?'

'No, is it still there?'

'Of course it is,' said Cronin, 'but it must be numb from the break. Here, drink this.'

'What is it?'

'Poppy milk,' said Cronin.' I don't have much but it will help.' He helped Hassan drink the opium from the leather cup and laid him back down to rest before joining the others to one side.

'How is he?' asked Jakelin.

'His leg is broken,' said Cronin, 'but I don't think he has any other serious injuries. The numbness is a blessing but I fear it is caused by something else beneath. We need to get him to a physician as soon as we can.'

'How?' asked Hunter.

'I don't know but he needs someone who knows what they are doing.'

'We can't move him as he is,' said Hunter, 'his injuries could kill him.'

'Then what are we to do?'

'I have seen many broken legs in my time,' said Hunter, 'some of which did not lead to the death of those suffering the injury. It is a painful thing to have done but if he is to have any chance, the bone needs to be reset in place and his leg strapped to a splint before we can move him anywhere.'

'I agree,' said Jakelin. 'To leave the broken ends of the bones apart invites further damage beneath the flesh.'

'Then that's what we will do,' said Cronin. 'Hunter, what do you need?'

'Just something to use for splints and ties,' said Hunter. 'I'll go and see what I can find.'

'Do you have any more poppy seeds?' asked Cronin, turning to Jakelin.

'No but I have willow bark. It is not as good but will ease the pain.'

'Anything will help,' said Cronin.

Ten minutes later, they were ready and all three gathered around Hassan's semi-conscious body.

'Hassan,' said Cronin, dropping to his knees alongside him, 'can you hear me?'

Hassan's eyes flickered open and he mumbled a response.

'Listen,' said Cronin. 'You have broken your leg and we need to fix it. It is going to hurt but has to be done so we can get you to a proper physician. Do you understand?'

Hassan nodded silently but there was fear evident in his eyes.

'Good, this is what is going to happen. Sir Jakelin is going to hold you while I straighten your leg so Hunter can apply a splint. It will hurt but once done, you should feel more comfortable and we will give you something for the pain. After that, we'll get you some proper help.'

'Do what you have to do, my lord,' said Hassan. 'God is watching over us.'

'He is,' said Cronin and placed a piece of wood in the boy's mouth. 'Bite on this, it will help.'

He nodded towards Jakelin who took his place behind Hassan. The knight reached under the boy's arms and locked his hands together, holding the torso firmly in place. Cronin moved down to the feet and took a firm hold of one ankle, while Hunter knelt alongside the break.

'Ready?' asked Cronin.

'Do it,' said Hunter and as Jakelin held the boy firmly, Cronin pulled on the leg to draw the broken bone back down into place.

Hassan cried out in pain and his teeth clamped down on the wood as Jakelin tightened the grip around his chest.

'A bit more,' shouted Hunter, his hands feeling around the bruised flesh of the break, 'almost there.'

Cronin leaned back, pulling the leg further until Hunter felt the bone move laterally back into place.

'That's it,' he said, 'hold it there. Quickly he grabbed the four pieces of wood he had stripped from a tree and strapped them to the boy's leg with strips of cloth torn from a saddle blanket.

'Make it tight,' said Cronin watching him work, 'we don't want the bone to move again.'

'I will,' said Hunter, 'but there must also be allowance for his blood to flow.' He finished tying the knots and looked up at the boy.

'That's it,' he said, 'how is he?'

'Unconscious,' said Jakelin, 'but alive.'

'We need to get a fire going,' said Hunter, 'and get him out of those wet clothes.'

'There should be some dry bushes under the overhangs out on the mountain,' said Jakelin, 'I will see what I can find. Here, wrap him in this.' He retrieved his pack from a ledge where it had escaped the worst of the flood and tossed it over to Cronin before disappearing out into the night. Cronin opened the pack and found Jakelin's Templar cloak inside.

'He brought it with him,' said Hunter, 'yet not once have I seen him wear it, even on the coldest of nights.'

'I didn't know either,' said Cronin, 'but he must have his reasons.' The two men stripped Hassan of his wet clothes and wrapped him in the Templar's cloak. 'Hassan always said that one day he wanted to wear the mantle of the order,' continued Cronin, looking down at the boy, 'it is unfortunate that this is how it came to pass.'

'There is colour returning to the boy's flesh,' said Hunter examining Hassan's foot, 'the blood is flowing again.'

'Then there is hope,' said Cronin. 'Now let's see what we can salvage while he sleeps.'

Chapter Four

The Negev Desert

December - AD 1177

Shirkuh ad-Din peered over the crest of the ridge into the valley below. Behind him, hidden amongst the rocks on the reverse side of the mountain, Salah ad-Din and several of his personal bodyguard rested alongside their camels, fatigued after their arduous flight from the defeat at Montgisard a few weeks earlier.

'There,' said Bakir-Shah, one of the Mamluk officers at Shirkuh ad-Din's side, and pointed north where a line of riders could be seen coming down a track into the valley.

'These men are harder to shake off than age itself,' said Shirkuh ad-Din

'They are led by a Bedouin tracker,' said Bakir-Shah, 'such people know every rock and path throughout the desert. It is impossible to keep hiding from such men.'

'We have no choice,' said Shirkuh ad-Din, 'our goal is to ensure Salah ad-Din gets to Cairo safely. Nothing else matters.'

'Then perhaps it is time to stop running,' said Bakir-Shah, 'and face them with steel in hand.'

'They outnumber us two to one,' said Shirkuh ad-Din, 'and are formidable fighters. I will not risk the Sultan's life.'

'I am Mamluk,' said Bakir-Shah, 'as are my men. Such numbers do not worry us. Give me your blessing and we will face the infidels while you and Salah ad-Din continue to Egypt.'

'And if you fail?'

'Then it will be Allah's will, but at the very least, we will delay them so you have more time to get to safety.'

'The camels are weary,' said Shirkuh ad-Din, 'as is the Sultan. We have hidden amongst these mountains for too long but there is an Ayyubid village less than a day's ride from here. If you can hold them a few hours, then perhaps we can get fresh mounts for the last push into Egypt.'

'Then that is what must be done,' said Bakir-Shah.

Two hours later, the column of forty Christian lancers wound their way across the valley floor. At their head was the scout, a weather-worn Bedouin hunter by the name of Abdal-Wahhab. Beside him, rode one of Raynald's best knights, Sir John of Margat.

'The ground is barren,' said Sir John, using a rag to wipe the sweat from his face, 'are you sure they came this way?'

'As sure as the sun is in the sky,' said Abdal-Wahhab, his body swaying as it matched the movement of the camel beneath him.

'Yet I see no signs,' said the knight, 'and I have enjoyed hunting since I was a boy in Margat.'

'If you were with a blind man, would it mean the sun does not hang, or would it be that he could simply not see the very thing in front of his eyes?'

'Your point is well made,' said John, 'yet I grow impatient that our quarry remains hidden to us. For many days you have said they are just ahead, but not once have I seen any sign.'

'Your impatience is a dangerous thing, John of Margat, be careful it does not get you killed.'

'Let me worry about my life,' said John, 'you just get us close enough to engage the Ayyubid.'

'I think you may get your wish sooner than expected,' said Abdal-Wahhab.

'What do you mean?'

'Do not slow your horse,' said Abdal-Wahhab, 'but we are being watched even as we speak.'

'Where,' said John, his eyes scanning the surrounding hills.

'Where the ridge dips like a horse's back. 'I suggest you tell your men to loosen the ties on their scabbards.'

John did as suggested and heard the murmurs of his men over his shoulder. Each one was a seasoned fighter and he had no doubt they would handle themselves well in any confrontation.

'Are they still there?' asked John eventually.

'They are,' said Abdal-Wahhab, as his head turned to scan the valley on either side, 'but something is wrong.' He reined in his camel and dismounted before walking over to a nearby boulder.

'What is it?' asked John as the Bedouin returned.

'Start moving, John of Margat,' said Abdal-Wahhab, 'and be prepared to ride like the wind.'

'Why?' asked the knight, 'we have come here to fight.'

'Because we have ridden into a trap. There are men hidden in this valley and I suspect the route back has been blocked off. If we are attacked, our only way is forward.'

'I think you are mistaken,' said John. 'This place has little in the way of cover and cannot possibly hide enough men to cause us a problem.'

'Your ignorance does you little justice,' said Abdal-Wahhab, and clicked his tongue to urge his camel forward.

'You listen to me,' growled John as he caught up with the tracker, 'we have come all this way to kill or capture those that fled Montgisard. Even if what you say is true and we are attacked, then we will do what has to be done.'

'Ordinarily, I would agree,' said Abdal-Wahhab, 'but things have changed.'

'How?'

Before Abdal-Wahhab could answer, a line of black-clad warriors emerged from the rocks ahead and spread out across the path. The Christian column reined to a halt and stared at the men blocking their way.

'There lies your answer, my friend,' said Abdal-Wahhab, 'they are not Ayyubid, they are Mamluk.'

John swallowed hard as the implications sunk in. Mamluks were the most feared fighters in the Holy Land and had few equals when it came to warfare.

'We outnumber them two to one,' said John, 'there is nothing to fear.'

'You are missing the point,' said Abdul, 'if there are Mamluk here, then Saladin is not far away, and they will fight to the death to protect the Sultan.'

'Saladin is near?' gasped John, his voice hardly disguising his excitement, 'if that is the case, we have a holy duty to take him prisoner.'

'Your mind gallops before starting to walk.' said Abdul. 'To even have a chance of getting near to Saladin, we have to spill Mamluk blood, and that, my friend, is no easy thing.'

Everyone stared at the Mamluk warriors. Every ex-slave that made up the feared army was highly trained and fearless in battle. Each was completely covered in black armour including black chainmail hauberks and steel plate cuirasses. On their legs were heavily-studded leather leggings and each wore a plumed steel helmet upon their heads. In their hands, they held the feared, razor-sharp scimitars that could behead a man with a single swipe. The Christian lancers spread out either side of Sir John and the valley fell still as each set of men weighed up the other.

'They are few in number,' shouted a voice from amongst the Christian line, 'why do we wait?'

'Well?' said John to Abdul. 'What is the answer, my friend, do you think they want to talk?'

'The Mamluk are wearing their battle armour,' said Abdul, 'so I fear there will be little talking.'

'Then so be it,' said John and turned to his men.

'Draw swords,' he roared, *'Prepare to advance.'*

'My Lord,' said Abdal-Wahhab, 'if you are going to do this, I suggest you dismount your men.'

'But why? Surely we have the advantage.'

'Look at the ground they hold,' said the Bedouin, 'it is covered with sharp rocks. Your horses will suffer and provide no platform for battle. You need to meet them on foot, or your mounts will be cut down from beneath you.'

John realised the scout was correct and ordered his men to dismount.

'Wait here,' said Abdal-Wahhab, 'I will see if there is room for parley.' He walked forward to within ten paces of the silent Mamluk line. *'As-Salaam-Alaykum,'* he said, nodding his head slightly in greeting.

The warrior at the front of the black-clad men nodded his head in reply but did not return the salutation.

'You block the road, my friends,' said Abdal-Wahhab, 'and we request safe passage.'

'There will be no safe passage for you this day,' said Bakir-Shah, 'only on the path that leads to your death.'

'We have no quarrel with the Mamluk,' said Abdal-Wahhab, 'and only seek he who is responsible for so much bloodshed at Montgisard.'

'But therein lies the quarrel,' said Bakir-Shah, 'we are sworn to protect the Sultan and will do so even unto death.'

Abdal-Wahhab stared at the man for a few moments before speaking again.

'I know you,' he said eventually, 'your face is familiar to me.'

Bakir-Shah returned the stare, his eyes narrowing as he examined the Bedouin's face.
'State your name, old man,' he said eventually.
'I am Abdal-Wahhab, son of Osama.'
'And your tribe is Heuwaitaat?'
'It is.'
'Then we do share a story. My family were slaves in your father's household.'
'I remember,' said Abdal-Wahhab. 'Your given name was Jaleel, but as a boy, you ran away in the midst of a desert storm. We thought you long dead.'
'I would happily have died in that storm rather than live another day in slavery. Now my name is Bakir-Shah. I serve only my commanders and the word of Allah.'
'Did my father not treat your family well?'
'It is irrelevant. I was a slave, now I am free.'
'But in a slave army,' said Abdal-Wahhab.
'Enough talk,' shouted Sir John from behind, 'there are matters to address. I demand you cede the road, Mamluk, or we will cut you down where you stand.'
'Your pet Christian has brave words for an infidel,' said the Mamluk without taking his eyes off the Bedouin, 'he must be in a rush to meet his god.'
'They are an impatient people,' said Abdal-Wahhab, 'but there is no need for anyone to die today. Let us through and we will be on our way.'
'You know I cannot do that,' said Bakir-Shah, 'so perhaps your friend is right. Perhaps we should seek the inevitable before the sun gets too hot.'
'And this is your last word?'
'It is.'
Abdal-Wahhab paused before turning and walking back to Sir John.

'Well, asked the knight, 'does he cede?'
'He does not,' said Abdal-Wahhab, 'and intends to fight.'
'So be it,' said the knight, 'but we need to make this quick. If Saladin is near, I want to be on his trail again as soon as we can.'
'I suggest you clear your mind of Saladin until this day is over,' said Abdal-Wahhab, 'there are more important matters to hand.'

'What could be more important than catching Saladin?'
'Surviving the onslaught that is coming your way,' said Abdal-Wahhab.
'Your pessimism is a fault,' said John donning his helmet. 'My men are well used to warfare and I see nothing to fear.' He turned to his command, drawing his sword. 'Form up, line abreast behind me. *Prepare to advance!*'

Many leagues away, in the cave near the coast of the Dead Sea, Cronin helped Hassan up into a sitting position.

'Here,' he said, offering a wooden bowl, 'Hunter has made a soup. It is rich with goatmeat and will help you to regain your strength.'

Hassan gasped as waves of pain pulsated up his leg and leaned back against the cave wall.

'I have let you down, my lord,' he said eventually, looking at the trickle of water still flowing through the middle of the cave. 'I should have realised the sand wall was at risk from the rain.'

'You could not have known,' said Cronin.

'But now I can't walk and will cause you to fail upon your quest. You should leave me here and go.'

'Nobody is going anywhere, Hassan,' said Cronin, 'at least, not without you. We will let you rest and then take you to a physician.'

'But that will take time and you know what the Grand Master said, we only have a few months to find and return the Courtney Cross.'

'Let me worry about that,' said Cronin, 'you just focus on resting and getting well while you can. Now eat your soup.'

He stood up and left the cave to join the others outside. The storm had passed, and the sun was high in the sky. Jakelin and Hunter had retrieved as many of their belonging as they could find and had spread them out onto rocks to dry.

'How is he?' asked Hunter as Cronin approached.

'Better,' said Cronin, 'but he is in a lot of pain.'

'To be honest, I'm surprised he's here at all,' said Hunter. 'I've seen men give up and die from far less.'

'He's nothing if not resilient,' said Cronin and turned to the knight. 'Sir Jakelin,' he said, 'I'm afraid he still clings to your cloak like a babe. I'll return it as soon as I am able.'

'It is nought but an earthly thing,' said Jakelin, 'and remains his as long as he needs it.'

'So what next?' asked Hunter. 'We can't stay here.'

'I've thought about going back,' said Cronin, 'but the distance to the nearest town is more than that we must cover to get to Segor. I suggest that we keep going forward and seek a physician when we get there.'

'And what about the boy?'

'We'll have to make him as comfortable as we can but there is no other option.'

'He can ride with me,' said Jakelin. 'My horse is stronger than the others and will take the two of us if needed.'

'There is no need for that,' said Cronin, 'he is my responsibility.'

'I am pledged to aid the afflicted in God's name,' said Jakelin.

'I thought your order was forbidden to share a mount with another man,' said Hunter.

'That is true,' said Jakelin, 'yet our crest shows just such a thing. I believe our holy pledge to aid the afflicted is of greater importance than the adherence to rules made by mortal man.' No, it is I who will bear the burden until we reach Segor. Then we will discuss how we will continue to carry out our quest.'

Cronin stared at the knight but knew there would be no changing Jakelin's mind. After all, as a Templar sergeant, he was outranked and in theory bound to do the knight's bidding anyway.

'As you wish,' he said. 'Perhaps we can let him rest this day and head out tomorrow at first light.'

'So be it,' said Jakelin and stood to go about his business.

'He's a strange one,' said Hunter when the knight was out of earshot, 'one moment he keeps himself distant, the next he volunteers to help the boy. I don't understand him. I also don't understand why is actually here at all.'

'Don't underestimate him, Hunter,' said Cronin, 'his reputation as a knight is second to none.'

'Is he here to make sure you carry out the order's commands?'

'In a way,' said Cronin, 'but his presence will ensure we get any help we need from other Templar outposts. It is through a misdemeanour that he is here in the first place.'

'What crime did he commit?'

'He broke the line,' said Cronin, 'and that goes against the most solid of Templar's rules.'

'I heard about that,' said Hunter, 'but did he not also return with the head of Saladin's nephew?'

'It matters not. Our creed demands we hold firm, for to break ranks risks the life of the men alongside us. Sir Jakelin broke the line and had to be punished. That is why he is here.'

'You are a strange lot,' said Hunter. 'In my eyes, that man should be hailed a hero, yet his own order condemns him. That is hard to understand.'

'He knows what he did was wrong,' said Cronin, 'and takes full responsibility. He may be a strange one, but it is to our benefit that he rides alongside us. Now, come, there are horses to tend.'

Back in the stony valley to the west, Sir John walked slowly forward, flanked by his men. Behind them stood the scout, his role now redundant until the fight was over.

When they were only twenty paces away from the Mamluks, John held his hand up and the advance came to a halt. Though the enemy's numbers were only half his own strength, he knew he had a fight on his hands. The Mamluks were fierce warriors and had not moved a muscle as John and his men advanced. He glanced around. Usually, he would have used archers, but he had none and hoped fervently that neither did his enemy.

'This is your last chance, Saracen,' he shouted, using the derogatory term the Christian forces reserved for most Arab tribesmen, 'cede the road or stain it with your blood.'

'The road is here,' said Bakir-Shah, 'and we are upon it. If you want the road, then you must wrest it from our dead hands.'

'So be it,' snarled Sir John. He was an experienced knight, but all enemies demanded respect, not least the Mamluk. 'Men of Jerusalem,' he called over his shoulder, 'you know why we are here. Beyond these Saracens hides the quarry sought by the king himself. Succeed this day and I personally guarantee your names will be feted in every hall from here to England.' He lifted his sword. *'For God, the king and Jerusalem'*, he roared, *'advance.'*

The men echoed his battle cry and broke into a run. The Mamluks stayed where they were but immediately adopted defensive stances, turned to one side, knees slightly bent with swords held high above their shoulders.

As the Christians reached the enemy position, many of the Mamluks stepped back and twisted to one side, allowing the attackers' own momentum to carry them unexpectedly through the defensive line.

The tactic bore dividends and as the first line of Christians stumbled past, the deadly Scimitar blades smashed into their backs. Despite the chainmail armour, the force of the blows were devastating with some cleaving right through the hauberks and into the flesh beneath. Men cried out in pain and seizing the advantage, the Mamluks ploughed amongst them, cutting left and right with their scimitars. Blood flew everywhere and for a few moments, the defenders had the advantage, but numbers soon told and as the rest of Sir John's men joined the fray, the Mamluks were forced onto the defence.

Steel smashed against steel and men fell on both sides but the cost on the Mamluk line was telling. Frantically they fought, cutting down attackers on all sides but their numbers dwindled rapidly until unexpectedly, the remaining dozen or so turned and ran.

The remaining Christians could hardly believe their eyes, and some started laughing and jeering.

'After them,' roared Sir John, caught up in the fever of battle, *'a dinar for every right hand you bring me.'*

'No,' shouted Abdal-Wahhab from behind, 'do not follow,' but it was too late, the rest of Sir John's men were in full pursuit of the Saracens.

'Sir John,' shouted Abdal-Wahhab frantically, *'call them back, it is a trick.'*

'They are beaten,' shouted the knight, turning to face the Bedouin scout, 'to the victor the spoils.'

'Listen to me,' roared Abdal-Wahhab, *'Mamluks do not run!'*

As the realisation sunk in, the knight turned to stare after his men.

'Hold,' he roared but it was too late and even as he watched, dozens more Mamluks appeared from amongst the rocks flanking the road to fall upon the confused Christians.

This time the fight was unequal, and the lancers were slaughtered by the fresher Mamluks. For a moment, John watched in disbelief but realising his men needed help, turned to those still at his side.

'*Don't just stand there,*' he screamed, '*help them.*'

What was left of his men ran forward to join the fray but it was useless and within minutes, all of the Christian force were dead or mortally wounded. Sir John and Abdal-Wahhab alone remained standing. A stillness fell around the battlefield, the silence broken only by the moans of the wounded from both sides. John stared at the leader of the Mamluks further down the road and rage rose in his heart like a thunderstorm.

'Don't do it, my lord,' said Abdal-Wahhab, seeing the knight adjusting the grip on his sword, 'seek mercy. He will take you prisoner and ransom you back to the king.'

'I will not suffer the humiliation,' snarled the knight, 'and if I am to die here today, my blood will mingle with that of my adversary.' Without another word, he strode towards the scene of the carnage. Over a dozen Mamluk warriors still stood, but each remained still, watching as their own commander stepped forward into the knight's path.

Neither men spoke, knowing that the fight would be to the death. Sir John raised his sword and broke into a run, but this time he anticipated the Mamluk's tactics and changed direction at the last moment to wrong-foot his enemy. As he passed, he swung his sword low and to the side, cutting through the leather leggings and deep into the Arab's thigh. Bakir-Shah cried out and dropped to one knee, his wounded leg unable to bear his weight. Sir John turned to finish him off, his eyes filled with cold hate and raised his sword to cleave the Mamluk's head from his shoulders, but Bakir-Shah was a seasoned warrior and still had fight in his heart. As the knight approached, the Mamluk grabbed a handful of dust and forcing himself up onto his one good leg. threw it in the knight's face, temporarily blinding him. It only lasted seconds but it was enough and as the knight wiped the dirt from his eyes, Bakir-Shah drew his knife and launched himself forward to knock his adversary to the ground.

Both men rolled in the dirt, but it was the Mamluk who had the advantage and as John tried desperately to reach his own knife, Bakir-Shah thrust his blade beneath the chin of his opponent's helmet and up through his mouth into his skull.

The knight gasped in pain and fell to one side, his whole body shuddering as he died.

For a few moments, everyone watched in silence before Bakir-Shah staggered to his feet and picked up the knight's longer sword. Using it as a support, he limped heavily towards the Bedouin as two of the other Mamluks walked over and forced the scout to his knees.

Abdal-Wahhab stared up at the Mamluk, his eyes calm.

'Why do you sell your soul to these devils,' asked Bakir-Shah eventually, 'these lands belong to your people, not the infidels who follow the teachings of Christ. You stain your ancestors' memory with every moment you give them aid.'

'Not all are as bad as you think,' said Abdal-Wahhab. 'Most are as pious as you or I. Do we not worship the same God?'

'Do not try to cloud my eyes with religious confusion,' said Bakir-Shah. 'There is no god but Allah and you should have your head removed for your blasphemy.'

'Do what you have to do?' asked the Bedouin calmly.

'I should,' said Bakir-Shah, 'but earlier you asked me a question about your father, Osama. You asked if he treated my family well and the answer is yes, he did. Many years after I escaped, I went back under the cover of darkness and spoke to my mother. She said she was well treated and happy with her lot, so for that reason alone, I will let you live. But there is a price to be paid.'

'There is always a price,' said Abdal-Wahhab.

Bakir-Shah held out his hand and took a knife from one of the guards, before ripping away the Bedouin's turban.

'You seem to believe there are two gods,' said the Mamluk, grabbing a handful of Abdal-Wahhab's hair and pushing his head to one side, 'so perhaps you should be made to listen to only one.' With a quick swipe of the blade, he severed the scout's left ear and threw it to the ground in front of his victim.

The two guards threw the scout to the floor as Bakir-Shah stood above him.

'Go in peace, Abdal-Wahhab, son of Osama, said the Mamluk as the Bedouin gasped in pain, 'but know this. If there was a debt to your father, then it is now repaid. The next time we meet, there will be death.' He turned and limped away, followed by his men and as Abdal-Wahhab lay in the dust, his hand pressing against his wound, the surviving Mamluks walked amongst the fallen, slitting the throats of every Christian not yet dead.

'Yes there will be death, Bakir-Shah,' moaned Abdal-Wahhab through gritted teeth, 'but it will not be mine.'

Chapter Five

The Castle at Ashkelon

December - AD 1177

The fires in the ante-chamber braziers were a welcome relief from the chill of the cold stone corridors when the warlords returned to see the king. This time they were not kept waiting and were ushered straight into his chambers. To their surprise, Baldwin was not only up and dressed, but sat on an ornate chair surrounded by courtiers and scribes.

Again the room was warm, but the smell of the ointments and incense used to mask the odour of the king's affliction lay heavy on the air.

'My Lords,' said the king looking up, his voice strong and commanding, 'there you are. Allow me a few more minutes to conclude the day's business and I will be with you. Please help yourself to refreshment.' He waived nonchalantly toward a table at the back of the room where jugs of watered wine lay snugly between platters of cold meat and fruit.

The four knights wandered over, leaving the hubbub behind them. Sir Humphrey of Toron walked over to join Amand while Sir Reginald of Sidon stood alongside Sir Raynald at the far end of the table.

'Such a difference in one day,' said Sir Humphrey quietly. 'Last night I met a sickly young man who could hardly stand. Today I see a stately figure exuding all the characteristics of kinghood. He is like a different person.'

'Do not be fooled by what you saw yesterday,' said the Grand Master, lifting a bunch of grapes from the table, 'Baldwin is a good and powerful king. Yes, there are days when his affliction weighs upon him like an anvil but there are others that make his commanders gasp in pride. At Montgisard, he was deep amongst the enemy alongside his men, his sword as busy as any, but he has a calculating mind and his heart can be as cold as any blade so do not underestimate him.'

'Do you think he will agree to our plan?'

'There is no way of knowing,' said Amand. 'He holds great store in the advice of the regent but ofttimes, Raynald just seeks conflict for the sake of it. The king is well aware of this trait, but my guess is that Sir Reginald holds the key to these negotiations.'

'Is he not an ally of the regent?' asked Humphrey, glancing over to the two other knights at the end of the table.

'In a way, but he is his own man and will speak from the heart.'

Eudes de St. Amand turned his attention back to the heavily laden table while Sir Humphrey turned to look around the room. The previous night, he had been tired from a long journey and the room had been dark and gloomy. This evening was different. He was well-rested and his mind fresh. The room was lit by hundreds of candles and a huge fire roared in the hearth. Despite this, the air was not overwhelmingly hot as some of the shutters were slightly ajar to allow the ingress of fresh air.

King Baldwin sat on his chair. Alongside him was a scribe and the ever-present William of Tyre. Before them stood a dozen or so men, each waiting their turn to present their business to the judgement of the king. As each man approached, he was given a few moments to present his petition before stepping back to await the outcome. Sometimes, William would lean forward and whisper in the king's ear before Baldwin gave his decision, but on every occasion, the outcome was written down by the scribe and never challenged by those seeking the king's edict. It soon became clear to Humphrey that everyone present held the monarch in great esteem and despite his feeble appearance, he was indeed a strong and respected ruler.

Eventually the last of the petitioners were dealt with and the court dismissed. The room cleared leaving just the king, William of Tyre and the four knights present.

'My Lords,' said Baldwin eventually as his quiet conversation with William came to an end, 'please approach.'

The four men walked up to the king, each nodding their heads in respect before he continued.

'I know you have duties to attend so I will keep this brief. Last night I spent many hours considering the petition to build a castle at Jacob's Ford. In essence, I believe it is a sound idea and deserves merit. However, Sir Raynald is my regent and as such is entrusted with many decisions regarding warfare on my behalf. His idea to immediately invade Egypt while Saladin licks his wounds also demanded great attention and both ideas caused me a sleepless night. However, these are troubling times and decisions have to be made.' He looked between Amand and Raynald. 'Sir Raynald,' he said eventually, 'you will have your war with Egypt...'

Before he could continue, Raynald stepped forward, the satisfaction evident on his face.

'Your Grace,' he said, 'you will not be disappointed, I swear I will...'

'Wait,' interrupted the king, holding up his hand, 'I have not finished.'

'Forgive me, Your Grace,' said Raynald, and stepped back into line.

'What I was going to say,' said the king, 'was this. Yes you will have your war, but Montgisard and the Arriere Bahn have drained my treasuries, so there will be a delay until I can fully fund such a venture. Our men also need to recover before committing to another fight, so I say this. Egypt will remain a target and you are to plan a campaign designed to conquer and occupy those lands. However, the instigation of such a campaign will not commence until such times as our treasuries are again full and can fully support the cost.'

'And how long will that be?' asked Raynald.

'We estimate, two to three years,' said William on the king's behalf.

'Three years,' gasped Raynald, 'Saladin will have rebuilt his army way before then.'

'I concede the fact,' said the king, 'but the financial reality is, we cannot afford another war at the moment.' He turned to face the Templar Grand Master.

'Bearing in mind that while we are in this weakened financial state,' he continued, 'and taking on board the threat from the northern and eastern Ayyubid, we have decided that a garrison at Jacob's Ford is a wise move and grant permission for it to be built with the following conditions.' He nodded toward William who unfurled a parchment and read aloud.

'Firstly, the castle will be fully built and paid for by the Order of the Knights Templar, with such cost being reimbursed by the administering of a toll upon all those who cross the ford, excluding those who cross on the king's business.

Secondly, the castle must be built with all haste, with the outer defensive walls to be finished no later than twenty-four months from the date of this decree.

Thirdly, the castle will be fully garrisoned by the order of the Knights Templar, or their subordinates, at their own expense for the term of five years from the date of completion.

And finally, upon the final repayment of the building cost, all further tolls will be forfeit to the kingdom of Jerusalem, less one-tenth, which will be paid to the order of the Knights Templar in perpetuity, in return for maintaining a garrison there controlling the ford and serving the king.'

William looked up at the four men and lowered the parchment.

'There are other details to be agreed,' said Baldwin, 'but in essence, this is what is acceptable to us. Eudes de St. Amand, how do you respond?'

'Your Grace, I must protest,' shouted Raynald stepping forward, but again the king held up his hand.

'Sir Raynald,' he said, his voice firm, 'you will have your war as promised but the facts are clear. We cannot fund nor sustain such a campaign at this time. This way, Jerusalem will have protection at minimal cost while we refill our coffers. Then and only then will we be able to mount an offensive.' He turned back to Amand. 'Well, Grand Master, are these terms suitable to you?'

'I will need to see the detail,' said Amand,' but based on what you have just said, I give my initial approval to proceeding with the agreement. However, I do have one question.'

'And that is?'

'The timescales are tight. To build a castle capable of defending Jacob's Ford within two years is a monumental task. The fortress will no doubt raise the ire of the Saracens so it must be formidable in stature.'

'I agree,' said Baldwin, 'and that is why we must move as quickly as possible. Can it be done?'

'With enough manpower, yes, but the cost will be prohibitive.'

'Spend what you must,' said the king, 'and add it to the ledger but if we are to continue, then I want my castle within the time specified.'

'In that case,' said Amand, 'you shall have a fortress like no other. Leave it to me, Your Grace.'

'Then it is settled,' said the king. 'I will have the details sent to your quarters for you to sign by dawn.'

'Thank you, Your Grace,' said Amand, 'we will not let you down.'

'Oh, I know you won't,' said Baldwin his voice lowering coldly, 'for if you do, I promise you, Grand Master, there will be consequences.'

The meeting dispersed and the four knights left the king's chambers. Amand and Humphrey walked alongside each other while behind them came Raynald and Reginald.

'Do you hide a smirk, Templar,' said Raynald, 'for your body manner betrays your thoughts.'

Amand stopped walking and turned to face the regent. Both men squared up in the corridor, each unafraid of the other.

'Why do you continue to be so aggressive, Raynald?' said Amand. 'We oft fight under the same banner yet always you seem to seek conflict with your brothers in arms.'

'The Templars are no brothers of mine,' said Raynald, 'nor, I suggest, to the kingdom of Jerusalem.'

'I will not reason with ignorance,' said Amand, 'perhaps your anger should be directed at those who threaten the kingdom, not those who protect it.'

'I kill my fair share of Saracens,' snarled Raynald,' as well you know.'

'Oh, your prowess at killing is well documented,' said Amand, 'and you truly have no equal. I just sometimes wonder how many of those were innocent women or children.'

'Every dead Saracen woman is one who will not give birth to a warrior, every dead child is one that will not grow up to wield a sword. I have no regrets, Amand, my conscience is clear.'

'God will be the judge of that,'' said Amand,

So what of you,' said Raynald, 'how do you justify bleeding the coffers of Jerusalem like a leech upon a sick man?'

'We are warriors of God and fight in his name,' said Amand. 'Our needs are minimal, but everything costs and all should pay their share. But I will not defend our piety to one who is too blind to see. Our record speaks for itself.'

'Perhaps you once were pious,' said Raynald, 'but now it seems you are just well-armed accountants who wield an abacus as often as a sword.'

'Jealousy is a pitiful state,' said Amand. 'I will pray for you.'

'Don't bother,' shouted Raynald as Amand turned and walked away, 'for I do not need your prayers. There are lands to protect and Saracens to kill.'

'You do what you have to do, Sir Raynald,' said Amand over his shoulder, 'I have a castle to build.'

Chapter Six

The Town of Segor

February - AD 1178

    Hunter made his way through the narrow alleyways of Segor, desperately seeking the alchemist they had been told lived in this quarter. They had been in the city just over a month and when Hassan had developed an infection in his leg, had sought out lodgings near the outskirts to enable him to get proper rest. Initial examinations by a physician confirmed that the leg had set as best as could be expected but the ongoing fight against infection was proving troublesome and taking far longer than they would have liked.
    Finally, the physician had suggested that either they remove the leg altogether or seek out the one person who may be able to provide a different treatment, the alchemist.
    To lose a leg would be devastating for a man so young and would commit Hassan to a life of begging or worse, so determined to give him every chance, Cronin had bid Hunter seek out the alchemist in the darker streets of the inner city.
    As he walked, those sitting in the shadowy doorways stared at him curiously, for though his skin was darkened by the sun, he was obviously a westerner and his presence drew suspicion. Soon he was lost amongst the alleyways and knew he needed help. He looked around and saw a boy staring at him from behind a damaged water barrel.
    'My friend,' he said walking across to greet the boy. 'I am in need of help.' His Arabic was basic but adequate. 'I seek the healer who lives in these parts. Do you know of whom I speak?'
    The boy didn't respond but just stared at the stranger through his huge, almond-shaped eyes.
    'The healer,' said Hunter again, 'does he live around here?'
    The boy remained silent but nervously held out his hand.
    Hunter delved beneath his jerkin and retrieved a Dinar before holding it up for the boy to see.
    'This is all yours if you take me to him, understand?'

The boy's eyes widened at the coin and nodded his head vigorously. He hadn't expected a coin and reached out to take the treasure.

Hunter snapped his hand shut and placed the coin back within his pocket.

'Take me to the healer first,' he said, knowing the boy could easily just disappear in the maze of alleyways, 'and the coin is yours.'

Again the boy nodded and stepping from behind the barrel, turned to run down a side street.

'Not so fast,' shouted Hunter and ran after him, desperately trying to keep him in sight. Despite his best efforts, the boy soon disappeared and Hunter was left standing at a convergence of tiny alleyways, totally lost. All around him, rough-looking men stared, knowing that he didn't belong and a few turned away from what they were doing to walk slowly towards him.

Hunter's eyes automatically went to the Jambiyas hanging from their belts, the curved daggers favoured by the tribesmen of the region, and he knew he was in trouble.

'The little dog tricked me,' he murmured to himself as the men neared and his hand sought out his own blade hidden beneath the folds of his cloak. He may have been outnumbered but if he was going to die, he would go down fighting. Without warning a door opened at his back and a voice spoke quietly.

'I wouldn't do that if I was you, stranger,' it said, 'they will cut you down before you have a chance to call out to your god.'

Hunter turned and saw a wizened old man in a doorway. Behind him stood the boy, peering from behind the safety of the old man's thawb.

'Are you the healer?' asked Hunter.

'I am not but you should come inside. To stay out here invites only death.'

With a final glance over his shoulder, Hunter ducked into the dark coolness of the house. The door shut behind him and he followed the man up a tiny winding stairway to a landing before stopping before a closed door.

'The boy says you promised him a coin?' said the old man. 'The debt should be paid before we continue.'

'Of course,' said Hunter and retrieved the Dinar before tossing it over to the boy.

'Thank you,' said the old man, and opened the door before leading Hunter into a windowless room, the air hot, and heavy with incense.

'Sit,' said the old man, indicating the single stool in the centre of the room.

Hunter did as he was bid, looking around nervously. The only door seemed to be the one they had entered through, though a curtain of silks covered the far wall.

'Now state your business,' continued the old man.

'My friends and I have lodgings at the edge of the city,' said Hunter. 'One of our number broke his leg a while ago, and though it has set well, the boy burns with fever and his skin is hot to the touch. We have plied him with poppy milk and Aloe but to no avail. The leg is poisoned and he is dying before our eyes.'

'Are you Christians?'

'We are.'

'And your God does not help you?'

'We have prayed constantly but it seems our pleas go unanswered.'

'Does this not concern you?'

'It is not our place to question upon whom our lord bestows his mercy. We will continue to pray but, in the meantime, we will also do whatever we can to help.'

'Have you considered removing the leg?'

'We are not physicians,' said Hunter, 'and don't want to see him lose his leg, but if it is the only way to save him, then that is what we will have to do.'

'How old is this boy?'

'We think about fifteen years but he is not sure.'

The old man nodded and thought for a few moments.

'Wait here,' he said, 'I will speak to the healer.' He disappeared through the veil of curtains and Hunter could hear the mumble of conversation in a rear room. Eventually, the man returned.

'We need to see the boy,' he said, 'can he be brought here?'

'I don't think so,' said Hunter, 'he is in too much pain and you saw those men outside, I fear we would not make it here alive.'

'Just local youths with frustration in their hearts,' said the old man. 'If you cannot come here, then the healer will come to you. Where are your lodgings?'

'Opposite the smaller tower on the northeast corner of the city. We are above the stable.'

'I know it,' said the old man. 'Return whence you came; we will be there by nightfall. Ensure you have a fire and plenty of hot water.'

'And the cost?'

'If he dies, there will be no cost.'

'And if he lives?'

'The price will be your best horse.'

'A horse?' sneered Hunter, 'you are surely no better than the brigands that ride the desert trails.'

'A horse for a man's life seems like a good trade to me. That is the healer's price.'

'Let me speak to him,' said Hunter. 'Perhaps I can agree a more suitable agreement.'

'It is forbidden for western men to lay eyes on a woman of Segor,' said the old man, 'there will be no other agreement,'

'The healer is a woman?' gasped Hunter.

'She is. But you will keep that knowledge between us. If it leaves this room, she could be killed.'

'Female healers are not allowed here?'

'Not in Segor.'

'Then I suggest you are halving the number of people able to save lives,' said Hunter, 'it is the way of the fool.'

'Yet it is these fools to whom you turn for help.'

'You have me backed into a corner,' said Hunter eventually. 'A horse is too much to pay but the boy is important to us. The arrangement is agreed.'

'Good. We will bring everything we need but you cannot go back the same way you came, the boy will take you a safer route for another coin.'

'At this rate, he will one day be a rich man,' said Hunter, reaching into his pocket.

'He is already rich with freedom,' said the man, 'now go and make the preparations. We will be there shortly.'

A few hours later, Hunter and Jakelin stood alongside the cot bearing the semi-conscious body of Hassan. Outside it was getting dark and both men had started to worry the healer wasn't coming.

'So what's so special about this healer?' asked Jakelin.

'I have no idea,' said Hunter, 'I only met her manservant.'

'Her?'

'Yes, the healer is a woman.'

'In this culture, a female physician is a rare thing.'

'So I understand. Perhaps she is some sort of witch.'

'The other physicians certainly referred to her as an alchemist,' said Jakelin,' so I would be interested in seeing what methods she employs when she gets here.'

'*If* she gets here,' said Hunter, 'it's already dark.' His hand wandered to the wooden crucifix hanging around his neck. 'If she arrives, we should be careful, that we are not caught amongst her spells and enchantments.'

'You believe in such things?'

'Where there is good, there is surely evil,' said Hunter. 'Perhaps that is why the others were so hesitant in recommending her. Perhaps the old woman is so deformed that she cannot walk the streets in daylight lest all who see her countenance drop dead from horror.'

'You listen to too many campfire tales, my friend,' said Jakelin, 'the only demons are of the soul, and it is they who make men evil.'

'Nevertheless,' said Hunter, 'I have seen many strange things in my time so will be on my guard. Where is Cronin,' he continued, 'he said he would be back by now?'

'Hassan was conscious a few hours ago,' said Jakelin, 'and gave us the name of the man who may be able to help in our quest. Cronin has gone to find him.'

'I hope he has his wits about him,' said Hunter, 'this city is not a place for strangers in daylight, let alone during the hours of darkness.'

'He is a resourceful man,' said Jakelin, 'I'm sure he will be fine.'

Across the city, Cronin stood in a dark doorway in the street of the jewellers. He felt uncomfortable in Hassan's thawb but knew he would have stood out like a sore thumb if he had worn his own garb. He looked along the street. Many stalls had gone, closed for the night but a few remained, hoping for a last deal from the many visitors that passed through the city.

He waited patiently until a harmless-looking old man wandered down the street towards him. He knew very little Arabic but had no other option but to engage him in conversation.

'My friend,' he said, stepping out into the gloom. 'I seek a man called Shamsur-Rahman. Do you know of him?'

The old man looked at Cronin suspiciously but eventually pointed to another man sat on a stool further up the street.

'Shamsur-Rahman?' asked Cronin again.

The old man nodded and continued on his way.

Cronin sunk back into the shadows and for a few moments, watched the man he sought, deciding how best to approach him. It was unlikely that he spoke French or English, but somehow, he needed to be able to communicate with him. Realising he was wasting time, he waited until the footfall had subsided and crossed the street to approach the Arab, his heart racing at the danger he was putting himself in. Slowly he walked toward him, trying to frame the few Arab words he knew into some sort of order. Finally, he arrived and the man looked up at him.

'You took your time, Infidel,' said the Arab, in broken English, 'I was about to go to my bed.'

'You speak our language,' said Cronin, in surprise.

'A man in my position knows many languages,' said the man, 'especially those that bear a profit.

'You have been watching me?'

'Of course.'

'For how long?'

'Since the moment you arrived.'

'How did you know I was English?'

'It could not have been more obvious if you had draped yourself in the flag of St George.'

'Are you Shamsur-Rahman?'

'I may be. It depends if there is a profit involved.'

Cronin looked around nervously.

'There is definitely a profit involved,' he said, 'and a handsome one at that, but can we talk inside?'

'Of course,' said Shamsur, and got to his feet. 'Are you alone.'

'Yes.'

'Come. We will eat and we will drink. Then we can discuss business.'

He led the way through the low doorway and Cronin followed him inside, bolting the door behind them.

Back above the stable, Hunter peered out through a crack in the door at the top of the steps leading up to their lodgings.

Walking down the street came an old man leading a woman by the hand. Although she was draped in layers of heavy veils, it was evident she was bent almost double by age and several people made a point of getting out of her way out of respect. Hunter groaned quietly, realising his worst fears had been realised.

'She's here,' he said quietly and unlocked the door as the visitors climbed the steps. 'Thank you for coming.' he said and stepped aside as the old man carefully led the old woman into the room. Hunter closed the door and turned to face the newcomers.

'Where is he?' asked the old man.

'Through there.' said Hunter and pointed towards the only other room in the building. 'He is asleep.'

The old man led the healer through closely followed by Hunter and Jakelin. All four stood around the semi-conscious boy until finally, the old man spoke again.

'Before we proceed, we need your word as Christians that what you are about to witness remains a secret amongst us. Is that clear?'

'Why would you accept our promises?' asked Jakelin. 'You are not Christian so surely they are meaningless to you.'

'If they are meaningful to you, that is all that matters. Now, do I have your word?'

'Aye,' said Jakelin.

'Anything,' said Hunter, 'just make him well again with your magic.'

'There will be no magic performed here tonight,' said the woman's voice, from under the veils, 'only the application of nature.' Without warning, the bent woman stood up straight and allowed her cloak to fall away. To Hunter's and Jakelin's surprise, the person who they had thought was an old hag only moments earlier, was a very beautiful young woman. 'Bring me candles,' she said, 'and hot water.'

Nobody moved, such was their shock.

'Well,' she said again, 'do you want your friend to live or not?'

'Of course,' stuttered Hunter and reluctantly tore his eyes away from the vision of beauty to go and find more candles.

'You,' said the woman, turning to Jakelin, 'remove his clothes and lay him on the table. I will also need bandages, as clean as you can find.'

'We have clean bandages already.'

'Then bring them to me.'

For the next few moments, Jakelin and the old man arranged Hassan on the table and removed his clothing, leaving only a draped cloth to cover his modesty.

The woman started feeling Hassan's leg gently, rubbing her hands either side of the break. Her fingers probed further into the flesh, causing the boy to whimper in pain as she homed in on the problem.

'What have you already tried?' she asked.

'The last physician tried potions to cure the ills,' said Jakelin as Hunter arrived with more candles, 'as well as bloodletting to drain the infection. We even allowed one of your holy men to pray over him in an effort to reach his own god, but nothing has worked.'

'I thought you said he was a Christian,' said the woman.

'He is,' said Hunter, 'but once worshipped Allah. We thought it prudent to leave no stone unturned.'

'Give me more light,' said the woman and waited as more candles were placed close to Hassan's leg.

'The break is healing well,' she said,' but the poison is on the inside. It needs to be cut out if he is to have any chance.'

'Have you done this before?' asked Hunter.

'I have.'

'And is it a successful procedure.'

'Some live, some don't. Each is different.'

'What do you think?' asked Hunter turning to Jakelin.

'It should be Cronin's decision,' came the reply, 'the boy is his responsibility,'

'But he is not here.'

'This boy will be dead by nightfall tomorrow if you do not do something,' said the woman. 'The choice is clear. Leave him as he is and he will die. Let me treat him and he may still die, or he may live.'

'Do it,' said Hunter.

'In that case,' said the woman, 'bring me the hot water. I also need bowls, four in total.'

Hunter disappeared down the stairs and came back with a steaming bucket and four clay bowls.

The woman placed the four pots on the table and waited as Hunter filled them from the bucket.

'Just fill three,' she said, 'but keep what is left of the water. We will need it later.' She opened a leather wrap and lowered several lethal-looking narrow blades into the first pot.

'When I say,' she continued, 'I want you to hand me the knives one by one. Do not touch the blades under any circumstances.'

'Why,' asked Hunter, 'are they bewitched?'

The woman stared at Hunter with a hint of humour on her face.

'No,' she said eventually, 'they are not bewitched, they are clean. Now be quiet and do as I say. Place half of the bandages in the second pot. The third pot will be used solely for the washing of hands.'

As they watched, she retrieved several clay bottles from the pack carried by the old man and proceeded to mix some of the contents into the fourth bowl.

'That smells like Garlic,' said Hunter.

'You have a good nose,' said the woman as she mixed the potion. 'When crushed it is a powerful weapon against the poison in your friend's leg, as is this.' She held up another jar. 'This is honey and you would do well to remember these things. Sometimes wounds, however caused, can cause the flesh to rot. Honey and Garlic, in the right consistencies, can help kill the poison but only if the circumstances are right.'

'And what circumstances are those?' asked Jakelin.

'The wound must be rid of all putrefying flesh, and then kept clean. Anything that touches it after the cleaning can cause the poison to return, and that includes dirty hands.' She placed her own hands into the third bowl of water, wincing at the heat but proceeded to wash them thoroughly. 'Now,' she said eventually, 'wash your own hands and give me the first knife. When I cut him, drain one of the bandages of water and use it to keep the wound clear of blood.'

Hunter did as he was told and as Jakelin and the old man held Hassan down, the woman gently dragged the first knife along the boy's swollen leg. The razor-sharp blade cut deeply and as they watched, an awful smell came from the wound, causing Hunter to gag.

'That is the poison,' said the woman, seemingly unaffected, 'the flesh is rotting and we need to cut it away.' Quickly she scraped away the infection as Hunter mopped up the thick black blood. 'We must get it all,' she said as she wielded the knife, 'to leave any invites further infection.'

For the next few moments, she cut away all the remaining infected flesh, peering closely to get at whatever she could find.

'The blood is red,' said Hunter.

'That is a good sign,' said the woman. 'Now pass me a clean knife.'

Using the next blade she gently scraped the wound clean before washing it with another bandage from the hot water. Finally, she picked up the pot containing the paste and nodded towards the old man.

Immediately he produced a small purse and undid the strings before pouring what seemed like fine dust into the mixture of honey and garlic.

'I knew it,' said Hunter. 'A magic ingredient.'

'It is pure silver,' said the woman without turning around, 'nothing more, but in powder form, it too helps to kill the infection. Combined with the garlic and honey, it is a powerful weapon against the poison.'

She smeared the paste thinly on the walls of the wound before finally producing a needle and sewing the wound back together.

'Is it done?' asked Jakelin

'It is,' said the woman. 'In the morning there will be more swelling and redness but that is normal. Use the rest of this paste on the wound for the next few days but only after you have washed him, and your hands with hot water. Understood?'

'Understood,' said Jakelin.

'Will he live?' asked Hunter.

'He is young, and seems strong so has a good chance,' said the woman, 'but he is in his God's hands now, whichever one he worships.'

'Who are you,' asked Jakelin, 'and why did you swear us to secrecy?'

'My name is Sumeira, and I am not of these people. I am from Greece and studied the art of medicine there but I am not allowed to use my knowledge in Segor.'

'Why not?'

'Because I treated one of their holy men a few years ago but he died and I was held responsible. They let me live but will not allow me to apply my skills further.'

'Why don't you leave?' asked Hunter.

'Because the man who was my husband disowned me and has now married someone else.'

'All the more reason to leave, surely.'

'I have a small child, a daughter. She lives with my husband and I see her once every seven days. If I left, then I would never see her again.'

'What would happen if they found out you helped us?'

'I don't know but I would fear the worst. At the very least I would be exiled.'

'Then they will not find out from us,' said Hunter. 'Whatever the outcome, your presence here this night will stay between us.'

'Thank you,' said Sumeira. 'I will leave now but return every second night to check on him. When the moon is next full, we will know if he will live and the price will be paid.'

'Your help is greatly appreciated,' said Jakelin and walked her and the old man to the door. Sumeira donned the veils and stooped into the guise of an old woman before descending the steps and heading out into the night.

An hour or so later, Cronin returned from his meeting with the Arab.

'Where have you been,' asked Hunter, 'you have missed the healer?'

'These things cannot be rushed,' said Cronin. 'How is Hassan?'

'Settled, and it seems the healer knew what she was doing. If he is not dead by morning, he should survive.'

'She?'

'Yes, a woman, and an attractive one at that but her presence must remain a secret between us.'

'Why?'

Hunter recounted what had happened as Cronin helped himself to cold meat and dates from the food bag. Finally, he stopped eating and drank watered wine from a goatskin.

'What of you?' asked Jakelin eventually. 'Was your business successful?'

'It was,' said Hunter. 'I found the man Hassan said may be able to help and the boy was right. Not only has he seen the cross but actually bought it from the thief.'

'So do you have it?'

'Unfortunately not, neither does he. He gave it to his brother to sell in a town called Al-Shabiya.'

'Why send it there?'

'Because each year, Al-Shabiya holds a market solely for the purpose of selling jewels and other artefacts. Traders and customers come from all over the Levant just to see the wares and strike a good bargain. The cross is obviously much more attractive to Christians and there will be many rich men there be willing to pay a good price.'

'I would have thought that the market would be an excellent target for thieves and bandits,' said Hunter.

'Normally yes, but there is a Christian castle nearby and the castellan there provides the village with protection for the three days the market is there. Obviously, there is a price to be paid but the collective cost is minimal when compared with the riches to be made,'

'What is the name of the castle,' asked Hunter.

'Krak de Moabites.'

'I know of it,' said Jakelin, 'but we call it Karak. We have a commandery there.'

'Even better,' said Cronin. 'We can obtain the money we need from our brothers and do the deal.'

'So are we going to Al-Shabiya?'

'Yes, but the market is not for another three months.'

'Just as well,' said Hunter, 'as Hassan is going to need some time to heal.'

'We will give him as much as we can,' said Cronin, 'but when the time comes, we will leave, with or without him.'

Chapter Seven

Jacob's Ford

March - AD 1178

Eudes de St. Amand sat astride his horse on a hill, examining the sight below him. Down in the valley, the River Jordan wound its way serenely through swampy land before the ground hardened and the flow increased before making its way south to the Sea of Galilee. Between the two extremes, a stretch of the river flowed slow and wide across a stony bed. The water was only knee-deep, and the only such place for leagues in either direction.

This was Jacob's Ford, the crossing place where the king had agreed to build a castle only a few months earlier. There had been great progress and the site had already been cleared and marked for the labourers to start digging out the huge amounts of spoil to accommodate the foundations. Since the initial meeting with the king in Ashkelon, the Templar architects had come up with a design that would rival any other castle in the Holy Land in both magnificence and solidity.

The walls would be over thirty feet tall and protected on all four corners by giant towers stretching another twenty feet above that. Along its walls would be further towers topping massive ramparts formed of stone and iron and the whole thing protected by a wide ditch on two sides with the steep slopes of the hill protecting the other two. Its location meant it could easily be defended against siege engines and the huge integral well already being dug at its centre would mean there would be plenty of safe water should it ever be besieged.

In all the planned castle could easily hold a garrison of over two thousand and when finished, would become one of, if not the best-defended castles in the Outremer, allowing the Templars to roam at will throughout the disputed territories east of the River Jordan.

'The work progresses well,' said Brother Valmont, the Templar Seneschal at Amand's side, 'the calculations have been made and the ground will soon be broken. Within the month the masons can start laying the foundations.'

'Have you sourced enough stone?'

'Aye, my lord,' said Valmont. 'Most will come from this very hill but we have identified another two quarries within an hour of this place. Hundreds of carts will bring stone day and night and word has been sent out far and wide that there is work to be had. Within weeks, there will be men upon this hill like flies on a corpse.'

'And you are comfortable that we can meet the deadline?'

'As long as Saladin leaves us alone, I see no reason why we cannot finish the task with time to spare.'

'It is a shame he managed to escape,' said the Grand Master, 'but I see no reason why he should bother us any time soon. I expect he is still in Egypt, spreading lies about how Montgisard was a great victory.'

'Actually, my lord,' said Valmont, 'I have heard whispers that he is already recruiting men to his banner and it is only a matter of time before he rides north again.'

'It is no surprise,' said Amand, 'but I am not unduly worried. Nevertheless, arrange more men to join us from our other fortresses. The construction of this castle presents a great opportunity for our order as well as the Holy Land itself. We cannot afford for its completion to be threatened in any way.'

'I will make the necessary arrangements,' said Valmont.

'And what of a potential castellan?'

'There are several that come to mind, but I suggest we elevate Simon of Syracuse. He is a pious man and has served us well these past five years as an Under-Marshal in both Blancheguarde and Karak. He also fought at Montgisard and acquitted himself well. He has earned the post.'

'I'm happy with your decision,' said Amand. Make the necessary arrangements.

'As you wish, my lord.'

'One more thing,' said Amand, 'have you any news of the king?'

'Aye,' said Valmont, 'we have received dispatches saying that he and his court are to relocate to the city of Tiberius.'

'Tiberius?' repeated Amand, mildly surprised. 'That is only half a day's ride away from here.'

'It is,' said Valmont, 'and you can guarantee he will have at least part of his army with him should we need reinforcements.'

'The military benefit is welcomed,' said Amand, 'but if I know Baldwin, then I suspect he is more likely coming to keep an eye on our progress. Anyway, we should be getting back to camp. Humphrey of Toron will be joining us tonight and I do not want to be found wanting for hospitality.'

'Of course,' said Valmont and both men turned their horses to return back down into the valley.

Several hundred metres away, another man stood on a hill, looking towards the crossing at Jacob's Ford. Behind him, hidden in a copse of olive trees, ten of his warriors waited with their horses as their commander talked quietly with the man at his side, one of the local labour overseers employed by the Templars to complete the groundworks for the castle.

The overseer had a parchment spread out on the floor and used his knife to point at the hill before referring to it on the sketch he had prepared for the Saracen warrior.

'Here,' he said, 'at each corner, there will be the four main towers. Along the walls there will be others, but smaller.'

'What are they building there?' asked the Saracen, pointing at a timber framework at the centre of the hill.

'They are sinking a well,' said the overseer, 'one that will fulfil all their needs in the event of a siege.'

'How will the walls be built,' asked the Saracen, 'of earth or stone?'

'Stone,' said the overseer, 'huge walls that no man will be able to breach. Two of the approaches are protected by cliffs but the others will have ditches to prevent the approach of catapults. I have few details yet but from I am told, they intend to make it the strongest castle throughout the Holy Land. Even at this stage, it is obvious that this fortress will be like no other and if allowed to be constructed, it will dominate the area for many generations.'

The warrior stared over to Jacob's Ford, realising the seriousness of the situation. He had to do something but with the Ayyubid army defeated and Salah ad-Din still in Egypt, his options were limited. The information was limited but if everything went to plan, there were plans afoot that would soon increase the flow of information.

'You have done well, Ramaz,' he said, 'and will be well rewarded. Go back to your work and learn whatever you can. If you find out something important, leave a message in the usual manner and I will come as soon as I can.'

'I will, my lord,' said Ramaz, glancing at the bird skull he had lodged in the fork of a tree a few days earlier.

The Warrior walked away, leaving the overseer on the hill behind him.

Ramaz watched them ride away, his heart at last slowing down after the stress of the last few hours. Working for the Christians was bad enough but being a spy on behalf of the Ayyubid was pressure like no other, especially as the man he reported too had the ear of the Sultan himself. The warrior was the most important man Ramaz had ever spoken too in his life. His name was Sabek ad-Din, one of the most powerful generals in Sala-ad-Din's army.

Chapter Eight

April - AD 1178

The Town of Segor

Cronin watched Hassan limp around the exercise paddock, leaning heavily on a stick as he carried out the daily routine given to him by Sumeira. It had been over two months since she had treated Hassan's broken leg and he had made good progress, just not enough.

'Look, my lord,' said Hassan, 'today I am even faster than yesterday and tomorrow, I will cast away the stick.'

'Is there any pain?' asked Cronin.

'A little, but I have borne worse. Now I can go to Al-Shabiya with you.'

Cronin looked at Hassan. Despite the boy's assurances, the sergeant knew he still struggled with his injury and would be a burden on the journey to come. It had already been agreed between Cronin and the stable owner that Hassan could remain and work for his keep as a groom until he was stronger, but the boy was desperate not to be left behind and worked every day to strengthen his leg.

'Hassan,' said Cronin, 'you will be better off here, you know that. The journey is hard and full of brigands and Saracen raiders. If we are forced to fight, we won't be able to defend you.'

'But I will also fight, my lord,' said Hassan, 'did I not prove myself at Montgisard?'

'Indeed you did,' said Cronin, 'and your mettle is not in question. The strongest of men would struggle with that injury but if we have to flee, you will become a burden.'

'But my lord, I am almost as good as I was. Look.'

Before Cronin could respond, Hassan cast away the stick and tried to run across the compound but hadn't gone halfway before his leg gave out beneath him and he collapsed into the dirt.

Cronin sighed and walked across to crouch beside him.

'Hassan,' he said, 'you know I would never leave you behind unless I had to but it is important that I get to Al-Shabiya before the market starts. Time is running out and I can wait no longer but there is also a role here for you to play.'

Hassan looked up at the man who had become his friend and mentor.

'What would you have me do?'

'There are rumours that Saladin is already recruiting an army from these parts,' continued Cronin, 'and if it is true, it would help if you could gather whatever information you could. You have already been accepted by the locals so why don't you stay here and be our eyes in Segor? What you learn may be of use to the king himself.'

Hassan stared at the Templar sergeant, fully aware that Cronin was only searching for ways to lessen the bitterness of his decision. His heart was heavy but he knew he could no longer make his friend feel worse than he already did.

'My Lord,' he said with a sigh. 'I wish with all my heart that I was going with you, but if that is your decision, then I will adhere to your will. Go to Al-Shabiya and retrieve the cross. When you return, I will still be here waiting.'

'It is the right thing to do, Hassan,' said Cronin, tapping the young man on the shoulder. 'When I return, I promise we will ride together back to Castle Blancheguarde.'

He helped Hassan to his feet and made his way back over to the stable where Jakelin and Hunter were waiting.

'How did he take it?' asked Hunter as Cronin approached.

'As well as you would expect,' said Cronin. 'He is not happy but accepts the decision.'

'Then we must be on our way,' said Hunter. 'Time is not on our side.'

'Are the horses ready?' asked Cronin.

'They are,' said Jakelin, 'we have enough food and water to get to Al-Shabiya but can restock in the commandery in Karak.'

'Good,' said Cronin. 'Now all we have to do is get there.'

'I have an idea,' said Hunter. 'I heard that a caravan left Segor this morning headed for Damascus. The route passes within a few leagues of Al-Shabiya so we could join them.'

'We will travel faster alone,' said Jakelin.

'Perhaps, but there is safety in numbers. The pace will be slower but we can trade with the caravan owners if needs be and share the protection a large caravan brings.'

'It sounds good to me,' said Cronin, and turned to face the knight. 'My Lord, the decision is yours.'

'This is your quest, Tom Cronin,' said Jakelin, 'and I am here to pay a penance for my sins. Until then I cede to your decisions.'

'So be it,' said Cronin. 'In that case, I agree with Hunter. We will take advantage of the safety of the caravan. If we leave now, we should be with them by nightfall.' Jakelin looked over Cronin's shoulder and the sergeant turned to see Hassan standing behind him.

'Hassan,' said the knight, 'it is time for us to go. Fear not for we will meet up soon but God has other work for you. Stay safe, my friend.' He offered Hassan a purse of coins but Hassan just turned and walked away.

'Hassan,' called Hunter, 'wait.'

'Leave him,' said Cronin. 'The words have been said so it is better that we just go. We can leave the purse upon his bed.'

Several minutes later, the three men mounted their horses and without looking back, headed north to the eastern coast of the Dead Sea. Behind them Hassan watched them go through a crack in the doors, angry that they had actually left him alone. He had already found the purse and though he wanted to fling it after them, he knew that life would be hard alone and he needed all the help he could get.

Outside the city, the three Christians encouraged their mounts to a trot, keen to catch up with the trading caravan before dark.

'You say there is a commandery in Karak, my lord,' said Cronin as they rode.

'Aye,' said Jakelin. 'I have never been there but I am told the castle is one of the best in the Holy Land and garrisoned by over a thousand men at arms including a hundred knights and twenty of our brothers. It is a powerful fortress that commands the road between Egypt and Damascus east of the salt sea.'

'Who is the castellan?' asked Hunter.

'Raynald of Chatillon,' said Jakelin.

'But surely Raynald is the king's regent,' said Cronin, 'and serves in Jerusalem. He led the king's army at Montgisard not a few months since.'

'Aye,' he did, said Jakelin, 'but he is the lord of the entire Oultrejordain including the castles at Karak, Montreal to the south and its outpost in the Valley of Moses. It is said he also commands the castle on the northern edge of the gulf of Aqabar, from where you can see into Egypt itself.

'The butcher is certainly a powerful man,' said Hunter with surprise.

'The butcher?' said Cronin, turning to face Hunter. 'I have not heard him called that before.'

'It is a name given to him amongst his own men,' said Hunter, 'though none would dare say it within earshot. He is known for his cruelty to all men, no matter what their allegiance. If you have cause to deal with him, tread as carefully as if you were in a pit of vipers.'

'I heard that he served over fifteen years in an Ayyubid prison,' said Cronin. 'I suppose hardship like that can do things to a man.'

'It can,' said Hunter, 'but the butcher made his reputation before he was imprisoned. Captivity just made it worse. He was released only two years ago, exchanged for Ayyubid prisoners as no man would pay a ransom, such was his notoriety. When he arrived in Jerusalem, he was penniless with neither fortune nor position. But look at him now, Baron of Hebron, lord of all the Oultrejordain and regent to the King of Jerusalem. To achieve that in little over two years takes a very special type of man. They say even Saladin trembles when he hears his name.'

'There's the caravan,' said Cronin staring into the distance as they reached the top of a hill. 'Let's just hope they are friendly to westerners.'

On the road ahead they could see a long line of carts, mules and camels, each piled up with all sorts of goods from pottery and gold to silks and spices. At the centre of the column walked two lines of slaves, each bound to the one in front by ropes attached to metal collars around their throats. A few hundred metres to either side rode dozens of Bedouin tribesmen, fearless fighters engaged to protect the caravan from brigands on the road to Damascus.

As the Christians descended the slope, several of the riders split from the flanking guard and rode towards them, each drawing Shamshirs from their scabbards as they neared.

'Take it easy,' said Hunter quietly as they neared, 'lift your hands so they can see we are no threat.'

His comrades reined in their horses and lifted their empty hands as the Bedouin horsemen rode around them in a circle.

'We are friends,' said Hunter in his broken Arabic, 'and seek safe passage to the village of Al-Shabiya.'

The riders stopped circling and one urged his horse a few paces closer.

'You are a long way from the safe roads, stranger,' he said, 'what business do you have this side of the salt sea?'

'One of trade only,' said Hunter. 'We seek a certain item stolen from Jerusalem yet seek no retribution. Instead, we offer a good price for its return and have been told it can be found in the markets of Al-Shabiya. In return for safe passage, we offer a good price.'

'The price is one hundred Dinars per person,' said the Bedouin, 'nothing less.'

Hunter turned to face his comrades.

'Three hundred Dinars, he said, 'do we have such an amount?'

'About half,' said Cronin. 'Offer him our services as mercenaries to cover the rest.'

Hunter passed on the information before turning around again.

'He wants to know how we can prove we are worthy fighters.'

Without speaking, Jakelin urged his horse forward a few paces and stopped directly in front of the Bedouin, pulling aside his cloak to show him the hilt of his sword. The Bedouin glanced down and saw the emblem of the Templars engraved into the pommel. He looked back up and turned to Hunter.

'The deal is done,' he said, 'follow me.'

'Your place will be at this cart,' he said, reaching the rear of the caravan, 'amongst the poor and the slave overseers. Keep your business to yourself and make no trouble. Tomorrow I will call upon you to take your place in the outer guard. Do not let me down.' He rode away leaving the riders standing in the dust of the last wagon.

'One hundred and fifty Dinars is robbery,' said Cronin.' We would have been better off risking the road.'

'You have a lot to learn, Thomas Cronin,' said Hunter. 'Out here the man with power decrees the price, the man without power accepts. We are the latter.' He dismounted and led his horse to the side of the wagon, tying the reins to a rail. 'Come,' he said, 'this pace will get no faster so we may as well unburden our mounts. We have a long way to go.'

Later that night all three men sat around a campfire on the side of the road. The cart-master had made a pot of mutton stew and shared it liberally. Despite Hunter's best efforts at conversation, the man just smiled in return, his toothless gums rotten with disease.

'I guess he speaks a dialect unknown to me,' said Hunter.

'It's a shame Hassan isn't here,' said Jakelin, 'he seems to know many of the Bedouin dialects.'

'I fear even he wouldn't be able to help,' said Cronin, 'the creature seems nothing more than an imbecile.'

'The reason your host does not talk, Thomas Cronin,' said a voice behind them, 'is that he has been forbidden to do so.'

All three men jumped to their feet and spun around, seeing an Arab standing before them dressed in a full white thawb.

'Do we know you?' asked Hunter, his eyes narrowing suspiciously.

'I am known to your friend,' said the man removing the hood from his head and uncovering his face, 'my name is Shamsur-Rahman, from the jewellery quarter of Segor. Your friend and I had business together.'

'What are you doing here, Shamsur-Rahman,' asked Cronin, 'I thought your brother attended the markets of Al-Shabiya on your behalf?'

'He does,' said Shamsur, 'but I do not place all my eggs in one basket. This is a dangerous road, my friend, and if his caravan was to be attacked and he lost all our items of commerce then my business would be finished. By sharing the merchandise between many caravans we cut our chances of catastrophic loss and our family still has a future.'

'So you are going to Al-Shabiya?'

'I am. It looks like we will be travellers together. Perhaps we can share refreshments on the journey.'

'I look forward to it,' said Cronin.

'As do I. Now, I will leave you to your meal. It seems you have an excellent host.'

The jeweller walked away into the night leaving the three Christians staring at his back.

'Is that the man you dealt with in Segor?' asked Jakelin.

'He is, my lord,' said Cronin, 'why?'

'Because there is something about him that makes me want to draw my sword,' said the knight.

'I agree that he makes the stomach turn,' said Cronin, 'but the success of our quest relies on me maintaining a good relationship with him. We have no other choice but to trust him.'

'Out here, my friend,' said Hunter, 'you would do well to trust nobody.'

Chapter Nine

April - AD 1178

The Town of Segor

Hassan spent the evening walking around the back streets and bazaars of Segor. Eventually, the night closed in and he headed back to the stable. Not even he, a Bedouin, was safe in the alleyways of Segor after dark.

He opened the stable door and went to comfort the horses, reassuring them in the darkness. Despite desperately wanting to go with his friends, his family's history meant he had an affinity with the beasts and at least he knew that until Cronin and the others returned, he would be gainfully employed doing something he loved. He walked to the ladder that accessed the loft where he was going to sleep and was halfway up when he heard a noise from one of the empty stalls.

Carefully he climbed back down and drawing his knife, crept to the far end of the stable before coming to a stop and listening carefully in the darkness. Horse theft was common in the area and quality animals brought a good price in the outer villages. Any injured or deemed not good enough were slaughtered for the meat and though Hassan was injured, he was willing to fight to the death to protect them.

Again there was a noise though this time, a rustle amongst the fodder. He crept forward and peered in. At the far end, he could just about see the pile of hay, piled up for the morning feed. As he watched there was another movement and he knew someone was hiding in the dark.

'Come out,' he said nervously, 'show yourself.'

The room fell deathly still and all movement stopped beneath the hay.

'I'm warning you,' he said, 'there are four of us here, all armed and it would go better for you if you surrendered right now.'

Again there was silence so Hassan picked up a hay rake and walked closer before stretching out and pulling half of the pile away.

A voice called out and Hassan jumped back in shock as he saw who it was hiding beneath the hay.

'Please,' said a woman, 'don't hurt us.'

Hassan gasped in astonishment. It was the physician who had healed his leg, and in her arms, a pretty girl no more than six years old.

'Sumeira,' he said, 'what are you doing here?'

'Hassan,' said Sumeira, her voice full of relief, 'is that you?'

'It is,' said Hassan, casting away the rake, 'let me help you.'

He took the child from Sumeira and waited as she got to her feet and brushed away the hay before taking back the child.

'Hassan,' said Sumeira looking around, 'where are the others?'

'They're not here,' said Hassan, 'it is just me.'

'But you said there were four of you,' said Sumeira, 'I heard it clearly.'

'That was when I thought you were a horse thief,' said Hassan, 'the truth is that they are well on their way to Al-Shabiya.'

'Al-Shabiya, why?'

'To retrieve something on behalf of the King of Jerusalem.'

'Yet you are still here?'

'I am. They said I was too weak to ride and had to stay until they returned, but what about you? Why do you hide amongst the hay like a criminal?'

'I had nowhere else to go, Hassan,' she said, 'I had to run away and find somewhere to hide us both.' She looked at the scared little girl. 'This is my daughter, Emani. Her father told me that today would be the last time I saw her as he was leaving for another place and would not tell me where. I cannot live without her, Hassan, I had to do something.'

'Do you not have friends in Segor where you can hide?'

'No, most are aware of my situation and will not help a woman against the wishes of her husband. I have to get away, Hassan, and thought your friends could help me.'

'They have long gone, Sumeira,' he said, 'but perhaps I can help. What is it you want?'

'I do not think there is anything you can do,' sighed Sumeira, her voice heavy with regret. 'Segor is no longer safe for us but with your friends gone, I fear this is no hope.'

'I don't agree,' said Hassan, 'surely there are those in the city who would gladly help for a price?'

'I have no money, Hassan,' said Sumeira, 'at least not the sort of coin needed to pay the kind of men you talk about.'

'Maybe not,' said Hassan, 'but I do. Come with me.'

Half an hour later, Hassan, Sumeira and the child all sat on Hassan's bed up in the roof space. On the blanket, they had counted out all the money Jakelin had left as well as the few coins Sumeira had brought.

'Almost two hundred Dinars,' said Hassan. 'It's not much but may get you to another city.'

'I cannot thank you enough,' said Sumeira, 'and I swear that one day I will pay you back.'

'You already have,' said Hassan. 'You saved my life, remember?'

'There is one thing more I need of you,' said Sumeira, 'I cannot go into the backstreets to find passage. It is far too dangerous. If it wasn't for Emani I would take the risk but I cannot risk her being left without a mother.' She looked up at Hassan. 'Can I place upon you this one last burden, to seek out someone willing to smuggle us out of Segor?'

'You know you can,' said Hassan, 'where is it you wish to go?'

'Alas I feel my options are limited,' said Sumeira. 'With so little money we must accept passage on wherever the next trading caravan leads.'

'Leave it to me,' said Hassan, scooping up the coins and placing them in the purse. 'When I go, ensure you lock the door from the inside and open it to nobody except me. I will be back by dawn.'

She followed him down the ladder and watched him go before returning to the loft and tucking the sleeping girl beneath Hassan's single blanket.

'Don't worry, little one,' she whispered, 'soon we will be as free as the birds in the sky.'

Several hours later, Sumeira woke to a gentle knocking on the door. She climbed down the ladder and let Hassan through before following him back up to the loft.

'Did you do it,' she asked, 'was there enough?'

'Not quite,' said Hassan, 'so I had to barter to get what we wanted.'

'Barter with what?' asked Sumeira.

'I had to tell him you were a physician.'

'Does he know my circumstances?'

'He does but that does not interest him. The deal was two hundred and fifty Dinars for the three of us as long as you served him as a physician and I as a hunter. In return, he would grant us safe passage and hide you if anyone comes looking.'

'You are also coming?' asked Sumeira.

'I am,' said Hassan.

'But I thought you said you were supposed to stay here?'

'I am,' said Hassan, 'but this is a chance too good to miss.'

'Why?'

'Because,' said Hassan, 'the caravan is going to Tiberius, but on the way, it will stop in Al Shabiya.'

The following night, Hassan, Sumeira and Emani made their way through the dark alleyways to the place where the traders' caravan had already formed up ready for the journey to Al-Shabiya. They kept to the shadows wherever possible and kept their hoods over their heads to hide their faces from any interested onlookers. Eventually, they reached the edge of the camp and asked one of the guards where they could find the caravan master.

'He will be here shortly,' said the guard, 'wait there.' He indicated a covered cart to one side and the three fugitives ducked gratefully into its shadow. An hour or so later, a large man emerged from one of the nearby alleyways and after talking to the guard, headed in their direction.

'Here he is,' said Hassan and stepped out to meet him.

'So you made it,' said the man, cutting short Hassan's greeting, 'where are the others?'

Sumeira stepped out of the shadows with her sleeping daughter in her arms.

'Come closer,' said the man, 'so I can see you.'

Sumeira walked into the moonlight causing a reaction from the caravan master.

'A beauty,' he said, 'yet also a physician. A rare find indeed. My name is Ahmed, what should I call you?'

'I am Sumeira, my lord,' she said, 'and this is my daughter Emani. We are forever in your debt for this and promise we will be no trouble.'

'Let's not get ahead of ourselves,' said the trader. He looked around the camp. 'There have already been men here asking about a woman and a child, and I am taking a great risk. It seems your husband is an important man and if I am caught smuggling you out of the city, my life could be at risk. I am in two minds to cancel the agreement.'

'Please,' said Sumeira, her voice shaking, 'do not change your mind, my lord. My life and that of my child both lie in the balance. I beg of you, please fulfil the bargain. In Tiberius, I can seek the protection of the Christians.'

'I don't know,' said the trader. 'As pretty as you are, it could be a choice between your life or mine.'

'I have money,' said Hassan suddenly. 'Much money. Fulfil the agreement and I will double the price.'

'That is quite a promise for a street rat,' said the trader, 'where is this coin you speak of?'

'I don't have it on me,' said Hassan, 'I have friends in Al-Shabiya with access to as much money as we need. Take us there and I swear upon my life I will pay that which I promise.'

'Al-Shabiya is a dangerous place for one so pretty,' said Ahmed.

'It is only I that needs to go into Al-Shabiya, my lord,' said Hassan, 'my lady will stay with you until I return.'

'Or you could all just disappear into the night the moment we are in reach of the city walls,' said the trader.

'That will not happen,' said Hassan. 'I am a man of my word.'

'Ah, how many times have people heard that before being betrayed at the first opportunity?'

'I can only give my word,' said Hassan, 'I have nothing else.'

'It is not enough,' said the trader, 'I need more.'

'His word is good,' interjected Sumeira, 'and I trust him with my life. So much so that if he does not return with the money, then I will stay with you until the debt is paid. When we near Al-Shabiya, keep me by your side, bind me in chains if you have to, but until Hassan returns with the payment, I will go nowhere.'

The trader's eyes widened at the generosity of the offer.

'You place a lot of trust in this boy.'

'I do.'

'Then it is done,' said the trader and walked to the back of the cart. 'You will travel on this cart. Make yourself a space amongst the sacks of grain and keep yourself hidden as much as you can. I will not reveal your whereabouts to anyone but this caravan has many eyes. I cannot vouch for them all. Come out only at night and do not wander. It will be a hard journey for you but it is the best I can do.

'Understood?' said Hassan.

'Thank you,' said Sumeira.

'Now,' said the trader looking up at the sky. 'Dawn is almost upon us. Make yourself as comfortable as you can and keep quiet. We leave as soon as it is light.'

Chapter Ten

May - AD 1178

East of the Dead Sea

A week after leaving Segor, Cronin and his comrades stood alongside their horses, staring at the magnificent fortress in the distance. The caravan had stopped near the village of Al-Shabiya to fill the water barrels before heading on to Damascus in the north.

'This is as far as we go,' said Shamsur-Raman, approaching the three men. 'The caravan will rest here tonight but tomorrow it continues to Damascus.'

'What about you,' asked Cronin, 'are you not staying?'

'I am,' said the jeweller, 'I have family in the village and will stay with them until the market in three days' time. Do you wish me to find you lodgings?'

'No, we will seek shelter in the castle,' said Jakelin. 'What about your brother, is he also in the village?'

'If Allah wills it, he will be here within two days.'

'Good. We must ensure we see him first before he sells the cross.'

'Come to the centre of the village on the first day and look for the stall with the red banner.'

'So be it,' said Cronin. 'We will seek you out. Do not sell it to anyone else.'

'Business is business, my friend,' said Shamsur-Ramon, 'and the cross is an attractive trinket. I suggest you get there early in case there are other buyers with heavy purses.'

An hour later, the three men rode towards the castle from the southern approach. Above them soared the immense fortress, built into and on top of a spectacular rocky hill. Towers soared majestically skyward and dozens of men at arms peered down from the many defensive positions atop the glacis walls, the steep stone slopes designed to easily repel any attackers. Arrow slits peppered the walls and carefully positioned wooden platforms spread out along the castellations, allowing the use of catapults in the event of an attack. As they approached, they crossed two deep trenches carved out of the rock, designed to slow down any attacking forces, a common feature in many castles at the time. Overall the effect was breath-taking, and they immediately knew that before them lay one of, if not the strongest and most majestic castles in the whole of the Levant.

'I have never seen such a thing,' said Cronin quietly, 'this place must be impregnable.'

'I agree,' said Hunter, 'surely no man could ever breach those walls.'

'No place is beyond the reach of man,' said Jakelin as they rode, 'it is only a matter of time before avarice or fervour encourages men to take what is not theirs.' As they rode, they saw one part of the defensive slope stained dark with blood above a pit dug at the base of the castle wall.

'I smell death,' said Jakelin, wrinkling his nose against the familiar stench. 'I heard that the castellan enjoys throwing his enemies from the walls onto the glacis. This must be the place.

As they passed the pit, they could just about see the rotting remains of broken bodies, entwined in death's embrace at the bottom. Clouds of flies swarmed out as they passed and the stench was overwhelming.

'Why doesn't he cover them up?' gasped Cronin, hardly able to breathe, 'they must be able to smell this inside the castle.'

'It is a warning to all,' said Jakelin, 'a promise of the fate that awaits them if they cross the castellan.'

'He truly is a butcher,' said Hunter as they passed the pit. 'Come on, I don't want to be in this place one moment longer than we need to be.'

They approached a pair of large gates between two towers, guarded by a dozen armed men.

'Hold there, strangers,' said one of the men as they approached. 'You are not of this garrison, 'state your business.'

'My name is Jakelin de Mailly,' said the knight, these two men are my comrades. We have business with the commandery within the castle walls.'

'You don't look like any Templars I've ever seen, said the guard. 'Your garb suggests common soldiers. What proof do you have?'

'My cloak is in my pack,' said Jakelin, 'but the pommel of my sword bears the emblem of our order. Will that suffice?'

'Such swords can be acquired by anyone with enough coin,' said the guard, 'do you have anything else?'

'I have this,' said Cronin and walked forward to show the ring given to him by the Templar Grand Master in the aftermath of the battle at Montgisard. 'This is the Grand Master's seal and gives us authority to seek assistance from any of our order throughout the Levant. Take it to the Templar quarters and they will authorise our entry.'

The soldier took the ring and passed it to one of his comrades.

'Do as he says,' he said, 'and return forthwith.'

The soldier disappeared into the tunnel beneath the heavy portcullis as the three travellers waited, talking quietly amongst themselves. The rest of the guards watched them closely, always wary of anyone seeking unauthorised entrance. It wasn't unknown for western mercenaries to change sides and even fight for the Saracens if the purse was big enough, and they were taking no chances.

Eventually, the soldier returned with a man in a brown tunic adorned with a red cross, one of the Templar's chaplain brothers dedicated to looking after the order's spiritual needs.

'Who bears this ring?' he demanded walking over.

'I do,' said Cronin, 'I am a sergeant of our order. This is Sir Jakelin de Mailly, a brother knight and our scout, Hunter. We are here on a holy errand from the Grand Master himself, Eudes de St. Amand.'

'And he gave you this ring?'

'He did, brother, and pledged we would be well received by any of our order throughout the Holy Land should the need arise.'

'Indeed you shall,' said the priest handing over the ring. 'Follow me.'

They entered the castle and headed along a narrow pathway designed to herd any attackers into a killing zone should they breach the formidable gate defences. Emerging out of the shadows into the lower bailey of the castle, they paused and stared in awe at the impressive fortress around them. The walls were obviously many metres thick and well-defended with dozens of towers interspaced around the entire perimeter, each well manned with lookouts. Rows of stone buildings lined the bottom of the walls, including armouries, stables and barracks for the garrison, all conveniently placed for rapid reaction should the call to arms come.

All around the lower level, people came and went through the secondary gates, going about the business of keeping the massive fortress operational. Carts laden with supplies queued to be unloaded by prisoners and a constant line of slaves carried water from the natural cistern built into the rock to other areas of the castle. Overlooking the whole operation were dozens of men at arms along the inner walls, each watching carefully for any form of deceit or treachery.

'This is an enormous place,' said Cronin,' how big is the garrison?'

'At full strength, fifteen hundred men at arms,' said the chaplain, 'though many of them are with Raynald in Jerusalem at the moment. On top of that, we have the families of the soldiers as well as civilian workers and the slaves. In all, in excess of two thousand souls, all needing to be fed and protected.'

'That must be a massive undertaking,' said Cronin. 'Where does it all come from?'

'Raynald of Chatillon is lord of all the Oultrejordain,' said the chaplain, 'and controls all the lands from the Zarqa river in the north as far down as Ayla near Egypt. He extracts a heavy tithe from all the villages and farms between and controls the trade routes from Egypt to Damascus, imposing a toll upon any who go that way.'

'I'll wager he is not a well-liked man,' said Hunter.

'It is the way of the world,' said the chaplain, 'and that is why this fortress is so heavily garrisoned. Nobody dares lift a hand against him or he responds with an iron fist. Raynald is of the view that Jerusalem exudes no control over the Oultrejordain and rules it as if he is a king in his own right.'

'And what does King Baldwin think of this?'

'What can he do? He has his hands full defending Jerusalem and certainly can't afford to wage war on one of the strongest barons in the Holy Land. Besides, the fact that he made Raynald his regent suggests he is comfortable with the situation.'

They approached a walled compound on one of the higher levels and walked through a gate into an inner courtyard.

'This is the commandery,' said the chaplain. 'We are fully self-contained and purchase what we need from the village or the castle stores. The stable is on the north wall as are the barracks.

The chapel is over there, along with the mess hall. We eat after vespers but you have journeyed far so must be hungry. Once you have tended to your horses, ask the kitchens for food on my authority.'

'Who is the Marshal of this place?' asked Jakelin.

'Sir Guy of Jaffa,' said the chaplain. 'He is on patrol but should be back tonight. Get some rest and we will meet again after Vespers.' He bowed his head and turned away, leaving them standing in the courtyard.

The three men led their horses over to the stables and only after their mounts had been fed, watered and fully groomed, wandered over to the mess hall to see if they could find some food.

A while later they sat at one of four wooden trestle tables in the small mess hall. Before them was a bowl of potage, a loaf of bread, and a platter of olives alongside a jug of watered wine.

'So, my lord,' said Cronin to Jakelin, 'do you know of this man, Guy of Jaffa?'

'I have heard his name spoken occasionally,' said Jakelin. 'I understand he is a quiet man but strong with valour. It is said he is humble yet a great servant to the lord.'

'I hope his treasury is healthy,' said Hunter, scooping more potage onto his trencher, 'for I suspect the price wanted for the cross will be a burden not many could bear.'

'Have no worries about money,' said Jakelin, 'all Templar outposts are able to meet any debt incurred on their behalf.'

'Yes, but with other people's money,' said Hunter.

'All monies held in our vaults are secured with promissory notes,' said Jakelin, 'and we are bound by our holy oath to honour those notes whenever and wherever they are presented. It makes a traveller's journey that much safer instead of carrying their wealth in coins or jewels where they are at risk from the thieves of the road.'

'I am surprisingly tired,' said Hunter eventually, pushing away his bowl, 'and think I will seek a cot in the barracks.'

'I'm going to have a look around this castle,' said Cronin, 'I have never seen anything like it.' He turned to Jakelin. 'What about you, my lord, will you join me?'

'No,' said Jakelin, standing up, 'I am going to see if there is somewhere to bathe. I stink like that pit of death we passed on the way in here and wish to greet the Marshal as a knight, not a beggar.' He walked out of the room leaving Cronin and Hunter sitting at the table.

'I still can't get used to him,' said Hunter, 'even after all this time.'

'I think he is fine,' said Cronin, 'though I struggle to remember that on this quest, it is he that answers to me, not the other way around. Lesser men would hold a grudge, yet he has accepted the role without question.'

'Well,' said Hunter standing up, 'another few days and all this will be over. We'll be in Jerusalem within the month.'

'I hope so,' said Cronin, 'but I have a feeling deep inside that something is wrong.'

'Like what?'

'I don't know, it's just a feeling.'

'Everything is going to be fine, Cronin,' said Hunter, 'we'll get the money from the Marshall, retrieve the cross, get Hassan and be in Jerusalem before you know it.'

'I hope you're right, Hunter,' said Cronin, 'I really do,' but as the scout left the room, the nagging feeling returned. He knew something was wrong, he just couldn't put a finger on it.

Chapter Eleven

May - AD 1178

The City of Tiberius

King Baldwin sat in a litter carried by eight of the court servants. Ordinarily, he would have walked down to the shores of the Sea of Galilee from his castle in Tiberius but recently he had suffered a deterioration in his health as the effects of the Leprosy took a firmer grip on his young body.

They reached a wooden platform standing on stilts that stretched out over the shallows and his servants helped him walk out to where a cushion-covered throne stood near the water's edge. A large cover had been erected on a frame above the throne and buckets of cooled water and wine lay in the shade, waiting to be brought by the servants at the king's whim.

Since arriving at Tiberius, his health had suffered despite taking in the cool air from the freshwater sea twice daily. His appearances at court were rarer and he often allowed William of Tyre to run proceedings in his absence, with any important questions or issues being relayed to him in his chambers, but today he had cancelled all petitions and just needed to rest.

'Where is the prelate,' he asked as two of his servants lowered him into the chair, 'he said he would be here?'

'I am told he had urgent business to attend, Your Grace,' said one of the servants.

'What could be more important than serving your monarch,' grumbled Baldwin, 'I should have the man flogged.'

The servant smiled. He knew the king was jesting for the closeness of Baldwin and his advisor was well known. Hardly any decision was announced by the young king without it having been run by the prelate first. William of Tyre had been with Baldwin since he was a boy, first as a teacher then advisor and chronicler, and enjoyed the sort of access other courtiers could only dream of.

'Bring me a bucket of water,' said the king, 'I will bathe my feet.'

'Of course, Your Grace,' said the servant and set about the task as Baldwin closed his eyes and sat back to enjoy the breeze.

For the next hour or so he relaxed at the water's edge, eventually being served a meal of duck breast and greens along with watered wine and ice from the mountains to the east.

'Your Grace,' said one of the servants as the king carefully chewed on a piece of meat, 'the prelate approaches. Shall I bid him wait until you have finished your meal?'

'Not at all,' said Baldwin. 'He was expected an age ago and needs to explain himself. Allow him through but offer no seat. He can stand in the sun as penance for making me wait.'

'Of course, my king,' said the servant and beckoned the waiting prelate forward.

'Your Grace,' said William dropping to one knee in front of Baldwin and kissing his hand, 'please forgive my lateness but there was a matter of urgency that needed my attention.'

'More important than the needs of your king?' mused Baldwin.

'It was in your interests that I made the decision,' said William. 'On my way here I was approached by one of the castle guards that said there was a man at the gates with a message for you alone. Of course, I assumed it was one of the many subjects who petition you on a daily basis but what he said next made me pause and take note.'

'What did he say?' asked the king.

'Your Grace, he said the messenger was a Saracen and wanted to meet with you directly.'

'Why under God's sun would an infidel think he would be granted an audience with me?' asked Baldwin.

'Because of who he is,' said William, 'his name is Farrukh-Shah.'

Baldwin's eyes widened and he sat up a little in his chair. Farrukh-Shah was Saladin's nephew and one of the Sultan's most trusted advisors. For him to come to Tiberius to seek an audience could only mean that he had been sent by Saladin himself.

'What does he want?' asked Baldwin.

'He said his message is for your ears only,' said the prelate, 'and insisted on an audience.'

'Where is he now?'

'He is waiting in the minor hall back at the castle. I have arranged suitable hospitality and have guards watching his every move but thought you would rather meet him there; such is his importance.'

'You thought correctly,' said Baldwin, 'is he alone?'

'He has two bodyguards with him and apparently has an escort of a hundred men waiting outside the walls of Tiberius, but nothing a swift attack from our forces couldn't deal with. Your Grace, this may be an opportunity to take Farrukh-Shah prisoner and use the threat of his safety against his uncle.'

'Let us not make any hasty decisions,' said the king. 'First, we will hear what he has to say and then decide what is appropriate.' He turned to the servant at his side. 'Summon my bearers immediately. I need to get back to the castle.'

'Of course, Your Grace,' said the servant and ran back to the shore where the men were resting in a tent out of the midday sun.

'William,' said the king, turning back to the prelate, 'send a runner to my quarters and have them arrange suitable regalia. In addition, prepare the audience room, I will welcome him as the King of Jerusalem, not some sickly child, unshod and suffering from the heat of the day.'

'It has already been arranged, Your Grace. All you have to do is get back and everything is waiting for you. That is why I am late, there was much to do.'

'You never cease to amaze me,' said the king. 'I have frequently considered having you beheaded for insolence but yet again you have managed to escape the fate you so often deserve.'

'Nonsense,' said the prelate with a smile, 'if you had me beheaded, Your Grace, then who would listen to your continued grumbling? Now come, let me help you up. Your litter is here.'

Just over an hour later, King Baldwin of Jerusalem sat on his formal throne in the audience chamber of Tiberius castle. To either side of him stood whatever nobles he could muster at such short notice and as usual, William of Tyre stood at his side. Lining the walkway to the throne were fifty of his personal bodyguards, each a trusted knight and fully armed in case of treachery.

'I am ready,' said Baldwin, 'let's see what he has to say.'

'Show him in,' said William and the two servants at the doors opened them wide before another walked out to greet the visitor.

'His glorious majesty, King Baldwin of Jerusalem will see you now,' he announced and turned around to escort the visitors into the chamber.

The sound of heavy footfalls echoed off the walls of the corridor before three men marched into the chamber and along the carpet between the two rows of soldiers. None of the three even acknowledged the presence of so many men at arms but just strode resolutely forward until being stopped by William of Tyre's raised hand. The room fell silent as everyone stared at the Saracens. Their garb was colourful yet practical and they wore none of the armour often seen by similar warriors on the battlefield. The two bodyguards had minimal facial hair while the one in the centre had a full beard. Lightweight cloaks hung from their shoulders, still bearing some of the dust of the road, and around their waist, everyone could see the feared scimitars hanging from their belts.

'Forgive me,' said the prelate, 'but I'm sure you understand that as we have allowed you to keep your weapons out of respect for your authority, any closer puts the life of the king at risk.'

The man at the centre looked around at the king's men at arms as if noticing them for the first time.

'I think you have us outnumbered,' he said with amusement, 'but please forgive me, I must introduce myself.' He turned back to face the monarch. 'King Baldwin, my name is Farrukh-Shah and I and here on the business of my uncle, Salah ad-Din, Sultan of all Syria and Egypt. He extends his warmest greetings and expresses hope that your affliction does not cause you too much discomfort. Indeed, he has sent ointments and potions to ease your pain. They have been left with your servants in the previous chamber.'

'You have my gratitude,' said the king. 'And where is your uncle these days?'

Farrukh-Shah smiled at the blunt attempt at gaining intelligence.

'I suspect he still celebrates our great victory at Montgisard,' he replied, 'but his whereabouts are unknown to me.'

'Victory,' murmured one of the nobles at the king's side, 'I was at the battle and I can tell you that...'

Baldwin held up his hand, cutting short the man's contradiction.

'Give him my best wishes when you eventually see him again,' he said with a false smile. 'Now, about your business here, shall we begin?'

'Of course,' said Farrukh-Shah. 'It has come to our notice that you are undertaking the construction of a fortress at the crossing of Vadum Iacob. This causes us great concern as for generations, the crossing has been shared by my people and those who follow the Christian God without conflict. Until now the only thing indicating the separation of our lands is an ancient oak, planted when Muhammad was yet a boy. We ask the king, why do you now see fit to desecrate this place when it was agreed by our forebears that no such thing would ever be built?'

'Decisions made by those who went before us were made without fear for the safety of our people,' said the king. 'Today, our lands west of the Galilee are often raided by your warriors and our women and children lie awake in their beds, worried that their lives may be taken by killers in the night. Should I, as a king, allow them to suffer this way or should I exhibit leadership in protecting them and what is rightfully theirs?'

'I know nothing about the events you speak of,' said Farrukh-Shah, 'only that by building this fortress you risk tearing apart the agreement that has existed since the time of our fathers' fathers. Continue on this path and there can be no talk or expectation of peace between our people.'

'You talk of peace,' said the king, 'yet the ground at Montgisard is still red from the blood of thousands, all dead because of your master's claim to that which is not his. This castle is being built to achieve peace, not destroy it.'

'The ownership of the kingdom of Jerusalem is a subject for a different conversation,' said the Arab, 'today I will concentrate only on the subject of my petition. Despite the anger, the construction of this castle brings, my master, in his wisdom and kindness has sent me here to offer you a trade.'

'What sort of trade?' asked the king, his interest piqued.

'If you agree to abandon the construction at Vadum Iacob, the Sultan will pay you the generous sum of sixty thousand golden bezants.'

There was an audible gasp in the room as everyone heard the amount. Gold coins were very rare in the Outremer and the few available were only minted in Byzantium. Only the highest of nobles had access to such riches but even so, sixty thousand was unheard of.

King Baldwin was also taken back by the amount but his face remained unmoved, determined not to show how much he was impressed by the offer.

Silence fell in the chamber and the king's eyes remained locked on those of Farrukh-Shah. William leaned forward from behind the king to speak into his ear, but Baldwin lifted his hand, stopping him short. The gold would immediately wipe out the huge shortfall in his treasuries and easily fund the campaign against Egypt that Raynald of Chatillon wanted so badly, but the thought of his policies being dictated by Saladin's riches made him feel sick to the stomach.

'The offer is admirable,' he said eventually, 'yet I cannot put a price on the safety of my people in the Outremer. Tell your master that if he comes to me with a pledge to forever cede his claim upon Jerusalem, and withdraw all his warriors back into Egypt, then we will dismantle the castle and return to our homes. That is my counteroffer.'

'And this is your final say in the matter?'

'It is,' said Baldwin. 'Now you may leave this place in safety to relay my thoughts to your master. My knights will escort you to the edge of the city.'

Farrukh-Shah took a step backwards and nodded his head slightly in respect to Baldwin's position before turning on his heels and marching from the audience chamber.

For a few moments, there was silence as the deputation left, only broken when the doors closed behind them.

'Your Grace,' gasped William as the rest of the gathered nobles broke out in astonished conversation, 'you do realise that sixty thousand golden bezants would probably fund your campaigns for many years to come?'

'Aye, William, I do,' said the king, 'but by accepting his offer, I become no more than Saladin's whore. Send a message to Jacob's Ford, tell Grand Master Eudes de St. Amand to double his efforts with the construction.'

'Your Grace,' said William, 'is that wise?'

'I think it is not only wise but a necessity,' said the king. 'If Saladin is willing to pay that sort of price to prevent the castle's construction, what cost would he willingly incur for its destruction?'

Chapter Twelve

May - AD 1178

Karak Castle

Cronin and Hunter sat in the ante-chamber of the Marshal's quarters in the Templar commandery in Karak Castle. The Marshal had not returned until after Vespers so now they had to wait while he prayed alone and ate his meagre meal before receiving their delegation.

'Where is Jakelin,' asked Hunter, 'it would be better if he was here to add weight to our request?'

'He will be here,' said Cronin, 'don't worry.'

A few minutes later the door of the Marshal's quarters opened and the chaplain stepped through.

'Sir Guy is ready to see you now', he said, 'please come with me.'

They followed the chaplain into the sparsely furnished room and stopped in surprise as they saw the Marshal talking to Sir Jakelin, now bedecked in all his full Templar finery.

'My Lord,' said Cronin, 'we were worried about your whereabouts.'

'The Marshal kindly invited me to pray with him due to the lateness of the hour,' said Jakelin and turned to the man at his side. 'My Lord, these are the men I told you about. Thomas Cronin is one of our brother sergeants and Hunter has been engaged by us as a scout.'

'It is a pleasure to meet you, my lord,' said Cronin. 'Your hospitality has been of the highest order.'

'We do what we can,' said Sir Guy sitting at a trestle table. 'Please, be seated so we can more comfortably discuss your business.'

The two men sat opposite the Marshal while Sir Jakelin remained standing, resplendent in his freshly cleaned Templar cloak.

'I am told you bear the Grand Master's seal,' said Sir Guy, 'may I see it?'

'Of course,' said Cronin and handed over the ring.

The Marshal held the ring to the light of a candle and examined it closely. Eventually, he was satisfied it was authentic and handed it back.

'Brother Jakelin has already explained the nature of your quest,' he said, 'and informs me you are aware of the location of the Cross of Courtney.'

'We know the bearer will be at the jewellers' market in Al-Shabiya,' said Cronin, 'and have been promised first access to purchase the piece. That is why we are here, to appropriate enough money to meet the cost.'

'Which is?'

'A thousand Dinars my lord,' said Cronin, glancing nervously over to Sir Jakelin.

'You want a thousand Dinars in coin,' said the Marshal with surprise, 'I think perhaps you overestimate the value of this cross.'

'My Lord,' said Cronin, 'it is not the value of the cross that demands such an amount but the reputation of our order. The cross was in our possession when it was lost and we have limited time to return it to the king.'

'The cross was in *your* possession if I understand correctly,' said the Marshal, 'is this not correct?'

'It is my lord, and I regret the loss deeply, but I do not regret the fact that by forfeiting the cross, I saved two innocent lives.'

'Saracen lives.'

'Yes, my lord, the mother and daughter of the boy who accompanied me on the mission.'

'Hmm,' said the Marshal and turned to face Sir Jakelin.

'Brother Jakelin,' he said, 'you have travelled with these men for the last few months. 'Do you consider them to be honest and trustworthy?'

'Indeed I do,' said Jakelin, 'and would march into battle alongside either.'

'And would you entrust them with a thousand Dinars?'

'I would, my lord, but if it makes you feel easier, I can take ownership of the purse and ensure the trade takes place as agreed.'

'I think that is sensible but tell me this. What is to stop us taking back by force, that which rightly belongs to the king?'

'There are two reasons, my lord,' interrupted Cronin, 'the first is that we do not know where the exchange will take place but we can be sure it will be well guarded, such is the nature of men who have it. I suspect that if any Christian forces are detected anywhere near the transaction, they will disappear like frightened rats, along with the cross. The second reason is a matter of conscience. Although the cross was stolen from me in the first instance, it was eventually given of my own free will in exchange for the lives of the two women. That means the ownership has transferred by right and it would be dishonest of us to take it by force.'

'Yet it was not yours to give.'

'I understand, my lord, but I was acting on behalf of the Seneschal when I made the decision. Whether that decision was correct or not, at that moment in time, I used my position as a brother Templar sergeant to make a trade. I believe that the arrangement should now be honoured.'

'I'm not sure I agree with you,' said Sir Guy, 'but the fact that the Grand Master has given you his seal suggests he is comfortable with the situation and happy for the trade to go ahead.' He paused for a moment before continuing. 'You will have your money, brother Cronin, as well as a promissory note for another five hundred Dinars in case of unexpected expenses. Any more than that I cannot authorise without being at the negotiating table myself. Understand?'

'Yes, my lord,' said the sergeant.

'In addition, I will want a receipt for whatever payment is agreed, witnessed by all present. Without it, I cannot reclaim the money from the Grand Master's treasury and you will become personally responsible for the debt.'

'I understand,' said Cronin.

The Marshal turned to face Sir Jakelin.

'Brother knight,' he said, 'I recognise the nature of your penance and encourage you to meet its terms with all piety, however, do not forget your calling. You are the senior person upon this commission, and it is you to whom I will turn for an explanation if anything goes wrong. Be the strength that this task needs and should the need arise, deal with it appropriately.'

'Of course, my lord,' said Jakelin with a nod.

'Good,' said the Marshall. 'Report to the treasury the night before the market, the funds will be waiting. You will be responsible for its security up until the actual transaction takes place. Once the cross is in your possession, return here with all haste. I will furnish you with an armed escort to get you and the cross safely back to Jerusalem as soon as possible.'

'My Lord,' said Hunter, glancing at Cronin, 'first we will have to go back to Segor to collect our comrade.'

'I understand your friend is a Bedouin,' said the Marshal, 'and though your loyalty is admirable, he can wait until this task is over. You will retrieve the cross and immediately take it under escort to Jerusalem. Once it has been handed over to the appropriate authorities, you may seek leave from the Grand Master to seek your comrade. More than that, I cannot promise.'

'My Lord,' started Cronin, but the Marshal cut him short with a raised hand.

'The decision is made,' he said, 'and this audience is over. You may leave.'

Cronin and Hunter left the two Templar knights alone in the room with the chaplain and headed back to the barracks.

'I can't believe we have to abandon Hassan,' said Cronin, 'he is one of us and should be treated so.'

'Hassan will be safe where he is for the time being,' said Hunter. 'We will go to him as soon as we can but in the meantime, at least we have the funding for the cross. One step at a time, my friend, one step at a time.'

Out on the road from Segor, another caravan trundled its way endlessly northward. The going was slower than the one Cronin and his comrades had joined and already they had been delayed as two wagons became stranded, each losing a wheel which had to be repaired. In one of the rear carts, Sumeira, and Hassan sat opposite each other, hidden behind a pile of sacks.

'This journey seems never-ending,' said Sumeira quietly. 'Every time we stop, I fear the carts are being searched at the behest of the girl's father. I fear my heart will stop long before we reach Al-Shabiya.'

'If that happens,' said Hassan, 'you and Emani must lie on the floor between two of the sacks. I will cover you with the others and pretend to sleep upon the top. They will be less likely to think there is anyone beneath.'

'But you will be seen.'

'They do not know you that you are with anyone else,' said Hassan, 'so I do not need to hide away. I will protect you, Sumeira, I promise you.'

The cart lurched forward again and Sumeira leaned back her head, closing her eyes as she prayed for the journey to be over.

Chapter Thirteen

May - AD 1178

Al-Shabiya

Cronin, Hunter and Jakelin all rode through the loose cordon of mounted guards surrounding the village. As far as they could see, people came along the paths leading donkeys or carrying their wares upon their backs, all heading for the market in Al-Shabiya. Any late carts were made to stop outside the village to avoid even more confusion in the crowded streets and riders were asked to leave their horses tied to the many rails on the village outskirts.

'The place looks busy already,' said Cronin, handing over a dinar to one of the many men tasked with caring for the horses.

'I am told the market lasts three days,' said Jakelin, 'and is the biggest of all such fayres, attended by people from across the Levant, Christian and Saracen alike. There is an agreement that all arguments are left outside of the village to allow commerce to take place without confrontation.'

'It's a shame that agreement doesn't spread outward,' said Hunter quietly, following his comrades into one of the streets.

Immediately they were caught up in a throng of people heading towards the village centre. All along the route, traders touted their wares from handcarts or from behind empty barrels or trestle tables. Many had rented the lower rooms of houses and set up trays upon the ledges of the windows, the shutters tied back revealing countless cords of coloured beads and necklaces. The noise was deafening with each trader vying with the next to attract custom but though the streets were packed with all sorts of goods from copper rings to golden chains, everyone knew it was in the village centre where the big money changed hands. Slowly they pushed their way forward, avoiding the hawkers with trays hanging from around their necks until eventually, they reached the place where Shamsur-Ramon told them he would be.

'There,' said Hunter, seeing a red pennant above a stall and led the way through the crowd.

'Ah,' said the vendor in broken Frankish as they neared the stall, 'Christian men. You wish for a nice ring for your wives, perhaps a necklace for your lover? You have come to the best place, let me show you what I have. Best prices only for you, my friends.'

'We are looking for Shamsur-Rahman,' said Cronin, 'we have some private business with him.'

'Alas my master is busy with other men,' said the seller, 'perhaps I can show you our best pieces.'

'No,' snapped Jakelin, before anyone could reply, 'we want to see your master now. You go and bring him here before I pull this stall down.'

'You are a very aggressive man,' said the vendor, a false smile upon his face, 'and you breach the agreement. This is a place where all men are friends.'

'We understand,' said Cronin quickly, 'but your master is expecting us. We need to see him urgently.'

'And what is the nature of your business?'

'We wish to purchase a cross,' said Cronin. 'He is keeping it for me.'

The man's expression changed and his stance softened.

'Ah, the buyers from Segor,' he said, 'why did you not say?' He turned to one of the young boys standing nearby. 'Take our friends to the master and do not linger, there is work here for you to do.'

The boy nodded and pulled Cronin's jerkin, leading the three Christians towards the dark and narrow side streets.

Cronin and his two comrades followed the boy through the quieter alleyways until they stood in a small square overlooked by mud bricked buildings, three stories high. Very little sunlight ever reached down into the courtyard and the oppressive feeling of claustrophobia made them feel nervous.

The boy pointed at a building in the corner of the yard and waited as Cronin walked over to bang his fist upon the door. A few moments later a face appeared around the doorway, looking at the three men with undisguised animosity.

'My name is Thomas Cronin,' said the sergeant in his limited Arabic, 'I am here to see Shamsur-Rahman.'

The man nodded and fully opened the door, allowing them through before locking it behind them. Without speaking he pushed past the three men and led the way to a back room where the trader was sat behind a table. Beside him sat a very fat man and to the side of him, two young men who looked like they would be happier cutting somebody's throat.

'Ah,' said Shamsur-Rahman, without standing up, 'my good friend has arrived. Thomas Cronin, this is my brother, Sayyid. We were just having a discussion about you.'

Cronin and the others looked at the fat man but there was no response, he just sat there, his arms linked across his fat belly.

'Sayyid is a man of few words,' said Shamsur-Rahman. 'Please sit, we have a busy day in front of us so will conclude our business quickly.'

The three men sat down, and Shamsur-Rahman nodded to his brother. With a sigh of resignation, Sayyid reached down to a bag under the table and produced a small package wrapped in silk. He unwrapped it and held the contents up into a shaft of dusty sunlight creeping in from a side window.

'Is this the trinket you seek?' asked Shamsur-Rahman.

Everyone in the room looked at the silver necklace, hanging from the trader's hands. At the bottom hung an exquisite golden cross embedded with gemstones of many colours. Sir Jakelin lifted his hand and made the sign of the crucifix upon his own chest, in awe of the symbolism as it spun slowly in the sun's light.

Cronin reached out to take the cross but Sayyid withdrew his hand quickly, denying the sergeant access.

'Show me the money first,' said Shamsur-Rahman.

Cronin looked over and nodded at Jakelin who reached beneath his cloak to retrieve a large purse of leather. He placed it on the table, but still within his reach.

Shamsur-Rahman nodded at his brother who placed the necklace alongside the purse. Cronin and Sayyid each reached out to retrieve the relevant item they were interested in and as the sergeant and his comrades examined the cross, Sayyid poured the coins onto the table and started counting.

'Well,' said Shamsur-Rahman eventually, 'are you satisfied it is the same one?'

'I am,' said Cronin, 'however before we conclude, I request that you sign a receipt stating that you have received the full amount.'

'A receipt?' said Shamsur-Rahman, with a laugh. 'You Christians do business in a very strange way. What worth is a parchment stating what we already know?'

'It is for our purposes only,' said Cronin. 'It will allow us to reclaim the cost from the vaults of the Templar treasury.'

'Ah, the Templars,' said Shamsur-Rahman, glancing towards Jakelin with a suspicious eye, 'I wondered if they were involved in any way.'

Cronin cursed inwardly at his mistake. Jakelin now bore the same plain garb as he had worn since leaving Jerusalem and outwardly bore no sign he was of the holy order, but his stature and demeanour would always suggest an air of superiority.

'They are the financiers,' said Cronin, 'but make no claim upon the ownership. The cross belongs to the King of Jerusalem.'

'Profit is profit,' said Shamsur-Rahman, 'no matter who the purchaser. Give me your document, Christian, I will make my mark.'

Before Cronin could retrieve the pouch containing the receipt and quill, Sayyid leaned across and whispered into his brother's ear. Shamsur-Rahman's demeanour changed and his voice lowered dangerously.

'There seems to be a mistake, my friend,' he said, 'the price we agreed in Segor was a thousand Dinars. We have only five hundred.'

'You are mistaken,' said Cronin, 'I agreed the price with the financier myself. Count again.'

'He is not mistaken,' said Jakelin, 'the purse contained five hundred Dinars.'

Cronin's brows crossed in confusion and he looked over at Jakelin.

'The price agreed was a thousand,' he said quietly.

'A thousand was discussed,' said Jakelin, 'not agreed.'

'What games are these?' growled Shamsur-Ramon. 'I expected a fair trade and am on the receiving end of treachery.'

'Five hundred is enough,' said the knight turning to face the trader, 'the value of the cross on the open market is less than half that and your possession stems from a theft by a brigand. Five hundred Dinars is the price we will pay.'

'My Lord,' said Cronin, 'I gave this man my word that he would not be double-crossed.'

'The price is five hundred,' said Jakelin coldly, 'not a Dinar more.'

Shamsur-Rahman turned to stare at Cronin.

'So this is the way you do business,' he said, 'give with one hand while bearing a dagger with the other. There is no deal, Christian, the trade is forfeit.' He reached over for the cross but Jakelin grabbed his wrist, making the trader wince with pain.

The men to either side of the trader drew their daggers and stepped forward but stopped in their tracks as Hunter and Cronin did the same. Jakelin stayed in his seat, gripping Shamsur-Ramon's wrist and staring into his eyes.

'Tell your men to stand down,' he growled. For a few moments there was silence, each man in the room on edge and ready to fight. Jakelin tightened his grip on the trader's wrist. 'There is no need for anyone to die here today,' he continued, 'but I will do what I have to do. Now, stand down or I swear you will be the first.'

'Do as he says,' said Shamsur-Ramon eventually and the men stepped back, slowly replacing their knives into their belts. Hunter and Cronin did the same but remained standing.

'Now,' continued Jakelin, easing his grip on the dealer's wrist, 'I say again. The deal is fair. We will pay five hundred Dinars for the cross or I swear there will be a disagreement within this very room, and that my friend, is something you do not want.'

The room fell silent again until eventually, Shamsur-Rahman tugged his hand from the knight's grip.

'This is the festival of light,' he said, 'and no man draws weapons against another. Take your cross, Christian, there will be many such others.' He scooped the coins into the bag and stood up before walking across to the door. As his brother and the bodyguards left the room he turned to stare at Cronin. 'I trusted you, Christian,' he said, 'I thought you were a man of your word. The consequences are now upon your head and one day, there will be a reckoning.' With that he left the room, slamming the door behind him.

For a few moments, nobody moved until finally Cronin broke the silence, still staring coldly at the cross upon the table.

'I gave him my word,' he hissed, 'as a Christian and as a Templar sergeant.'

'That pledge was not yours to make,' said Jakelin. 'The cross belongs to the Kingdom of Jerusalem and that trader should be happy he left with what he did. If I had my way he would have been carried out of here minus his head.'

Without another word Cronin got to his feet and walked out of the room, leaving Hunter and Jakelin behind him.

'He has a point, my lord,' said Hunter as the knight picked up the cross and hid it about his person, 'sometimes, his word is all a man has. Take that away and what worth does he have?'

'Brother Cronin is a Templar sergeant,' said Sir Jakelin, 'and has sworn an oath to serve God and the temple. I suggest that today, despite his self-doubt, he served both with equal measure. Now, let us begone. I suspect those rogues are devoid of morals in any form and may seek retribution.'

They walked through the tiny courtyard and into the street, pushing their way through the still growing crowd. They reached the edge of the town and saw Cronin mounting his horse.

'Wait,' said Hunter, 'we should ride back to the castle together.'

'I'm not going to Karak,' said Cronin.

'Where are you going?'

'I'm going to get Hassan,' he said. 'The cross has been retrieved, the order's reputation has been protected, and the king will have his trinket. My task here is done.'

'You cannot just ride away, Cronin,' said Sir Jakelin, 'you are still a brother sergeant and have your duty to uphold.'

'At the moment, my lord,' said Cronin, 'I feel like I am no better than a common thief. Unless you intend stopping me with your blade, I am going to Segor to get my friend. That, at least, is one promise I *can* keep.'

'They will look for you,' said Jakelin. 'You will have to answer to the Grand Master for your absence.'

'Tell them to save their horses,' said Cronin. 'When I have got Hassan, I will ride to Jerusalem and face the consequences willingly, and though it may mean nothing to you, my lord, I promise you I am a man of my word.'

Before any of the other two men could respond, Cronin dug his heels into his mount's flanks and galloped south towards Segor.

'I'm going with him,' said Hunter, untying his own horse.

'Wait,' said Jakelin, 'ride with me to the castle and I will join you as soon as the cross is in the hands of the Marshall. He will ensure it gets safely to Jerusalem and we will catch up with Cronin upon the road. When he has cooled down, perhaps he will see the necessity of my actions.'

'I will ride to you as far as the castle gates,' said Hunter, 'but only to ensure the cross gets to where it needs to be. After that, I am going after Cronin, alone. You must do what you have to do but my loyalties lie elsewhere.' He mounted his horse and turned to look down on the knight. 'You are a Templar,' he said, 'part of the greatest brotherhood in the known world. Today I would suggest you do not know the meaning of the word.'

Chapter Fourteen

May - AD 1178

The Southern Road

Cronin road southward, his shame hanging upon him like a sodden cloak. The road was busy, so he turned east for a while, needing to stay away from what he saw as accusatory eyes. It seemed that everyone was aware of his dishonour and he sought out the solitude the smaller paths afforded.

He slowed his horse to a walk and followed the trail, alone with his thoughts. The day passed slowly and as night approached, he turned west again, seeking the more popular road back to Segor. He had ridden away from Al-Shabiya without much thought and would need food and water for the journey, as well as fodder for his horse, something he hoped he could get from one of the many caravans upon the road. As darkness fell, he made a camp amongst the rocks and sat back to stare at the stars as if seeking absolution for the wrong that he had done. Eventually, his eyes grew heavy and he laid down upon the still-warm sand, wrapped in his blanket against the coolness of the night.

Despite his worry, sleep enveloped him wholly and the sky was already beginning to lighten when he woke. He packed his things and sorted out his horse before heading back onto the main track heading south.

The sun had only just made an appearance when he saw the group of riders heading towards him. There was nothing unusual about that in itself because the road was well travelled but there was always a risk of trouble. Mentally he prepared himself for any outcome. If they were brigands then they would find him no easy target for in his current frame of mind he was more than happy to fight any man. If they were traders, then he had an excellent Templar knife that would more than cover the cost of all the food and water he needed. Slowly they came closer, four men on horseback who, as they neared, spread out line-abreast to block the path.

He reined in his own horse and waited until they stopped ten paces ahead. One of the men looked familiar but Cronin struggled to place him.

'Greetings, traveller,' said the familiar rider. 'You are early about your business.'

'The day waits for no man,' said Cronin. 'I need to get to Segor and have little time.'

'You westerners always seem in a rush,' said the rider. 'Perhaps you should slow down and enjoy Allah's great gift.'

Cronin didn't answer, knowing that to enter religious argument only invited trouble.

'The thing is,' continued the rider, 'we have a problem. The road belongs to us and there is a toll to pay.'

'The road belongs to no man,' said Cronin, 'except God Almighty.'

The rider turned and looked up as a fifth man appeared on an adjacent slope just a few dozen paces away. The new rider wore a black thawb, his face wrinkled into a thousand folds by the effects of the desert sun. His skin matched the colour of his clothing and across his saddle, he carried a hunting bow, already nocked with an arrow.

'That man's ancestors,' continued the rider nodding towards the nomad, 'hunted these hills, and travelled these roads long before either Muhammad or your Christ god was born. Since the mountains rose from the seas, his people have lived and died beneath this sun. Now the hunting is sparse, for too many travellers disturb the balance. Do you not think that it is only fair that he is compensated for his people's hardship?'

Cronin fell silent. Though every sinew in his body wanted to fight, he knew that against five men and an archer he stood little chance. He had little to trade except for his knife and sword, and he could never yield the latter.

'If I was to agree,' said Cronin, 'how much is the toll?'

'You have two choices,' said the man, 'and it is very simple.' He paused and stared at the sergeant, his voice lowering menacingly. 'The price is a golden cross on a silver chain or five hundred Dinars.'

Cronin swallowed hard as he stared the speaker.

'Who are you,' he asked, 'you are familiar to me?'

'You have a short memory, Christian,' said the man, 'for we met only yesterday. My name is Naseem, Shamsur-Rahman's brother.'

'The fat man was his brother,' said Cronin, remembering at last, 'you were one of the guards at his side.'

'Our family is extensive,' said Naseem, 'with many brothers.'

Cronin thought furiously, he knew his life was in danger but could do nothing to escape the situation.

'I do not have the cross,' he said again. 'By now it safe behind the walls of Karak Castle and beyond the reach of either of us.'

'We are not unreasonable men,' said Naseem, 'the balance of the agreed price will be acceptable. Five hundred Dinars.'

'I do not have it,' said Cronin. 'I was betrayed just like your brother.'

'Your oath was yours to honour, the fault cannot lie elsewhere.'

'The situation was not foreseen,' said Cronin, 'let me go and I promise will press the Christian king for recompense.'

'Another worthless promise,' spat Naseem. 'Do not take us for fools, my friend, my brother bid me return with one of three things. The cross, the purse,' he paused again staring into Cronin's eyes, 'or the man who betrayed him. Which is it to be?'

Cronin thought furiously. There was no way he could fight all five men and hope to survive but he could not risk being taken prisoner. Coming up with a rudimentary plan, he nodded and reached beneath his cloak.

'So be it,' he said with a sigh, 'perhaps this will suffice.' He withdrew his hand but instead of producing a purse, pulled out a knife and in one sudden manoeuvre sent it spinning towards Naseem's heart. Immediately, he kicked his horse hard and rode at the nearest two men, the air resounding with the roar of his challenge.

The sudden action took Naseem's men by surprise and Cronin burst through them without response. Behind him, Naseem had managed to lean to one side at the last moment and the knife had plunged into his shoulder instead of his chest. His men turned their horses to race after their quarry but even as they urged their mounts into a gallop, the nomad calmly stood up in his stirrups and lifted his bow.

'Do not kill him,' shouted Naseem, 'my brother wants him alive.'

'So be it,' said the nomad and took aim. A second later an arrow soared through the morning air and Cronin's horse crashed to the floor, an arrow embedded deep in his stomach. Cronin was hurled onto the road, his face smashing against the rocks, knocking him momentarily senseless. The pursuing riders reined in their horses and dismounted. They dragged him to his feet and threw him against a boulder, doubling him up with a heavy blow to the stomach before lifting him back up and forcing his head back against the rock, the grip under his chin exposing his throat. One of the men checked he had no other hidden weapons as Naseem rode up to join them.

'It seems treachery and you go hand in hand,' he said, looking down at the knife in his shoulder. Gritting his teeth he grabbed the hilt and withdrew the blade before pressing his thawb tighter against the wound. He stared at the blood on the blade. 'You have no idea how much I wish to open your throat,' he said looking up, 'but my brother has other ideas for you.'

One of the men punched Cronin again and as the Christian fell to the floor, the others came over, kicking the sergeant into unconsciousness. The nomad walked over and slit the wounded horse's throat before proceeding to cut large chunks of meat from the carcass.

'Bring me his sword,' said Naseem and the Nomad unclipped the scabbard from the saddle before passing the weapon up to the rider.

Naseem examined the hilt and swore under his breath.

'I suspected the taller man was a Templar knight, my friend,' he said quietly, staring at the carved pommel, 'but this sword has just increased your value tenfold.'

Half an hour later, the four riders headed back towards Al-Shabiya, the nomad riding parallel with them along the higher ground. Cronin staggered behind them, his wrists tied, and secured to the rear horse with a length of rope. Blood poured from his face and he struggled to breathe, such was the pain of his two broken ribs.

'Keep up, Christian,' shouted Naseem, over his shoulder, 'and don't die yet. There is a profit to be made from you, I can feel it in my blood.'

Back in Karak Castle, Jakelin de Mailly stood in front of the Marshal in his quarters. Before them, on a table lay the cross and the second purse of five hundred Dinars.

'It looks like you traded well,' said the Marshall, 'and only paid half the price. What of your comrades?'

'Alas, they did not see the benefit of the situation and have left to retrieve their comrade in Segor.'

'But brother Cronin is one of us and should have returned here.'

'I reminded him of his duty, my lord, but he insisted on making the journey. He gave his word that upon completion, he would report to the Grand Master in Jerusalem.'

'In that case,' said the Marshal, 'your penance has now been served. Rest here in Karak for a few days and then return to Jerusalem with the cross. I will send an escort with you to ensure it's safe passage.'

'As you wish, my lord,' said Jakelin with a nod, but as he left the Marshal's chambers, he had a heavy feeling in his heart such as he had never experienced before.

The following morning on the southern road, Sumeira sat amongst the sacks in the covered cart. Emani was still sleeping, her head in her mother's lap while Hassan sat at the tailgate, staring out over the Negev desert in silence. The rocking of the cart was almost hypnotic, and the warmth of the rising sun driving away the cold night air was a welcome luxury, one that they knew would soon turn into a burden as the sun rose higher.

For an hour or so, the caravan trundled onward and though the cart master had told them they would be at Al-Shabiya by nightfall, it still seemed a lifetime away. Sumeira opened her eyes and sighed deeply as the wagon stopped for what seemed like the hundredth time.

'What now?' she asked.

'I'll go and see,' said Hassan and jumped from the cart to walk towards the front of the stalled caravan. As he neared, he saw a group of Arab women gathering around something at the side of the road.

'What's happening?' he asked one of the cart masters.

'There's a dead horse at the side of the road,' came the reply, 'killed only a day or so ago by an arrow. The wagon master has sent the mercenaries outward to check we are in no danger of attack.'

'What about them?' asked Hassan, pointing at the women.

'Slave women,' said the cart master, 'the predators have had their fill but the carcass still has some meat left on the bones.'

Hassan walked down out of interest but stopped a few paces short when he saw the distinctive marking on the skin still hanging from the horse's neck.

'Wait,' he shouted as the women set about retrieving the meatier bones for soup, *wait!*'

He ran forward and examined the rest of the dead horse's skin, his mind racing as he recognised all the marks. Getting back to his feet he scanned the surrounding desert before examining the dust in the floor where the horse had fallen.

'What's the matter?' asked the cart master, 'have you lost something?'

'No,' said Hassan, 'but I recognise this horse, it belonged to a good friend of mine.' He looked up. 'Has anyone seen a body?'

'Not that I have heard though there is blood over there by the rocks.'

Hassan walked over and sure enough, saw the black stains where someone's blood had been spilt into the sand. He walked around slowly, closely examining the ground, soon realising that a group of riders had headed eastward, dragging a man on foot behind them.

The tracks indicated that the prisoner had been wearing western boots and the scuffs on the ground told him he was injured. He looked up towards the hills, his face creased with concern. Unless Cronin had sold his horse, the only other explanation he could come up with that his master was hurt, and in serious trouble. He ran back to the last cart and climbed aboard; the worry evident upon his face.

'What's the matter,' asked Sumeira, 'you look like you've seen a spirit?'

'Something's wrong,' said Hassan, 'my master's horse is dead at the side of the road and there are signs that he has been dragged off. I need to help him.'

'Are you sure?' asked Sumeira, 'it may not be his.'

'Perhaps but everything says it is. He loved his horse and would never part with it. It looks like he was attacked by brigands but is still alive.'

'What about the others, his comrades?'

'I see no sign of other western horseshoes,' said Hassan, 'it looks like he was alone and was on his way south.'

'Why would he do that?'

'He promised he would come and get me when his business was concluded,' said Hassan, 'I can only think he was fulfilling his pledge.' He looked up at the woman. 'I have to follow them, Sumeira, he said, while the tracks are fresh.'

'But you have no horse and your leg has still not healed.'

'I will survive, my lady,' said Hassan, 'I am Bedouin and know where the desert hides her secrets. With a little luck, I will find them and perhaps help my friend.'

'What about us?'

'Stay with the caravan and go to Karak. Jakelin and Hunter must still be there. Seek them out and explain the situation, they will help you.'

'Hassan, no, it is too dangerous. You will die out there.'

'I have to take the risk, Sumeira, and my only regret is that I have to leave you and Emani.'

'If your heart is set, then do not worry about us,' said Sumeira. 'Do what you must and when I find your friends, I will tell them what happened here.'

Hassan nodded and picking up his water skin and cloak, climbed down from the cart to hide amongst the rocks at the side of the road.

Within the hour the slave women had stripped the carcass of all they could and the wagon master gave the order to continue. The caravan headed north once more, watched silently by Hassan from his hiding place. As soon as they were out of sight, he emerged to study the ground in more detail. Finally, he stood up and after taking a drink of water from the skin, headed eastward, deeper into the Negev desert.

Chapter Fifteen

August - AD 1178

Jacob's Ford

Eudes de St. Amand walked around the perimeter of the huge new castle. The Seneschal, Brother Valmont, walked beside him along with Simon of Syracuse, the newly appointed castellan.

The massive glacis walls around the boundary were already well underway and stretched high above their heads, vast sloping slopes of hewn rock that would eventually bear the massive defensive walls. Everywhere they looked, men swarmed over the site. Labourers brought the never-ending supply of slabs from the quarries to face the angled construction while teams of masons placed them carefully in place, ensuring there was no gap or protrusion any attacker could get a hold on.

'How is the well progressing?' asked Amand as they walked.

'We expect to hit water in the next few weeks,' said Simon, 'the dig is a massive undertaking and we have men upon it day and night. The spoil is mostly solid rock so we are using it between the walls on the outer curtain.'

'Are we on schedule?'

'We are, my lord. Since the king's instruction to increase the pace we have almost doubled the workforce.'

'And the cost?'

'It works out just over four Dinars per block laid including the labour. Our men bring the weekly purse from the temple in Jerusalem under a strong guard.'

'Expensive,' said Amand putting one foot up onto the Glacis wall and leaning forward to run his hand over some of the joints, 'but the quality is good and the king has sworn we can reclaim all expenses via the toll. How long until we start the walls?'

'The architects have already finished the plans for the walls and the four corner towers. I estimate the Glacis will be finished by Christ's Mass so the walls will quickly follow. Their construction will be far quicker and we should see them reach castellation six months after that. All the inner buildings will be constructed last and will take another three months, well within the king's time specification.'

'Excellent,' said Amand. 'As soon as you have this outer wall completed, have them focus on the entrance so the inner baileys can be secured. I will muster every knight we can spare from across Jerusalem so you can command the crossing without fear of opposition. In addition, the king has said he will supply lancers and I'm sure we can complement the garrison with mercenaries if needs be.'

'Your plans are welcome, my lord,' said Simon. 'Has there been any more contact from the Saracens?'

'Not that I am aware of but I'm sure there are eyes in every tree. Stay alert and have your men available to fight at a moment's notice. Saladin sees this place as a threat to the Saracen empire and I suspect he will not let us build it unchallenged.'

'We have an armed force on constant standby,' said Simon, 'as well as manned lookout posts a league distant in all directions. If anyone comes, we will know of it in plenty of time.'

'I have seen enough,' said Amand, 'and will report back to the king accordingly. Keep up the good work, Brother Simon, your dedication has not gone unnoticed.' He turned away but stopped as the castellan spoke again.

'My Lord, I have one last question.'

Amand turned back around to face the knight.

'My Lord,' said Simon again, 'I was wondering if the king has yet named the castle.'

'Aye,' said Amand, looking up at the already formidable defences, 'he has called it Chastellet.'

Twenty leagues to the northwest, Hassan staggered towards a Bedouin encampment. His skin was blistered from the sun and his tongue swollen in his mouth from lack of water.

It had been a hard and frustrating few months for Hassan. At first, the tracks left by Cronin's attackers had been clear and easy to follow, but as he was on foot, the trail soon ran cold and he had to use what knowledge he had of the area to anticipate where they may be headed at any given time. Many of the small villages he encountered had no knowledge of the party he sought but occasionally, a snippet of information from a shepherd or traveller gave him the confidence to carry on. Starving and exhausted he had finally crested a hill and saw the encampment below, recognising the tents as belonging to one of the tribes he had grown up amongst as a child.

He walked down the hill and was greeted by a group of young women wearing the black abaya, adorned with colourful embroidery sparkling in the midday sun. On their heads they wore Tarhas, the thin veils always worn outside of any dwelling.

'As-Salaam-Alaykum,' said Hassan, stopping to greet the women, 'my name is Hassam Malouf of the tribe of Nazar. I am weary from the road and seek assistance from my brothers, the Heuwaitaat.'

One of the women returned the greeting and offered a skin of water. He drank gratefully, raising his blistered face to the sky as he poured the warm water down his throat. When he had drunk his fill, he lifted the waterskin and poured more over his head, letting it run down his face to soak into his filthy thawb.

'You look exhausted, traveller,' she said in his native Bedouin, 'and must have travelled a long way. Where is your camel?'

'I have neither camel or horse,' said Hassan, after taking another drink, 'and have walked here from Al-Shabiya.'

The women looked at each other with surprise. The expanse of desert between Al-Shabiya and their encampment was barren and few would be able to cross it alive.

'Do you seek one of our people?' asked the woman.

'No, I seek a group who have come this way with a prisoner and would speak to your chief to see if he knows if where they are.'

'Come,' said one, 'this is not the time for such talk. We will take you to see the elders but first, you must rest.'

Hassan followed the women into the coolness of a tent, knowing that to press the urgency upon his hosts would be seen as rude. The heavy fabric kept out the heat of the desert sun and he collapsed onto the floor, exhausted and desperate for sleep. Several minutes later, a pretty slave girl came into the tent carrying a leather bucket of water and a fresh Jellabiya, the long loose garment preferred by the desert Arabs.

'Clean the dirt of the road from your skin,' she said, 'in a while, I will return with food and drink.'

Within the hour, Hassan sat cross-legged on the beautifully embroidered rug filling most of the tent. Before him was a plate of tender mutton and dates as well as a flask of surprisingly cool goat's milk. The slave girl waited until she knew he needed nothing else and turned to leave.

'Wait,' said Hassan, 'what is your name?'

'Kareena, my lord,' she said with a bow of her head, 'and I am at your service.'

'Thank you, Kareena,' said Hassan and waited until the girl had left before turning to the platters. The fruit tasted delicious, as did the meat, but by the time he had finished, he was struggling to keep his eyes open. Eventually, he laid down, using his hands as a pillow, intending to just shut his eyes for a few moments, but the exhaustion caught up with him and he fell into a deep and dreamless sleep.

By the time Hassan awoke, the sun had already reached the horizon and outside the tent, the men could be heard returning to the camp with their goats and sheep. The familiar sounds of his childhood created a strange longing within Hassan's chest, and he ducked out through the doorway, watching the scenes he had grown up with playing out all around him.

Children ran over to take over the responsibility of the herd while others brought water for the camels and horses. Some men headed for their tents, greeted by their women with buckets of water for washing while others walked to the edge of the small camp to report to the elders.

Hassan stayed where he was, knowing that when they were ready, he would be summoned. Gradually the activity died down and as night fell, several small campfires appeared outside the tents, many shared with neighbours to cook their evening meals. The smells were wonderful and Hassan's mouth watered at the thought of the spice-filled food of home.

Eventually, Kareena returned, giving him a pretty smile as she approached.

'You are awake,' she said, 'we thought it better to let you rest.'

'Thank you,' said Hassan, 'I feel much better.'

'Then come,' said Kareena, 'the chief is waiting.' She led the way through the camp to a tent standing slightly apart. Several men sat around a larger campfire, talking amongst themselves.

As he approached, one of the men stood up and walked to greet him. Hassan immediately knew he was the chief and as he neared, leaned forward to hold the man's shoulders and touch noses, the traditional greeting for all Bedouin tribes in the area.

'Hassan Malouf,' said the chief, 'my name is Najm al-Din, chief of this goam. The Heuwaitaat welcomes our friend from the Nazar, brothers of Banu Adnan under the gaze of Allah.'

'The honour is mine,' said Hassan, 'and I am grateful for the shelter and food.'

'Come and sit,' said Najm, indicating a place near the fire, 'first we will eat together and then discuss your business.'

For the next two hours, Hassan shared cups of warm spiced tea along with platters of aromatic rice dishes, slow-cooked in the traditional tajines hanging above many of the smaller fires around the camp. The food was delicious and the hospitality welcoming but he was desperate to find out what, if anything, they knew about Cronin. Finally, the platters were taken away and replaced with yet another ceramic kettle of tea and a platter of dates. Najm leaned forward and helped himself to a date before sitting up and turning to face Hassan.

'So, my friend,' he said at last, 'tell us about your journey and how it is we can help.'

Hassan took a deep breath and recounted the tale of how he had found Cronin's horse dead upon the road and how he had lost the trail of the men who had taken him.

'You say that the moon has been full three times since then,' said Najm. 'The probability is that they have long reached their destination and your friend is already dead.'

'I think not,' said Hassan, 'for he is worth far more alive to his captors.'

'Why?'

Because he is a Templar sergeant,' said Hassan, 'and will bring a pretty price. I suspect his captors intended to sell him to the highest bidder.'

'If that is so, why do you seek them out here? We are many leagues away from the travelled roads.'

'I do not know,' said Hassan, 'but their tracks led east. On the way here I passed through many camps that gave them shelter or seen them upon the mountain paths. They even tried selling him to some of the Emir's but the agreement between Bedouin and the Christian king is honour bound and they refused. Now I believe they are headed back this way to seek a buyer less worried about the consequences.'

'I have heard whispers of such a group,' said the chief, 'though did not know their prisoner was a Christian. The man you need to speak to is one of our hunters but he is still out working as a scout for the Christians. I think he will be able to furnish you with what you need to know.'

'When will he return?'

'Tomorrow, ten days, a month, who knows?'

'I cannot wait that long,' said Hassan, 'my friend is in great danger and needs my help.'

'He will take as long as it takes,' said Najm.

'Then I should leave,' said Hassan.

'Where will you go? You have no food, no camel, no horse and no idea where to look. Stay here and gather your strength. When he returns, I will furnish you with a horse and a guide to take you where you wish to go. That way, if he is still alive, you have a chance to find your friend.'

Hassan was frustrated but knew it was the sensible thing to do. If he left now, in his present state, he could be dead within days. Cronin's best chance was for Hassan to get strong.

'You are a wise man, Najm ad-Dim,' he said eventually, 'and I cede to your greater wisdom.'

The rest of the evening went slowly for Hassan, but he stayed amongst the men until only the embers remained.

'The new dawn approaches on hawk's wings,' said Najm, at last, getting to his feet, 'it is time for me to make my peace with the day.' He turned to Hassan. 'The tent in which you rested belongs to a family but the next one along is used by the single men of the tribe. You will find a space and blanket within where you can rest until you leave. My table is your table Hassan, so until that day, go about the camp with my trust upon your shoulders.'

'Thank you, Najm,' said Hassan and waited for the old man to disappear before heading off to find the allocated tent.

Chapter Sixteen

September - AD 1178

Jerusalem City

    Hunter sat in a tavern outside the citadel walls in Jerusalem city. The room was full of soldiers of fortune, most spending their latest wage obtained by serving a local lord, or even the king himself. Most were from Christian countries except for the occasional beggar who managed to sneak in while the landlord's attention was elsewhere.
    Hunter nursed a jack of thick and fruity ale, a heady concoction brewed by the monks in the citadel. Already he was beginning to feel its effects and he knew that one or two more would see him end up in a dangerous state while walking back to his lodgings amongst the back alleys of the city.
    Next to him sat a group of men, each merry after too many ales, and courted by the whores of the tavern due to the bulging purse of coins sat on the barrel that served as their table.
    'With my share,' announced one after a particularly loud belch, 'I'm going to find the first ship home to England and find myself a village where a good day's work will earn a good day's wage. It's not too much to ask for, I just want to get away from this place as soon as possible.'
    'Not for me,' responded another, just as drunk, 'there are still Saracens to kill so I'm staying here.'
    The largest man in the party, heavily bearded with a scar above and below his left eye from some long-forgotten knife fight, watched on, enjoying the camaraderie yet still sober despite having drunk the same as his comrades. He turned to the youngest man in the room.
    'What about you, my friend, you have paid your passage and acquitted yourself well on the field. What will you do with your share?'
    'I'm staying in Jerusalem,' said the young man looking up lovingly at the woman caressing his shoulders from behind. 'I'm going to spend my time with this beauty and who knows, perhaps we will settle down and raise children together.'
    The rest of the men roared with laughter at the young man's naivety.

'She is a whore,' roared one, 'and is only after your coin. I had her myself not two day's since and a pretty penny it cost me too.'

'I don't care,' said the drunken man, 'those days are behind her and we have a future together.'

The bearded man turned to look around the room, his eyes pausing to stare at Hunter.

'What of you stranger,' he said, 'have you also just been paid?'

'I have not,' said Hunter, 'so cannot share your merriment.'

'Who do you serve?'

'I serve nobody but myself.'

'Everyone serves somebody,' said the man, 'else how can you afford to drink that ale in your jack?'

When Hunter didn't answer, the man turned his chair to face him and held out his hand in greeting.

'My name is Arturas,' he said, 'and you, my friend, look like a man with a lot on his mind.'

Hunter returned the stare, wondering whether to just drink up and leave. Instead, he gave a sigh, placed his jack on the table and leant forward to take the man's wrist.

'James Hunter,' he said, 'from England. 'I served with Baldwin at Montgisard but am now free to ply my trade elsewhere.'

'You look like a man of the road,' said Arturas, 'yet have the look of a fighter about you. Who do you call comrade?'

'The men I rode alongside have taken different paths,' said Hunter. 'One has returned to service in the name of the king, one has disappeared from the town of Segor to the south and the one whom I looked upon as a brother, disappeared on the road to Damascus east of the salt sea.'

'Did you seek him out?'

'I did, for many days but nobody saw anything of him. I found the remains of a freshly killed horse but it had been butchered and the bones scattered by predators. I fear it may have been his.'

'The Damascus road is known for brigands,' said Arturas. 'Perhaps it was inevitable for a rider alone.'

'Aye, I fear he is long dead.'

'So,' continued Arturas, 'without employment, how does a man eat bread and drink ale?'

'I live frugally and work when needed,' said Hunter.' One day I will head home but my funds are depleted so I no longer hold the fare.'

'What is your trade?'

'Scout,' said Hunter, 'and though it may be self-praise, I see no shame in saying that I am better than most.'

'There is no shame in a man proclaiming his own worth,' said Arturas, 'for few others will take the time.' He paused for a moment, staring at Hunter. 'A scout, you say,' he continued eventually, I may have need of a man such as you.'

'I thought you and your men have recently been paid off,' said Hunter.

'Aye, we were,' said Arturas, 'we were recently engaged by Reginald of Sidon protecting Ashkelon from Saladin. After Montgisard our services were no longer needed and this is our severance pay.' He nodded at the coins now spread out across the top of the barrel. 'Soon it will be gone and we will need new employment.'

'In Jerusalem?'

'No. We have heard that the king is recruiting men like us to protect a project in the north. Apparently, he is building a castle at Jacob's Ford and fears that the Saracens may attack before it is built. Me, I doubt that very much for after the rout at Montgisard, I think Saladin is done, however, it seems like easy money to me so in a few days we ride north. If you are as good as you say you are, I could find a place for you amongst my men.' He nodded towards the young man with the whore now straddling his lap. 'Some can't see further than who will warm their bed tonight, but me, I know there is still a fortune to be made in the Outremer.' He drank the rest of his ale and stood up to let out a deep belch. 'I could do with a good scout,' he said, 'and the pay is fair. If you are interested, be outside here the day after tomorrow with a horse and three days rations. After that, I will take care of the rest.'

Without another word he turned and left the tavern, leaving Hunter deep in thought behind him.

Many leagues to the east, Hassan sat near a pool in a tiny oasis watching Kareena collecting water in two leather buckets.

It had been several weeks since he had first arrived at the goam and for the last ten days had stayed with them as they travelled north to find new pastures for their herds. At first, he had become increasingly frustrated when the hunter that Najm had said would be able to help failed to arrive but though he wanted to continue his search for Cronin, he knew his body was weak and needed to recover. Consequently, he had stayed with the goam, helping out with the herds to pay his way.

Slowly he had grown stronger and he knew he would soon be able to leave but over the weeks, something strange had happened, he had grown attracted to the slave girl.

'Kareena,' he said, walking over with a smile, 'let me help you with those.'

'Thank you,' said the girl, 'but I may be called lazy and beaten by my master.'

'Does he beat you?' asked Hassan with surprise.

'No,' said the girl with a giggle, 'in truth he does not, and never has, but often he threatens me with such a punishment. I suspect it is no more than a game he plays.'

'I agree,' said Hassan, 'for when you are not looking, I see him gaze upon you like a father does his daughter.'

'I have been here as long as I can remember,' said Kareena, 'and they have been very kind to me.'

'Do you not know of your own people?'

'I do not. Najm has told me I was found as a baby amongst a slaughtered caravan, still clinging to my mother's breast. He says that I was amongst the slaves so it is a title I always carry but if I am honest, they do not treat me as such.'

'Then there is little to worry about,' said Hassan, taking the buckets, 'and anyway, if he sees us, I will speak on your behalf.'

They walked back to the camp, talking quietly to themselves and sat on a rock for a while, chatting and laughing between themselves. Finally, Kareena stood up to leave.

'Now I really have to go,' she said, 'there is much for me to do.'

Hassan watched her go and for the first time, realised that he actually had feelings for the girl. The realisation was overwhelming and for a few moments, his mind ran away with the possibilities. Never had he even considered any sort of relationship but now, due to circumstances out of his control, the possibility became real and everything he had ever thought possible, changed. The girl was supposedly a slave probably from one of the tribes of Egypt and though there was nothing stopping them being together on race or religion grounds, she was owned by the chief and Hassan was no more than a traveller passing through. To even hope of being together, he would have to persuade both her and the chief that it would be a good thing and that he could provide as a good husband. For a moment the possibility lightened his heart but like a storm cloud covering the sun, the feeling died as he remembered his commitment to finding Cronin. While that quest remained unfulfilled, there was no room in his life for anything else.

With a heavy heart, he stood up and headed back to the pool where the flocks were being brought to drink. For the next few hours, he joined the young men of the tribe, tending the camels and riding the few horses they collectively owned. Eventually, they headed back to camp but on the way saw a man descending a nearby hill, leading two horses, both piled high with what seemed like animal skins. Hassan stopped and stared, before turning to the young boy at his side.

'Who is that?'

'Abdal-Wahhab,' said the boy, 'the man for whom you wait.'

Hassan breathed a sigh of relief as he watched the hunter walk his horses into the camp. Trotting alongside him were his two beautiful Saluki, the lithe and powerful hunting dogs that were the pride of all Bedouin tribes in the Negev and on the second horse, a pair of hunting falcons perched upon the piled load of furs.

As he entered the village, women and men alike emerged from the tents to welcome the hunter and children ran alongside his horse, excited to see the man again after so many weeks.

Hassan took his own horse to the corral before walking back to the camp but as was usual, the welcome and hospitality took precedence and the hunter did not endeavour to talk. Instead, he greeted all who knew him before being taken away to rest and to be fed.

Hassan knew the custom and though it was frustrating, remained calm. After all this time, a few more hours meant nothing.

Later that evening the camp put on a feast for the return of Abdal-Wahhab and everyone gathered around a large campfire to sing their welcome and hear his stories. The hunter regaled them with tales of wonder, including how he killed a lion after being cornered in a ravine. Hassan was dubious about the truthfulness of the tale but was surprised when the hunter produced an adult male lion's pelt to back up the story, presenting it to Najm's wife as a gift.

More surprises and gifts followed, along with parcels of meat from snake to impala, all dried in the hot sand of the desert for preservation and wrapped in palm leaves ready for transportation.

Finally, the time came that everyone had been waiting for and Abdal-Wahhab turned to the chief.

'Najm al-Din,' he said, 'to you I bring the greatest gift of all. Across the kingdom of Jerusalem and throughout the Oultrejordain, the Christians deploy powerful warriors in the name of their God. They are religious men, devout and pious in their worship yet fearless upon the field of battle. It is said that even Salah ad-Din shakes at the sound of their footfall. They fear no-one and dedicate their lives to protecting Jerusalem, a band of brothers that would die rather than lose one of their own.' He turned around slowly, building the tension amongst the watchers. 'Yet, despite this,' he continued, 'I have obtained something precious to those men, something they will pay a pretty price to have returned.'

He bent down and unwrapped a long package at his feet, holding up the contents up for all to see. The firelight glistened off the Christian sword, but as they all gathered around the hunter for a closer look, Hassan stood back, sick to his stomach. As soon as Abdal-Wahhab had held up the weapon, he had known it was more than just a sword, it was a Templar sword, and had once belonged to Thomas Cronin.

The following morning, Hassan was summoned to the chief's tent. Upon entering he saw the chief sitting upon an ornate rug opposite Abdal-Wahhab. Both men sipped on tea and picked from a platter of dates.

'As-Salamu-Alaykum,' said Hassan, touching his hand to his heart and lips.

'Wa-Alaykum-Salaam,' came the reply from both men.

'Please,' said Najm, indicating an extra cushion on the carpet, 'join us.'

Hassan sat and waited as one of the chief's women poured him a goblet of tea. When she had finished, he sipped the drink and placed it back on the platter before turning to the chief.

'Hassan Malouf,' said Najm, 'of the tribe, Nazar, brothers to the Heuwaitaat, this is Abdal-Wahhab, the greatest hunter throughout the Negev. I am proud to call him brother and a valued member of this Goam.'

'It is my honour to meet you at last,' said Hassan. 'It has been said you have the heart of a lion and last night I bore witness to why you bear that tribute.'

'The respect is mutual, Hassan Malouf,' said Abdal-Wahhab, 'for I hear you walked across the Negev with neither horse nor camel in search of a friend. That is an achievement far greater than killing any lion.'

'Thank you,' said Hassan.

'You have waited a long time to speak to Abdal-Wahhab,' said Najm, 'now you should ask what you wish to know before he leaves to wander the desert once more.'

'Thank you,' said Hassan again and turned to the hunter.

'Abdal-Wahhab, it is said you have eyes like a thousand hawks and nothing happens without your knowledge. I seek a man, a Christian who used to bear the blade you brought to the fire last night. He was taken by brigands many moons ago but I believe he still lives and I am sworn to find him or die trying.'

'The Templar knight?'

'He is no knight,' said Hassan, 'but one of the lower orders called sergeants.'

'But a Templar nonetheless?'

'Yes. He is a good man with honour as high as any.'

'And who is this man to you?' asked Abdal-Wahhab

'He has saved my life twice,' said Hassan. 'Once when I was accused wrongly of spying for Salah ad-Din and again when I was going to be killed by brigands. He also willingly failed his master in exchange for the lives of my mother and sister. My oath is to serve him until the day I die.'

'A great debt indeed,' said Abdal-Wahhab.

The boy nodded while the hunter continued to stare at him.

'Hassan,' he said eventually, 'I am no friend of Salah ad-Din. I walk the desert, my own man and judge another by his deeds, not his words. I have been told of your journey and how you almost died in the Negev in your search for your comrade. I also see into your soul when you sing this Christian's praises. I believe you are true in faith and intent so will give you what you want.'

Hassan swallowed hard as Abdal-Wahhab took a drink from his goblet.

'Before the last moon,' continued Abdal-Wahhab, 'I came across those you seek camped in a wadi many leagues to the west. With them, they had a man, gagged and bound against a tree. It was obvious to me he was hurt and needed a physician, but their business is their own, not mine. First, they tried to sell him to me as a slave, but I have no respect for men who sell other men. I refused so they offered me the blade instead in return for meat. I made the trade but not before sharing tea and finding out where they were going.'

'Where?' asked Hassan.

'Damascus,' said Abdal-Wahhab.

'But why were they out the way out here?'

'They feared being followed by the Templars so hoped to sell the man to one of Saladin's patrols, but his forces are busy fighting the eastern tribes. Now they know there is little chance of finding the sultan or his men, they have turned their heads back towards Damascus. It seems your friend is a great prize and will command a healthy ransom.'

'Thank you, Abdal-Wahhab,' said Hassan and turned to the chief.

'Najm al-Din,' he said, 'your hospitality is a shining light to be held up for others to follow, and it pains me that I can never repay you enough, but now Abdal-Wahhab has shown me the path, it is time for me to finish that which I have started. I beg permission to take my leave and proceed with all haste to Damascus.'

'Your commitment to your vow does you justice,' said Najm, 'and though I fear the outcome, you go with my blessing. I am a man of my word, Hassan, and will furnish you with a horse. You have the choice of my herd except for the black stallion. In addition, Abdal-Wahhab will take you to the outskirts of Damascus, though what you will do when you get there only Allah knows.'

Hassan leaned over and took the chief's hands, kissing them in gratitude before standing up.

'I will say my goodbyes,' he said, 'your people have become family to me.'

'One more than most, it seems,' said Najm.

Hassan's face reddened and he struggled to find a response.

'Go to her,' said the chief, 'and say what has to be said. You have my blessing but be warned, if you promise that which you do not intend to deliver, there will never be a welcome for you amongst the tents of this goam.'

'I understand,' said Hassan.

'Be ready at dusk,' said Abdal-Wahhab, 'we will travel through the night and shelter when the sun is at its highest tomorrow.'

Hassan nodded and left the tent to find Kareena.

When he was gone, the chief looked over at Abdal-Wahhab, with curiosity in his eyes.

'Your offer of help was generous,' he said, 'especially to one who is so young and perhaps ignorant.'

'I admire his heart,' said Abdal-Wahhab. 'For one so young to try and honour a life-debt, at the probable cost of his own is a value seldom seen. The boy is brave.'

'The chances of him finding this man and being successful are small.'

'Perhaps, but he deserves his chance. I will track the men he seeks but limit my involvement their discovery only. What he does after that is his own business.'

'You will not fight alongside him?'

'No,' said Abdal-Wahhab, 'for I have other business to attend.' His hand crept up to the still-raw wound where his left ear used to be. 'It is said that Salah ad-Din has returned and with him, the man who did this to me.'

'And you seek retribution?'

'I do,' said Abdal-Wahhab, 'my honour demands it.'

Kareena sat outside one of the tents washing rice for the evening meal. She smiled as Hassan approached and wiped her hands before inviting him to sit upon the rug alongside her.

'Hassan,' she said, 'As-Salamu-Alaykum.'

'Wa-Alaykum-Salaam,' responded Hassan, lowering himself to sit beside her.

'I see you have been with the chief and Abdal-Wahhab,' she said, 'was it the news you hoped?'

'It was,' said Hassan,' and that is why I came here to see you. I have to leave, Kareena, and will probably not return for a long time.'

The girl's face fell and she lowered her eyes.

'When?' she asked quietly.

'This very day,' said Hassan. 'Abdal-Wahhab will take me to where I have to be.'

'I expected it,' said Kareena looking up, 'I just hoped it would not be for many days yet.'

'If I am honest with myself, I too was hoping for more time,' said Hassan. 'Every day I am here you make my time easier and I find myself seeking you out at every opportunity.'

'I know,' said the girl with an embarrassed smile, 'I fear I am falling behind on my work due to our conversations. But I do not care, Hassan. My time with you is worth any punishment I may receive.'

'So like us being together?' asked Hassan.

'I savour every moment,' said Kareena, 'and though I know you have to go, I wish with all my heart that this was not the case.'

Hassan paused his own heart racing. He had come to Kareena, with thoughts tumbling through his head about how he would express his feelings for her, but here she was, expressing those very same thoughts.

'Kareena,' he said, hardly daring to breathe, 'if I was to promise that I would return as soon as I can, would you wait for me?'

'Of course,' said Kareena, taking his hands in hers, 'until my dying day, if needs be.'

'And would you be happy to take me as a husband?'

'Happier than any other woman in this world,' said the girl with a beaming smile.

Hassan thought his heart was going to burst, such was his joy. He jumped to his feet and started walking away.

'Where are you going?' laughed Kareena.

'To see the chief,' said Hassan.

'Why?' asked Kareena.

'To ask for your hand,' shouted Hassan. 'Why else?'

The sun was setting when Hassan and Abdal-Wahhab finally led their horses through the Goam. The people came out to say goodbye and as they reached the edge of the camp, Kareena called quietly from the shadows of the last tent.

'Hassan, please, come here.'

Hassan hesitated, knowing that now they were promised, he was not allowed to be alone with the girl.

'Please,' said Kareena, 'I must say goodbye.'

'Be quick, boy,' said Abdal-Wahhab, quietly, 'my attention has been drawn elsewhere.'

'Thank you,' said Hassan and gave him the reins of his horse before running over to join the girl in the shadows.

'Hassan,' she gasped, 'the women told me the chief said yes. I am so happy I could burst apart.'

'As am I,' said Hassan taking her hands, but there are restrictions.'

'What restrictions?'

'Najm has promised that one year from today, he will bring this goam back here, to this same oasis. I have until then to finish my business and return to claim your hand. If I am not here by sunset on that day, then you will be released from your promise and free to marry another man.'

'I don't want any other man.'

'I understand but that was the price I had to pay. It is a good, thing Kareena, for if I die, at least you will be free to live the rest of your life.'

'You will not die, Hassan,' said the girl, 'Allah will not allow it.'

'In that case,' said Hassan, 'a year is less than a heartbeat compared to the time we will have together.'

'Come on boy,' said a voice in the gloom, 'we have to go.'

'Be safe,' gasped Kareena as Hassan's hands started to slip from her own.

'I will be back,' Kareena, he said as he walked back into the darkness, 'I swear it upon my soul.'

Chapter Seventeen

October – AD 1178

The Castle of Chastellet

Arturas led his force of twenty mercenaries along the hilltop track towards Jacob's Ford. Since leaving Jerusalem a few days' earlier they had made good time and apart from seeing a few Saracen riders in the distance, had encountered no trouble. Behind him, his battle-hardened men rode in a double file, talking quietly amongst themselves. The mood was light, for the work they had signed up to seemed easy compared to other tasks they had undertaken, especially as there was no sign of Saladin or his armies.

The young man who had declared his love for the whore in the tavern rode at the rear, his pride still hurt after being discarded as soon as his share of the purse was gone. With no other option, he had finally begged his laughing comrades to allow him back into their fold, a little bit wiser, and a whole lot poorer.

Up ahead, Hunter waited on the highest hill in the area, drinking warm water from his leather flask as he looked over at the construction site on the other side of the valley. Already it was a magnificent sight and with the advantage of the higher ground, he could see the entire footprint of the half-built castle.

Arturas called his men to a halt and rode forward to join Hunter. For a few moments, there was silence as he stared at Chastellet, momentarily taken aback at the magnificence of the proposed fortress and its powerful position overlooking Jacob's Ford.

'I had heard it was going to be an impressive castle,' he said eventually, 'but I had no idea it was going to be anything like this.'

'It reminds me of Karak,' said Hunter, 'but much bigger.'

'You have served in Karak?' asked Arturas looking at the scout.

'I have visited there once,' said Hunter, 'and thought it was the biggest fortress I would ever see, but it is nothing compared to this.'

The two men continued to stare in wonder at the activity on the opposite hilltop. Men swarmed all over it like ants and as far as they could see, columns of carts carried the pre-dressed stone from the quarries.

Hunter looked down the hill and saw a column of armed men riding up towards them, the banner of the king flying high from atop one of the riders' lances.

'We have company,' he said, and the two men waited until the lancers arrived.

'State your business,' stated the knight at the head of the column.

'We have been engaged by the king's office to serve as guards to the workforce,' said Arturas, pulling out a parchment from beneath his cloak. 'A twelve-month contract for twenty men at arms and their mounts, to include all food, fodder and lodgings.' He handed over the document and waited as the knight read the detail.

'Mercenaries,' he said looking back up at Arturas as he rolled up the parchment.

'Is that a problem?' asked Arturas.

'Some may say you are overpaid,' said the Knight, 'and your only allegiance is to the highest payer.'

'Are these thoughts also yours?'

'I only care that you are able to fight Saracens,' said the knight.

'Have no worry on that score, Sir knight, my blade has been reddened by Saracen blood as often as any man down there.' He nodded towards the construction site.

'We will see,' said the knight tossing the parchment back to Arturas. 'Follow me, I will show you where to go.'

Half an hour later, the knight led Arturas and his men into a compound near the base of the hill.

'I've seen towns smaller than this,' said Hunter as they rode between row after row of tents and makeshift huts.

'The builders are on a tight timescale,' said the knight, 'King Baldwin wants it completed before next winter.' He stopped at a paddock containing a few goats and a mule. 'You can keep your horses here,' he said, 'and there should be enough room for your tents on the far side. Meals are served at dawn and sunset at the kitchens near the ford. Take your authorization from the king with you the first time you go else you will be refused entry.'

'When do we find out about our tasks?' asked Arturas.

'Break your fast tomorrow and report to the command tent at the entrance to the castle. I'll inform the Marshal you are here, and he will allocate your duties.'

'Will do,' said Arturas and watched the knight turn to ride away.

'You heard him,' he said turning to his men, 'we'll set up camp here. Someone organise water for the horses, the rest of us will break out the tents.'

The following morning, refreshed after a good night's sleep, Arturas and Hunter walked up the approach road to the command tent outside the half-built gate towers. Other men were on their way down having already been issued their orders for the day by the Marshal. They stood outside, waiting their turn before being summoned inside.

Tables lay end to end all around the edge of the huge tent, each covered with plans for the castles, lists of provisions or maps of the region. Scribes sat on chairs recording events or writing down lists of what was needed by the masons in order to continue the never-ending construction. The place was a hive of activity and at the centre, the castellan stood leaning over a deerskin map of the area, barking out his orders as the various commanders reported for duty. Despite the bustle, Hunter had eyes for only one man, a Templar knight stood in conversation with a squire at the rear of the tent.

'Hunter,' said Arturas, 'come, we need to see the map.'

'Ah,' said Simon of Syracuse, looking up as they approached. 'You must be the men who arrived yesterday, I was expecting you sooner. Have any of you ever ridden east of the Jordan?'

'Aye,' said Hunter, 'I rode to Karak alongside your man there.' He pointed at the back of the Templar knight.

The knight at the far end of the tent straightened up as he recognised the voice and turned slowly to stare at the scout. It was Jakelin De Mailly.

'Hunter,' he said, eventually, 'it has been a while. Is Cronin with you?'

'He is not,' said Hunter coldly, 'and I suspect his corpse rots somewhere east of the salt sea. Still, I see you are safe and well amongst your brothers. I hope you are content.'

De Mailly didn't answer, he just stood there staring at Hunter as the castellan glanced between them both.

'Is there an issue here?' he asked.

'Not with me,' said Hunter. 'I'm here to do the job I've signed up for. I just hope your so-called brotherhood does the same.'

'What do you mean by that?' asked the castellan.

'He means nothing,' intervened Tartarus, 'just some insignificant squabble from way back.'

'Well keep your pettiness to yourselves,' said the castellan, 'and do the job you are getting paid for. There is no room out here for score-settling.'

'We understand,' said Arturas, sending a cold stare towards Hunter, 'don't we, my friend?'

'Aye,' said Hunter eventually and turned his attention back to the map. 'Now, where are we going?'

'What was all that about?' growled Arturas as they marched back down the hill half an hour later.

'That was the knight that betrayed us,' said Hunter, 'and my comrade is probably dead because of him.'

'You said nothing about being in conflict with the Templars,' hissed Arturas, 'and if I had known that was the case, I would never have signed you up.'

'You have nothing to fear on that score,' said Hunter, 'I'll do my job as promised but when all this is over, there will be a reckoning.'

Arturas looked over at him with surprise.

'You intend to take on a Templar knight in combat?'

'They are men like you and me,' said Hunter, 'nothing more. This one has a price to pay.'

'Then you are already a dead man,' said Arturas, striding away from Hunter, 'your body just doesn't know it yet.'

For the next few weeks, Arturas led his men on daily patrols to the east and west of the River Jordan, acting as the eyes and ears of the king. News had arrived that Saladin's forces were busy fighting the eastern tribes so Saracen interference was minimal but the king insisted on maintaining the perimeter, painfully aware that the Sultan was more than capable of organizing an attack at any moment, especially from Damascus which had been ruled by Saladin since the death of Nur ad-Din four years earlier.

On the rare days between the constant patrols, Hunter would rest in the olive groves a few leagues west of Chastellet or wander throughout the castle building site, in constant awe of the vision and ability of those men responsible for its construction. It was on one such day that he came across Jakelin de Mailly, staring eastward over one of the partly constructed walls.

For a moment he stared at the knight's back, controlling his anger but knowing this was neither the time nor the place, decided not to initiate conflict. Instead, he walked up to stand alongside Jakelin, taking in the same view.

'He's still out there, you know,' he said, causing Jakelin to glance across.

'Who?'

'Cronin. Somewhere, out there in the Oultrejordain, our friend's remains are probably laying somewhere, his bones bleached by the desert sun.'

'All men die,' said Jakelin.

'Aye, we do. But few as a result of betrayal by a friend.'

'I did not betray him, Hunter, I did what I had to do and as a Templar sergeant, he would have understood my motives.'

'And what motives would they be,' asked Hunter, 'greed, envy, or the pursuit of profit.'

'That trader was paid five hundred Dinars,' said Jakelin, 'it was more than enough.'

'And what about the other price, the life of a friend?'

Jakelin turned to face Hunter and the scout braced for a verbal backlash. For a few moments, they stared at each other, two men of war who had lived their lives knowing nothing but conflict. Finally, the knight took a deep breath and sighed.

'You cannot say anything to me that I have not already thought,' he said. 'At the time, I was carrying out my duty to the Temple and the king with little thought of consequence. There is no way I could have known he would ride away and though that is no fault of my own, there is not a day that goes by that I don't regret my actions or pray for his soul. My decision was the right one, Hunter, the outcome was not. We can stay here all day while you cast your accusations and insults, but it will not bring him back. Now, say what you have to say, or do what you came to do. I tire of your constant crying like a hurt maiden.'

Hunter shook his head in disgust.

'And that's it?' he asked.' The story is done, our friend is dead so we must move on.'

'What do you want of me?' shouted Jakelin taking a step towards the scout with clenched fists, *'I cannot bring him back.'*

'You can, my lord,' said a voice behind them.

They both spun around to see a young man standing behind them. It was Hassan Malouf, and he looked exhausted.

'Hassan,' gasped Hunter. 'Where have you been these past months? What happened to you?'

'We have no time,' said Hassan, 'we have to go.'

'Go?' asked Hunter, 'go where?'

'To rescue Cronin, my lord,' said Hassan, 'my master is still alive, *and I know where he is!'*

Chapter Eighteen

November – AD 1178

The Castle of Chastellet

Hunter and Arturas once more stood in the command tent outside the gates of Chastellet castle. Before them was the castellan, listening to their tale with concern.

'So, you are telling me,' he said, 'there is a Templar sergeant in captivity not far from here and you want to go and get him.'

'Aye, my lord,' said Hunter. 'He is being held in a prison camp south of Damascus and we think that a small group of men can get in and out without being seen.'

'Saladin holds many men prisoner,' said Sir Simon, 'yet we do not undertake rescue missions for them. What makes your friend so special?'

'The jails of Damascus are beyond our reach,' said Arturas, 'but Cronin has not yet been sold to Saladin. If we move quickly, we can get him out of there and back amongst his brothers where he belongs.'

'And the risks?'

'There are always risks,' said Hunter, 'but on this occasion they are minimal. Saladin is more concerned about the eastern tribes, so his attention is elsewhere. The men who hold our brother prisoner are not men of war, they are slavers who profit on his misfortune. It would be unjust if we did not at least try to rescue him.'

'I don't know,' said the castellan. 'The rescue of one of our own brothers would send a strong signal to all, but the task would need many men and could leave our defences weakened. We can't risk the safety of these workers or the castle.'

'Me and my men are happy to undertake the task,' said Arturas. 'The constant patrolling and lack of conflict are driving them crazy anyway. Let us go with him and we can be back within days.'

'Your role is protecting the workers,' said the castellan, 'not riding on what could be a suicide mission to rescue a man that may already dead.'

'My Lord,' said Hunter, 'Cronin is one of your own. He was sent on a mission by the Grand Master himself, one that he managed to undertake successfully, and if it hadn't been for the betrayal of one of your own knights in Al-Shabiya, he would still be here now. I reckon he deserves some sort of loyalty and even if we die trying, then at least we do so with clear consciences. If it is the cost of such a venture that holds your arm, then I will forfeit my share of the purse due to me at the end of the contract.'

Sir Simon looked between the two men. It was true that the situation was relatively peaceful and the construction of Chastellet surging ahead, but there was always a chance that Saladin could turn up at any moment and if that happened, he would need every sword he could get.

'I will let you go,' he said eventually, 'but I have to protect the king's investment. Take ten of your men and be sure you are back here by the next full moon, whether you have brother Cronin or not. If you have not returned by then, the agreement you signed in Jerusalem will be forfeit and your remaining men enrolled into the royal army without recompense to you. Is that understood?'

'Aye, my lord,' said Arturas, glancing at Hunter, 'ten men should be more than enough.'

'There will be eleven,' said the castellan, and nodded to the man who had just entered the tent.

Hunter and Arturas turned around to stare at the Templar knight standing behind them.

'Sir Jakelin,' said Hunter eventually, the distaste obvious in his voice.

'Aye,' said Jakelin, 'I am coming with you.'

Two days later, Arturas and Hunter stood alongside their horses in the paddock, loading the remainder of the supplies they would need for the journey. Around them, another ten men, handpicked by Arturas, did the same, each keen to get away from the monotonous daily regime of patrolling the surrounding hills.

'Here he comes,' said Hunter glancing up from his task.

Arturas looked up to see the imposing figure of Jakelin de Mailly leading his own horse into the paddock.,

'He looks different without his Templar garb,' said Arturas, seeing the rider's drab brown cloak and surcoat, 'at least he had the common sense to leave it behind.'

'To ride so close to Damascus without being seen will be hard enough,' said Hunter, tightening the girth strap around his horse, 'the last thing we would need is a self-important knight bedecked in attire bearing the emblem hated by everyone east of the Jordan.'

'As long as he can fight,' said Arturas, 'then I will be happy. Have you seen him with a sword in hand?'

'I have not, but it is known he fought well at Montgisard. I think he will not be found wanting should it come to conflict.'

'Yet you still hold him in low esteem.'

'I hold him responsible for the capture of my friend and unless Cronin is free, I have a duty to ultimately settle the score.'

'And if we succeed in releasing your friend?'

'We will see,' said Hunter and turned to face Jakelin as he stopped beside them. 'Sir Jakelin,' he said, 'you are late. We were about to leave without you.'

'I am here now,' said Jakelin, looking around. 'Where is the boy?'

Hunter pointed at Hassan riding down the slope from the castle astride a fresh horse.

'In that case', said Jakelin, 'we should move out. There are only ten days until the moon is full.'

'We will ride upon the road for today,' interjected Arturas, mounting his horse, 'and continue throughout the night while we are still fresh. When the sun rises, we will find somewhere away from the eyes of those who would report our journey to the Saracens. If God is with us, we should be somewhere near the camp within four days.'

'That's fine with me,' said Jakelin and mounted his own horse.

Arturas led his men out of the paddock and onto the path heading eastward into Syria. Hunter rode his own horse alongside Jakelin's and turned to stare at the knight.

'You may be a Templar,' he said, 'but until you prove otherwise, you are no higher than a traitor in my eyes.'

'Think what you will, Hunter,' said Jakelin, 'for only God can judge the trueness of my soul. Now come, there is the Lord's work to do.' He nudged his heels into his horse's flanks and followed the mercenaries out onto the path.

Back in the castle, the chaplain and the castle's only physician, John Loxley, walked between the cots in the hospital tent situated within the upper bailey. Several patients lay on straw-filled mattresses, some with injuries caused by work accidents, others suffering from the ague or some other unknown illness. Two young women also moved amongst the patients, sitting on their cots and cooling their brows with flannels while slaves brought them buckets of fresh water from the well.

John Loxley stopped alongside the cot of a young man whose leg had been badly crushed by a falling rock. They had given him poppy juice for the pain but they both knew he was dying.

'Can we not remove the leg?' asked the chaplain.

'I could have,' said the physician 'but by the time they brought him from the quarry, it was too late. If they had sent word, I could have even gone over there to see what I could do.'

'The castellan would never allow it,' said the chaplain, 'your place is here.'

'I know, and that is why I have requested extra help from the king. The population of Chastellet grows by the day and if you include all those working in the quarries, it is far too big a responsibility for one man.'

'How will you cope? '

'The king has promised me another physician will arrive in the next few days.'

'The sooner the better,' said the chaplain, 'I'll return later to give this man the last rights.'

Later that day, a caravan arrived from Tiberius carrying various supplies for the garrison. Most of the carts carried barrels of arrows and spare crossbows but some carried skilled masons and their apprentices, men desperately needed to increase the speed of the construction. To the rear of the caravan were several carts carrying camp followers, the people who made their living from following armies or relocating to remote outposts to trade their wares. These could range from washing and cooking services to labouring or nursing. Others offered sexual services; a commodity highly valued by the many single men encamped within the garrison.

To the rear, a single cart was piled high with rolls of linen to be used as bandages as well as a box of new surgeons' tools and several bottles of poppy juice. John Loxley walked along the column, desperate to find his much-needed supplies. He walked up to the cart and looked up at the two men on the seat.

'Is this the cart for the hospital?' he asked.

'Aye, my lord,' said one of the men,' and well-stocked it is.'

'Which of you is the physician?'

'Not, us my lord,' said the cart driver, 'we are cart masters only and trade where the money takes us. The one you seek is in the back.'

'Thank you,' said the physician and walked around to the tailgate to look inside. Towards the far end, he saw someone amongst the sacks of supplies, sitting in the shadows.

'Hello,' he said, peering in, 'I'm John Loxley, physician of Chastellet. Have you been sent by the king to aid me in caring for his subjects?'

'I have not, my lord, 'said the half-hidden person, getting to their feet and stepping over some boxes to approach the rear of the cart, 'I am, however, a healer. My name is Sumeira and this is my daughter, Emani.'

'So, you have come from Tiberius,' said Loxley as they walked towards the inner bailey ten minutes later.

'We have,' said Sumeira. 'We have been there for a short while having journeyed from Segor in the south.'

'Why did you leave Segor?'

'It is too complicated to explain, but our lives were at risk. We managed to get safe passage on a trading caravan to Tiberius. The master was a good man and though I was bound to his service, he set me free on a promise that one day I would pay my fare, a promise I vow to keep.'

'So why have you come to Chastellet?'

'Tiberius is not secure from those who pursue me,' said Sumeira. 'Out here, Emani and I should be safe. Those that wish us harm will not be welcome here. '

'Saracens?'

'Not men in the service of Salah ad-Din but they support his cause. At first, we hid amongst the back alleys of Tiberius but when I found out there was a caravan headed out here, I offered my skills as a physician in return for passage. They agreed and placed me in the medical cart where you found me.'

'So, you have not been appointed by the king?'

'No, my lord, and I am aware that there is no other person in the caravan with that role.'

Loxley sighed in frustration. Despite the king's promise, it seemed he was still on his own.

'My Lord,' said Sumeira, sensing his doubt, 'my family have been healers for as long as I can remember. I learned the secrets of the herbs and medicines from my mother and my grandmother and assure you I can help. If you will trust me, I will work endlessly in return for just a little food and water, and perhaps a dry corner to lay our heads at night. I implore you, my lord, give me a chance and I swear you will be well served.'

'I don't know,' said Loxley. 'This is a busy place, and many are falling to an ague I cannot control. I have little time to nurture a newcomer.'

'I need no mentoring, my lord,' said Sumeira. 'Let me go amongst the afflicted and see what I can do. If I can help, then your load will ease and if not, then you are in no worse a position than you were this morning.'

Loxley stopped and stared at the woman.

'I'll tell you what I will do,' he said eventually. 'I will let you work alongside the women in the hospital tent. The work is hard and the hours long,' he looked down at Emani, 'and while you work at the hospital, perhaps your daughter can be given work as a messenger or a water carrier.'

'Thank you, my lord,' said Sumeira again. 'We will not let you down.'

'Make sure you don't,' said Loxley, 'now follow me. I'll show you where you can sleep.'

The following morning, Sumeira stood near a fire alongside the hospital tent. A large cooking pot hung from a tripod and she and two others were busy cutting the rolls of linen into strips for bandages.

'Sumeira,' said Loxley, striding towards her, 'I have engaged you to heal, not to cook. What's all this?'

'My Lord,' said Sumeira, 'I have been waiting for you.'

'Aye, I received your message but was busy. What's going on?'

'My Lord,' said Sumeira looking at the pot, 'this is just boiling water to cleanse the bandages.'

'You wash the bandages before use?' said Loxley. 'Why?'

'Because infections can be transferred by anything and only boiling water can kill them. Everything we use should be treated this way.'

'You are changing things already?'

'Yes, my lord, but there are other changes I suggest we make.'

'Like what, exactly?'

'First, we need to turn the tent around, so the openings face the east.'

'But that means the entrance will face directly into the wind.'

'Yes, and that is a good thing. The tent is full of flies and the air is foul. There needs to be fresh air and plenty of it. The breeze itself will keep away many of the flies so will go a long way to treat the infections.'

'How?'

'Because they fly from wound to wound, spreading their diseases. We have to keep these people as clean as possible even before we start to treat them.'

'And how will that help?'

'Disease breeds in filth, my lord,' said Sumeira. 'If we keep everyone and everything as clean as possible, we have a chance. If not, everything we do is a waste of time as no sooner do we treat someone than the infection spreads again.'

'And will this help those with the ague?'

'There is not a lot we can do for those, except keep them cool. Willow bark also helps but they are in the hands of Allah.'

Loxley stared at Sumeira for a few moments, surprised at her choice of god.

'You are Muslim,' he said quietly.

Sumeira swallowed hard, realising her slip of the tongue had put herself at risk.

'My Lord,' said Sumeira, 'it was a mistake. I have lived amongst the Muslims for many years, but all my family are Christian.'

'And what of you, Sumeira?' said Loxley, 'in who's house do you worship.'

The woman stared back, not knowing what to do or say. To answer either way put her at risk.

'My Lord,' she said eventually. 'I truly do not know what to believe, but what I do know is this. I care for those whom God, whoever that may be, places in my care. Be they Muslim or Christian, all life is precious, and I will treat all the afflicted the same. If that is not enough for you, then perhaps I have made a mistake in coming here and will leave.'

The physician stared at Sumeira, considering everything she had said. If he reported her to the castellan then she would be limited to working only outside the walls of Chastellet, but she seemed sincere and he needed whatever help he could get. With a heavy heart, the woman dropped her gaze and turned to leave before she was expelled.

'Sumeira, wait,' said Loxley, 'you are right, there is no room for religion when it comes to medicine. You may stay though I suggest that in future you are careful with what you say aloud.'

'Thank you, my lord,' said Sumeira bending down to kiss his hands, 'I will not disappoint you.'

'I'm sure you won't,' said Loxley, 'now come, let's find some men and get this tent turned around.'

For the next few days, Sumeira oversaw the repositioning of the tent as well as placing the patients' beds in some sort of order. Each mattress had the straw replaced and any blankets were taken away to be washed in the river. Every patient was stripped and washed, and all bandages removed so the wounds could be cleaned and dressed with aloe. Finally, the injuries were re-covered with fresh bandages and the nurses instructed to change them regularly and keep everything as clean as possible.

Those with the ague were also washed and though there was little to be done to fight their fevers, they were kept cool by applying regular soaked cloths of well-water to their bodies, much cooler than the water brought up from the river. Sumeira also administered doses of crushed willow bark where necessary to ease the pain, and within a few days, the whole hospital tent felt completely different.

'You have worked hard,' said Loxley, walking through the tent alongside the woman. 'You have my admiration.'

'These are basic provisions,' said Sumeira, 'and not the whole answer but at least they are comfortable.'

'On the contrary,' said Loxley, 'I see an improvement already, though the castellan has questioned why our stocks have depleted so quickly.'

'What is more important,' asked Sumeira, 'a strip of linen or the return of a warrior to service?'

'A point well made,' said Loxley. 'I will be sure to ask him that myself when next he questions my requisitions.'

Chapter Nineteen

November – AD 1178

The City of Tiberius

King Baldwin once more sat upon his throne in the lesser hall in the castle at Tiberius. Around him were a selection of knights and noblemen from across the Outremer, all waiting patiently for the Saracen messenger to arrive. It had been six months since Baldwin had turned down Farrukh-Shah's offer and they had long thought the matter closed.
'What do you think he wants this time?' asked Baldwin to William of Tyre, standing at his side.
'Perhaps he has had second thoughts,' said William, 'and will relinquish all claims on Jerusalem in return for the abandonment of the construction of Chastellet.'
'As much as I hope that is true,' said Baldwin, 'I fear the opposite. Saladin bases his entire rule on his vow to rid the Outremer of Christians and to retract from that promise will fatally weaken his rule. No, I think he will threaten us with war unless we capitulate.'
'And if he does?'
'I do not fear Saladin. We showed him at Montgisard what cold Christian steel can do in the hands of pious men. Let him make his threats and I will treat them with the disdain they deserve. Is everything ready?'
'It is, Your Grace.'
'Then let him approach. Let us see how the mind of the sultan works.'
William nodded to the servants who turned to open the giant doors leading into the huge chamber.
'His glorious majesty, King Baldwin of Jerusalem and the Oultrejordain will see you now,' said one, and turned around to escort the visitors into the chamber.
As the king and his entourage watched, Farrukh-Shah once again strode into the hall, his head held high, his demeanour confident. Like his previous visit, he was flanked by his two bodyguards and they all walked forward, stopping exactly in the same place as they had stood months before. All three nodded their heads slightly in acknowledgement of the king's status, though all

kept their eyes firmly placed on those of the monarch, avoiding the suggestion of subservience implied if they had lowered their gaze.

'Farrukh-Shah,' said William eventually, 'once more you grace us with your presence. I hope your journey was uneventful and you are well-rested.'

'The king's hospitality leaves nothing unattended,' replied Farrukh-Shah, 'and I will be certain to relay my thoughts to the sultan.'

'Thank you,' said William and turned to the king. 'Your Grace?'

Baldwin had been staring at the impressive warrior. As usual, the Saracen was impeccably dressed in colourful leggings and tunic, along with a turban wrapped around his head. Around his waist, he bore a black leather belt holding an impressive scimitar along with a lethal-looking Jambiya. Although the weapons were ceremonial, Baldwin was under no doubt that the Saracen would gladly use both, given the chance.

'Farrukh-Shah,' he said eventually, 'welcome to Tiberius. My home is yours for the duration of your stay and the safety of you and your men is guaranteed, upon my word.'

'You have my gratitude, King Baldwin,' said Farrukh-Shah with another slight bow, 'but I will be no burden upon you. My business here is short and I will ride back to my people before the sun sets.'

'I understand,' said the king. 'So, in that case, if you are rested, and have been fed and watered, perhaps we could get down to the business you speak of.'

'Of course,' said Farrukh-Shah and turned to one side to receive a scroll from one of the men to his side.

The king and the court waited patiently as Farrukh-Shah unfurled the scroll before reading it aloud.

'To King Baldwin, fourth in his line', he announced, *'king of all Christians throughout Jerusalem. I, Salah ad-Din, Sultan of all Egypt and Syria, offer greetings, wealth and good health upon you.*

I extend my gratitude for your counteroffer and report to you I have given it serious consideration. Like you, I also put my people first in such matters and like you, I have concluded that the agreement under discussion was not acceptable.

Since then I have given the matter further thought and in the interests of avoiding further bloodshed, have amended my first offer accordingly.'

Farrukh-Shah lowered the scroll momentarily as one of his bodyguards gave two claps of his hands. Behind them, three more Saracens ran into the room, one holding a roll of black silk while the other two carried a small chest between them.

The court waited quietly as the first man unfurled the roll of black silk on the castle floor in front of Farrukh-Shah. When it was done, the two remaining men placed the chest on the silk and undid the clasp before looking at their master, waiting for the signal to continue.

Farrukh-Shah raised the parchment again.

'To the King of the Christians,' he continued, *'I present an improved agreement. In the interests of peace, I propose that the castle at Vadum Iacob is abandoned within one month of today, and all claim to ownership of the ford relinquished by both sides.'*

He paused as a hint of sarcastic laughter rippled around the gathered knights, each knowing full well that the request would be impossible to agree. The king held up his hand and the room once again fell into silence.

'Your Sultan asks a lot of me,' said Baldwin, staring at Farrukh-Shah. 'Am I to assume he has a further offer to sweeten the pain of such an agreement?'

'He has,' said Farrukh-Shah, and lifted the parchment again.

'Assuming the agreement is accepted,' he continued, *'one day after the last Christian soldier leaves the castle, my men will occupy, and dismantle the fortress, spreading the building materials far and wide so they can no longer be used for any construction at Vadum Iacob. This cost will be borne by the Ayyubid.*

In addition, I offer an unconditional truce between our people for the term of five years, to be renegotiated at that time.

Finally, as I am aware that you have incurred serious expense in the construction, I offer the following recompense.'

Farrukh-Shah looked up again and nodded towards the men holding the casket. With a flourish they swung the container, emptying the contents across the silk sheet.

Everyone in the room gasped in astonishment as the gleam of highly polished gold coins contrasted against the blackness of the silk. Nobody had ever seen such an amount, and everyone stared in awe, momentarily struck dumb by the sight of so much wealth. Even the king had to swallow hard, such was his shock, but he remained silent, knowing that to show any emotion would be a sign of weakness.

'My master, Salah ad-Din, Sultan of Egypt and Syria,' continued Farrukh-Shah, 'offers the King of the Christians the sum of one hundred thousand Golden Bezants as recompense for the expenses incurred so far.'

Again, the room fell silent and all eyed turned on Baldwin, awaiting his response. The sight of so much gold, representing so much wealth was impossible to ignore, and every man present knew the offer was almost too good to decline.

Again, the king swallowed hard, thinking furiously. His coffers were already low, having been seriously depleted by the battle at Montgisard and his rule was currently being propped up by extended credit from the Templars. This sort of money would clear the kingdom's debts and present a healthy surplus to concentrate on other issues across Jerusalem. In addition, the offer of five years truce was almost unheard of and again, would allow him the luxury of time to rebuild Jerusalem's strength.

Farrukh-Shah saw the doubt in the king's eyes and spoke up again, increasing the pressure.

'King Baldwin,' he said. 'This along with the rest of the Sultan's offer is a good proposition. Not only will it provide you with recompense but also has the benefit of stopping all bloodshed between our peoples for at least five years. Whatever you decide, you must realise we cannot allow your castle at Vadum Iacob to remain unchallenged. Whether it falls through negotiation or through violence, fall it will, of that you can be sure.'

The thinly veiled threat of violence caused Baldwin to look up. For a moment he had been considering the benefits of acceptance but the change in manner from the Saracen caused him to pause.

'If I was to accept,' he said, 'and the castle destroyed, what is to stop Saladin sending an army from Damascus to invade Jerusalem?'

'We have not done so yet and you have the word of my master that the truce will be honoured for five years.'

'Truces can be broken,' interjected William.

'By men of lesser honour, perhaps,' said Farrukh-Shah, 'but my master is willing to believe that King Baldwin has no less moral strength than himself. If the Christians adhere to any agreed terms, so will the Ayyubid.'

Again, the room fell silent as all men stared at the riches on the floor. Finally, Baldwin looked up and stared at the messenger.

'Farrukh-Shah,' he said. 'In your parchment, Saladin refers to me as King of the Christians. My title is King of Jerusalem and the Oultrejordain. Why does he not refer to me as such?'

Farrukh-Shah paused, realising where the conversation was heading.

'King Baldwin,' he said eventually. 'We are all men of the world and fully aware that Jerusalem is claimed by both sides. Therefore, it will be no shock to you to that we Ayyubid do not accept the Christian rule over the kingdom of Jerusalem. Since first your ships landed on these shores, our ancestors have warred over the Holy Land. As it was then, so it is now. On behalf of Salah ad-Din, I can assure you we mean no slight on your kingship over your own people, we just do not acknowledge your right to rule Jerusalem.'

'There is only one King of the Christians,' said Baldwin, 'and that is Jesus Christ. I am king only of Jerusalem and the Oultrejordain.'

'I am not here to argue your right to kingship,' said Farrukh-Shah, 'only to press my master's proposition. It is more than fair and cannot be bettered. With all due respect, King Baldwin, I urge you to accept, if only to protect the lives of thousands of men, on both sides.'

Again, Baldwin fell silent, considering the arguments for and against. Finally, he looked up to speak, his mind made up.

'Put away the coins, Farrukh-Shah,' he said, 'and return whence you came. Relay to Saladin the following. You have my gratitude for your generous offer, but until you cede that Jerusalem belongs in the hands of Christianity, no amount of gold can buy my commitment to protecting our people there. My hope is that we can still agree to a truce but if not, then you must do what you must do. I will pray that further bloodshed will be avoided but whatever happens, the castle of Chastellet at Vadum Iacob will remain.' He stepped down from the dais. 'Fare ye well, Farrukh-Shah,' he said. 'It is my hope that the next time we meet it will be in different circumstances. Until then, go in peace.' Without waiting for an answer, the king left the chamber, followed by his court, leaving only men at arms watching as the Saracens collected their coins.

Farrukh-Shah stared after the king, silently furious at the snub.

'We will meet again,' King Baldwin he said under his breath, 'but next time there will be blood instead of gold.'

Back in the king's chambers, William helped Baldwin remove his regal robes as the servants came running with balms and ointments to ease his painful skin. Throughout the audience, he had shown no sign of discomfort but now, in the privacy of his own rooms he almost collapsed with pain, such was the effect of his illness.

'Let me sit,' he gasped when at last he was draped within the coolness of silk.

William helped him into a soft chair before preparing a cold drink laced with poppy juice.

'Here,' he said, 'take this,' and watched as the king slurped at the goblet greedily before sitting back to allow the medicine to work its magic.

'Has he gone?' asked Baldwin eventually, opening his eyes.

'I assume so,' said William. 'I will send for word about his whereabouts.'

'I was tempted, William,' continued the king, 'I was moments away from falling to the temptation of Satan.'

'You overcame, Your Grace,' said William, 'and the Outremer will know that Saladin is so worried about the strength of Christianity he resorts to cheap bribery to achieve the devil's work. Lucky for us we have a monarch who marches with Jesus at his side.'

'A hundred thousand golden Bezants,' said the king. 'Never has anyone been offered such an amount. He must be really worried about the effect that the castle will have on the Outremer.'

'All the more reason to revel in your decision, 'Your Grace,' said, William. 'I feel that Chastellet will be a turning point in the wars against the heathen.'

'Nevertheless,' said Baldwin, 'I fear my decision has put the fortress at risk. Send word to the castellan there.' He looked over to the southern window. 'The risk of attack has just risen tenfold.'

Chapter Twenty

November – AD 1178

South of Damascus

The night was almost spent when the figures of Hunter and Hassan appeared out of the darkness, returning to the small column of men making their way slowly through the hills towards Damascus.

They had been on the road for three days and nights, riding when it was dark and hiding during the day. Every night, Hunter and Hassan rode ahead of the column, seeking the wadi where Cronin was being held. Luckily, the ravines and canyons crisscrossing the area meant hiding places were numerous and they had so far remained undetected.

Arturas headed the remaining column, closely followed by Jakelin and the rest of the men. As Hunter and Hassan got closer, the mercenary held up his hand, calling for a halt before untying the waterskin from around the horn of his saddle and taking a long drink.

'Hunter,' he said eventually as the scout reined in his horse, 'I was getting worried. Was there a problem?' He offered Hunter the waterskin.

'No problem,' replied Hunter eventually after slaking his thirst. 'The shadows are many and concealment will not be difficult this coming day, but we are later than anticipated as we have news. The wadi is less than two leagues from here and there are campfires to the northern end. It looks like there is a large encampment within that holds many men.'

'Are you sure it is the place we seek?'

'It is,' said Hassan, 'I am sure of it.'

'In that case,' said Arturas, 'we will rest here today and go forward as soon as it is dark. Hunter nodded and they followed the mercenary into the adjacent hills where they could rest without being seen.

Several hours later, Hunter, Hassan, Arturas and Jakelin lay hidden on a ridge over a deep wadi a few leagues to the north.

Below them, they could see a well-established camp holding over a dozen huts and a paddock containing several horses and mules along with at least a dozen empty carts. To one side, a pile of bulging sacks lay waiting to be loaded onto the carts while further on, two emaciated men laboured in over several broken wooden sledges, working in the unforgiving heat to try and make the repairs needed.

All through the wadi, they could see dozens of wooden cages, obviously designed to hold men against their will but even from their viewpoint, they could see they were empty.

A few guards patrolled between the tents and the smell of something cooking wafted up from a fire where two wizened old women laboured over the evening meal, but apart from that, the camp was relatively quiet.

'Where is everyone?' asked Jakelin eventually, 'the place is deserted.'

'When I was last here,' said Hassan, 'Cronin was in one of those cages, as were many men. Now they are empty.'

'I think I know what's going on here,' said Arturas, adjusting his position, 'I have seen something similar a few years ago, and it's not good.' He crawled to one side, peering through a clump of undergrowth for a better view. 'There,' he whispered, pointing further down the wadi, 'just as I thought.'

The others joined him and stared at a small hole in the base of the rocky walls on the far side of the wadi.

'What are we looking at?' asked Jakelin. 'All I see are two armed men standing alongside a cave.'

'That's no cave,' said Arturas, 'it's the entrance to a mine.'

'I have heard no reports of mines out here,' said Jakelin. 'If there was gold or silver to be had or even tin, I suspect that this place would be flooded with men from Damascus. What could they be mining of any value?'

'Something more important than gold or silver,' said Aruras, glancing over at his comrades, 'salt.'

For the next few hours, they watched as pairs of emaciated men dragged wooden sledges piled with great chunks of rock salt out of the tunnel mouth to where others waited to load it into sacks. Each time they unloaded a sledge, the men were allowed to drink their fill from a horses' trough before heading back into the underground hell.

'There will be overseers in the mine itself,' explained Arturas, 'brutal men who will beat a man to within an inch of his life should he not pull his weight. They ensure the quotas are met and the demand for fresh slaves is never-ending. That explains why he has not been sold to Saladin; he is worth more as a slave. If Cronin is in there, I fear he is already dead to us.'

'Why?' asked Hunter. 'Surely all we need to do is wait until they return to the cages and set him free under the cover of darkness.'

'Because, my friend,' said Arturas, 'the cages are for fresh slaves. Once they are inside the mines, few ever see the light of day again. They live and die down there, and there is no way we can even hope to get in. Even if we could, it is said they are labyrinths that can stretch for leagues in all directions. We would be lost within a few heartbeats.'

'What about those men?' asked Hunter pointing to another team of two who had just emerged with their sledge piled with salt. 'They can come out.'

'Only a selected few,' said Arturas, 'and the chance that your friend is amongst them is very small.'

'Don't they sleep,' asked Jakelin staring at the scene below.

'They work in shifts. If that mine is anything like the one I saw a few years ago, there are men already sleeping inside, waiting to take their turn. Don't forget, they have no knowledge of day or night and work by candlelight. It is truly hell on earth.'

As they watched, another six slaves emerged, this time with empty waterskins and headed towards the troughs to fill them before returning to the tunnel entrance.

'Come,' said Arturas, 'we have seen enough. There is nothing we can do.'

'Wait,' said Hunter, reaching out and grabbing Arturas's arm, 'I have an idea.'

Several hours later, Hunter lay amongst the rocks to the rear of the water trough along with Arturas. At first, his idea had been met with derision by his comrades but as they thrashed it out, a plan had begun to emerge and though it depended on a lot of luck, it was the best they could do.

When night fell, the rest of the column came forward to hide amongst the undergrowth covering the slopes of the wadi, their horses hidden well to the rear. Down below, Hunter waited for the water bearers to emerge, knowing full well that in order for men to keep working in the mine, they had to have a constant supply of water, and that meant there was a possibility of getting a message inside.

Eventually the men they had been waiting for loomed out of the darkness and started to refill the waterskins.

'Here we go,' whispered Hunter and crawled forward to the trough. Slowly he lifted his head, staring into the face of a man devoid of all hope. Before the man could react, Hunter pulled him down to the floor.

'*Shh,*' he whispered, his hand clamped over the slave's mouth. 'I am here to help. Do you understand?'

For a moment the man just stared in confusion but eventually nodded his head, his eyes wide with fear.

Hunter slowly removed his hand and helped the man up into a sitting position.

'Who are you?' Asked the worker. 'What do you want of me?'

'I am a friend,' said Hunter. 'We are here to help but first, we need your aid. Are you willing to help me in return for your freedom?'

'I'll do anything,' gasped the man looking over his shoulder, 'just get me out of here.'

'We will,' said Hunter, 'but first I need to know if a comrade of mine is in those salt tunnels.'

'A comrade?'

'Aye, a man who goes by the name of Cronin. Do you know of him?'

'Names are a luxury we do not share,' said the man. 'We are forbidden to speak and communicate only in whispers when the overseers' backs are turned.'

'This man is of western descent,' continued Hunter, 'he has a distinctive accent and would have been here only a few months.'

'There are many franks down there,' said the man, 'I can't know all of them. Please, just get me out of here.'

'I cannot,' said Hunter, 'not until I know my comrade is either dead or alive. Think well, my friend for if your memory serves you well, you could regain your freedom before this night is out.'

'Describe him,' said the man, 'everything you can think of.'

'Reddish hair, large build. He has been a soldier all his life so his body will be toughened and used to hard work.'

'There are several such as he,' said the man, 'but there is one who the overseers give a harder time than the rest of us.'

'Why?'

'Because they have been told he is a Templar sergeant.'

Hunter's heart raced at the reply.

'That's him,' he said, 'do you know where he is?'

'Aye, I do. But how will that help?'

'Because I want you to get a message to him. Tell him that tomorrow night, Hunter will be waiting outside. All he has to do is get himself out and we will do the rest. Tell him that we can wait for one night only. After that, we have to go, with or without him.'

'It's not possible,' said the slave. 'The overseers watch us like hawks and if we try anything, they are just as likely to kill a man as beat him.'

'Listen to me,' hissed Hunter, grabbing the prisoner's arm. 'All men must have water, right? All I need you to do is when you give him his ration, pass on the message and give him this.' He pressed a small sheathed dagger into the water bearer's hand. 'There is no need for you to fight, just leave it to Cronin. He has very special skills and can match any man with a blade. If he is successful and you both make it out, I swear I will take you with us.'

The water bearer looked down at the knife and then up at Hunter.

'If I do this, the chances are I will die down there,' he said.

'You are already a dead man,' said Hunter.' This way you at least have a chance.'

Again, the man stared at the knife before finally placing it inside the neck of the water skin.

'I will do it,' he said, 'just don't forget your promise.'

'I swear by all that is holy,' said Hunter, 'if you make it out alive along with my friend, I will carry you to safety upon my own horse.'

'So be it,' said the man looking over his shoulder. 'Now I must be gone or suffer a beating.'

Hunter watched him go before crawling back to where Arturas lay waiting.

'Is it done?' asked the mercenary.

'Aye,' said Hunter, 'the water bearer will pass on the message. All we can do now is wait.'

'We can do no more,' said Arturas. 'You get some sleep; I will take the first watch.'

Deep inside the mine, Cronin sat naked against a wall, tethered to several other prisoners by a rope around his neck. His hair and beard were matted and rivers of sweat ran down his emaciated body. The air was stifling and most of the men took the opportunity to grab what sleep they could before they were forced back to the never-ending task of digging out the rock salt. Opposite them was another row of men, each similarly tethered but they were different, they were all Muslim.

He looked up at the ceiling, no higher than a standing man's shoulders. He had tried to sleep but his thirst was too great. A fight between two of the slaves the previous night had ended with one of them being killed and the overseers, furious at the loss of a good slave, had withheld their water ration as punishment. Now they now all suffered collectively. He closed his eyes again, trying to forget his torment for even the fleetest of moments.

'Can't sleep, Christian?' asked a voice and Cronin opened his eyes to look at the prisoner opposite. The man was new to the mine having only been brought in a few days earlier. His manner was brash, still unbroken by the rigours of the mine.

Cronin stared, too tired to answer.

'You are strangely quiet for an infidel,' said the man opposite, 'or does the thirst claim your voice?'

Again, Cronin remained silent, not rising to the taunt.

'I have heard you are a Templar,' continued the prisoner, 'perhaps if you pray to your false God, he can cause rivers of water to burst from the walls. Is that not what he does, create miracles to the devout?'

'What do you want?' asked Cronin eventually.

'Ah, he talks,' said the man. 'Tell me, infidel, what does it feel like knowing you are going to die so far from home in a land where you do not belong?'

'I am not going to argue with a Saracen,' said Cronin, 'I suggest you get some sleep.'

'To sleep is to waste what time I have left,' said the prisoner. 'I will be dead soon enough.'

'Then you are the same as the rest of us,' said Cronin, 'flesh and bone, nothing more.'

'Ah, but I will die knowing that the land of my ancestors will soon be free of the infidels. My heart soars at the thought of so many Christians about to fall beneath the swords of Shirkuh ad-Din.'

'You must already be asleep,' said Cronin, 'for you are truly dreaming. Jerusalem belongs to us and always will.'

'You are wrong, Christian,' said the man, 'even as we rot down here, the eastern tribes gather under Salah ad-Din's banner. Soon the earth will tremble beneath the sound of their horses as they ride on Chastellet.'

'Chastellet?' said Cronin. 'I know of no such place.'

'Then you have been down here too long,' said the man. 'You have been forgotten already, Christian and the world moves on without you. Jerusalem will be ours soon enough, especially as it is your own men who help us achieve the inevitable.'

'What do you mean?' asked Cronin.

'What I mean,' said the man, 'is despite your claims to the contrary, even Christians are beginning to see the error of their ways and make pacts with us to end the occupation of Jerusalem. They want to go their homes across the sea and need gold to pay the fare.''

'You talk of spies?'

'Call them what you will. The fact is, they recognise the futility of your occupation and work towards its end. Chastellet is only the first, Christian, others will follow. Even your king will be blinded by Gold and when he does, we will fall upon him and expose his weakness. You are all the same, Christian, every man has his price.'

'Why should I listen to a Saracen slave,' asked Cronin, 'you are nothing more than a braggart?'

'My present state is nothing more than Allah's will,' said the Saracen, 'and I accept it with an open heart. But before this, I rode with Shirkuh ad-Din himself and had status amongst my fellows. I know what I am talking about, Templar, and it gives me great pleasure to see you doubt your own kind.'

'Even if you are telling the truth,' said Cronin, 'why would you share this information with me?'

'Who are you going to tell,' laughed the Saracen,' these men here? We are all dead men, Templar, and I want you to go to hell knowing that you died in vain.'

The conversation ended abruptly as another man crawled into the cavern carrying a waterskin. Everybody sat up, desperate for the single cup of water each was allowed. Cronin waited his turn, his mouth dry. The water bearer approached but as he handed Cronin the cup, he leaned forward and slipped a knife into his hand.

'Someone awaits you outside,' he whispered. *'You have one night only to escape.'*

Cronin stared at the water bearer in shock, momentarily forgetting about his thirst.

'Hurry up,' shouted another prisoner further down the line, 'we are dying here.'

'What do you mean,' hissed Cronin, *'who gave you this?'*

'A man called Hunter,' said the water bearer. *'Now give me the cup before these men strangle me with their bare hands.'*

Cronin drank the rest of his water before sitting back and hiding the knife behind him.

'It seems we all have secrets, Christian,' said the Saracen opposite, 'what did he have to say?'

'Nothing that concerns you,' said Cronin and closed his eyes to make his plans. Somehow, no matter what the risk, he had to get out.

Outside the mine, there was little movement except for the coming and goings of the sledge men and water bearers. The following day, Arturas and Hunter rejoined the rest of the men hidden amongst the undergrowth, waiting again for night to fall. When at last it was dark enough, everyone regained their positions, placing their weapons of choice close at hand.

As the hours passed, the camp fell silent with only the movement of occasional guards breaking the silence.

Chapter Twenty-One

November – AD 1178

The Salt Mine

Inside the mine, men toiled relentlessly in the tiny tunnels, using well-worn tools to hack lumps of rock salt from the walls before passing them back to be placed on the sledges waiting in the main passages.

In one of the groups, Cronin used his metal spike to drive deep into a crack in the wall, levering a chunk of salt out to crash onto the floor. He passed it through the hands of his fellow prisoners, knowing that time was running out. It had been several hours since the water carrier had passed him the message and although he had no idea of time, he guessed it must be approaching dawn. If he was to have any chance of making his escape, he had to move now.

'Are you ready?' he whispered quietly to the man furthest into the side tunnel.

'Aye,' came the response, 'but I swear if you try to leave me behind, I will kill you with my own bare hands.'

'Just do as I asked,' said Cronin, his face encrusted with salt and sweat, 'after that our fate is in the hands of God.'

The man lowered himself down to the floor and lay still as Cronin and the other two men looked between each other, their eyes full of nervousness and no little fear.

'Do it,' he said, and the prisoner turned to shout into the main passage a few steps to his rear.

'Master,' he called, 'we have a man down.'

For a few moments, nothing happened until they heard the heavy breathing of one of the overseers approaching.

'Shut your mouth,' growled the overseer, 'or lose what teeth you have left.'

The overseer was a skinny man, himself a prisoner, but unlike the others, would be freed should the quotas in his section be achieved within twelve months. Each overseer was selected carefully for his brutality and carefully placed to control a group whose religion or allegiance was far from his own.

'My Lord,' said the prisoner who had called out, lowering his face to touch the ground, 'forgive me, but we think he has died from his injuries.'

'I did no lasting damage,' said the overseer peering into the candlelit tunnel, 'the beating was his own fault.'

'My Lord,' said the man without looking up. 'He started coughing up blood and a seizure fell upon him. Now we cannot move him to continue the dig.'

'I swear by Allah himself,' growled the overseer, 'that if he feigns illness, I will kill him here and now. Drag him out.'

The other three men turned to grasp the rope and shuffled backwards out of the tunnel, pulling the fourth across the rocky floor. As the body emerged, the overseer stepped forward to swing his boot hard against his head, checking for signs of life. Despite the casualty's determination to remain silent, the sudden pain made him cry out and the overseer smirked in cruel satisfaction.

'You waste my time, infidel,' he growled, 'now you will know real pain.' He pulled a cudgel from his waistband and bent low to administer a beating but before he could land the first blow, he felt his head being forced back and the unmistakable agony of a sharp knife being dragged across his throat.

'*Hold him.*' gasped Cronin pushing the knife deeper into the struggling victim's throat to cut through the artery. Blood spurted over his fellow prisoners and ran down the salt-encrusted walls until finally, the overseer fell still, and Cronin allowed the body to fall to the floor.

Quickly he cut the rope from around his comrades' necks and helped the injured man to his feet.

'How fare you?' asked Cronin.

'I'll live,' said the man and picked up the overseer's cudgel from the floor. 'What now?'

'Now we just run for the exit,' said Cronin. 'There is no time for subterfuge or trickery, we will not win any fight against men well-fed and well-armed. Keep going and charge down any that step in our way. At least some of us may make it.'

'And if we get out?'

'My friends are outside. They will help.'

'I hope you are sure,' said one of the other men, 'for death is the only punishment for what we have just done.'

'Then let us not get caught,' said Cronin, 'now come. There is little time.'

He turned and headed along the narrow passage that led in the direction of the wadi. Although he had been here a long time, he didn't know the exact layout of the mine and had to rely on instinct. Within moments they reached the cavern where the men were allowed to sleep for a few hours between shifts. All along the walls, prisoners slept fitfully, aching in pain from the daily rigours and constantly hungry from the meagre rations they were allowed. At the far end, two guards talked between themselves, unaware of the situation playing out behind their backs.

Cronin stopped and stared at the prisoners who had shared his fate over the last few months. The mix was varied from Franks and Venetians to Syrians and Bedouins.

'Why have you stopped?' hissed a voice behind him.

'We can't leave them,' said Cronin eventually. 'Their fate is a death that no man deserves.'

'We don't have the time,' said the voice, 'keep going.'

Without reply, Cronin crouched and made his way over to the first prisoner. Holding his fingers to his lips to demand silence, he cut the rope around his neck before giving the man the knife and indicating he should do the same to the prisoner alongside him.

The man nodded and did as he was asked. Within minutes almost all of the men around the walls were freed from their bonds, though stayed where they were, looking towards Cronin for an indication what to do next.

As the blade reached the last few men, one of the guards turned and immediately saw the danger. With a shout he ran forward, drawing a cudgel from his belt but one of the prisoners tripped him up, sending him sprawling to the floor.

Immediately all hell broke loose as the prisoners fell upon their captors, their victims' screams echoing through the tunnels.

Shouts of alarm came from other tunnels and within moments, more guards and overseers poured into the chamber to try and control the revolt, but it was no use, the released slaves were rabid in their desire for revenge.

'What now?' shouted one of the men at Cronin's side, 'which way do we go?'

Cronin looked around the artificial cavern. There were several tunnels leading out but only one which led to the entrance.

'I don't know,' he said, 'they all look the same.'

'This way,' shouted a voice and they turned to see the water carrier standing in one of the smaller tunnels.

Cronin ran through the throng closely followed by his allies. One fell to a well-aimed sword blow from a guard while another tripped, smashing his head on a rock.

'Leave him,' shouted the water bearer, seeing Cronin pause, 'we have no time.' Realising his own life was at imminent risk; Cronin forced his way through and into the exit tunnel. Several men followed him, and they ran as fast as they could towards the entrance, bending low to avoid the rocky ceiling.

'Almost there,' shouted the water bearer over his shoulder, 'it's just around the bend,' but before he could say another word, an archer appeared in front of him and sent an arrow straight into his chest.

With nowhere else to go, Cronin charged forward as the bowman notched another arrow into his bow. The sergeant roared his defiance and just as the archer released the arrow, charged into him at full speed, knocking him down onto the rocky floor. Unleashing months of pent up rage and frustration, he grabbed the archer's head and smashed it repeatedly against the floor.

Many of the freed men ran past him, determined to get out and as he came to his senses, Cronin got to his feet. He was almost there.

Outside in the Wadi, the remaining guards realised something was wrong and lined up facing the tunnel entrance. Within moments the first of the escaping prisoners appeared, staggering towards freedom but was cut down by an arrow before taking half a dozen steps. More men followed and though many died, there were just too many and the escapees poured out of the tunnel into the wadi.

The guards laid into them with their cudgels, outnumbered, but stronger and well-armed. Men fell everywhere and it was clear the prisoners stood no chance.

'We have to help them,' said Hunter standing up, 'come on.'

He and Arturas drew their swords and ran across to join the fray. At first, because of the darkness and confusion, nobody saw the threat and the guards just concentrated on running down the prisoners but within moments they realised what was happening and turned to fight the intruders.

Despite being outnumbered, Arturas and Hunter fought furiously, creating panic in the guards' ranks but were soon on the defensive as they lost the advantage of surprise. With things going against them, they had to retreat but had gone no more than a few paces when an imposing figure ran past them into the thick of the advancing guards, Jakelin de Mailly.

For a few seconds, they watched in awe as the knight's sword swung in all directions, skillfully wielded by a warrior used to the heat of battle. Men fell all around him and he fought like a demon, unafraid and lethal to all within range. Hunter and Arturas caught their breath and ran back towards the fight. Behind them, the rest of their men poured down from the banks of the wadi to aid their comrades.

'Leave this to us, Hunter,' shouted Arturas, rejoining the fray, 'you find your friend.'

Hunter swerved away and headed for the entrance of the mine, closely followed by Hassan. There were still a few men coming out, but they pushed them aside and ducked into the tunnel. Within moments they found the sergeant, breathless and injured having been trampled underfoot by the panicking prisoners.

'Cronin,' gasped Hunter and knocked another escapee aside as he leant down to aid his comrade, a look of concern on his face.

'I'm fine,' gasped Cronin, 'just help me up.'

Hunter and Hassan reached beneath Cronin's arms and pulled him to his feet before helping him towards the entrance.

Outside, the mercenaries had dominated the battle and stood victorious in the light of the slowly dawning sun.

'Bring the horses,' shouted Arturas, taking advantage of the sudden lull in the fighting, 'some of the guards have escaped but there may be others nearby.'

Hassan and Hunter carried Cronin over to sit against a rock. The sergeant looked up; his hair and beard matted and his face haggard with salt-encrusted into every crevice.

'Water,' he said simply, and Hunter quickly gave him his flask, watching as his comrade drank it all without taking a breath.

'How did you find me?' asked Cronin eventually.

'It was the work of Hassan,' said Hunter, glancing at the boy,' 'he never gave up on you and followed your trail through the desert until he found you here. It is to him you owe thanks for your life.'

Cronin looked at Hassan but before he could say anything, Arturas shouted a warning and dozens of arrows thudded into the ground throughout the wadi. Hunter and Hassan dragged Cronin behind the rocks, covering him with their bodies.

The experienced mercenaries reacted immediately, running from boulder to boulder towards the archers' position, forcing them back until they were out of range. Eventually, the rain of arrows stopped, and Hunter got to his feet.

'We have to get out of here,' he said, looking over to where Arturas and his men were returning, 'we are deep into Ayyubid territory, 'the horses are on their way.'

Nobody answered and Hunter looked down to where Cronin was still lying on his back. Across his chest, still pinning him to the floor lay Hassan, with a Saracen arrow sticking out of his back.

'*Hassan,*' shouted Hunter, and he pulled the boy from Cronin to lay him on his side in the dirt.

'What's wrong with him?' gasped Cronin, getting to his knees.

'He's been hit by an arrow,' said Hunter, 'just below the shoulder. We have to get the arrowhead out as soon as we can.'

'*Don't worry about me,*' gasped Hassan through his pain, 'just get Master Cronin out of here. You don't have much time.'

'We are going nowhere without you,' said Hunter and turned to shout across the wadi. 'Arturas, we need help.'

Arturas ran over and saw what was happening.

'He's been hit,' said Hunter, 'but we can't get that arrow out here, we need to get him to the physician in Chastellet.'

'He'll never make it,' said Arturas, 'the pain will be too great. It has to come out now if he is going to survive.'

Hunter paused and stared at Arturas, knowing exactly what the mercenary intended.

'In that case,' he said, 'you get him ready while I sort Cronin out. I'll be back as soon as I can.' He got to his feet and helped the sergeant up. 'Can you ride?' he asked.

'I'll manage,' said Cronin weakly.

'Good, let's get you to the horses.' The two men staggered across the wadi and as they neared the far side, saw Jakelin de Mailly standing over one of the dead guards.

'Brother Jakelin,' said Cronin weakly, staring as the knight wiped the blood from his heavy sword, 'you are the last man I expected to see here.'

'It is not a quest I foresaw myself, Brother Cronin,' replied Jakelin, 'but since that day in Al-Shabiya, my conscience has allowed me no rest. This was an opportunity to settle my mind.'

'You have my gratitude,' said Cronin. He looked around all the men still standing near. 'As do you all.'

'We have to be going,' said Jakelin sheathing his sword. 'You will share my horse.'

'The order forbids such an action,' said Cronin, 'as well you know.'

'Sometimes, it is better to listen to God's will than rules made by men,' said Jakelin. 'Now come, we have to get back to Chastellet. There you can be taken back into the care of our order and receive treatment from our physicians.'

Cronin stared at the knight.

'Where?' he asked.

'Chastellet, the castle at Jacob's Ford.'

Cronin stared at the knight again, his mind spinning at the revelation.

'Are you sure it is called Chastellet?'

'I am. The king named it himself only a few months ago. You will see it for yourself soon enough.'

'No,' said Cronin, as everyone turned to leave. 'I cannot go to Jacob's Ford; I have to get to Jerusalem.'

'Jerusalem?' said Jakelin, turning back to face the Sergeant. 'Why Jerusalem?

'Because I have urgent information that needs to reach the ears of the king.'

'Baldwin is not in Jerusalem,' he said, 'he sleeps safely within the walls of Tiberius. Can we not send this information via a messenger?'

'I cannot entrust it to any other man,' whispered Cronin, 'I have to deliver it to the king himself. You have to trust me on this, Brother, I need to speak to Baldwin.'

'I believe you,' said Jakelin after a pause, 'and in that case, Chastellet will have to wait. Today we head back towards Jacob's Ford with the rest of the men but tomorrow we will leave our comrades and head for Tiberius.'

'Thank you,' said Cronin, 'this matter is of the utmost urgency.'

As Jakelin helped Cronin over to the horses, Hunter returned to where Arturas and one of his men were still working on Hassan. They had cut away the cloth from around the wound and had snapped the arrow shaft just a few inches away from the skin. Hassan was still conscious despite the pain but sat up as straight as he could, hardly daring to move.

'We have to go,' said Hunter as he arrived, 'are you done?'

'Not yet,' said Arturas, and handed Hunter a rock the size of his fist. 'He is your friend; it is better if you were the one to do it.'

Hunter nodded and took the rock before kneeling down beside Hassan.

'Hassan,' he said, 'this is going to hurt, a lot, but it just might save your life. Are you ready?'

'God is with me,' whispered Hassan in fear and he closed his eyes in anticipation of what was to come.

'Hold him tight,' said Hunter and as Arturas held Hassan around the shoulders, Hunter swung the rock to drive the arrow straight through the boy's body.

Hassan screamed in pain but as the arrow emerged through his upper chest, Arturas grabbed it and drew the rest of the shaft completely clear. This time there was no scream, just a gasp as the boy passed out and fell back into Hunter's arms.

'Bandage the wound,' said Arturas getting to his feet,' and get him on a horse. He may not last the journey but at least he now has a chance.'

Chapter Twenty-Two

December – AD 1178

Tiberius

King Baldwin walked along the castle walls alongside William of Tyre. Down below, the city of Tiberius stretched away to the shores of the Sea of Galilee. The weather was crisp, but it was the first time in several weeks that the king had walked outside, having suffered a particularly bad bout of illness.

William walked slowly, matching the king's steady pace, knowing that to rush such things invited only setbacks.

'Have we heard from Grand Master Amand about Chastellet's progress?' asked the king eventually.

'We receive regular dispatches, Your Grace,' said William, 'and are informed that the castle progresses well.'

'Why I have not seen these messages?'

'With respect, Your Grace, you have been in no fit state to concern yourself with trivial matters of court administration.'

'I would hardly call my new castle trivial,' said Baldwin, 'far from it.'

'Agreed, but the day to day details need not worry your ears. You should just concentrate on getting well.'

'Well?' said Baldwin, looking out to the sea in the distance, 'I fear that day will never grace us with its presence.'

'Admittedly there is no cure for your affliction, Your Grace,' said William, 'but with regular treatment and plenty of rest there is no reason you will not live to be as old as your father.'

Baldwin stopped and looked down at the approach road to the castle.

'Who's that?' he asked.

William looked down and saw three men leading two horses towards the castle gates.

'The taller one looks familiar,' said William, 'I believe he is a Templar, though the Grand Master would be less than impressed that he approaches the king unburdened with the attire usually associated with the order.'

'Why do you hold the Grand Master in so little esteem?' asked the king, glancing at William.

'Because he acts as if he answers to no authority,' said William, 'neither king nor God.'

'His manner is forthright, I agree,' said the Baldwin, 'but is that not the way of all such men?'

'In general, yes, but Amand's pride manifests itself like the highest mountain. He seeks only advancement for himself and his order, losing sight of why it was formed in the first place.'

'A talking point for another time,' said the king looking down at the men now in the outer bailey, 'but for now, let us see who our visitors are.'

Half an hour later, the king sat on a chair one of the antechambers, the ever-present William at his side.

'Bring them in,' said William and two guards escorted the three travellers into the room. Each stopped in front of the king and bowed low in deference.

'Stand tall,' said the king, 'and introduce yourselves.'

'Your Grace,' said Jakelin, 'I am Sir Jakelin de Mailly of the Knights Templar. My comrades here are Brother Cronin, sergeant of the same order and our scout, James Hunter.'

'It looks like the road has been unkind to you,' said the king, 'are you here seeking shelter or is your presence the result of a more meaningful task?'

'Your Grace,' said Jakelin, 'we are on our way back to Chastellet to serve our duty there, but my comrade has information that he needs to share with you. We beg your attention for moments only before heading on our way.'

'Granted,' said the king and turned his attention onto Cronin. 'It seems you are in a far poorer state than your friends, do they not feed you in Chastellet?'

'I have never been in Chastellet, Your Grace,' replied Cronin, 'and it is true that not much food has passed my lips for many months, but I am thankful to be alive and back amongst comrades. My body will soon recover.'

'So, where have you been?'

Cronin glanced at Jakelin before telling the king the story of how he was taken prisoner and sold into slavery, but deliberately omitted the detail of the knight's betrayal in the jewellers' market in Al-Shabiya.

'So, you two rescued this man and brought him here,' said the king, looking between Hunter and Jakelin. 'A tale of honour indeed.'

'Us and ten others, Your Grace,' said Hunter, 'they have now returned to Jacob's Ford.'

'And what is this information that you deem so important?' asked the king, returning his attention upon Cronin.

'Your Grace,' said Cronin, 'during the time I was a prisoner, I toiled alongside men of all nationalities and religions. Some were Christian, some were Muslim. There were men there from countries I have never even heard of. The work was backbreaking with little in the way of food or water. Ours was a miserable existence.'

'I don't think the king needs to hear the finer detail,' said William, 'just get to the point.'

'I only expand in order to justify the circumstances in which I came into this information,' said Cronin. 'When men are in such a desperate situation, they often form a strained comradeship that transcends origin. This happened to me and I often found myself alongside a Saracen who recently served under one of Saladin's generals.'

'And what did this Saracen do to warrant being sold into slavery?'

'I heard he exhibited cowardice, Your Grace, but cannot be sure.'

'So why is he important?'

'Because he was new to the mine and boasted of many things. Most were trivial and meant nothing but one night he told me that his people would soon bring down Chastellet. At that time I did not know it was the name of the castle at Jacob's Ford so paid it little heed but when my comrades rescued me and I overheard its name for the second time, it all made sense and I knew I had to get here to warn you.'

'Warn me of what?'

'About the Saracen plans to attack the castle.'

The king leaned forward and peered at Cronin.

'Wait, are you telling me that this Saracen knew of plans to attack Chastellet?'

'He did, Your Grace, and was vocal in the claim. He said that while the Christian king was blinded by Saracen Gold, Saladin would take the opportunity to fall upon Chastellet.'

'Why would a Saracen share this information with you?' asked William.

'Because he was a braggart, my lord, and thought I would never see the light of day to betray Saladin's plans.'

'He was mistaken,' said the king quietly

'He was, my lord,' said Cronin, 'thanks to my comrades here. If they had not turned up when they did, I would have taken this information to the grave.'

'And you are sure this man was telling the truth?'

'I cannot be sure, Your Grace, but there was no reason to lie and I had no prior knowledge of any castle called Chastellet. What I do not understand is the reference to Saracen Gold.'

'Oh, there was Saracen gold, 'said the king, 'enough to buy a kingdom but I turned it down.'

'So, the tale rings true,' said Jakelin.

'Possibly,' said the king and turned to William. 'Have we heard anything about Saracen incursions south of Damascus?'

'Not much,' said William. 'There have been reports about some smaller patrols but nothing worth noting.'

'With respect, Your Grace,' said Jakelin, 'in my experience I have found that small Saracen patrols have the habit of coming together to form larger fighting units, especially when they are in enemy territory. I would suggest the reason their numbers are low is to avoid detection.'

'These were also my thoughts,' said the king. He turned to face Cronin again. 'Do you know the name of the man who was so free with his tongue?'

'No, Your Grace, but I do know the name of the general responsible for this plan, someone who goes by the name of Farrukh-shah.'

'Farrukh-shah,' said the king as William gasped in shock at his side, 'I should have known.'

'You know of him?' asked Cronin.

'He stood before me just a few weeks since, plying me with gold and offering peace across the Outremer in return for the destruction of the castle. His manner was honest, and I believed the offer was true, yet all the while he was scheming to take Chastellet by other means.' He sat back and stared at the three men before him as his mind raced.

'I have heard enough,' he said eventually, 'and there are many things to consider. If what you say is true, we may still have time to thwart the Ayyubid's plans.'

'Your Grace,' said Cronin, 'there is one more thing. The reason why I had to convey this message myself and could trust no other.'

'And that is?'

'Your Grace, the Saracen claimed that Saladin has a spy working within Chastellet.'

'Spies are a common thing in such a situation,' said Baldwin, 'but that is the risk we take when using the local workforce. Besides, we have already caught and hung two. Why should we worry about this one?'

'Because, Your Grace,' said Cronin, glancing between the king and William, 'if what the Saracen said is correct, this spy is one of us. *He is a Christian.*'

'Nonsense,' said William after several seconds' silence, 'any man of God would never betray his religion to sell us out to the heathen. He would surely burn in the fires of hell for eternity.'

'That may be so,' said Cronin, 'but the Saracen was adamant and took great delight in his boast. He said the man relays information via one of the labourers and in turn receives gold to pay for his passage home.'

'Home?'

'To a land across the sea.'

'So, he is not someone born in the Holy Land but has come here after taking the cross?'

'So it seems,' said Cronin, 'It may be true, it may be false, but I thought you should know.'

'There are over a thousand men stationed at Chastellet,' said Jakelin, 'from labourers to knights, half of which have come from overseas. It could be anyone.'

'Including the both of you,' said William quietly.

'My Lord,' said Cronin, turning to face the prelate, 'is it not I who am bringing this matter to the king's attention? Why would I do that if I was the traitor?'

'A cunning ruse perhaps,' said William and turned to the knight. 'What of you, Sir Jakelin, are you above suspicion?'

'I am a Templar,' said Jakelin. 'That in itself should be enough to answer your question.'

'Enough,' interrupted the king. 'We don't even know if this information is true so let us not start casting suspicion on those who have already served Jerusalem with distinction. That way engenders only fear and mistrust.'

'So, what are you going to do?' Asked William.

'There's not much we can do about any spy,' said the king, 'at least not yet, but one thing is abundantly clear. The construction of Chastellet causes Saladin greater worry with every stone that is laid, and he is determined to have it stopped. That means even he can see its strategic importance. Once finished, it will be indestructible but at the moment, while it is still under construction, it is vulnerable. I know this and Saladin knows this.'

'So, do we send men to reinforce the walls?'

'We will do better than that,' said Baldwin, 'I will relocate my army there to garrison the fortress along with whatever mercenaries I can muster. It will also mean we can set about finding this so-called spy, whoever he is, and make an example of him for all to see. In the meantime, we will send a message to Grand Master Amand, warning him of Saladin's plan and demand he deploys as many Templars as he can to Chastellet. He is as committed to this arrangement as any and it is about time he was reminded of his obligations.' The king stood up and turned to face Cronin and his comrades. 'You have done well, all three of you. Before this month is out, I will lead an army to Chastellet, and you will accompany me.'

'Your Grace,' said Jakelin, 'with respect, I would like to leave for Jacob's Ford at first light tomorrow, especially if it is likely to be attacked any time soon.'

'Three men will make no difference, either way,' said the king, 'so you will stay here with me. Besides, I have heard your name oft mentioned and would welcome your opinion on any military response I plan. It will also give your emaciated friend there, time to recover.'

'As you wish, Your Grace,' said Jakelin.

'Good. My castle steward will see to your immediate needs and you will be quartered with my personal bodyguards. Tonight, you will dine with me so until then, get some rest.'

'Of course,' said Jakelin and all three men bowed as Baldwin and William of Tyre left the room.

Jakelin and Cronin both turned to leave but paused as they realised that Hunter was still staring at the empty chair on the dais.

'Well,' said Jakelin, 'are you coming or not?'

'I have concerns,' said Hunter without turning.

'It is indeed a worry,' said Jakelin, 'if what Cronin said is true then we could be facing Saladin's warriors within days and I don't think we are ready.'

'No, it's not that,' said Hunter.

'Then what?'

Hunter turned to face the other two men.

'Did you not listen,' he said, 'does the title Templar rend you both deaf to the important things?'

'Spit it out, Hunter,' said Cronin, 'I am exhausted and need food and sleep, in that order. What did we miss?'

'Well I suggest that you not overindulge, my friend,' said Hunter, his eyes wide with wonder, 'for if I heard correctly, tonight we dine with a king.'

In Chastellet, the mercenaries rode into the lower bailey and dismounted, exhausted after a hard ride. Arturas helped Hassan down from his horse before looking at the curious people who had gathered around.

'Where's can I find the physician?' he demanded

'At the far end of the upper bailey,' replied one of the women, pointing the way.

Arturas headed towards the upper levels carrying the semi-conscious boy in his arms. He ducked into the hospital tent and seeing no empty cots, walked over to where a man was being treated for a broken hand.

'You,' he shouted, 'get up, I need the bed.'

The injured man needed no more bidding and jumped up, allowing Arturas to lay Hassan on the cot.

'Where's the physician?' he shouted, 'someone get him for me right now.'

One of the women ran from the tent to find John Loxley, just as Sumeira entered the tent.

'I'm a healer,' she said, 'what's going on?'

'This boy needs help,' said Arturas, 'and fast.'

Sumeira walked over and stared down at Hassan. Her face dropped as she recognised him and she looked up at Arturas.

'I know him,' she gasped, 'what happened?'

'Hit by an arrow,' replied the mercenary. 'The shaft has been removed but the wound is dirty.'

'Remove his upper clothing,' said Sumeira, 'quickly.' She turned around to one of the other women. 'Hot water,' she demanded, 'and plenty of it. Somebody bring me my medicine basket.'

She turned back around to smooth Hassan's brow. His skin was damp and hot to the touch.

'He has a fever,' she said, 'the wound must be infected.'

'How do you know him?' asked Arturas.

'He saved my life,' said Sumeira, 'not a few months since.'

'In that case,' said Arturas, 'this is your opportunity to return the favour.'

Chapter Twenty-Three

February – AD 1179

Castle Chastellet

Four weeks later, Eudes de St. Amand stood alongside Simon of Syracuse, each man looking down into the valley below. For the first time since the castle had been started, construction had come to a halt. Workmen who toiled for hours on end, now enjoyed a couple of hours rest as they lined the road linking Tiberius to Jacob's Ford. Up above, hundreds of men at arms lined the outer wall of the castle while two hundred Templars, resplendent in their finery lined the approach to the recently finished castle gates, all waiting for the arrival of King Baldwin of Jerusalem.

'He's late,' mumbled Simon, eager to continue the works on the castle.

'It is the king's privilege,' said Amand, 'he will be here soon enough.'

'Have you ever met him?' asked the castellan.

'Many times.'

'What's he like?'

'Once you see past the disfigurement, you will find him a young, yet able monarch.'

'I have heard he looks like a monster.'

'Appearances does not a good king make,' said Amand. 'I have seen Baldwin sword in hand, deep amongst the fray while knights of good standing retreat from the fight. His face may be one of nightmares, but his mind is sharp and his sword arm strong. Do not underestimate him.'

'Here he comes,' said the castellan and both men stared towards the end of the valley where the first of the outriders had appeared flying pennants bearing the king's colours.

Over the next few minutes, the full column came into full view, over a thousand horsemen and foot soldiers, closely followed by the endless carts and mules needed to support an army on the march. The workmen lining the road cheered as the army passed, some with relief as they realised their safety would now be guaranteed, others only in response to earlier threats from their overseers.

Once the initial outriders had passed, Baldwin himself was easily recognisable, even from high on the castle mount. He rode alone, several paces in front of the army, adorned in fiercely polished chainmail and a brightly coloured tabard. Despite the increasing heat of the mid-morning sun, he wore an open-faced helmet upon his head and a heavy cloak hung from his shoulders. His magnificent horse, bedecked in the finest caparison pranced to the beat of the drums while behind him, five hundred lancers, also bedecked in their finery, stared coldly forward, ignoring the cheers from the surrounding crowd as they passed.

'He certainly knows how to make an entrance,' said Sir Simon.

'Nothing but a show for the masses,' said Amand. 'He knows that Saladin has eyes and ears in the workforce and wants to send him a message.'

'Do you think the Ayyubid will attack?'

'According to the dispatches from Baldwin, he is in possession of information that suggests the question should be when, not if.'

'Well, we'll find out soon enough,' said the castellan as the king turned his horse to head up the hill.

'Aye we will,' said Amand.

In the upper bailey, Hassan sat on the edge of a cot, waiting to have the last of the dressings removed from his shoulder. Since being brought to the hospital tent weeks earlier, he had made a good recovery and although there was still a weakness in his shoulder, he had spent the last few days helping Sumeira and the other women tend the injured.

'Hassan,' said Sumeira, walking into the tent, 'you are looking well today.'

'Thank you, my lady.' he said as she sat on the cot next to him. 'The pain has almost gone.'

'Good,' said Sumeira. 'We'll remove your bandages and as long as the wound is fully healed, I see no reason you can't return to your normal duties.'

'My normal duties?' asked Hassan. 'Alas, that cannot be, unless I ride to Tiberius and seek out Master Cronin.'

'Tiberius?' said Sumeira, stopping what she was doing and looking at Hassan with surprise. 'Haven't you heard? The king is coming here, and if I understand correctly, so is your friend.'

'Master Cronin is coming to Chastellet?' gasped Hassan.

'Apparently so,' said Sumeira, 'and in fact, he is probably here already.'

Several hours later, the king walked along the castle walls alongside Amand and the castellan. Down below, within the castle walls, the army from Tiberius was busy erecting their tents as the masons had concentrated on finishing the defensive walls rather than the inner buildings. Outside, the workforce had returned to their duties and the construction had restarted in earnest.

'Impressive,' said the king eventually, 'your men have worked well.'

'The masons work dawn till dusk,' said Simon, 'and we use the hours of darkness to bring up fresh materials for the following day.'

'And the well?'

'We have at last hit water,' said the castellan, 'all that needs to be done in that respect is to construct a cistern for storage.'

Baldwin looked towards the corners of the castle.

'I see the main towers have already been started.'

'They have,' said Simon, 'and will be completed within months. The lesser towers will follow and lastly the inner buildings. Barracks, stables, that sort of thing.'

'Yes,' said the king, looking at the temporary camp already appearing below the walls, 'a tented garrison is never a good idea.'

'We have arranged timber to build temporary barracks and a commandery,' said Simon. 'They should be completed within weeks.'

'How long do you intend staying, Your Grace?' interjected Amand, 'you mentioned in your dispatches that you have word that Saladin is up to something?'

'Aye, I do. In fact, it was two of your own men who furnished me with this information.'

'Sir Jakelin and the sergeant?'

'Indeed. The one called Cronin fell into circumstances where he found out some of Saladin's intentions.'

'Not for the first time,' said Amand, 'for it was Cronin who found out the Sultan's location before Montgisard and relayed that information to Sir Gerald of Jerusalem and the garrison at Blancheguarde. '

'So I understand,' said Baldwin. 'He is either blessed with good luck or is watched over by God himself. I have made use of their extensive experience this past few days.'

'What did Cronin find out?'

'Apparently, the Ayyubid are turning their attention to Chastellet and intend to attack within months.'

'Was this not always likely?'

'Aye, but this time they are preparing the ground. First, their attention will fall upon our cattle herds to the east. The intention is to deny us access to food and thus weaken our position. After that, his nephew, Farrukh-Shah will raid westward into the lands of Sidon to do the same. Once the food and water are scarce, they intend to attack.'

'So, you have come to reinforce the castle?'

'In part. I will maintain a force here, but I cannot allow Saladin to steal our stock so I will lead a campaign eastward to protect our farmers while they round up the herds. I want you to provide me with a squadron of Templars as extra protection.

'I will lead it myself,' said Amand.

'Good. Once the castle is finished, we will talk of a more permanent garrison. Until then, tell your men that we will no longer sit back and allow Saladin to dictate our policies, from today, we will decide who and where we fight, on our terms.'

'Aye, Your Grace.'

'One more thing,' said the king, looking around to see he could not be overheard. 'We have come into information that there may be a spy amongst us. Someone who is passing vital information about what's happening here onto Saladin.'

'A spy?' said Simon in disgust. 'Do you know who he is?'

'Not yet but we suspect he may be one of the men at arms recently arrived from overseas. All we know is he is not native to the Holy Land and passes messages through the hands of one of the native labourers.'

'Then we must flush him out,' said Sir Simon. 'I will round up the tribal elders and punish them until they turn the messenger over. Once we have him, we can catch the true traitor.'

'No,' said the king. 'This must stay between ourselves, at least for the moment.'

'Why?' asked Amand. 'Should we not announce our knowledge and see what rat breaks cover?'

'No, not yet. First, let's see if we can find out who he is by subterfuge. If so, we can feed him false information and lead Saladin astray. The Brothers Templar are the only ones I trust in all this, so it is to you I turn to entrust the mission. Ask your men to make discreet enquiries but tell them to tread lightly. We don't want to scare him off, whoever he may be.'

'He should be tortured by the foulest means,' growled Amand, 'until he begs for death.'

'And he will be, but first, we need if we can find out who he is. Besides, he may be one of several and I would rather burn the nest instead of a single snake.'

'What man of God could possibly be tempted to betray his fellows in return for heathen gold?' said the castellan. 'The thought turns the stomach.'

'You'd be surprised, Sir Simon,' said the king, thinking back to his recent encounter with Farrukh-Shah, 'you'd be surprised.'

An hour or so later, in the corner of the castle where the Templars had already set up their own separate camp, Sir Jakelin and Cronin handed over their horses to the squires and headed into the command tent. Waiting for them was the Templar's Seneschal, Brother Valmont of Lyon.

'Ah,' said Valmont, his manner suggesting he was far from pleased with their appearance, 'you are back. I hope you enjoyed your time at the king's court while the rest of us toiled to build his fortress.'

'My Lord,' said Sir Jakelin. 'The decision was the king's, not ours. I asked to return on several occasions but was denied.'

'And you,' he continued, turning to face Cronin. 'It's been over a year since I saw you last. It seems that trouble follows you like a shadow.'

'I was on a mission for the Grand Master himself,' said Cronin, 'as well you know. I would have been back sooner but was taken prisoner.'

'Perhaps,' said Valmont, 'but the fact is, our order has invested a lot of time in every man who takes the vow and needs those men to call upon when required. As it stands, you have spent little time amongst your comrades. Perhaps it is time you thought about your future with us.'

'With respect, my lord,' said Cronin, 'I am as committed as ever and seek only the chance to prove myself alongside my fellows. The misfortune with the Cross of Courtney apart, have I not conducted myself with honour?'

'Ah yes, the cross,' said Valmont. 'A total waste of time and finance, again caused by your poor choices.'

'What do you mean?' asked Cronin, 'we retrieved it as tasked. Sir Jakelin here delivered it with his own hands.'

Valmont stared at Cronin and then back at Jakelin.

'Have you not told him, Sir Jakelin?'

'I have not,' said the knight. 'I believed the knowledge would do more harm than good.'

'What knowledge?' asked Cronin. 'Did you receive the cross or not?'

'Oh, I received the cross, alright,' said Valmont, 'but it turns out that it was fake, and the real cross had been delivered to the king by other means weeks earlier.'

'What?' gasped Cronin, 'I don't understand.'

'It's quite simple,' said Valmont, 'the pope sent two versions of the cross to Baldwin. One was the real thing, the other a fake, designed to ensure the king received at least something should anything happen to the other. As it turns out, that is exactly what happened and though you succeeded in locating and retrieving the one you lost, the real one was already in the king's hands.'

'So, all that was for nothing,' said Cronin. 'We nearly died out there just for some trinket worth nought more than a jug of ale.'

'Perhaps so,' said Valmont, 'but here you are alive and kicking. The only damage done is to our treasuries which, by the way, are several hundred Dinars lighter thanks to your escapades.'

Cronin stared at the Seneschal. More than anything he wanted to knock the dislikeable
man to the ground but he knew to do so was to incur instant dismissal from the order and flogging at the hands of the castle jailer.

The Seneschal turned to face Jakelin.

'Brother Jakelin,' he said, 'as you know, the king intends to lead a campaign eastward to oversee the gathering of the herds.

The Grand Master will command a patrol of our own men in support, but you will accompany the king with the main army.'

'With respect, my lord,' replied Jakelin, 'my place is amongst our own order.'

'Your place is anywhere where I command you to serve,' said Valmont, 'and as King Baldwin has specifically requested your presence, approved by the way, by the Grand Master himself, you will be seconded to his command until further notice.'

Jakelin did not answer, but his demeanour suggested he was far from happy with the situation.

'As for you, Brother Cronin,' said the Seneschal, turning to the sergeant, 'as much as I want to send you on patrol, I can see you are still not fully recovered from your time in captivity. You will stay here in Chastellet while you regain your strength.'

'My lord,' interjected Cronin, but the Seneschal held up his hand, cutting him short.

'There will be no argument,' said Valmont, 'at the moment you would be a liability if we have to fight and we need everyone at full strength. Besides, a spell on the walls will allow you to regain some humility.'

'Yes, my lord,' said Cronin with a sigh.

'So,' continued the Seneschal, 'if there is nothing else, Sir Jakelin, I suggest you get some rest and then ready yourselves for the campaign. Sergeant Cronin, first thing tomorrow you will report to the castellan for sentry duty.'

Both men nodded slightly in deference and left the tent.

'A posting alongside the king himself,' said Cronin as they walked. 'An honour indeed.'

'I am a knight,' said Jakelin, 'and should be fighting Saracens, not herding cattle.'

'I suppose it is an important role in the greater scheme of things.'

'It is a menial task. There is no knowing where Saladin will strike next and we should be ready to react as soon as he moves, not roaming the cattle fields.' He turned to face the sergeant. 'Brother Cronin,' he said, 'you have spent a great while in chains at the hands of our enemy, a fate that few men escape. The responsibility for that situation lies with me and I accept the blame. Nobody would judge you if you now sought retribution.'

'Yet you were one of those that saved me,' replied Cronin.

'Nevertheless, the original fault was mine. In light of what now lies before us, this may be the only chance you will have to seek a reckoning, so, if that is your inclination, strike now for I will not retaliate.'

Cronin returned the stare, eventually softening it with a slight smile.

'Nah,' he said eventually, 'I think we can safely say we are even.'

'I'm going to the chapel to give thanks,' said Jakelin. 'Do you care to join me?'

'Not yet,' said Cronin, 'first I'm going to find Hassan. I'm told he has made a good recovery and I still haven't conveyed my gratitude for what he did.'

'Give him my best regards,' said Jakelin, 'that boy will one day make a good squire.'

'I'll tell him you said that,' said Cronin, as the knight walked away, 'It will mean a lot to him.'

Chapter Twenty-Four

March – AD 1179

The Grazing Fields South of Damascus

King Baldwin rode alongside Sir Jakelin at the head of a strong military column. Behind him came fifty Christian knights and a further five hundred lancers from his relocated army at Chastellet. To the north, a further force of two hundred mounted men guarded his left flank, led by Humphrey of Toron while over to the right rode fifty Templars and a hundred Turcopole lancers commanded by Eudes de St. Amand himself.

'Does it feel good to be back on campaign?' asked the king as he rode.

'It does, Your Grace,' said Jakelin, his body swaying with the rhythm of the warhorse beneath him, 'it why I took the cross, to ensure the safety of our Christian brothers in the Holy Land. All men should be allowed to worship their Gods in peace.'

'That's interesting,' said the king, 'you say *'their gods,'* so do you believe there are more than one?'

'No, Your Grace, but if others believe otherwise, that is their business.'

'And the claim to Jerusalem?'

'Jerusalem is in Christian hands and should stay that way.'

'You proclaim a peaceful outlook yet are renown for your prowess on the battlefield,' said the king. 'Is that not a contradiction for a man such as yourself?'

'As I said, as long as they leave Christians alone, they will get no argument from me or my comrades. Inflict hurt upon them or our faith and I will smite them with everything I have in the name of God.'

'Hmm,' said the king glancing over at the knight. 'You are a strange mix, you Templars. There is no doubt about your abilities or indeed your piety, yet I often wonder why you focus so much on matters of finance.'

'Questions for the Grandmaster, Your Grace,' said Jakelin without looking over, 'I am a man of the sword, not the purse.'

The column continued weaving its way along the track towards the pastures where the Christian farmers grazed their cattle and the men of war relaxed in their saddles as the sun rose higher in the sky. Finally, the scouts returned and reported a shaded valley where the column could rest from the midday sun.

Several leagues away, another army sheltered from the afternoon sun, a force of two thousand Saracens, hidden deep within the forests of Banias.

At the centre of the camp, Farrukh-Shah sat cross-legged on a rug, one of three men in a council of war. The other two, Bakir-Shah and Shirkuh ad-Din had joined him from Saladin's main camp a mere twenty leagues away to the west.

'How fares my uncle?' asked Farrukh-Shah, taking a glass of tea from a slave.

'He is well,' said Shirkuh ad-Din, 'and back astride the warhorse. Egypt is now settled and his attention is firmly back on the Franks.'

'Is his army at full strength?'

'It is, my lord,' said Shirkuh ad-Din, 'since he united the eastern tribes, warriors are not hard to muster. He only awaits the right opportunity and the castle at Vadum Iacob will be trampled to dust beneath the hooves of his cavalry.'

'So he awaits my diversion?'

'He does. Our scouts tell us that as suspected, Baldwin has sent out a force to protect the Christian herdsmen but Allah has blessed us with a gift like no other.'

'Which is?'

'It seems that Baldwin himself heads the Christians.'

'The Christian king is out here,' gasped Farrukh-Shah, 'why?'

'Who can read the minds of such men?' asked Shirkuh ad-Din. 'But the fact is, he is there and more vulnerable than he has ever been.'

'And Salah ad-Din knows this?'

'He does, my lord, that is why he sent us here. Your uncle wants you to attack immediately.'

'To capture King Baldwin?'

'Yes, my lord. Our master says that even if you fail, an attack on the king's column will create a thunderstorm in the minds of those garrisoned at Vadum Iacob and they are likely to send a relieving column, leaving the fortress under defended.'

Farrukh-Shah nodded silently. His role was to have been one of harassment only but he was loyal without question to Salah ad-Din and would have ridden through the gates of hell if such was the command.

'Did he state when?' he asked.

'Within the next two days while they are at the furthest point from Vadum Iacob.'

'It makes sense,' said Farrukh-Shah. 'Return to the Sultan and tell him that Allah willing, we will attack the Christians when the sun is at its highest tomorrow before they have a chance to water and corral their horses.'

'I will report back,' said Shirkuh ad-Din, 'but Bakir-Shah will stay here on the orders of Salah ad-Din. He brings fifty Mamluk with him and was responsible for our master escaping with his life after Montgisard.'

'You are welcome,' said Farrukh-Shah. 'I'm sure your extra men will make all the difference.'

'Thank you, my lord,' said Bakir-Shah. 'We will not let you down.'

Shirkuh ad-Din got to his feet.

'I must go but leave knowing the Sultan's plans lay in the hands of a great warrior.'

'Travel well, my friend,' said Farrukh-Shah, getting to his own feet. 'Hopefully, we will meet again amongst the rubble at Vadum Iacob.'

'If Allah wills it,' said Shirkuh. 'As-Salaam-Alaykum, my friend.'

'Wa-Alaykum-Salaam,' replied Farrukh-Shah and waited until Shirkuh ad-Din had left the clearing.

'Tell your men to rest well tonight, Bakir-Shah,' he said turning towards the newcomer, 'for tomorrow we fight the King of the Christians.'

The following morning, King Baldwin and the rest of his army were on the road early, determined to travel as much distance as possible before midday. Baldwin travelled in his cart having suffered a bad night and though he had bathed in warm water and had all the usual ointments applied by his servants, his skin was tender and he couldn't face wearing his armour.

William of Tyre rode alongside him in the cart, wishing he had accepted the offer to stay behind at Chastellet, such was the discomfort of the rough road.

At the head of the column, Jakelin was now accompanied by the Grand Master who had taken control of the army while the king was indisposed and the two men rode side by side, their eyes peeled for any sign of trouble. The morning passed, uneventfully and eventually, Amand called a halt to water the horses.

'It's strangely quiet around here,' said Amand, looking around the valley before taking a drink from his waterskin.

'I noticed,' said Jakelin. 'You would have thought we would have seen a goatherd or shepherd but the hills are empty and have been since we set out.'

'I don't like it,' said Amand. 'It's as if they know something we don't. I'll organise a scout party to ensure there are no surprises waiting for us on the other side.'

'Of course, my lord,' said Jakelin, 'I'll tell the men to stay alert.' He turned away and rode back along the Christian column, talking to the lancers. Some were seasoned fighters, especially the king's bodyguard but many were new to warfare as the best of the men had remained at Chastellet to defend against any attack. Their lack of experience was a concern to Jakelin but they had to make do with what they had.

'Sir Jakelin,' called a voice and the knight turned to see the prelate approaching from the king's cart.

'Father William,' said Jakelin, 'what can I do for you?'

'The king wants to know why we have stopped. He is keen to continue.'

'We are watering the horses,' said Jakelin, 'but also need to send out scouts. We will be here a while yet.'

'On whose orders?'

'The Grand Master.'

'That is not an option,' said William. 'The king is suffering and would benefit from the coolness of a stone building. I understand there is a village a few leagues away, we need to get him there before the sun is at its highest.'

'With respect,' said Jakelin, 'the king may be uncomfortable but his life is more important and we dare not advance until we know the way is clear.'

'I don't think you understood me,' said William. 'This is not a request but a royal command from the king himself. Tell your master to get this column moving at once or he will be replaced with someone who knows his place.'

Without waiting for an answer, William turned away and returned to the row of royal carts at the midst of the column.

With a sigh, Jakelin returned to the head of the column and relayed the message to Amand and though both were of the same mind, they had no other option but to do as the king commanded.

For the next hour or so they continued along the path, the unease growing in their hearts and just as they neared the end of the valley, two of the advance scouts came racing back towards the column.

Amand raised his hand to halt the column and waited as the scouts reigned in their exhausted horses.

'My Lord,' gasped one, 'there are Saracens upon the road less than a league from here.'

'How many?' asked Amand.

'About two hundred in all and they are coming this way.'

'Cavalry or foot soldiers?'

'Cavalry,' said the scout, 'and it seems over half are Mamluk.'

'The only reason Saladin deploys his Mamluk,' said Jakelin, 'is if there is fighting to be done. I suggest we stand to the column.'

'No,' said Amand, we will take the fight to them.'

'My Lord,' said Jakelin,' don't forget Baldwin is indisposed and unable to ride. If we fight this force and come off second best then the king himself is at risk.'

'They will get nowhere near the king,' said Amand looking around the valley. His Templars were on the right hill and he knew Humphrey of Toron and his men were somewhere over the hill to the left. 'This is what we will do,' he said turning back to face Jakelin. 'I will take the Templars to face the Saracens. They will probably withdraw at our approach but just in case, you will form a defensive position here with the rest of the column. Send a message to Sir Humphrey to draw in to reinforce the position and wait here until I return.'

'Should we be splitting our forces?' asked Jakelin. 'We have no idea if these two hundred Saracens are alone or part of a greater force.'

'In the unlikely event we are routed,' said Amand, 'you have more than enough men to make a stand here. Tell the king's guard to close in around the royal wagons and form an outer cordon with the rest of the men. I will be back as soon as I can.'

Without another word, the Grand Master turned his horse and galloped towards the Templar force on the right flank.

'You heard him,' said Jakelin turning to the nearby officers, 'let's get this defensive position sorted.'

The officers hurried off to their tasks while Jakelin headed towards the king's cart.

'Is there a problem?' asked William as he approached.

'There may be,' said Jakelin, 'there are Saracens up ahead. Grand Master Amand has set out to engage them while we wait here until the road is clear.'

'What do you mean he has ridden out to engage them? Who has he taken in support?'

'The rest of my comrades as well as the Turcopoles.'

'What?' gasped William, 'he has taken the Templars?'

'Aye,' said Jakelin, 'but worry not, they are more than capable of defeating a force of only two hundred Saracens.'

'I care not about their prowess,' snapped William, 'only about the safety of the king. While your master rides out to fulfil his personal quest for glory, Baldwin is left at risk.'

'With respect,' said Jakelin, 'we still have over five hundred men at arms and another two hundred under the command of Humphrey less than a league away. Nothing is going to happen to the king.'

'I hope you are right,' growled William. 'The Templars were engaged to secure Baldwin's safely and here we are, at risk from attack and all I can see of your comrades is the dust left behind by their horses.'

Before Jakelin could respond, William strode away, knocking aside a young squire as he went.

'King's guard,' shouted Jakelin walking down the column, 'stand to. Close in to protect the royal wagons. The rest of you, listen to your officers and keep your eyes open.'

Up on the hill, two men lay deep amongst a clump of sun-dried grass, transfixed by the activity in the valley below. Everything was going exactly to plan but the fact that the Templars themselves had taken the bait was better than they could have hoped. The first turned to the man at his side.

'Allah is truly with us,' he said quietly, 'send the signal.'

The second man lifted a small mirror from the ground and twisted around to reflect the sun's rays across the hills to his rear.

Two leagues away, another group of men hid amongst the rocks, waiting for exactly this moment.

'There it is,' said Bakir-Shah, seeing the bright flash of light and turned to walk through the narrow passage splitting the rocky outcrop. After a few hundred paces he emerged onto a ledge overlooking a valley and stared down at the impressive sight below, almost two thousand Saracen warriors, each standing beside their horses as they waited for the signal to mount up.

'They have taken the bait,' announced Bakir-Shah walking over to his own horse, 'send the signal.'

Two men walked from the shadows and as Bakir-Shah rode away to join the waiting army, the signallers waived a giant flag high in the air. Down below, Farrukh-Shah saw the signal and turned to his officers.

'The infidels have taken the bait,' he said. 'Send a message to Salah ad-Din. Tell him that the battle is about to commence.'

Chapter Twenty-Five

March – AD 1179

The Battle of Banias

Two hours later, Jakelin approached the scout commander at the head of the column, concerned that the messenger he had sent to Humphrey still had not returned.

'Any sign of them?' he asked.

'Nothing,' said the scout sergeant. 'They should be back by now. '

'My Lord Jakelin,' said a voice and the knight turned to see two riders approaching.

'Hunter,' he said as they neared, 'I thought you were still at Chastellet.'

'I asked for this posting,' said Hunter, 'but was attached to Sir Humphrey's command as lead scout.'

'How are you back here?'

'We have noticed something strange,' said Hunter, 'and thought we should report it to the Grand Master.'

'What have you seen?'

'Green pastures with not a single sheep upon them,' said Hunter, 'and these valleys are usually infested with rogues feeding their cattle on the king's grass.'

'There is a Saracen patrol a few leagues away,' said Jakelin. 'Amand has taken our knights to disperse them but something tells me such a small number would not have had the effect we are talking about.'

'What's the plan?' asked Hunter.

'We are going firm here until the Grand Master gets back, but we could do with more men. Can you ride back and brief Sir Humphrey?'

'Aye,' said Hunter. 'Furnish me with fresh horses and we can be back here with his men by nightfall.'

'Do that,' said Jakelin, 'and in God's name, do not fail. I have a very bad feeling about this.'

'Leave it to me,' said Hunter and turned his tired horse around to head towards the temporary paddock.

Over the hill on the right flank of the Christian column, two hundred Saracens waited patiently for their commander to give the signal. Although the slopes were rocky on both sides, the gradual incline meant they could advance over a wide front and they spread out accordingly. The Emir rode his horse a few paces up the hill until he could be seen by every warrior. There was no need for rousing speeches or calls to arms, every man had been thoroughly briefed and they knew just what to do.

He drew his Scimitar and every warrior immediately did the same. This was the moment they had been waiting for, the time when at last they could inflict a devastating defeat on the Christians.

'Allah Akbar,' he roared, his voice echoing around the valley and as his men responded with the same cry, he turned and galloped his horse up and over the ridge.

In the valley on the other side of the hill, several men stopped what they were doing and lifted their heads.

'What was that?' asked one.

'What was what?' replied his comrade.

'That noise, did you not hear it?'

Before the man could reply, one of the squires shouted out, his voice laced with fear.

'My Lords, *look.*'

Everyone in earshot turned to face the way the young boy was pointing and immediately their faces fell as two hundred riders appeared on the top of the hill.

'Saracens,' gasped one of the men, and turned to face into the camp. 'Sound the alarm, we are under attack.'

Three leagues away, the Templar column emerged from the valley onto an open plain. To their front, two hundred Saracen riders spread out, line abreast facing the Christian patrols.

Amand reined his horse in and stopped to stare at his adversaries. Behind him, the column automatically fanned out to form a wedge formation facing the enemy. Brother Tristan, the Templar Marshal rode up to join the Grand Master.

'What are they doing?' asked Brother Tristan, 'surely they know that is the weakest defensive formation. Man on man we will triumph with hardly a sweat.'

'I don't know,' said Baldwin. 'Either their commander is very stupid or very brave. Either way, I'm not going to wait to find out. Form up line abreast, close order. Tell the Turcopoles to protect our flanks.'

'Aye, my lord,' said Tristan and gave the orders to form the classic Templar fighting formation. One by one the knights rode their horses up to join the extended line, each within touching distance of the man to either side. At their centre, Amand drew his sword while the other knights withdrew their lances from their leather sockets ready to be lowered in the charge.

'I have neither the time nor inclination for parley or negotiation,' shouted Amand to his men. 'We will hit them head-on and return to finish them off with our blades. Take no prisoners.' He lifted up his sword. 'Templar brothers,' he shouted, *'forward.'*

As one the line of fifty knights advanced, each keeping in tight formation with those to either side. Behind them came the Turcopole lancers, fanning out to form the wings of the blunt wedge-shaped attack formation.

'Prepare to charge,' shouted Amand as they neared the Saracens and all the warhorses increased speed, responding to the subtle nudges from the heels of the Templars.

'Templars, present,' shouted Amand, and as the knights lowered their lances to aim at the enemy, he roared the battle cry, calling the squadron to the charge, *'Beauséant alla riscossa.'*

Back in the valley, the defensive cordon responded to the signal horn and leapt onto their horses' backs, immediately ready for battle. As one they turned to face the enemy racing down the hill and without hesitation, dug in their heels to meet the Saracens head-on.

Seconds later the two forces clashed, and men fell on both sides, but momentum was with the Saracens and many broke through the line to continue the charge towards the king's wagons.

Further along the position, Jakelin had already anticipated the risk and sat astride his horse at the head of two hundred of the king's lancers.'

'Prepare to move,' he shouted, *'advaaance.'*

The column responded and spurred their horses onward, cutting off the advance of the Saracens who had breached the outer line. As one the lancers swung left and charged at the enemy, now down on level ground. Steel again met steel but this time, the Christian cavalry got the better of their opponents and slowly but surely, forced them back up the hill.

'My Lord,' shouted a voice, 'foot soldiers.'

Jakelin looked up and saw men running down from the ridge to form up in a line.

'Archers,' he gasped and turned to face his scattered force. If they retreated now, they would be cut down but to advance was just as risky. Unchallenged, archers would just send volley after volley into the column's position as soon as it was in range but the ground above was rocky and no place for horses. 'Sir Michael,' he shouted to one of the nearby knights, 'take half the men and reinforce the king's guard. The rest of you, dismount and follow me.'

Within moments he and a hundred other men were running to the protection of the nearest rocks.

'We have no time to waste, 'shouted Jakelin, 'those archers need to be routed. Ready?'

'Aye,' roared the men in reply.

'Then let's get it done,' shouted Jakelin and holding up his shield as protection, broke cover to head up the hill.

Immediately the archers turned their attention on the approaching men but the combination of the rocky cover and skillfully used shields meant few fell to arrows. Slowly but surely Jakelin and his men neared the enemy position but as suddenly as it started, the rain of arrows stopped, and the Christians peered over their shields in confusion.

At the top of the hill, they could see the last of the archers fleeing back to their horses, their work done.

'After them,' shouted one of the knights but Jakelin knew something was wrong.

'Hold,' he roared and looked around the hill in confusion. All across the plain below, men lay dead or dying but apart from the enemy casualties, not a single Saracen remained in sight.

'They are beaten,' shouted a voice, 'the enemy has fled the field.'

'No,' said Jakelin to himself, 'it can't be that easy.'

As if in answer to his doubts, a movement on the far hill caught his eye and his heart sunk as he realised they had been tricked.

As far as he could see, lines of Saracen Cavalry emerged from the tree line to face the Christian column on the road below and with the bulk of the king's army spread out across the valley, there were not enough men to form a solid defensive wall.

'*Back to the column,*' roared Jakelin but as his men broke into a run, the enemy on the far hill responded, charging down towards the weakened defences surrounding the king.

'*Close in,*' roared the knight in charge of the inner cordon, 'form a shield wall, present lances.'

Everyone in earshot ran to their positions, each determined to protect the king at all costs and within moments, a wall of lance bearing defenders surrounded the wagons, each braced with shields to the fore. An inner rank of crossbowmen stood to the rear, ready to release their own arrows at the charging enemy but despite the obvious strength of the position, nobody was under any impression it would be strong enough against the thousands of horsemen racing to the attack.

'Make ready,' shouted the knight as the riders neared, 'archers, *loose.*'

Immediately a hundred bolts sliced through the air, cutting down men and horses alike but it was too slow and by the time they had reloaded, the front ranks of the Saracen force were already smashing into the defending wall. Many tried to leap the hedge of metal-tipped lances and though those to the fore were impaled, many broke through with few injuries.

Immediately the crossbowmen dropped their weapons and fell upon them with swords and daggers but even as the adjacent men closed in to seal the gap, they knew the weakness of the line had been exposed.

Inside the king's cart, Baldwin was struggling to stand.

'My armour,' he demanded, 'William, get my sword, I need to get out there.'

'Your Grace,' said William, 'you can hardly stand. Stay here and leave the fighting to your men.'

'I am useless in here,' shouted the king,' get me my sword,' but the words were no sooner out of his mouth when he collapsed in a coughing fit, struggling to breathe.

'Your Grace,' said William dropping to his knees and grabbing the monarch, 'you are safer in here. Should the defences fall, we will be taken prisoner, that is all. There is no way Saladin will kill a king and you will be released within weeks.'

'I am not afraid to die,' growled Baldwin, 'my place is beside my men not hiding in here like a woman. Get me out there.'

'Your Grace,' said William, 'listen to me. Your bravery is not in question, but you are as weak as a kitten. If you go out there now, not only will you make little difference, but good men will have to be posted to your side, weakening the defences. Let them do what they have to do and see how this attack plays out. Sir Jakelin knows what he is doing.'

As the main attack continued, Jakelin and the remainder of the men raced down the opposite slope to join the fray but despite their desperation, their progress was slow.

'Come on,' he roared at the men spread out all around him, 'they are breaking through the lines.' With renewed energy, the knights increased speed but by the time they reached the column, the outer defences were already scattered, and men fought one on one against the throng of Saracens pressing forward towards the caravan.

'The king's guard still holds,' shouted Jakelin, 'head towards them and add your swords to their number.'

Slowly but surely the lancers and knights headed towards the inner position. Despite their exhaustion, their strength and prowess told, and Saracens fell all around, many cleaved open by the weight and force behind the Christians' heavy two-handed swords.

Jakelin reached the inner wall and forced his way through.

'How fares the king?' he demanded.

'The king is safe,' responded a knight, 'but we can't hold on much longer.'

Jakelin looked around desperately. The knight was right. Already their forces had been depleted by over a quarter and though those that still survived fought courageously, there were still hundreds of Saracens on the hill above, all waiting their chance to join the fray.

'We can't stay here,' said Jakelin eventually. 'We'll all be dead by nightfall.'

'Where can we go?' asked the knight, 'they'll cut us down before we got out of the valley.'

'Up there,' said Jakelin pointing to the edge of a forest spreading down from a nearby ridge. 'That forest goes on for leagues. If we can get up there, at least we will be safe from their cavalry.'

'We'll never make it,' said the knight.

'It's the only chance we have,' said Jakelin. 'Rally the men, I'll brief the king.'

Minutes later, a group of the king's guard gathered around the rear of the king's cart, each turned outward to present their shields against any incoming arrows. When they were in place, William climbed down the steps and waited as Baldwin followed. Despite his attempts to stand tall, it was obvious to the men he was weak and unable to fight.

'What now?' asked William.

'We've made a litter,' said Jakelin. 'If the king will sit upon it, we'll carry him up to safety.'

'I can walk,' said Baldwin.

'I meant no disrespect, Your Grace,' said Jakelin, 'but it would be easier if you allowed us to carry you. You will be protected by a shield wall held tightly around the litter.'

'My Lord,' shouted a voice, 'the Saracens are reforming.'

'We have to move now, 'urged Jakelin, 'we can't hold them out much longer.'

'Then get it done,' said the king and the knight spun away to issue his commands.

'Listen to me,' he roared, 'we will no longer stay here as target practice for their archers. Upon the signal, every man is to head up to the forest above us. Those without injury will form a rearguard for the others to escape. I, along with those still with horses, will do what we can to delay their cavalry. Does everyone understand?'

'Aye,' came the shouted reply and Jakelin ran over to where a hundred men sat upon their horses.

'Is this it?' he asked looking around.

'The rest are either dead or scattered around the valley,' said a knight.

'It will have to do,' said Jakelin. 'When I give the signal, we will spread out and charge straight at the centre of their line. They will not be expecting a counterattack so the element of surprise will be with us. Strike where you can but do not stop to engage any man in combat. Any of us who survive are to immediately swing around and ride back to join the rearguard. Victory is beyond us this day so our focus must be on saving the king. Is that clear?'

'My Lord,' said a young lancer, 'there must be a thousand of them up there, we have no chance.'

'Our aim is not to defeat them,' said Jakelin struggling to control his skittish horse, 'but to gain time for the king to escape. The Saracens cannot deploy their whole army at once due to the steepness of the slope, nevertheless, they will outnumber us at least two to one.'

He looked around the mounted men.

'Make no mistake,' he continued, 'the king's life is in our hands. If we can hold them up even for a few moments, then he has a chance to escape.' He turned to the signaler at his side. 'As soon as we move, sound the attack.'

The young man nodded and raised the horn to his mouth as Jakelin and the rest of the men drew their swords.

'Are you ready?' he roared.

'Aye,' roared the men in reply.

'Then in God's name, *advaaance.*'

The sound of the horn echoed through the valley and with an almighty roar, the hundred remaining Christian cavalry followed the Templar knight up the hill, straight at the heart of the enemy.

Behind them, those responsible for protecting the king heard the signal and turned to their own tasks.

'There it is,' shouted one of Baldwin's officers, 'move out.'

With three men on each of the four arms of the makeshift litter, the king's guard immediately set out across the open space to the nearby slope. The remaining men at arms ran alongside, ready to defend the king with their lives.

'When we reach those two boulders,' shouted Sir Michael, 'we will form a defensive line facing back down this way. The ground to either side is too rough for horses so if we are pursued by cavalry, they will have no other option but to come through our lines.'

Up on the hill, Jakelin led his makeshift mounted force directly at the enemy position.

Up above, the Saracens reacted quickly and with only seconds to spare, sent a line of their own warriors down to meet the Christian charge. Both lines crashed into each other with blood spurting everywhere as steel blades cleaved through flesh and bone. Many fell on both sides, but the Christian knights did not pause to continue the fight, instead, they forced their way through and headed on up the hill.

'What are they doing?' asked Farrukh-Shah at the top, 'they must know they are facing nothing but death?'

Without waiting for an answer, he gave a hand signal and a second wave of warriors prepared to head down to face the oncoming knights, but before they could move the attackers suddenly swerved away to head back down the hill.

'What sort of tactic is this?' asked Farrukh-Shah, 'they just attacked for no reason and now withdraw with no ground being gained. It makes no sense.'

'Look, my lord,' said Bakir-Shah at his side, 'the rest of the Christians are trying to escape.'

Farrukh-Shah stared across the valley, seeing the main group heading up the far slope as others formed a defensive line to their rear.

'A diversion,' he said eventually, 'I should have known.' He turned to Bakir-Shah. 'This is the moment you have been waiting for,' he said. 'I suspect our quarry lies at the heart of those heading for the trees and the Christians are in disarray. The lies the king, Bakir-Shah, bring him to me.'

'As you wish, my lord,' said Bakir-Shah and turned away to give the commands. Moments later, five hundred Saracen horsemen poured down the hill and headed across the valley, straight at the Christian rearguard.

Jakelin led his men through the newly formed defensive line before spinning around and leaping from his horse.

'Dismount,' he roared, 'support the wall.'

His men did as ordered and turned to face the oncoming Saracen army.

'Dear God almighty,' mumbled one of the knights, making the sign of the cross upon his chest, 'deliver us from evil.'

'He is with us, my friend,' said Jakelin, 'and guides your blade.' He turned to shout along the lines. *'Keep low,'* he roared, 'and strike at their horses' legs. Wait for no orders from me or any other, this day you fight alongside your comrade and the Lord himself. Have no fear, my friends, God is with us.'

'*God is with us,*' roared the men and turned back to face the oncoming enemy.

Within moments the first of the Saracens smashed into the defending wall, destroying the front rank before heading towards the next. The Christians fought back with everything they had to hand. Swords cleaved into horse flesh and lances speared men, their screams of pain mingling to echo around the valley. Still, the enemy came, encouraged by the emirs to their rear, wave after wave of Ayyubid horsemen, seasoned warriors well used to the carnage of war.

'*Hold the line,*' roared Jakelin and as his heavy sword flew through the air, cutting deep into horse and human flesh alike. Blood saturated his Surcoat and dripped from his helmet to cover his face. He fought like a man possessed, no sooner killing one man than racing to engage another. Dozens fell to his blade and encouraged by his valour; the defensive line rallied to force the Ayyubid back down the hill.

'*They're running,*' gasped a knight at Jakelin's side.

'A temporary reprieve,' said Jakelin, looking around the battlefield, 'there are ten times as many waiting to take their place and we will not withstand the next attack.' He looked up the hill to his rear. 'The king is not yet safe,' he said, 'they need more time.'

'My Lord,' shouted a voice,' look to the east.'

Jakelin spun around to look further up the valley. To his dismay, he saw a force of fifty Mamluks picking their way up the rocky slope to outflank the Christian lines.

'We have to get up there,' he said.

'If we retreat now, their horsemen will fall upon our backs and the day lost.'

Jakelin thought furiously. His comrade was right. The defensive line was still strong and needed to stay in place, but the king's life was in danger.

'Sir Michael,' he said at last, 'there is only one thing we can do. I will take one-third of our men and head off the Mamluks. You stay here with the rest and hold off their lancers as long as you can.'

'I fear that will not be long enough,' said the knight.

'Just do what you can. Once they break your line, disperse the men and try to find us in the forest. Hopefully, it will be enough to ensure the king reaches sanctuary.'

The knight stared at the Templar, both fully aware that it was unlikely any man still in the line when it broke would survive long enough to escape.

'So be it,' he said eventually and turned to address the watching men.

'First rank, retire to the command of Sir Jakelin,' he roared, 'the rest of you close in and prepare to defend the line.'

Everyone did as ordered and as Jakelin's allocation assembled a few paces to the rear, the Templar held out his arm to Sir Michael in a token of comradeship.

'Thank you, my friend,' he said, 'history will remember every man who fought and died here this day.'

The knight looked down at the proffered wrist and then back up to stare into Jakelin's eyes. The look was one of resignation, but his words were strong.

'We do this not for you nor scholars of history,' he said,' but because it is our duty to the king and to God. Now go before we change our minds.'

Jakelin withdrew his arm and nodded silently. Though the knight's refusal would usually be deemed rude, it warranted no judgement, coming as it did from someone almost certainly fated to die within the next few minutes.

'God be with you,' he said simply and turned to race up the hill, closely followed by his allocated men.

'My Lord,' shouted one of the men alongside King Baldwin's litter, 'the enemy is closing on our right flank.'

Everyone turned to see the Mamluk horde clambering over the last of the rocks to the right and it was soon obvious they would block off the escape route long before the king's group could reach safety.

'Form a cordon,' shouted one of the defending knights, 'defend the king at all costs.'

Everyone ran to place themselves between the king's litter and the black-clad attackers determined to sell their lives dearly, but all knew it was a hopeless task, they would just be no match for Mamluks.

Down below Jakelin and his reinforcements doubled their efforts.

'*It's no use,*' gasped one of the men at his side, 'we'll never make it.'

Jakelin paused and looked up the slope. The knight was correct, they were just too far away. His heart sunk as he realised there was no way they were going to get to the king in time. He let out a roar of frustration and was about to continue when another voice rang out.

'My Lord,' look to the ridge.

Jakelin spun his head and saw a fully armed squadron of men galloping along the ridgeline, headed directly towards the king's position. For a few seconds, his heart sunk but then saw the flag flying at the head of the force. It was Humphrey of Toron and his men.

'*God be praised,*' he gasped as the patrol galloped past the king to engage the Mamluk.

'We are saved,' said one of the men but Jakelin knew different. The arrival of Humphrey and his men was indeed welcome, but it bought them time only. They were still heavily outnumbered, and it was only a matter of time until the main Saracen army overran their positions.

'Keep going,' he shouted, 'get to the king.'

Up above, Humphreys men smashed into the Mamluk infantry, but the enemy was well trained and more than a match for the Christian cavalry. Heavy fighting broke out again, but it gave Jakelin time to reach the king's litter.

'Why have you stopped?' he shouted, 'you need to keep going.'

'My men need to rest,' gasped the knight in charge, 'they are as exhausted as you.'

'To stop is to die,' said Jakelin, 'keep going.'

The men got to their feet but had gone only a few more paces when one of the poles supporting the litter snapped, sending the king tumbling to the ground.

'Your Grace,' shouted William and ran to his side.

'Get off me,' snapped Baldwin, 'I am unhurt.'

'Your Grace,' said Jakelin,' you'll have to walk the rest of the way.'

'Aye,' nodded the king and turned to start walking up the hill but Jakelin could see he was in a terribly weakened state.

'Are you mad,' shouted William to Jakelin, 'can you not see he is ill?'

'What's going on here,' shouted a voice and everyone turned to see Humphrey of Toron approaching alongside one of his knights, Rénier de Maron. 'You need to get going,' he continued, reining in his horse. 'We can't hold them much longer.'

'The litter has broken,' shouted William, 'and the king is too weak to walk.'

Humphrey looked around in desperation. His own men were just about holding out but down below he could see the first of the Ayyubid cavalry had already breached the defensive line.

'We have no more time,' he said and turned to the knight riding at his side.

'Sir Darius,' he said, you have the strength of two men, and we are out of options. Leave your horse here and carry the king up the last of the slope? I and your fellows will fight as rear guard.'

'Aye, my lord,' said the knight, and dismounted before walking over to Baldwin.

'Wait,' shouted William, 'you cannot lay hands on the King of Jerusalem.'

'What would you have us do?' roared Humphrey, 'it is either this or see him fall into the hands of the enemy. Make your mind up, priest, for we are a heartbeat from defeat.'

'William,' said the king weakly. 'These men know what they are doing. Let them do what has to be done.'

'So be it.' said William turning to face Sir Humphrey, 'but I hold you personally responsible if he comes to any harm.'

Without pausing further, the knight turned towards Baldwin.

'Forgive me, Your Grace,' he said and leaned forward to lift the king into his arms.

'Just get on with it,' said Baldwin from his undignified position.

Without further ado, the knight started trotting uphill, along with his royal burden.

'Well,' shouted Humphrey, 'what are you waiting for, they will need your protection before this day is done.'

The rest of the men followed the knight leaving Jakelin standing alone alongside Humphrey.

'You too, Templar,' said Humphrey.

'I still have fight left in me,' said Jakelin.

'I suspect you have fulfilled your duty more than most,' said Humphrey staring at the blood-soaked knight, 'and besides, is your oath not to God and the king?'

'To God and the protection of Christianity,' said Jakelin.

'Well the King of the Christians in Jerusalem needs your help,' said Humphrey, 'so I suggest you get going.'

'And you?'

'I will do what I can back here. We will meet again you and me, of that I am sure but for now, you have a king to protect and I, Saracens to kill. Fare ye well, Templar.'

Jakelin watched him go and knew Humphrey was right. He was nearing the last of his strength and would be no use against fresher men. He turned to face uphill and with a deep breath, followed the rest of the king's bodyguard up to the tree line.

For the next hour or so, the Christians fought desperately for their lives as the Saracen forces poured up the hill. Jakelin and the king's guard managed to reach the trees due to the bravery of Humphrey and his men but even then, the assault did not stop. Mamluk foot soldiers followed them in and the fighting continued, hand to hand.

Darius ploughed on relentlessly, slowed by neither obstacle nor fatigue. Around them ran the terrified servants and Baldwin's personal bodyguard while the remainder of the patrol sought to slow their pursuers. Everyone was exhausted and Jakelin knew they could not go much further.

'Enough,' he shouted eventually, as they saw a pile of rocks in a clearing. 'We will go firm here.'

'Why?' asked William.

'Because our men are spread out over too far an area. If we reform our lines here, we can hold out until dark.'

'But they are too many.'

'They won't send their cavalry in here,' said Jakelin. 'The ground is uneven and to do so means losing too many horses. If they come, they will do so on foot and I still maintain Christian knights are more than a match for Saracens in single combat.'

'We should keep going,' said William, 'at least until nightfall.'

'William,' said the king, now sitting on the ground and leaning against a fallen tree, 'Sir Jakelin is right. We can go no further. Recall our men but know this. If the Saracens come in great numbers, I will seek negotiations with their commander.'

'*A surrender?*' gasped Jakelin.

'Too many men have died in my name,' said Baldwin. 'Enough is enough. Call the men in, Sir Jakelin.'

Jakelin sought out one of the signalers and the sound of a horn resonated amongst the trees. Those already in the clearing set about creating a makeshift barrier by felling smaller trees. If nothing else, it would at least slow any attackers down.

Slowly, one by one the stragglers appeared and joined their comrades amongst the rocks. By nightfall, there were almost two hundred exhausted men forming the flimsiest of cordons around the king, but it was the best they could do.

Gradually the forest fell quiet and despite the risk, many of the men succumbed to their exhaustion.

'Let them sleep,' said Jakelin when the problem was pointed out by one of the men, 'at least for a little while. There are enough of us with eyes peeled.'

'You should get some rest yourself, 'said the knight, 'you have done more than most.'

'In a while,' said Jakelin.

The following morning the sound of hopeful voices murmured amongst the rocks. The anticipated attack had not materialized in the night and though they were not yet safe, they were in far better shape than they had been only hours earlier.

'Sir Jakelin,' said a voice and Jakelin turned to see Baldwin walking towards him.

'Your Grace,' said Jakelin standing up. 'How are you this morning?'

'As well as can be expected,' said the king. What do you think happens now?'

'I'm not sure,' said Jakelin, 'but I'll go and check the valley. If it is clear, we'll see about heading back to Jacob's Ford.'

'What about our dead and wounded?'

'We are in no state to recover the dead,' said Jakelin, 'but will take the wounded with us. It will be difficult but doable.'

'Why do you think they stopped?'

'I have no idea,' said Jakelin, 'but we must thank the Lord that they did. We were a whisker away from being routed.'

'My Lord,' shouted a voice, 'someone's coming.'

They looked over to the trees at the edge of the clearing and saw fifty or so men walking towards them. All were exhausted and most carried wounds of some sort. In the centre, four men carried another on a makeshift stretcher.

'Who are they?' asked the king.

'I believe they are Sir Humphrey's men,' said Jakelin, 'or what's left of them.' He walked out to greet the survivors, pausing when he recognised one of the stretcher-bearers.

'Hunter,' he said, 'you are still alive.'

'I don't die easily,' said hunter and the four men lowered the stretcher to the ground.

Jakelin looked down, recognising the wounded man on the stretcher. Lord Humphrey of Toron.

'What happened to him?' he asked.

'His chest has been sliced open by a scimitar,' replied Hunter, 'and he took two arrows to his back but still he fought. It was only when he was hamstrung by a Saracen knife did he fall. We have stitched his wounds and removed the shafts, but the arrowheads are still beneath his flesh. He is in a bad way.'

Jakelin looked down to speak to Humphrey but he was unconscious.

'Take him amongst the rocks,' said Jakelin. 'Our medic has been killed but we will see what we can do for him.' He turned away and returned to the king.

'Your Grace, I'm going to see if it's safe to move out. I'll be as quick as I can.'

'You do that,' said Baldwin, 'but make sure you return. Without you, I feel our chances of reaching Chastellet are significantly less.'

Jakelin bowed and turned away, beckoning Hunter to join him.

An hour later, they both stood at the top of the valley where the main battle had taken place. Below them the hillside was littered with bodies, the crows already feasting on the eyes of the dead.

'It makes no sense,' said Jakelin, 'they had us beaten. Why withdraw at the last moment when the king was almost in their hands?'

'I know why,' said Hunter, 'look.' He pointed along the valley and in the distance, they could see a strong Christian column riding up the road. The heavy cloaks of the first fifty riders stood out in the morning sun, pure white embossed with a red cross, and above them flew the Baucent, the war flag of the Knights Templar.

'It's Grand Master Amand,' said Jakelin, 'the Saracens must have seen them coming and withdrew from the field.'

'It's a bit late,' said Hunter, 'we needed them yesterday, not now when the fighting is done.'

'Such is the way of war, my friend,' said Jakelin. 'Fret not for what might have been but rejoice in their arrival.'

A while later, Grand Master Amand and his Marshal stood before the king, relating how the Saracen force that had initially drawn them away had been nothing more than a decoy and they had pursued them to no avail.

The king listened intently and though he was unimpressed with how easily the Grand Master had fallen for the ruse, did not pursue the matter.

'What is done, is done,' he said after hearing the Templar's report. 'What matters now is what are we going to do about it?'

'I'll make sure you get back safely, Your Grace,' said Amand, 'and then we will seek out the pigs that did this to you with no quarter given.'

'No,' snapped Baldwin. 'Our forces are too few at Chastellet. Take me back to Tiberius where I can recruit more men to replace those we have lost. In addition, send dispatches to Raymond of Tripoli and tell him to assemble an army in my name.'

'To what end, Your Grace?' said Amand.

'Farrukh-Shah will see this as a great victory,' said the king, 'and even as we speak, I suspect he is heading west towards to continue Saladin's plan. If that is the case, we need to be ready for him.'

'Farrukh-Shah was responsible for this?' asked Amand.

'I suspect so,' said Baldwin. 'Saladin would never have let us escape so easily.'

'So where is Saladin?' asked Amand.

'I have no idea,' said Baldwin, 'but I would wager he is somewhere near.'

The following day, the ravaged column headed back the way they had come. Less than half of the men who had set out from Chastellet still lived and many of those carried wounds. Most of the horses had either been taken by the Ayyubid or had scattered during the battle but the few Jakelin and his men had managed to round up were allocated to any man still able to fight. The remainder walked while the most seriously injured lay in the looted carts that had previously carried the possessions of the king on the way out.

The Templar force under the command of the Grand Master had split in two, one half to the front and the rest to the rear, determined to protect the column should they come under further attack. For hours the column headed westward, heading for Tiberius and despite William of Tyre's protestations, the king insisted on sharing his wagon with the wounded.

The pace was slow but as the day progressed, the tension eased as they got closer and closer to Tiberius. By the time nightfall came, they were over halfway to their destination and had made camp under the shelter of an escarpment overhang with only one possible approach, a location that Amand and his men found far easier to protect.

King Baldwin and William sat behind a few boulders, away from the prying eyes of the rest of the men. One of the two surviving servants applied what ointments they had left to the king's open sores while the other washed his used bandages in a leather bucket of cold water. It had been a hard journey so far but at least they were alive.

'Your Grace,' said one of the servants quietly, 'the Grand Master approaches.'

'See what he wants, William,' said the king, 'I am too tired for discourse.'

'Of course, Your Grace,' said the prelate and got to his feet before heading out to meet the Templar.

'Grand Master Amand,' he said blocking the path. 'How can I help you?'

'I want to talk to the king,' said Amand.

'The king is indisposed,' said William. 'You can talk to me in his stead.'

'My words are for the king,' said Amand and barged past the prelate.

'*What do you think you are doing?*' shouted William reaching out to grab the Templar's cloak but Amand pulled clear and marched around to where Baldwin was sitting.

'Your Grace,' he said coming to a halt, 'I have grievous news.'

'You have no right to do this,' shouted William catching up with the knight, 'just who do you think you are?'

Baldwin lifted his hand to silence his advisor.

'Your Grace,' continued Amand, 'a rider just arrived from Chastellet. Last night the castle was attacked.'

Chapter Twenty-Six

March – AD 1179

The Castle of Chastellet

Thirty leagues away, Simon of Syracuse marched along the outer wall of the castle, bedecked in full chainmail. In his hand, he carried a shield though his sword was still sheathed. Alongside him came Sir Rénier de Maron, his appointed Under-Marshal.

At the base of the heavily manned wall lay dozens of dead Saracens, the result of an unsuccessful attack the night before where a hundred Ayyubid had attacked the castle gates under the cover of darkness.

'Are the gates now secured?' demanded the castellan without looking at his Under-Marshal.

'Aye, my lord,' said Rénier, struggling to keep up. 'The carpenters have worked the night through to install the locking bars. That should be enough for now, but we are constructing more as we speak.'

'And the portcullis?'

'It won't be ready for a few days. It is ready to be fitted but the masons need to finish the channels.'

'I want it done by tomorrow at the latest,' snapped Simon. 'We have no time to waste.'

He looked down to the base of the wall, seeing one of their own men lying amongst the Saracen bodies.

'Who's that?'

'I don't know his name, 'said the Under-Marshal, 'he fell to a Saracen archer last night.'

'Any other casualties?'

'One more dead,' said Rénier, 'and seven wounded. One of those will likely die before the day is done.'

'And the civilians?'

'Some have dispersed but most are in the inner bailey. We have enough food and water for a month if needed, but after that, we will have to resort to horse meat.'

'It won't come to that,' said Simon, 'there is no way they can maintain a siege more than a few days.'

'Why not?'

'Because I have sent messages to the king along with all the castellans within fifty leagues. There will be reinforcements riding this way within days so all we have to do is hold the enemy out until they arrive.'

'I thought the king was on campaign?'

'He is but is only a few days hard march away. I have no doubt he will about-face and head back with all haste as soon as he gets the message.' He looked down at the bodies at the base of the wall. 'Tell me how this happened.'

'There was a commotion in the workers camp,' said Rénier, 'and everybody's attention was turned upon the outcome.'

'Even our sentries?'

'Aye. By the time someone realised what was happening, there were Saracens upon the scaffolding. Luckily, we are well manned, and our men dispatched them in short order.'

'We were fortunate,' said Simon, 'nothing more. I want those who neglected their duties punished heavily.'

'Exile my lord?'

'No, that is too easy. Have them whipped and placed on heavy duties for a month.'

'And the guard commander?'

'That is different,' said Simon. He paused and watched as a unit of twelve heavily armoured knights left the castle by the postern gate and headed out to retrieve the body of the man who had been killed in the night.

'That man is only dead because one of our own men neglected his duties,' he continued eventually, 'and it is only by the grace of God that hundreds more have not shared his fate. Chastellet itself could have fallen had it not been for his divine intervention. There is a war in front of us, Sir Rénier, and we cannot afford any more mistakes.'

'Your recommendation?'

The castellan turned to face the Under-Marshal.

'We need to set an example,' he said, 'tell the carpenters to build gallows.'

Deep in the heart of a forest a few leagues away, Salah ad-Din sat cross-legged with Shirkuh ad-Din and Sabek ad-Din. Alongside them sat Abu al-Qassim, the Emir tasked with the assault on Chastellet the night before. The Sultan waited patiently as the Emir gave his report.

'I hear that we lost a dozen of our warriors with little return,' said Shirkuh ad-Din.

'It is true that twelve men were martyred,' replied the Emir, 'but their lives were not wasted. Their sacrifice will be repaid a thousand-fold when the walls fall.'

'What did you learn?'

'While our men assaulted the east wall, others got close enough to inspect the rest of the defences.' He leaned forward and drew a square in the sand. 'This is the main castle. The walls are almost completed and stand the height of seven men. They are heavily built and though there is only one tower completed, any assault would be easily repelled, causing the loss of countless lives.'

'Can they be destroyed with siege engines?' asked Shirkuh ad-Din.

'No, my lord, or at least not quickly. The walls slope steeply at the base as is the way of the Christian builders so even if the walls above are destroyed, our men would still flounder at the base, easy targets for archers.'

'This much we already know,' said Salah ad-Din, 'tell me our warriors did not die for information already in our possession.'

'Not at all, my lord,' said Abu al-Qassim, and drew another square outside the first. 'This is the outer wall surrounding the castle. It is a timber palisade backed with an embankment of earth. Any concerted attack would see it easily destroyed.'

'Even so,' said Shirkuh ad-Din, 'once inside the outer perimeter, how are we to breach the main walls?'

Abu al-Qassim looked between the other three men. He had carried out the task required of him with minimal losses but had no answers to the main question.

'There must be a way, 'said Salah ad-Din and turned to face the generals. 'Sabek ad-Din, you have eyes within the castle. Can our songbird not provide us with more information?'

'He could have,' said Sabek ad-Din, 'but he is now within the castle itself so has no way to send a message.'

'The Christian is quick enough to take Ayyubid gold,' said Salah ad-Din, 'and so far, has provided minimal benefit. Perhaps now is the time for him to prove his worth. Can you contact him?'

'We can,' said Sabek ad-Din,' but for him to respond risks his identity being revealed.'

'He is a man with no honour,' snapped Shirkuh ad-Din, 'we will lose no sleep if he dies at the hands of his own kind.'

'Nor I,' said Sabek ad-Din, 'I only voice concern because if he is discovered, we may never get another bird who is willing to sing so loudly.'

Salah ad-Din fell silent, his gaze going between the three men.

'It is a price I am willing to pay,' he said eventually. 'Nothing takes precedence over the fall of this fortress and I have no doubt that many will die before this matter ends. Send your message, Sabek ad-Din. Let the Christian traitor earn his blood money.'

In Chastellet, Simon of Syracuse stood in the upper bailey, looking down at the developing situation below. Four men stood stripped to the waist; their heads bowed as they awaited their fate. A fifth was already tied to a post, his mouth dry with fear. Behind him stood a giant of a man holding a whip formed from a timber handle with a plaited thong of dried leather hanging from the end.

The Under-Marshal walked through the gathered soldiers and civilians and made his way to the centre before turning to address the crowd.

'Last night,' he announced, 'the lives of everyone inside this castle were put at risk because a few men failed to do their duty and it is only by a holy miracle that we are here to tell the tale. These men,' he said his voice rising as he pointed to the prisoners, 'are the guilty parties and they should be thankful that they are not dancing at the end of a rope. That is what they deserve but the castellan in his mercy has decreed that each will receive twenty lashes for every one of their fellows who died as a result of their failures.'

The man already tied to the post, swallowed hard as he realised he would be on the receiving end of sixty lashes. Most men rarely had more than a dozen and few survived fifty.

'Let this be a lesson to all,' continued the Under-Marshal and turned to face the first victim. 'Let the punishment commence.'

The castellan stared coldly down as each man took their place at the whipping post. The crowd fell silent as the crack of the whip rang out over the courtyard, accompanied by the associate cries of pain from the victims. After the first dozen lashes, each victim fell silent as they fell into unconsciousness, only to be revived by having a bucket of water thrown over them. By the time the punishment ended, the ground at the base of the whipping post had turned into a blood-soaked quagmire and at least one of the men had drawn their last breath.

Sir Simon watched as the body was dragged away but turned to see Thomas Cronin walking towards him.

'My Lord,' said the sergeant, 'there is something you should see.'

The castellan followed Cronin, coming to a stop on the wall overlooking the hills to the north.

'There,' said Cronin and pointed to a wooded hilltop in the distance. For a few moments, Simon could see nothing and then, suddenly, there it was, a series of flashes from high on the ridge.

'A signal,' he said, eventually. 'Someone is using a mirror to send a message.'

'The light is directed at us,' said Cronin, 'of that I am sure. It has been flashing for quite a while. It must be the Saracens but why would they be signalling the Castle?'

'I don't know,' said the castellan, 'but call the garrison to arms, I'm taking no chances.'

For the rest of the day, every man in Chastellet took turns up on the ramparts, each as alert as they could be after witnessing the punishment of those who had failed their duty the night before. Finally, night came again and though the outer wall glowed in the light of a hundred burning torches, the upper bailey fell deeper into shadow as the sun disappeared and the clouds covered what little moonlight there had been.

Hours passed and only the sound of the men returning from their stints on the walls broke the silence.

At the far end of the upper bailey, Ramaz looked nervously around him, his heart racing at the danger he was in. His eyes flitted everywhere, suspicious of every movement until finally, the man he had been waiting for joined him in the darkness, his head covered by the hood of a heavy cloak.

'What took you so long?' whispered Ramaz.

'None of your business,' said the newcomer, 'what do you want?'

'My master wants information.'

'What sort of information?'

'He wants to know the weak points of the castle walls.'

'*What?*' gasped the hooded man, 'I'm not going to tell him that.'

'We have no option.' said Ramaz, 'you know what he is capable of.'

'Saladin is an honourable man. He will not sanction the assassination of an ally.'

'*I'm not talking about Saladin,*' hissed Ramaz, 'I'm talking about Sabek ad-Din. He will cut our throats as soon as look at us.'

'I have an agreement,' said the hooded man, 'and have honoured my side of the bargain. In a couple of months, I will be gone from here and your master can do whatever he wants.'

'It's not,' enough said Ramaz. 'He wants information or the agreement is off. The money will disappear, and your identity will be revealed to your masters.'

'*This is a betrayal,*' hissed the first man again. 'I will not do it.'

'Wait,' said Ramaz running to catch the man up as he walked away. 'One last time, that's all we ask. Furnish him with this information and there will be no more requests, I swear.'

The hooded man dragged Ramaz back into the shadows. 'You do not know that,' he said. 'This will never end.'

'I do,' said Ramaz. 'They have promised that if you do this, they will double your purse and never ask anything of you again. In addition, in the event the castle falls, as it will, they have promised safe passage to any place of your choice.'

The man stared at the overseer. The lure of more money was tempting but his conscience gnawed at him like a hungry rat.

'I cannot tell him any fault of the castle itself,' he said, 'for there is none, but I will say this. If it was I who sought a way to bring the fortress down, I would start by looking between the southern walls. Now never contact me again.'

'What is he looking for?' hissed Ramaz as the man walked away, but it was too late, the informer had already disappeared into the shadows.

Frustrated, Ramaz skulked off into the night. The meeting had been risky, but the hardest part was yet to come. Keeping to the shadows he headed to a quiet corner and scraped away some earth to reveal a small box. Inside were several pieces of parchment, a quill, a small bottle of ink and strangest of all, a bird's skull. Quickly he wrote a message and placed it inside the bird's skull before hiding it within his thawb and replacing everything else back where it had been. Knowing there was nothing more he could do until daylight, he headed back to the overcrowded tent allocated to him and the other overseers.

The following morning, Ramaz reported for duty with the rest of the workforce. Despite the high level of alert through the night, no attack had come, and the castle was returning to a semblance of normality. The huge amount of people within the fortress meant that the unfinished well struggled to meet the demand for water and many of the labourers were tasked with bringing a constant supply from the River Jordan in the valley below. Over and over again, Ramaz made the trip down to the river but each time returned having been unable to do what he had to do. Finally, in the late afternoon, he found himself away from the others with no knights within sight. Quickly he retrieved the bird's skull from beneath his clothes and wedged it in the fork of a tree next to the ford before heading back up the hill to the castle. His work was done.

Later that night, Sabek ad-Din once more stood in front of Saladin. In his hands was the note written by Ramaz the previous night.

'So, the bird has sung,' said Saladin.

'He has,' said the general. 'Though the message is unclear. He says find the route between the outer and inner walls on the southern side.'

'Do we know what he means?'

'We do not and need to get closer to find out.'

'And how do you intend to do that?' asked Saladin.

'There is only one way, my lord,' said Sabek ad-Din, 'we must breach the outer wall.'

Chapter Twenty-Seven

March – AD 1179

Chastellet

Sir Simon of Syracuse was fast asleep when the alarm came, horns and bells mingling with shouts of fear resounding around the castle summoning the garrison to arms.

Immediately he jumped up and grabbing his chainmail with one hand and his sword belt with the other, ran out of the tent to head towards the outer walls.

'What's happening?' he roared as he ran, 'Someone brief me.'

'My Lord,' shouted one of the knights,' the Saracens are attacking the southern wall.'

'At night?' gasped the castellan pulling his hauberk over his head. 'What are they playing at?'

'I don't know,' said the knight, 'but they are everywhere. 'This is no feint, my lord, it looks like the entire Saracen army is out there.'

As if in response to his comment, the air suddenly lit up with hundreds of flaming arrows, flying over their heads to land in the lower bailey of the castle.

'Fire,' shouted dozens of voices as many of the tents caught aflame, 'bring water.'

Simon continued out through the gate to the outer palisades and climbed the ladder to the ramparts. At the top, Rénier de Maron marched back and forth, his voice echoing in the night as he directed the defenders. Immediately Simon could see the scale of the attack and knew they were in trouble. Outside, hundreds of men raced from the trees, many carrying scaling ladders. Behind them, rows of Saracen archers kept the defenders' heads down with volley after volley of iron-tipped arrows.

'What's going on?' shouted Simon as he neared Rénier de Maron.

'I don't know where they came from,' said Rénier, 'but we have seen no sign of any siege engines. Without Mangonels there is no way they can even think of breaching the inner walls. It seems they seek conflict for the sake of it.'

Simon peered over the palisade. He knew his men would put up a good fight but the wooden walls were far from finished and were difficult to defend. The structure of the main castle, on the other hand, had already reached its full height and was impregnable at the base. It would be far easier to defend and would cost far fewer lives.

'Listen,' he said to Sir Rénier. 'There is little point in losing men for this unfinished wall. Fight back as long as you can but if it looks like we are to be breached, withdraw immediately. We will be far better placed behind the walls of the main castle.'

'Are you sure, my lord?' asked Rénier. 'We can make a stand here.'

'We have reinforcements already on their way,' said the castellan. 'It's pointless losing men for no reason. I'll take half back up to the main battlements and cover your withdrawal from there, out here there is only death, for nothing but a wall of wood and a few paces of rock. They cannot get into Chastellet, so let the castle do what it is designed to do.'

Before the Under-Marshal could respond, the castellan turned and walked away, calling many of the men away from the palisade as he went.

Within minutes, the main assault hit the walls. Saracen arrows hailed down, filling the night sky and most of the defenders were forced to take refuge beneath their shields. Siege ladders thumped against the wall and Saracen foot soldiers swarmed up onto the unfinished battlements. Rénier's men emerged from cover and stormed into the fray, fighting furiously to gain the advantage. Saracens fought Christians with no quarter shown, such was the savagery and men fell everywhere, their cries echoing in the night. For a while it looked like the defenders would prevail but as the Under-Marshal glanced over the wall, his heart sunk and he knew they could not emerge the victors. A few hundred paces away, waiting for their chance stood thousands more Saracens, each fully armed, waiting for their chance to attack. With half of his men already redeployed into the castle with the castellan, Rénier knew the time had come and ordered the signaller to sound the retreat.

Again the sound of a horn rang around the defences and as the castellan's archers on the higher ramparts of the inner fortress filled the air with their own arrows to cover the retreat, the men on the outer walls turned and fled towards the gates.

Rénier and his men ran through the giant gate and headed straight up to the battlements to spread out along the walls. Immediately he could see the sense in the withdrawal and looked down as the main Saracen army poured over the outer walls.

'I still don't understand it,' he said to Simon, 'why does he commit so many men to a strip of land of no use to him? Without siege engines, it is nought but a waste of men.'

'I don't know,' said Simon, 'but the tide has turned in our favour. They are like trapped fish in a barrel and we should not waste this opportunity.' He turned to call out along the parapet. 'All archers to the wall,' he called, 'never will you have easier targets.'

Every archer jostled for a place as squires and servants ran behind them with baskets of arrows.

'Give me one of those,' said Rénier as a boy passed carrying two spare crossbows. He took a bolt from one of the baskets and loaded up the bow.

Down in the killing zone, the Saracen archers continued their rain of arrows though this time, their targets were much higher and their intended victims much harder to see. Other warriors ran forward to the gates carrying buckets of pitch to set the fires. Others carried bundles of bracken and wood to fuel the flames but even though many succeeded in reaching the gates, those above knew it was nowhere near enough.

'My Lord,' shouted Abu al-Qassim, lifting his shield to block a Christian arrow, 'we have secured the ground. What do we seek?'

Sabek ad-Din looked down from the parapet recently torn from the possession of the Christians. His gaze searched the killing ground, desperate to find what it was the songbird had referred to in his note, but he saw nothing. Time was running out as his men were succumbing to the constant hail of arrows from above. He knew he had to make a decision.

'Allah uncover my eyes,' he whispered. All around the outer bailey, dead and dying lay on the rocky floor, surrounded by thousands of arrows from both sides. Dozens more bounced off the rocks, sent spinning sideways amongst the attackers.

'My Lord,' shouted Abu al-Qassim again, lowering his shield, 'what are your orders?'

High up above, Rénier de Maron saw the Emir lower his shield and seizing the opportunity, lifted his crossbow to his shoulder. He aimed carefully, easing his breath and lowering his heartbeat. He knew he was an excellent shot, but the distance meant he would have to allow for the drop of the bolt. Gently he pulled the trigger and with a thud of released tension from the twisted bowstring, the bolt flew down through the night air.

'My Lord', roared Abu al-Qassim again, 'my men are getting slaughtered, *'what are your orders?'*

Sabek ad-Din looked down but before he could respond, the Emir staggered forward and fell to his knees. For a moment his gaze remained on the general before he fell forward, a crossbow bolt embedded deep into his back.

Sabek ad-Din stared in shock as a pool of blood grew around the dead emir's body, but slowly his look of horror changed to confusion and he looked sharply around the rest of the killing field. Realising the difference his head spun back around, and he stared down at the Emir again though this time not directly at the dying man, but at the forest of arrows embedded deep into the ground around him.

'That's it,' he gasped to himself, 'it's the ground. It's softer!' Without waiting a moment longer, he turned to his signaler. *'Sound the retreat,'* he roared, 'we have what we came for.'

Several hours later, Sabek ad-Din once again stood before Salah ad-Din and Shirkuh ad-Din.

'I hear you were successful in your mission,' said the sultan.

'I was, my lord. At first, I was blinded but Allah himself became my eyes and the knowledge was revealed.'

'So you found the weakness in the walls?'

'No, my lord, for there is no weakness, they are truly formidable. But Allah in his wisdom has given us a different route.' He paused and looked between the two men. 'My Lords, the castle is built on a rocky crag on solid foundations, but on the spot where Abu al-Qassim fell, the ground is soft and easily worked. We don't go over the walls, or even through them, we go under them.'

Salah ad-Din stared at the general, his heart lifting at the revelation. Tunnelling had been discounted previously because of it would have taken just too long to cut through the bedrock, and Christian reinforcements would probably arrive before they could get halfway, but the news that there was an area of soft ground meant his sappers could quickly reach the foundations and set fires to bring the walls down.

'*Allah, Akbar,*' he said quietly.

'My Lord,' said Shirkuh ad-Din. 'What do you wish us to do?'

'We will withdraw,' said Salah ad-Din, 'and pick our moment carefully.'

'My Lord,' said Sabek ad-Din, 'should we not press our advantage while the castle is weakened?'

'No,' said Salah ad-Din. 'Our sappers are in Damascus and besides, I have just received news that Farrukh-Shah has failed in his attempt to capture Baldwin and the Christians are on their way back, along with the Templar column.'

'The Templars do not scare me,' said Sabek ad-Din, 'they die just like all men.'

'They should scare you,' said Salah ad-Din, 'and you are wrong. They do not die like all men; they are devils that fight on until they are hacked apart and their body parts scattered to the four winds. Even then I would not turn my back upon them.'

'So, what are your plans?' asked Shirkuh ad-Din.

'We will withdraw to the forests of Banias,' said Salah ad-Din, 'and send for more men. In the meantime, Farrukh-Shah has headed west and will ravage the lands of Sidon. This will not be countenanced by the king and he will no doubt retaliate. When he does, we will be waiting.'

Chapter Twenty-Eight

May – AD 1179

Chastellet

  Brother Cronin headed across the upper bailey and headed for the Templar Commandery, one of the few areas now completed within the castle walls. The buildings within the enclosure consisted of a stable block, a barracks, a kitchen and mess hall along with the obligatory chapel, all constructed from timber until such time as they could be replaced with stone.
  At his side walked Hassan, now fully recovered from his ordeal in the desert. The boy was growing stronger by the day, but his demeanour had changed and was a concern to Cronin.
  'I have a surprise for you,' said Cronin as they walked, 'today you, along with the other squires will be allowed into the hall for the briefing.'
  'But I am no squire,' said Hassan.
  'You may not bear the formal title,' said Cronin, 'but there is no other person that fulfils the necessary requirements as well as you. The Grand Master himself has granted permission and I reckon it is just a matter of time until the position is yours by right.'
  'My Lord,' said Hassan after a few moment's silence, 'there is something you should know.'
  'What's that?' asked Cronin without breaking stride.
  'My Lord,' said Hassan again, 'there are things in my life that you do not know, things that have happened these past few months that have changed my view on the world.'
  Cronin stopped and turned to stare at Hassan.
  'What do you mean?'
  'When I was searching for you,' said Hassan, 'I spent a long time in a camp out in the desert. There I mingled with people of my own race, speaking the language of my childhood, eating the food I remember. For a while, I was desperate to leave but the chief knew better and made me stay until I was stronger. With every moment I stayed, my devotion to your service grew weaker and I fear if I had stayed any longer, I may have abandoned my search.'

'But you did not,' said Cronin, 'and that's the reason I am standing here.'

'I know, my lord, but I was tempted and that's what worries me.'

'Why,' asked Cronin, 'you overcame the temptation?'

'I did, but though my mind says I did the right thing, my heart aches to return.'

Cronin stared in surprise. For almost two years, ever since he had met the boy on the dockside in Acre, Hassan had declared only one interest, to become a squire to one of the Templar knights.

'I don't understand,' he said eventually, 'you are closer to your dream than ever. Why would you change your mind so easily?'

'I don't know,' said Hassan. 'It is not something I welcome but it is a pull that I feel when I finally lay down my head at night, greeting me again with my first breath of the day.'

'And do you intend to act upon this impulse?'

'I do not yet know,' said Hassan. 'I ask God every day to guide my will, but he has remained silent on the matter.'

'Free choice is a gift from God,' said Cronin. 'I think perhaps he waits until you know yourself what will make you happy.'

'I want to serve him,' said Hassan, 'I truly do, but my allegiance is also to you. This extra desire adds only confusion. I know not what to do.'

'Only you will know the answer,' said Cronin

'There is another deadline, my lord,' said Hassan, 'something else that clouds my judgement.'

'And that is?' asked Cronin.

'A girl,' said Hassan, 'one with eyes like the prettiest flower and hair that floats on the slightest breeze. Her smile lights up the dawn better than any sun and she is as gentle as a lamb. I fear I may be losing my heart to her.'

'I think you already have,' said Cronin, 'yet still you hesitate. I suggest that you take the time to consider everything before making your mind up. You are still young and there is no deadline, at least not until the Grandmaster allows you to take the oath of the order.'

'There was a time when I dreamed of that day,' said Hassan, 'now I think of it with dread.'

Cronin sighed and looked at the boy. Even though Hassan was now a Christian, he knew that the pressures of being Bedouin born was a conflict he faced on a daily basis.

'Come,' he said at last, 'there are no decisions to be made out here. We will go to the briefing and face whatever the day brings.' He tapped the boy on the shoulder, and they turned to head into the hall together.

Seven leagues away, King Baldwin stood gazing out of a window in his chambers, listening in silence as William of Tyre read the latest dispatches from the various lords and barons around the kingdom of Jerusalem.

Since the defeat in the cattle fields to the south of Damascus, he had hardly left Tiberius, knowing that he had little strength to walk, let alone fight. Instead, he had dispatched Eudes de St. Amand and his Templars back to Chastellet, determined to discourage any further attempt on the castle by the Saracens. The brief assault several weeks earlier had been strange, but nevertheless a reminder that they were constantly at risk and they needed to push ahead with the completion of the castle.

Eventually, William came to the last of the parchments and cut open the seal to unfurl the document.

'Your Grace,' he said, 'yet another from Sir Reginald of Sidon. He says that the raids on the farms and villages within his lordship continue and he struggles to defend them from the attentions of the Saracens. He begs reinforcements else his people may not meet the tithe.'

'It's the work of Farrukh-Shah,' said Baldwin, 'and Sir Reginald is correct, we cannot allow him to continue unchecked. However, Raymond of Tripoli has reported that he has recruited well and is now only days away from being able to field an army of considerable size. I have already sent a messenger to Grand Master Amand at Chastellet and commanded him to join us at the castle at Beaufort ten days hence along with the strongest force he can muster.'

'Is that wise?' asked William

'In what way?'

'To leave Chastellet with a weakened garrison.'

'The inner walls of the castle are now at full height,' said the king, 'and even though the towers are yet to be built, it is more than strong enough to repel any assault. Was not this proven when the Saracens last attacked?'

'It was but it was no prolonged siege.'

'And neither will be the next. We can be there within days if needs be and that is not enough time to bring down a fortress such as Chastellet.'

'You say, we,' said William, 'do you intend to join the campaign?'

'I do. '

'And are you sure you are strong enough?'

'I feel as well as I have in a long time,' lied the king, 'and yearn to be back in the saddle. I will take our own army to Beaufort and lead the fight against Farrukh-Shah. We have unfinished business, that man and I.'

'One more thing, Your Grace,' said William.' I have been having some thoughts about the traitor at Chastellet.'

'Go on,' said the king.

'Lately,' said William, 'I have had thoughts about whom it may be.'

'And do you have any ideas?'

'I do, but it may not be something you wish to hear.'

'Spit it out, William.'

'Your Grace, ask yourself this. Who choose the route to the cattle fields south of Damascus?'

'Grandmaster Amand,' said the king, 'at my direction.'

'And who was tasked with providing the first response in the event of an attack?'

'The Templars.'

'Aye, again the Templars. The very the same people who were absent when the attack came.'

'Where are you going with this, William?'

'Your Grace,' said the prelate, 'if you recall, it was Jakelin de Mailly, who told us that the Grand Master had left the column to pursue a Saracen patrol, leaving us undefended on the right flank.'

'It was, but only after receiving the information from one of our own scouts.'

'One of the T*emplar* scouts,' said William, correcting the king, 'and we only had his word for it.'

'What do you mean?'

'Did any of our own men actually see this Saracen force with their own eyes, or even hear the report directly from this unknown scout? Because I didn't, nor did any man I spoke to. Only the Templars seem to have any knowledge about the perceived risk.'

'Are you saying there was no Saracen patrol?'

'I don't know,' said William, 'it's possible.'

'But why would Amand pretend there was a risk if there was none?'

'Perhaps to keep us in one place,' said William. 'Is it not interesting that we stopped exactly where the Saracens had prepared the ambush?'

'But that doesn't make sense. He would be risking the lives of his own men for no reason.'

'Only a few were risked,' said William. 'The majority were with him several leagues away from the fighting, a convenient absence that remained the case until the following day when the battle was over. It is also very convenient that Saladin attacked Chastellet at the same time as the Templars were leagues away. How would he have assembled such a force so quickly if he had not been informed well in advance?'

'The attack was weak,' said the king, 'and easily repelled. I suspect they were just testing the defences.'

'I agree, but Saladin's warriors would have got nowhere near as close had the Templars been there to respond. There just seems to me that there are an awful lot of coincidences where Amand's influence could have had a large bearing on the outcome.'

'Eudes de St. Amand is one of the most loyal men I have met,' said the king. 'Yes, he can get above himself at times but his hatred for the Saracens is well known. Why would he now turn traitor?'

'Every man has his price,' said William. 'Perhaps his was met.'

'You make a compelling case, William,' said Baldwin, 'yet I cannot forget that you have long borne a grudge against him. Why I do not know but it is an issue that clouds your judgement. I have seen the man fight and bleed in service of the Lord and until the day I see his treachery with my own eyes, then I will trust him.'

'As you wish,' said the prelate with a nod,' I just hope it is a decision you do not come to regret.'

Back in Chastellet, Cronin and Hassan filed into the mess hall and sat on a bench at the rear. The other knights and their squires filed in to take their places until finally, the room was full. At the far end of the hall, Grand Master Eudes de St. Amand stood in quiet conversation with Brother Valmont and Brother Tristan.

Hassan looked around the hall in amazement. It was the first time he had seen all the Templar knights and brother sergeants in one place and the sight filled him with awe. Men who would usually pass him by without a second glance, now sat alongside him, waiting for the briefing to start. Some of the squires looked at Hassan with suspicion but those who had known him at Montgisard knew of his ability and nodded to him in welcome.

Hassan looked around the hall itself. Although it was only a few weeks old, it was already adorned with the emblems of the Templars and many weapons retrieved from various fields of battle hung from the walls and rafters, trophies claimed in the service of the lord.

'To your feet,' announced the Marshal as one of the chaplain brothers entered in his plain brown robe. Silence fell as the chaplain said a prayer before standing to one side, allowing Eudes de St. Amand to take his place.

'Be seated,' said Amand and waited until the noise died away.

'You have been summoned here,' he said, 'to be briefed on a campaign we are about to undertake on behalf of the king.' He started walking around the room, talking as he went. 'As you know, a few weeks ago, the king's column was ambushed near the forests of Banias by a Saracen army led by Saladin's nephew, Farrukh-Shah. It was a well-planned attack and the king was lucky to escape with his life. At the same time, another army led by one of the sultan's generals, Sabek ad-Din attacked Chastellet, an assault that we now believe was purely launched to gather intelligence. Eventually, they retreated but we have no idea what, if anything they learned.' He looked around the room. 'The point is,' he continued, 'both of these men, Farrukh-Sha and Sabek ad-Din, would not have attacked without the immediate and express order of Saladin himself, which means, he is close, and probably planning an attack on Chastellet itself.' A murmur rippled around the room. 'Now,' said Amand, 'it will be of no surprise to any man here that this castle is a thorn in the Sultan's side and will eventually become a target, but the fact that Saladin is already here means the assault may be sooner than we think. Work details have been doubled and though we have no fear that the walls can be breached, we cannot wait around until he decides that the time is right. We have to face him on our terms.' He turned to the Marshal. 'Brother Tristan, perhaps you could continue.'

'Of course, my lord,' said Tristan and walked over to stand before the gathered men.

'For a few weeks,' he said, 'Farrukh-Shah has ravaged the lands of Sidon, destroying farms and stealing anything he can get his hands on. The lord of Sidon has done what he can to limit the damage, but his forces are few and the Saracens are gaining the upper hand. '

He paused as grumblings of anger passed through the hall.

'However,' he continued, 'the tide is about to turn. Recently, we have come into the knowledge that Farrukh-Shah intends to head back east to sell his plunder in the markets of Damascus. Not only this, but we also know he intends to go via the valley known as Marj Ayum.'

Again, there was a reaction in the room, though this time one of determination and controlled rage.

'Therefore,' said the Marshal, raising his voice, 'tomorrow at dawn, we, as an order, will head out of Chastellet in full battle order. From here we will head to Beaufort Castle on the Litani river, there to meet the combined armies of King Baldwin and Sir Raymond of Tripoli. We will stay at Beaufort until we have confirmation that Farrukh-Shah is within striking distance, and when we have that, we will ride out to smite him in the name of our Lord, Jesus Christ.'

This time there was an uproar in the hall, with many men banging their fists on the table in agreement.

'There is something else,' he said when the noise had abated, 'something that leaves a bitter taste in the mouth. We all know what happened near Banias. Our Grandmaster led many of you with honour and bravery, each avowed to protect the king, and it was unfortunate circumstances that kept you away from the fight. Indeed, if things had been different and we were there at the point of ambush, Farrukh-Shah would probably already be dead. However, God moves in mysterious ways and that did not happen.

Now, men not worthy to wipe your shoes whisper in the shadows that we were afraid of the fight and kept away until the killing was done.'

'*No,*' shouted some of the men, getting to their feet, '*that's not true.*'

'*No, it is not true,*' roared Tristan in reply, 'and no man would dare repeat that accusation to any within this room without fear of violent retribution. But that is the burden being placed upon us, a burden we can only discard by proving them wrong. So, to that end, this time, there will be no chasing of shadows, nor will there be tactical withdrawals or feints of intention, this time they will feel the full force of Templar steel head-on, as did their fellows at Montgisard. This time, we will wade in Saracen blood and the name of Farrukh-Shah will be remembered only by those lamenting his death.'

This time every man in the room got to their feet and roared their approval.

'*I hereby charge every man present,*' roared Tristan, 'to get thee hence and prepare your equipment. Sharpen your blades, brothers and look to God for his blessing for tomorrow, *we ride to war.*'

The room erupted into roars of approval and squires climbed upon the tables, cheering wildly as the officers made their way through the mass of warriors to leave the hall, closely followed by the knights and then the sergeants.

Finally, only a few were left, and Cronin turned to speak to Hassan.

'I was wrong to say earlier that there was no rush for your decision,' he said, 'this makes all the difference. If you are to leave, then it must be this very night. I will not hold you back and you will go with my blessing, but if you remain, Hassan Malouf, you will ride to war alongside me.'

Hassan nodded silently and as Cronin left the mess hall, he turned to stare at the giant crucifix hanging on the far wall.

'My Lord, Jesus Christ,' he said quietly, 'guide me in thought and deed.'

The following morning, two hundred Templar knights stood alongside their horses in the upper bailey, along with the many sergeants and lancers attached to their unit. Most of the knights were attended by squires, each in control of their masters' weapons and spare horses while the sergeants shared servants between them. Cronin looked around for Hassan, but he was nowhere to be seen and the sergeant assumed he had made the choice to stay behind.

Eventually, the gates of the commandery opened and Grand Master Amand emerged riding his warhorse, flanked by the Marshal and Seneschal. Behind them came the banner bearers and they all rode through the assembled army to wait at the top of the slope leading down to the lower bailey.

The Marshal turned and faced the men.

'Brothers Templars, mount up,' he shouted and turned away to reclaim his place at the side of the Grand Master. When every man was in the saddle, Eudes de St. Amand raised his fist in the air and without turning around, gave the order everyone was waiting for, Brother Templars, *advance!'*

The impressive column wound their way slowly through the castle and out through the main gate. As they went, many workers stopped and stared at the impressive sight, some cheering while others just watched in silence, knowing that some may not be coming back. They rode down to cross the river but as Cronin waited his turn at the ford, another rider jostled into position beside him. Cronin turned to offer a rebuke but smiled when he saw it was Hassan.

'You decided to stay,' he said.

'I did,' said Hassan, 'for it would be traitorous for me to leave you in such a way.'

'I told you,' said Cronin, 'you are free to make your own choices.'

'I know, and this is my choice,' said Hassan. 'I will ride by your side until Christ's mass. When that day comes, I will say my goodbyes and head back to my own people. Only then will my conscience be clear.'

'That sounds like a good plan,' said Cronin.

'Do you not have a squire?' asked Hassan looking around.

'I do now,' said Cronin, urging his horse forward, 'come on, let's go to war.'

Chapter Twenty-Nine

June – AD 1179

The Litani River

Ten days later, Grand Master Amand and his Templars stood at the bottom of a valley, watering their horses from the Litani River. Further downstream they could see the flags of Jerusalem flying high over a tented camp while up above, lancers from the army of Raymond of Tripoli covered their flanks, allowing their comrades to drink in safety. King Baldwin, along with Raymond had already been at the river for several days and had established camps along its banks while their patrols sought any sign of Farrukh-Shah. The Saracen and his army were certainly in the area but by the time any Christian patrol could respond to a sighting or the scene of an attack, the perpetrators had already moved on, making it difficult to confront them.

Since leaving Chastellet, the Templars had also sent out scouts far and wide to try and find Farrukh-Shah with little success and had now linked up with King Baldwin and Raymond to create an impressive force of over five thousand men.

'My Lord,' said the Seneschal at the Grandmaster's side, 'look.'

Amand looked up to see two riders approaching, one of whom bore the king's standard.

'I have a message from the king,' announced one of the men, reining in his horse, 'you are to attend him immediately.'

'Do you know why?' asked Amand.

'I am not privy to the king's thoughts,' said the messenger, 'I'll tell him you are on your way.' Without waiting for an answer, the two men turned their horses around and headed back down the valley in a cloud of dust.

'Brother Tristan,' called Amand, 'send a patrol up to relieve Sir Raymond's men. We will set up camp here.'

'Aye, my lord,' said the Marshal.

'Brother Valmont,' said Amand turning to the Seneschal, 'you're with me.' The two Templars mounted their horses and headed down the valley, following the river into the heart of the king's camp.

Ten minutes later they joined a group of men in conversation with the king around a trestle table. Amand was surprised to see Sir Raymond was already there.

'Your Grace,' said Amand, striding towards the gathering, 'you summoned me?'

'I did,' said Baldwin, 'grab yourself a drink and join us.'

'I would prefer not to, Your Grace,' said Amand, 'if you don't mind.'

'It matters not,' said the king, 'come, join us for we have information you will wish to hear.'

The Grand Master and the Seneschal joined the others as the king turned to face the Count of Tripoli across the table.

'Lord Raymond,' said the king. 'Perhaps you can repeat the news for the benefit of our newcomers.'

'Of course, my lord,' said Raymond and turned to face the Grand Master.

'As you know we have sent scouts out to find Farrukh Shah with little success. However, today one of our Bedouin trackers found them camped not far from here.'

'Where?' asked Amand.

Lord Raymond pointed his knife at a mark on the map covering the table.

'Here,' he said, 'at a place called the Valley of springs.'

'It's less than a half day's march away,' said the Seneschal, staring at the map, 'how were they not seen sooner?'

'They are constantly on the move,' said Raymond, 'and though the valley had already been checked, it seems that they arrived there yesterday morning.'

'How many?' asked Amand.

'About a thousand,' said Raymond, 'and they are laden down with booty.'

'Christian chattels no doubt,' said the Seneschal.

'We should march on them immediately,' said Amand, 'while they are still unaware of our presence. I will muster my men.'

'Wait, Grand Master,' said the king, 'we have already made plans.'

'Without me?' asked Amand.

'You were not here,' said Lord Raymond.

'We were busy clearing the ground to the east,' said Amand.

'You need not justify your absence, Grand Master,' said the king, 'nevertheless, the plans have been made. Tonight, we will light no fires or cause any commotion that may draw the attention of their outriders. Before the sun is up, Lord Raymond will lead his men along this upper valley and stay hidden while I lead my army to attack from the west. Once they have been engaged, Lord Raymond will fall upon their flank and split their lines into two. We outnumber them three to one and will crush them like ants.'

'And my men,' asked Amand, 'what about them?'

'They will provide the rear guard,' said the king, 'and ensure we are not attacked by forces yet unknown.'

'With respect, Your Grace,' said Amand, 'my men are primed to spearhead any attack and must be allowed to do so. To deny them this task would be foolish.'

'I'm sorry,' said a voice, 'did I just hear you call the king foolish?'

Amand turned to see William of Tyre standing amongst the ring of noblemen.

'You know what I meant,' growled Amand, 'my men were good enough at Montgisard when the enemy forces were ten times as large and yet, now the Saracen numbers are poor and we are guaranteed victory, it seems we are no longer required.'

'Grand Master,' said the king, 'I can assure you that is not the case. It is simply a matter of priorities and logistics. Sir Raymond's army was mustered specifically for this task and it would be traitorous of me to now deny him this opportunity. Besides, there is a bigger battle to come and your men will be needed for that.'

'Nobody knows where Saladin is,' said Amand.

'No, but you can wager that he will make his move in the next few months and when he does, The Templars will lead our combined armies against him. That I promise.'

'And there is no movement in your decision?' asked Amand.

'No,' replied the king, 'there is not. Have your men ready before sunrise and take them to this valley here.' He pointed at the map. 'It lies adjacent to the valley of springs. I have allocated you one of my Bedouin trackers to take you via a hidden pathway amongst the hills.'

'We are more than capable of finding our own way,' said Amand.

'I'm sure you are, but this man was there as recently as last night, and we cannot afford to be discovered.'

'Can he be trusted?'

The king turned to a Bedouin standing near and beckoned him forward.

'This is Abdal-Wahhab,' he said, 'a hunter and scout who has worked with us for many years, as did his father before him. I trust him with my life.'

Amand walked forward and stared at the Bedouin. Abdal-Wahhab returned the stare without flinching.

'What happened to your ear?' asked Amand.

'I lost it to a Mamluk officer,' said Abdal-Wahhab, 'someone who I believe now rides with Farrukh-Shah.'

'So you want retribution?'

'If Allah wills it, I will take the gift.'

Amand stared at the Bedouin for a few seconds longer before spinning around to face the king.

'Your Grace, is that all?'

'I think so,' said Baldwin, 'just be in place by dawn and ensure we are not falling into some sort of trap.'

'As you command,' said Amand with a nod and turned to stride away, closely followed by the Seneschal and Abdal-Wahhab.

'That went well,' said Raymond sarcastically as soon as the Templars had left.

'It is his way,' said the king.' Do not worry, he will deliver what we ask despite his demeanour.'

'I hope you are right,' said Raymond and turned back to the map. 'Now, let's talk about tactics.'

The following morning, one of the king's scouts peered down into the enormous valley of springs from his hiding place amongst the rocks. Half a league away, the Saracen army were preparing their horses for the day's ride, many piled high with booty from the raids throughout Sidon.

The scout turned and signalled one of his comrades further back who passed the message on to a rider on the reverse side of the hill. Within moments, the rider was galloping down to the huge Christian army hidden in the smaller valley below.

'My Lord,' he said reining in his horse. 'They are still there.'

'Excellent,' said the king and turned to his commanders. At their head was the Templar knight, Jakelin de Mailly.

'God is with us,' he said, 'and we owe the people of Sidon retribution for the terrible crimes performed upon them. Take this day and strike a blow in the name of Christendom.'

'Aye my lord,' said the knights and all turned away to their units. Almost immediately, rank after rank of mounted lancers passed the king to form lines abreast, filling the smaller valley from slope to slope and with Jakelin to the fore. When they were all in place, Jakelin turned to face the king, awaiting the final command.

Standing up in his stirrups, Baldwin drew his sword and held it in the air.

'Men of Jerusalem,' he roared, *'advaaance!'*

On one of the hills overlooking the Saracen camp, another hidden scout saw the king's army wheel into the valley of springs and sent his own signal back to Raymond of Tripoli hidden amongst the trees to his rear. Raymond received the message and passed the word along to his own commanders. The attack had started, and their own role was about to begin.

Jakelin de Mailly trotted his horse down through the valley with his visor open. Behind him came a thousand lancers and another two thousand men at arms, all battle-hardened fighters used to the ravages of war. To his front, he could see that the enemy camp had already spied their approach and was rushing to arms to meet the threat.

'Men of Jerusalem,' roared Jakelin, *'present!'*

Everyone in earshot heard the command and lowered their own visors before lifting their lances out of the sockets and digging their heels into their horses' flanks. The pace increased and as everyone roared their battle cries, a thousand lancers crashed into the Saracen army.

The sounds of battle rend the air as the Christian army tore into the still assembling ranks of the Saracens. Men without armour poured from the tents bearing nothing but their scimitars and launched themselves into the fight, desperate to repel the sudden attack. Screams of pain echoed around the valley, mingling with roars of aggression and the clash of steel upon steel. The attack was overwhelming with over half the camp destroyed on the first pass, but the Saracens were fearless and quickly recovered to form their own lines.

The Christian lancers tore through the camp to re-assemble on the far side, lining up again for a second attack. In the distance, they could see their own foot soldiers still approaching and knew that whatever happened, there would be no defeat this day.

'This is too easy,' shouted a knight at Jakelin's side, 'where are their cavalry?'

Before the Templar could respond another knight called out from amongst the ranks.

'My Lord, look to the north.'

Jakelin turned his head and saw hundreds of Saracen lancers bearing down on his own position. Up above he could see their commanders, sitting astride their horses watching the events unfold from the safety of a ridgeline.

'Farrukh-Shah,' he hissed under his breath.

'My Lord,' said the knight at his side, 'what are your orders, do we attack the camp or face their cavalry?'

'We wait,' said Jakelin, 'for if Raymond of Tripoli is worth his spurs, this is exactly what he was waiting for.'

Everyone stared at the approaching army in anticipation, each man getting more nervous the nearer the enemy got.

'My Lord,' said the knight again,' we should attack.'

'Wait,' ordered Jakelin, 'just a few moments more.'

The Christian army faced the Saracens knowing that to be hit by such a force while they were stationary invited certain defeat. Hands flexed around the hafts of lances, desperate to lunge their horses forward but just as it seemed it would be too late, Jakelin's patience paid off.

'God be praised,' gasped the knight at Jakelin's side and watched as hundreds of Raymond's lancers poured out of a side valley to smash into the Saracen army, tearing their ranks apart.

'Do we join the fray, my lord,' shouted a knight.

'No, leave them to Raymond,' responded Jakelin, 'our task is to break the defences of the camp. Our foot soldiers are almost upon it so let's make it easier for them. About face, lancers, *advaaance.'*

For the next few hours, the battle spread throughout the Valley of Springs. Men fought head to head with no quarter asked nor given. Hundreds died on both sides, but it was by far the Saracens who suffered the most. Despite receiving more reinforcements from another returning patrol, their army was torn apart by overwhelming numbers and a carefully thought out strategy. Despite this, they fought on with many escaping up the rocky slopes to hide amongst the trees of the adjacent hills.

By noon, the valley was relatively quiet with only the cries of pain from the wounded still scattered throughout the valley. At the heart of the destroyed enemy camp, King Baldwin met with Raymond of Tripoli and Sir Jakelin to discuss their victory.

'In the name of God,' said the king as the two men approached, 'I offer my gratitude and admiration. The battle was truly great, and our men fought well.'

'Thank you, Your Grace,' said Raymond. 'Our casualties are less than expected and we have recovered dozens of carts laden with the spoils of war, all ripped from the heart of Christian citizens.'

'Excellent,' said the king, 'we will ensure they are returned to their rightful owners as soon as we can. He turned to the blood-sodden Templar alongside Raymond. 'What of you, Sir Jakelin, how fared our own men?'

'A few hundred dead, Your Grace,' said Jakelin, 'double that number wounded.'

The king grimaced. It was a heavy price but one that needed to be paid.

'The main thing is,' said William at the king's side, 'the victory is ours and we have struck a huge blow for God against the heathen.'

'We?' asked Jakelin turning to stare at the prelate. 'I do not remember you with sword in hand?'

'We all have our roles to play,' responded William, 'mine is on the spiritual level, not that of mortal man.'

Jakelin reached out his arm and silence fell as he ran a blood-soaked finger down the prelate's cheek.

'There.' he said, eventually, 'now you can pretend are one of us.'

'Enough,' said the king. 'William of Tyre is right, this is a day to be celebrated. Our defeat at Banias has been avenged and Farrukh-Shah's army destroyed but there is still work to be done. Get the prisoners to dig graves for the dead and send a message to

Beaufort castle, we need carts for our wounded. What about Farrukh-Shah, is he counted amongst the dead?'

'Alas no, Your Grace,' said Jakelin. 'He and his commanders watched the battle from an escarpment. When he realised the day was lost, they disappeared into the forest. We have men seeking them out but fear they have long gone.'

'His time will come,' said the king, 'but for now, see to the aftermath. The rest of us will form a camp two leagues north of here to recover. In a few days, we will continue but until then, we will see to the wounded and rest the men and horses.'

'As you wish,' said Jakelin and nodded before turning away with Raymond of Tripoli to attend their duties.

'They are all cut from the same cloth, those Templars,' said William, wiping the blood smear from his face.

'They proclaim to be God's soldiers,' said the king, 'and are truly magnificent warriors.'

'That may be so, Your Grace,' replied William, 'but apart from the ability to wage war they are graceless men and I struggle to see what the Lord sees in them.'

A few leagues away, Grand Master Amand walked along the crest of a hill with the Seneschal. Their army had provided the necessary rearguard and had been waiting for hours to be deployed but had ultimately not been needed.

'It was a good victory for Christendom,' said Amand, as he walked, 'yet the men's mood is sour.'

'As is mine,' said Valmont. 'There is not a blade amongst us that has been drawn in anger.'

'I suspect Brother Jakelin has spilt more than his share of Saracen blood,' said Amand.

'I expect he acquitted himself well,' said Valmont. 'He is a true knight. Perhaps now Farrukh-Shah is no longer a threat, King Baldwin will allow him to return to the order.'

'Perhaps,' said Amand, 'but it does not concern me. To have one of our own so close to the king may one day be an advantage.'

'What now?' asked Brother Valmont. 'Do we return to Chastellet unchallenged?'

'Not yet,' said Amand. 'I have received a message that he and Raymond are to encamp their armies a few leagues north of here and wish us to attend him at dusk.'

'The last thing I need is an evening filled with boasting and revelry,' said Valmont.

'A sentiment shared,' said Amand, 'but nevertheless, he is the king and we will comply. Once the men are fed and watered, we will head north but perhaps make our camp away from the others.'

'I agree,' said Valmont, 'and will make the necessary arrangements.'

The two men descended from the hill and rejoined the Templar column in the valley. It had been a frustrating few hours for everyone, but little did they know, Farrukh-Shah was not yet done.

Chapter Thirty

June – AD 1179

North of The Valley of Springs

Several leagues away, Farrukh-Shah and Bakir-Shah, commander of the Mamluks rode quickly along the hidden forest tracks, watched every step of the way by fellow Saracens hidden amongst the undergrowth. Soon they reached their destination, a heavily guarded clearing containing several tents. They dismounted and waited as their horses were led away to be watered. One of the guards turned away and entered the larger tent to report their arrival and a few minutes later, he emerged to hold the tent flap aside.

'The Sultan will see you now,' he said.

'Wait here,' said Farrukh-Shah to his comrade and headed inside.

The decoration inside the tent was exquisite with rich fabrics draped from the tent walls and sumptuous rugs upon a wooden floor. A dozen servants knelt on silk cushions around the perimeter, waiting to meet the sultan's every request. At the centre stood Salah ad-Din, drinking water from an ornate silver goblet.

'Farrukh-Shah,' he said after the usual greetings, 'I was not expecting to see you until I returned to Damascus.'

'I know, my lord and can only offer my apologies but we have suffered a terrible defeat and I have come here to throw myself on your mercy.'

'Tell me,' said Salah ad-Din staring at the Emir.

'My Lord,' said Farrukh-Shah, 'this very morning in the valley of Marj Ayyun, the Christian armies led by Baldwin himself caught us unawares and defeated my men in a long and bloody battle.'

'Your column has been destroyed?' asked Salah ad-Din with surprise.

'It has, my lord, and I humbly accept your judgement for my failure.' He dropped to his knees and waited in silence as the Sultan digested the news.

'How many men have you lost?' asked Salah ad-Din eventually.

'Over five hundred, my lord.' said the Emir, 'though it may be more. Many escaped to the mountains.'

'How many men were in this Christian army?'

'I estimate upward of four thousand lancers and foot soldiers.'

'And you say the army was led by Baldwin?'

'He was not to the fore, but we saw his colours on a hill overlooking Marj Ayyun. He was there.'

'Get up,' said Salah ad-Din and walked around the tent, thinking furiously. 'This happened this morning?' he asked eventually.

'It did, my lord, less than two hours hard ride away.'

'And you say he has four thousand men in total.'

'As far as I could estimate.'

Silence fell as the Sultan continued his thoughts until finally, he turned around and walked quickly to stand directly before the Emir.

'This may not be the disaster you think it is,' he said, 'in fact, it could be a gift from Allah himself.'

'I don't understand,' said Farrukh-Shah, 'most of my command are dead because I failed in my duty.'

'They are truly martyrs,' said Salah ad-Din, 'but this presents an opportunity too precious to ignore.'

'In what way, my lord?'

'The Christians will see this as a great victory, correct?'

'Yes, my lord.'

'Well knowing them as I do, I suspect they will immediately relax and be off their guard, thinking there is no more fighting to do.'

'I have no more men to counter-attack,' said the Emir.

'No, but I do,' said Salah ad-Din, 'six thousand warriors within two hours of Marj Ayyun. They have been assembled with a view to attacking the castle at Vadum Iacob, but if the king is at the head of this army you speak of, then this situation is too important to ignore.'

'What do you intend to do?'

'What I must do,' said the Sultan, 'attack the Christians with everything at my disposal.'

The sun was heading towards the horizon when Baldwin's army finally reached the green valley designated for their overnight camp. Unlike the valley of springs, the hills to either side were gentle with no steep crags or rocky slopes to hide anyone intent on setting an ambush. The mood amongst the combined armies was relaxed although several scouts had been sent forward to check the area.

'This will do,' said Baldwin, reining in his horse, 'we will set the camp here. Tell the men to dismount and erect a perimeter. Pitch what tents we can before dark and make sure they get something to eat.'

The officers turned away to their tasks as William helped the king from his horse.

'How do you fare, Your Grace?' asked the prelate, as the king struggled to walk.

'As well as can be expected,' said Baldwin, 'but I look forward to my cot.'

'I will have it brought up from the supply caravan immediately,' said William. He walked away as Raymond of Tripoli turned up and approached the king.

'Your Grace,' said the count, 'you look exhausted. It has been a long day.'

'But a fruitful one,' said the king. 'Perhaps Saladin will now realise he cannot just ride into Christian lands without fear of retribution.'

'You would have thought he had learned his lesson at Montgisard,' said Raymond.

'Aye,' said the king with a laugh, but his demeanour changed, and a look of concern spread across his face as he stared past Raymond and into the distance.

'What's that?' he asked.

Raymond turned and saw a group of men riding hard from one of the far hills.

'Some of our scouts,' said Raymond, 'and they look worried.'

One of the riders galloped into the centre of the watching army and reined in his exhausted horse.

'Your Grace,' he gasped, 'there are Saracens headed this way, thousands of them.'

'Saracens?' asked the king. 'But we destroyed the only Saracen force this side of the Jordan just a few hours since. Who are they?'

'Your Grace,' said the scout nervously, 'unless I am mistaken, the banners belonged to Saladin himself.'

Baldwin swallowed hard, struggling to take in the information. Saladin was supposed to be many leagues away to the east of the Jordan, not here at the Litani River.

'Are you sure of this?' he asked.

'As far as I can tell, Your Grace,' said the scout, 'but one thing I can be sure of, it's the biggest Saracen army I have ever seen.'

The king looked around and saw Sir Jakelin walking briskly towards him.

'What's going on?' asked the knight, seeing the worried look on their faces.

'It seems Saladin has outthought us,' said Baldwin, 'and heads an army this way.'

'How far away is he?' asked Jakelin to the scout.

'He will be here before dark,' said the scout, 'we have to get away from here.'

'There's no time,' said Jakelin, 'our wounded will slow us down and we can't leave them here.'

'What do you suggest?' asked Baldwin, 'our men are exhausted.'

'Your Grace,' said Jakelin, 'if what this man says is true, we are heavily outnumbered and can't hope to match the Saracen army in a pitched battle. We need time to regroup.'

'How?'

'Send a message back to the Grand Master. Ask him to ride here with his men with all haste. Even my fellow Templars will not be strong enough to engage the enemy this strong but at least they are fresh and can help us strengthen the shield wall until nightfall. After that, we can withdraw to somewhere easier to defend.'

'I agree,' interjected Raymond, 'Sir Reginald and his army are also on their way from Sidon with the intention of joining us at Beaufort Castle. If we send riders to meet him, he can change course and be here by midday tomorrow. All we have to do is survive the night.'

'It's not the best,' said Baldwin, 'but we have no choice.' He turned to the scout. 'You and your men continue down the valley and brief the Templar commander. Tell him to report to me with all haste. Once done, continue downstream and find Sir Reginald of Sidon. Tell him I need him and his army here as soon as possible. Tell him to ride through the night if necessary. Our lives may depend on it.'

'Yes, Your Grace,' said the scout and turned to lead his men out of the camp.

'The rest of you,' said Baldwin, 'get your men to form defensive lines, and may God protect us.'

Chapter Thirty-One

June – AD 1179

Marj Ayyun

Grand Master Amand and his eighty Templar knights rode hard up the valley, the veins in their horses' necks bulging with the effort. They had just received the king's message and were galloping as hard as the terrain allowed. Behind them came the mounted Sergeants and the two hundred turcopole lancers, each struggling to keep up with the better-mounted knights. The pace was punishing but, at last, they turned a bend and the camp came into view less than a few hundred paces to the front. Amand held his hand up to rein in his men as he assessed the situation.

'They've set up defensive lines,' he said, looking at the rows of men on the shield wall at the far side of the camp.

'I suspect they feel defence is their best option,' said the Seneschal at his side, 'look.'

Both men looked up and in the distance saw thousands of horsemen riding slowly towards the king's position. The Saracen army filled the northern half of the valley and beyond them, them, on the far slopes was a second force of riders waiting in reserve. Above them on the crest of a hill, a dozen or so men sat on their horses beneath the banners of the Sultan.

'Saladin,' growled Amand, 'how dare he show his face after what we did to him at Montgisard.'

'This is not good,' said the Seneschal, assessing the situation. 'It looks like the king's horses have been taken to the rear and Baldwin is relying on the shield walls to keep the Saracens out. Even allied with Raymond's army, I fear they are too exposed and will be overwhelmed.'

'That's why they sent for us,' said Amand. 'They need our steel to cut the enemy down.' He turned to Brother Valmont. 'We got within touching distance of Saladin himself at Montgisard, but he escaped by a dog's whisker. This time I want him at the end of my sword.' He turned to face the column. 'This is what you have been waiting for,' he called, 'once we have passed the camp, extend into line abreast. We will smash through their vanguard and head for Saladin himself.' He drew his sword and held it up high as his horse strained to be away. 'Brother Templars,' he roared, 'the king and Jerusalem is in peril, *Beauséant alla riscossa!*'

'*Beauséant alla riscossa!*' roared the column of knights in response and spurred their warhorses to join the battle.

Everyone in the shield wall stared at the huge army of Saracens sweeping down from the hills. The enemy numbers were enormous, and the defenders swallowed hard, knowing that without help they stood little chance of surviving the night.

The front rank kneeled with their lances aimed between their shields towards the enemy while those immediately behind rested their own spears on the kneeling men's shoulders. Those in the third rank did the same to those in the middle, presenting a wall of hardened spears to the oncoming Saracens.

Behind the first three rows, seven more ranks of men waited to replace those who would die in the first assault, a fate that awaited many.

'*Do not fear their numbers,*' roared Jakelin, as he marched back and forth behind the first three ranks, 'they are men like you and I and bleed just as easily. Hold fast to your spears until they are wrested from your hands and then fight with sword and knife. Remember Montgisard where many of you fought an army three times this size and emerged the victors? This is no different. We will prevail, my comrades, for God is with us.'

'*God is with us,*' roared the men in reply.

To the centre of the camp, King Baldwin and Count Raymond stood upon an upturned cart to get a better view of the impending battle. Fresh horses were already saddled nearby in case the fight went the wrong way and they were surrounded by a personal bodyguard of a hundred of their best knights.

'I don't understand,' said Raymond, 'how could he have amassed such a force without us knowing?'

'Many of the people living amongst the hills pledge allegiance to us,' said the king, 'but turn to Saladin as soon as they are threatened. The forests of Banias are huge but someone must have known about this.'

The Saracens continued their advance until they were only a few hundred paces away. Suddenly they stopped and the valley fell into relative silence.

'My Lord', said a voice to one side, 'the Templars approach.'

King Baldwin turned to see the column galloping up the valley.

'At last,' he said, 'with them in support the shield wall should hold until dark.' For a moment he stared at the galloping column and as it got closer, his relief turned to concern. 'Where are they going?' he asked as Grand Master Amand led the column wide to skirt around the camp, 'we need them here.'

'What is he doing?' roared Raymond of Tripoli, as the Templars lowered their visors, 'did you not send a message saying he was to support our position, not attack Saladin? Someone sound the recall.'

The sound of a horn rent the air and many men in the shield wall looked around in confusion. To them, the Templar army to their front was the most welcome sight they had ever seen and the last thing they had expected to hear was the signal to withdraw.

In the centre of the closely formed Templar line, the Seneschal heard the signal and turned to the Grand Master.

'They sound the recall,' he said, 'the king wants us back amongst the lines.'

'Let him command his own men,' said Amand quietly,' this is our concern and I'm not going to enclose our brothers like rats in a barrel. Saladin and I have unfinished business.' He lifted his lance from the holder and lowered it into position pointing towards the massed ranks of Saracen warriors. 'Fellow Templars,' he roared, *'advaaance.'*

'The man is a liability,' spat William of Tyre from his place at the base of the king's vantage point, 'I have been saying it all along.'

'There is no way he can take on an army of that size,' said Raymond, 'he will be wiped out before the battle has begun.'

'Give him a chance,' said the king quietly. 'He faced a far greater foe at Montgisard and led us to victory. Perhaps he can do the same here.'

'Your Grace,' said Raymond, 'with respect we had ten thousand men at arms ready to follow him into battle at

Montgisard. Here we have none except the exhausted and the wounded. Whatever his intention is, he will have to do it alone.'

The king looked up at the far hill and saw the distant banner of Saladin fluttering in the wind.

'Oh, I know his intention,' he said quietly, 'I know *exactly* what he wants.'

The Templars thundered towards the Saracen lines, roared on by the thousands of men to their rear. To their front, the Saracen commanders responded and to the cacophony of hundreds of horns echoing through the valley, launched their own warriors into the attack.

The clash of men and horses was immense with neither side giving ground. The Templar's tactic, as usual, was to smash the front line across a wide front and use the shock to drive a wedge into the heart of the enemy position, followed up immediately by their sergeants and Turcopoles, but the tactic that had worked so well at Montgisard had been anticipated and instead of splitting apart as was expected, the enemy lines held.

Saladin had learned his lesson well and rather than place his better men on the flanks to offer a counterattack option, he had packed them in the centre, meeting the Templars head-on. Despite this, the first few ranks still fell beneath the hooves of the Templars' war horses and warriors screamed in pain as they were impaled on pennant bearing lances, but those to either side were seasoned warriors, used to death and mayhem and they immediately closed in from the sides to launch flanking assaults on the Templars.

At the same time, those on the outer flanks also turned inward and headed straight for the knight's supporting forces, the sergeants and the Turcopoles. Within moments the whole of the Templar column was engulfed, and it was obvious, there had been a terrible miscalculation.

Men and horses screamed in the dying light and despite the impact of the Templar attack, their advance ground to a halt as they were surrounded by Saracens.

Unhorsed knights and Saracens fought hand to hand and though the Christian chainmail was stronger and thicker, the lighter Saracen armour allowed ease of movement. All around the valley men fought furiously, with Christian sword smashing against Saracen scimitars. Men fell to blades and clubs and though both sides had archers in their rear lines, neither side could deploy them in case they hit their own men. Even horses, well trained to fight in battle, reared up on hind legs to smash their iron-clad hooves down onto whoever was in front of them and it soon became obvious that any thought of reaching Saladin must wait, this was a fight for their lives.

Cronin fought desperately, drawing on every moment of his military experience to stay alive. His sword smashed through Saracen flesh, dropping men to the ground before following up with a stamp to the face or a thrust from his blade into the enemy's chest. Hassan stayed close behind but as he was unskilled with a sword, used his knife to finish off any still alive. Other squires did the same and the field became a cauldron of pain and fear. The noise was deafening with screams of men and horses filling the air. No quarter was given or expected, and blood flew in all directions, covering everyone in its path.

Cronin stopped, desperately trying to catch his breath. Already he and his comrades had accounted for dozens of Saracens but hundreds more lay before them. He looked around seeing no way out and no sign of reinforcements. For once in his life, he was desperate and knew there was no way any of them could ever hope to escape the onslaught.

'It's no good,' he gasped, 'we are beaten. We have to get out of here.'

'How,' shouted Hassan, 'we are surrounded?'

'This way,' shouted Cronin, stepping over a fallen comrade amongst, 'stay close.'

Hassan followed the sergeant, his heart racing with fear. Cronin cut his way through the mayhem until they reached another group of fellow soldiers.

'Cronin?' shouted one, 'where are the knights?'

'They have their own problems,' shouted Cronin, 'they've been engulfed by Saladin's cavalry.'

'Can we get to them?'

'No,' shouted Cronin, 'we have been cut off and there are thousands of Saracens between us.'

'Then we have to get out of here,' said his comrade.

Cronin looked around. The enemy was everywhere and no matter which way they went, they would have to fight their way out.

'Close in,' he shouted, 'and maintain a tight all-round defence. We'll head for the rocks.'

The rest of the group came together and started to fight their way across the valley. Saracens attacked from all sides, but the Templar sergeants' training paid off and slowly, step by step, they neared the cover of the rocky slopes.

The men at the shield wall stared in shock. Moments earlier the Templars had raced past them to confront the Saracens in a glorious charge. They were well known for their prowess in battle, warriors unmatched in the skills of warfare and many battles over the past seventy years had been swung as a result of their bravery. The very sight of them charging towards the enemy had sent fear deep into the hearts of countless men, but this was different, this time they had been engulfed like a pebble in a stream.

'What's happening?' asked William, now standing alongside the king on the upturned cart, 'why have they not emerged?'

'They have been matched,' said Raymond on the far side of the king. 'The idiot has wasted his own men by thinking he was something more than he is.' He turned to the king. 'Your Grace, we should think about getting you out of here. Even if any of the Templars escape, their force will be spent, and this camp is at risk of being overrun.'

'Not yet,' said the king, 'there is still a chance.'

Deep in the heart of the battle, the Templar knights fought furiously. Some were still on horseback, but many were now afoot, using what little space they had to kill anything in range. Men hacked at men, half-blinded by blood and rage with no thought of quarter. Screams for mercy were ignored as those terrified for their own lives hacked other human beings apart.

'My Lord,' shouted the Seneschal, 'we have to retreat,' but there was no answer. The Grand Master was like a man possessed, hacking his way through the Saracen lines as he fought his way ever forward, determined to reach Saladin.

'Leave him,' shouted the Marshal at his side, 'he has lost his mind.'

'I cannot,' replied Valmont, 'he is our leader and I will not fail him nor God,' but even as watched, the next wave of Saracen warriors surged forward, completely engulfing the Templar Leader.

'*He is down,*' roared Brother Tristan, 'there is no more we can do except save ourselves and what is left of our men. *In the name of God, Valmont we must retreat.*'

The Seneschal gasped in horror as he saw the Grand Master fall, and knew the Marshal was right. Their fight was done.

'*Retreat,*' he roared, '*everyone back to the shield wall.*'

The command was repeated throughout the shattered column and the surviving knights started heading back, their swords still flying in all directions as they forced a passage through the sea of Saracens.

'My Lord,' shouted a knight back at the shield wall, 'the Templars are retreating.'

Almost a hundred men from the initial Templar force turned to flee back to the Christian lines while the Turcopoles fought a rearguard action to give them what little time they could. Knights battled furiously, their overwhelming strength and skill accounting for many Saracen warriors but one by one, even they fell to the inevitable, a defeated force totally dominated by the unrelenting power of the Saracen army. Men spread out across the battlefield, running as fast as they were able, desperate to live, but behind them all came the Saracens, thousands of warriors determined to cut them all down.

'*Be ready to let them through,*' shouted Jakelin.

'*No,*' shouted Count Raymond, running over, 'hold the line fast. If we open the wall, the Saracens will pour through and get to the king.'

'We cannot leave them out there,' shouted Jakelin, 'every one of them will die.'

'*The king is more important,*' roared Raymond, 'hold fast the lines.'

Jakelin stared at the hundreds of men staggering back towards the safety of the shield wall. Many he knew personally, and he knew he could not stand fast and see them cut down.

'Sir Jakelin,' shouted Raymond again, seeing his doubt, 'I am warning you, hold this line or this position will fall. There is nothing we can do for your comrades.'

'Oh yes there is,' said Jakelin quietly and turned to face the massed ranks. 'All men to their feet,' he shouted, 'present lances and draw swords. *Prepare to advance.*'

'No,' gasped Raymond, 'what are you doing?'

'The only thing we can do,' shouted Jakelin, 'something we should have done as soon as Brother Amand led the Templars into battle.'

'You hold fast,' shouted Raymond as all the men presented their lances or drew their swords.

'If we stay here, we will all die,' roared Jakelin, 'this way at least some of us will live. Get the king out of here, Raymond, this battle is lost.'

'Do not do this,' shouted the count as Jakelin raised his sword in the air, but it was too late. Even as the last word left his lips, the Templar knight's sword slashed downward, and he roared the battle cry that would cost the lives of thousands of men.

'For God and the king,' roared Sir Jakelin, *'advaaance!'*

Chapter Thirty-Two

June – AD 1179

Marj Ayyun

The following day, the sun rose on a scene of devastation and despair. All across the valley, thousands of men and horses lay dead or dying, the soil dyed red from the rivers of blood spilt in the name of religion. The valley was strangely silent with only the distant cries of the circling crows and hawks breaking the silence, waiting to partake in the unexpected feast below.

Saracen soldiers walked amongst the carnage, retrieving their own dead and slitting the throats of any enemy wounded trying to hide amongst the bodies. The main Saracen army had long gone, once more safely hidden amongst the forests of Banias.

The battle had been a disaster for the Christian army. At first, the unexpected countercharge had stopped the enemy attack in its tracks, but the overwhelming Saracen numbers soon took their toll and it wasn't long until they regained momentum to break the Christian army apart. As soon as the lines had broken, all mayhem was let loose and the defenders had scattered like a giant flock of startled birds. The Saracen cavalry took advantage of the undisciplined retreat, riding amongst them with impunity, killing at will without thought of giving quarter.

King Baldwin and his entourage had fled the field with only minutes to spare and even then, his bodyguards had to fight their way through to escape the valley and make their way to Beaufort Castle.

The morning dragged on and the heat of the day rose. The Saracens finally left the field, taking their dead and wounded with them until eventually, the crows and birds of prey swooped down to take their place, staking their claim to the bodies they had left behind.

Throughout the valley, nervous men began to emerge from any place of refuge they had managed to find. Slowly they walked out onto the battlefield, shocked at the scale of the killing with many silently giving thanks to God that they had survived.

Over on one of the hills on the far side of the valley, Cronin emerged from a hollow beneath a rock, his hair matted with sand and blood from a wound across his scalp. His left arm hung uselessly at his side, the result of a scimitar strike when he and Hassan had fought their way furiously through the darkness. He looked around, looking for the Bedouin boy.

'Hassan,' he said quietly, 'where are you?'

A rustle in a nearby tree made him turn and he watched in relief as Hassan dropped from its branches.

Somberly they stared around the battlefield. Bodies lay everywhere, slaughtered to a man. Over two thousand men brutally cut down by Saracen steel and left to rot in the midday sun.

Cronin looked around the hill. More men were emerging from their hiding places, many with wounds and they walked aimlessly across the battlefield, still shocked at the scale of the defeat.

'Is everyone else dead?' asked Hassan quietly.

'I don't think so,' said Cronin. 'This is probably only half the men we fielded. The others must escaped.'

'Do you think they still live?'

'It was getting dark,' said Cronin, 'many should have escaped in the night.'

'And the king?'

'I saw him and his bodyguard flee the field as soon as the shield wall advanced, so unless the Saracens had more men to the south, there is every chance he made it.'

What now?' asked Hassan, eventually.

'First, we will find our friend's body,' said Cronin.

'Sir Jakelin?'

'Aye, he was in the midst of it all and would never have run. After that, we'll make our way to Beaufort Castle. I expect most of the survivors would have headed there.'

'It was a terrible defeat,' said Hassan, looking at the thousands of bodies around the valley.

'It was more than that,' said Cronin, 'it was a massacre.'

By the middle of the afternoon, several dozen men had gathered around a damaged pennant at the heart of the battlefield. The flagpole had been snapped in half and it listed to one side, but it was a recognisable beacon to which all the survivors rallied.

'Any luck?' asked Cronin, as he and Hassan met up again near the flagpole.

'No, my lord,' said Hassan, 'I looked everywhere. Many of your brother knights have fallen but Jakelin was not amongst them.'

'Looking for a comrade?' asked a soldier standing nearer the flag.

'Captain Bullard,' said Cronin, recognising the officer, 'You survived the onslaught.'

'Aye, me and a few others. Who is it you seek?'

'Sir Jakelin, the Templar who led the shield wall.'

'Ah, him. The last I saw of him he fell under a storm of steel. You are wasting your time.'

'I can't find him,' said Hassan. 'Perhaps he escaped?'

'Ran away more like,' said the man, 'along with his comrades.'

'I counted over fifty Templar corpses,' hissed Hassan, 'they fought harder than any.'

'It was they who got us into this mess in the first place,' replied the officer, 'and I saw Templars run away with my own eyes.'

'Jakelin de Mailly would never run, 'shouted Hassan, 'he would rather die than retreat.'

The soldier stared at Hassan, his face creasing in anger.

'Why don't you just shut that mouth of yours,' he growled, 'I have seen you around the castle pretending to be one of us. In my opinion, you are just another useless mouth that needs feeding. Look around you, Saracen, it was your own countrymen who did this and I wouldn't be surprised if you used your own blade against us in the night.'

'I am no Saracen,' shouted Hassan, 'I am a Bedouin and a Christian.'

'Bedouin or Saracen,' said the captain, 'it matters not. In my eyes, you are all the same. Now get out of my face before I lose my temper.'

Hassan lurched forward, his hand reaching for his knife, but Cronin grabbed his shoulder and pulled him back.

'Enough,' he said, 'too many men have already died on this field. Let's not add to their number.'

'You just keep your pet Saracen under control,' said the captain, 'Or I swear I'll slit his throat myself.' He stared at Hassan again before spitting on the floor at the boy's feet and turning away to join the sorry group of survivors drifting away from the battlefield.

'You should not have held me back,' said Hassan, 'that man is known to everyone in Chastellet as a coward and a scoundrel. He forces the women of the workers to his bed and threatens to hurt their children if they report his deeds.'

'I have heard the rumours,' said Cronin, 'but he is also a good fighter. You would never have bettered him.'

'Despite everything I believe,' said Hassan, staring at the back of the departing soldier, 'despite everything I do or say, it is never enough. I will never fit in.'

'Don't think that way, Hassan,' said Cronin, 'that man is just ignorant. You are a true Christian and as important to Jerusalem as any. Now come, we need to get to Beaufort.'

Several leagues away within the walls of Beaufort Castle, King Baldwin sat on a simple wooden bench. His elbows were on the table and he cradled his head in his hands.

William of Tyre stood near the fireplace and several knights either sat on stools or stood leaning against the walls while Raymond of Tripoli stamped around the room, his face contorted with anger.

'What was he thinking?' he shouted. 'He should have known to attack meant our lines would be put at risk.'

'Which one,' asked William, 'Sir Jakelin or Grand Master Amand?'

'Both of them,' said Raymond, 'for both employed the same tactics, abandoning the king's army in favour of personal glory. A futile, self-serving attempt that cost the lives of thousands of men.'

'They did what they had to do,' said the king with a sigh as he lifted up his head. 'Taking the attack to the heart of the enemy in order to divide and conquer.'

'And look what it achieved?' said Raymond, 'a defeat on the scale never before seen in our lifetime.'

'Did we not praise the same tactics at Montgisard,' said the king, 'and the countless other times their bravery has delivered victory from the jaws of defeat? Are we so blind that the very men that are held up as our champions are then vilified as soon as they fail? No man is perfect, Count Raymond, and neither are the Templars.'

'If I may, Your Grace,' said William, 'this is the third time in as many months a Templar decision has caused the deaths of many men. On top of that, we know there is a traitor in Chastellet and despite your assurances, I still maintain it could be one of the brotherhood.'

'They did what they had to do,' said the king, 'and fought the only way they know how, by attacking the enemy.' He sighed and stood up. 'I have had enough of this self-destruction, how many men do we have left?'

'About two thousand within the bailey,' said Raymond,' and another five hundred or so safe on this side of the river.'

'Five hundred,' said the king, 'there were far more than that last night. Where are they?'

'Most are dead, my lord,' said Raymond, 'others are probably on their way to Damascus.'

'What,' gasped the king. 'Half of our army was over there and Reginald of Sidon tasked with covering their withdrawal. What happened?'

The room fell silent as most eyes turned away. Nobody wanted to be the one to tell the king about yet another failure.

'Well,' said the king, 'anybody?'

'Your Grace,' said a knight getting to his feet. 'Sir Reginald and his army were less than a league from here but came across a group of our own men fleeing from the battle. They told him that all was lost and that both our armies, as well as the Templars, had been routed. Faced with such news and having been assured that there was nothing he could do; he turned his army around and headed back to Sidon. When he turned away, the Saracens realised our men were undefended and attacked those still on the far side of the river. Many were killed and those who survived, taken prisoner.'

'This is a disaster,' said William from the corner.

'William, shut up,' roared the king. 'I have had enough of your naysaying. Do not speak again unless I address you directly.'

The hall fell silent as the king turned to lean on the table, his mind racing. Eventually, he stood up straight and turned to face the knights.

'I agree this campaign has fallen short,' he said, 'and there have been many failings by many men, but it strikes me that almost all those decisions were made in good faith, not realising the consequences their actions would have. In different circumstances, we would have hailed them as tactical brilliance. Alas, this time it was not to be.' He looked around the room. 'However, let it be known that I hold no man responsible for this defeat other than myself. It was I who issued the call to arms and I alone that will take the blame.'

'Your Grace,' shouted the prelate getting to his feet, 'I must protest.'

'I told you to be quiet,' roared the king, 'and if you speak unbid again, I will have you removed from my court. Do you understand?'

'Yes, Your Grace,' mumbled William.

'Good, now sit down and maintain your silence.' He turned around again. 'As I said,' he continued, 'let it be known that this defeat lies upon my shoulders alone, not the Templars, not Sir Reginald, and certainly not on any the men who fell in the shield wall. The responsibility lies with me, and me alone, is that understood?'

'Yes, Your Grace,' said the gathered men.

'Good. Now spend some time with our men. Tend the wounded and speak to the castellan about re-arming those who can still fight. As soon as it is safe, send out patrols to gather up any stragglers.' He turned to the Count. 'Sir Raymond, when you are ready, take your men home with my gratitude. See that your wounded are well-tended and give compensation to the families of those who died. My treasury will pick up the cost.' He turned away. 'The rest of you, as soon as we are able to move, we will return to Chastellet and subsequently Tiberius to lick our wounds. This battle has been lost, but the war has just begun.'

A few days later, a column of men rode back through the gates of Chastellet. The mood was sombre with no fanfare to welcome them home. This time the stares from the workers were of shock and fear as they learned of the heavy defeat. Families whose loved ones did not return cried at the side of the road as soon as they received the news while others stared down the line, hoping against hope they would see a familiar face.

King Baldwin headed the column and he remained stone-faced the whole time, his gaze not veering off the path as he led the survivors through the gates and up into the upper bailey.

Grooms and slaves came running to take the horses while servants rushed to offer aid to those who needed help.

Amongst the injured walked Hassan and Cronin, the former helping the wounded sergeant whenever he needed aid. As they approached the hospital tents, Sumeira came running down the line towards them.

'Thank God you are alive,' she said, 'I heard the Templars lost many men and I feared you would be amongst them.'

'Our brothers paid heavily,' said Cronin. 'We were amongst the lucky ones.'

'What about Hunter?'

'I have not seen him since leaving Chastellet,' said Cronin. 'I don't even know if he was there.'

'And Sir Jakelin?'

Both Hassan and Cronin stared at Sumeira without reply but she could see in their eyes, they feared the worst. She walked closer to examine the bandages around the sergeant's head.

'How bad is it under there?'

'Nothing that won't heal,' said Cronin.

'Have you kept it clean?'

Cronin shrugged his shoulders but did not reply.

'Hassan,' said Sumeira turning to the boy, 'you know the importance of this, tell me you applied what you have learned.'

'There was little time,' said Hassan with a shrug of his own, 'we did what we could.'

'In the name of God,' sighed Sumeira, exasperated, 'will you people never learn? Take him to the furthest tent and tell them to give him a cot near to my quarters.'

'I am no child,' said Cronin, 'and can speak for myself.'

'I disagree,' snapped Sumeira, 'it seems to me that a child would know how to wash themselves, especially if there is a wound. Now get up there, I'll be with you as soon as I can.'

Back in his chambers, Baldwin's servants raced to disrobe the king and bathe his body to ease the pain from his sores. The final few leagues had drained the last of his strength and he was weaker than he had been for a long time.

'Bring me Poppy milk,' said William marching into the chamber, 'and plenty of hot water.'

'What are you doing here?' asked the king seeing the prelate. 'I have still not forgiven you for your outbursts in Beaufort. Get out.'

'I'm going nowhere,' said William. 'You need help, and nobody knows you or your ailments like I do. I'm staying right here until you recover so if you want me out, then call the guards.'

The king stared at the prelate with anger in his eyes, but he didn't answer. William had been with him since he was a boy and he was right; nobody knew him as well as he did.

'Good,' said William, realising he had gotten his own way. 'Now you stay there, and I will arrange a warm bath and silk robes. Once your sores have been treated, I suggest you sleep as long as you can.'

'I have to get back to Tiberius,' said Baldwin as his servants helped him gently into a chair,' there are things to do.'

'What things?' asked William.

'Like rebuilding my army,' said Baldwin, 'and seeking reinforcements from the other Templar outposts throughout the Outremer. We need to get back to full strength as soon as possible.'

'I will send the appropriate messages immediately,' said William, 'giving all the castellan's advance notice of your intentions. That way they can get the process started. Once you are well, we can go wherever you want but unless you rest, I fear you may not recover.'

'Do what you have to do, William,' said the king with an exhausted sigh, 'I am done here.'

William nodded and turned to one of the servants.

'Summon the scribes,' he said, 'we have messages to write. '

The servant hurried away and William turned back to face the king. Baldwin now sat back in his chair with his eyes closed, his body wracked with pain.

The prelate stared for a few moments. He knew he should tell him of the rumours that were already rife throughout the castle, but the king was exhausted, and it would have to wait.

Chapter Thirty-Three

August – AD 1179

Chastellet Castle

Four weeks later, life at the Chastellet had almost returned to normal. Those who had died of their wounds had been buried and those still recovering, given light duties around the castle. Cronin had recovered most of the use of his arm and Sumeira's timely intervention had prevented the infected wound in his head from getting any worse.

Simon of Syracuse had increased the workforce even more since the defeated army had returned, desperate to finish the castle before the attack that everyone suspected was coming. Those soldiers not on patrol or manning the walls were tasked with helping the masons but as the weeks had passed, the threat had diminished until eventually, King Baldwin had returned to Tiberius, half a day's ride away.

The castellan walked around the battlements above the upper bailey with the Under-Marshal at his side.

'A few more months, that's all I need,' said the castellan, 'and the towers will be finished. As soon as they are complete, we can concentrate on the outer walls and this place will become impregnable.'

'I suggest it already is,' said Rénier de Maron, looking around the impressive defences. 'There is no way any man can take these walls without Mangonels; I don't care who they are.'

'Saladin is a resourceful man,' said Simon.

'Perhaps so, but we have many allies to call upon in the event of a siege. Warriors alone could never scale these walls and by the time he got his engineers to build any siege engines, Baldwin's army would be amongst them.'

'Is that supposed to give me confidence,' asked the castellan.

'The king has recruited well,' said Rénier, 'and his army is almost back at full strength. Do not judge him by what happened at Marj Ayyun for they were taken by surprise. That will not happen again and along with the men we have garrisoned here; we are more than a match for the Saracens.'

'I hope so,' said Simon, 'for it seems that Saladin is in no mood for peace.'

'You sound like you doubt the strength of your own fortress.'

'On the contrary, I reckon these walls are as strong as you will get anywhere. It is the weakness of men that gives me cause for concern.'

'You talk of the traitor?'

'Aye.'

'And you still have no idea who he is?'

'No. We have questioned every man here three times over but whoever it is, hides his treachery well.'

'We will get him,' said Rénier. 'Rats always reveal themselves eventually.'

'Aye,' said Simon, 'and when he does, I will personally cut open his flesh and revel in his screams as the dogs rip out his insides.'

The two men continued their inspection, pausing occasionally to inspect fields of fire from the castellations or a well-placed arrow slit.

'I see your comrades arrived yesterday,' said Rénier, referring to the column of Templars who had arrived from Blancheguarde and Gaza.

'Aye, almost a hundred knights and another two hundred turcopoles. Their arrival takes our garrison up to almost two thousand.'

'The cost must be prohibitive,' said Rénier.

'It is but the king has unlimited credit from the Templars until Chastellet is finished. Even so, the debt is rising by the day.'

'Any sign of the Saracens?' asked Rénier.

'No, they have long gone. We have scouts patrolling the lands around Chastellet in every direction and will have plenty of warning should they come.'

'In that case,' said Rénier, 'I suggest you get some rest. You have surely aged a hundred years, my friend, take to your cot and sleep for a week. I will ensure that at the slightest news of Saladin, I will wake you.'

'I have too much to do,' said the castellan. 'This castle needs finishing, Sir Rénier, and it is my responsibility to do it.'

'As you wish,' said Rénier and they continued the inspection, each unaware that Saladin was closer than anyone could ever have imagined.

Two days later, Shirkuh ad-Din stood at the map table in Saladin's campaign tent deep in the heart of Banias forest. Alongside him stood the two generals who had fought alongside him at Marj Ayyun, Sabek ad-Din and Bakir-Shah.

All three waited until the sultan appeared through a flap at the rear of the tent and dropped to their knees with their foreheads touching the rich carpet.

'On your feet,' said Salah ad-Din, his manner more curt than usual.

The three men stood but remained silent as the sultan looked at all three in turn.

'My friends,' he said eventually, 'you have all delivered many victories in the name of Allah and have all lost friends and allies to Christian blades. But the time has come to ask you once again to ride against the infidels.'

'We are always at your service, my lord,' said Shirkuh ad-Din, 'so please tell, what is our target.'

'It seems that a great Christian king has landed in Acre along with a huge army,' said Salah ad-Din. 'His name is Henry of Champagne and he comes to join forces with Baldwin of Jerusalem. As we know, Baldwin is in Tiberius and as soon as this new king finds out, I suspect he will come this way. If we allow this to happen, the fortress will be completed, and we will never again have a chance to tear it down.'

'Are we to attack this king?' asked Shirkuh ad-Din.

'No. Before he arrives, I want you to besiege the monstrosity they call Chastellet.'

'Do we have access to siege engines?'

'We will need neither catapult nor rams,' said Salah ad-Din, 'for we have to do this in just a few days before King Baldwin has a chance to muster his army in Tiberius.'

'You ask a great thing of us' said Shirkuh ad-Din.

'I know, but if Allah is with us, then it is possible. All I need you to do is get us into the outer bailey and provide a wall of arrows to keep the defenders' heads down. Do that and we have a chance. Send word to our men, we will attack at dawn.

'As you wish,' said Shirkuh ad-Din and all three men bowed low before exiting the tent.

Salah ad-Din turned to the one other man who had been sitting quietly at the far end of the tent.

'It is done, my friend,' he said, 'muster your sappers.'

The following day, Cronin and Hunter stood alongside their horses in the outer bailey waiting for final instructions from the castellan. The weakness in his left arm meant the sergeant still could not resume patrolling duties with the rest of his comrades but for the past few days, he had been used as one of the messengers between Chastellet and the other castles in the area. Today he was tasked alongside Hunter with taking a message to the castellan of Beaufort Castle on the Litani River. Hassan was staying behind, as every spare set of hands was needed to help the masons.

'So, where have you been?' asked Cronin as the two men waited.

'I had to go Acre on an errand for the king,' said Hunter. 'Apparently, Henry of Champagne is due to arrive with a vast army under his command and Baldwin wanted him briefed as to the situation in Jacob's Ford. We left the dispatches with the castellan in Acre and headed back as soon as we could. By the time we returned, the battle was over.'

'Just as well,' said Cronin,' Marj Ayyun was not a good place to be.'

'I heard you were lucky to escape with your life.'

'I was. God was watching over me that day.'

'Here he comes,' said Hunter and they turned to see the Simon of Syracuse striding towards them. The castellan handed a sealed parcel up to Cronin.

'The route is safe,' he said, 'and has been ridden many times these past few days so I see no need to send an armed escort.
'

'We will be fine,' said Cronin.

'If you ride hard,' said Simon, 'and change your horses in Beaufort, you can be back by nightfall.'

'As you wish, my lord,' said Cronin. They turned their horses away but before they could leave, another rider came galloping up the hill towards the castle.

'Wait here,' said the castellan and walked down the path to meet the rider at the outer wall. Although they could not hear what the messenger had to say, it was obvious he was agitated and by the look on the castellan's face, it was not good news. Within moments, Simon of Syracuse came running back up the slope to stop before Cronin and Hunter.

'A change of plan,' he gasped. 'You are to ride to Tiberius with all haste with a message for the king. Tell him to mobilize his men. Saladin is on the move at the head of a huge army. He is less than a day away and this time, his target is Chastellet.'

Chapter Thirty-Four

August – AD 1179

The Siege of Jacob's Ford – Day one

Several hours later, Simon of Syracuse and Rénier de Maron stood atop the one finished tower on the inner wall of Chastellet. Beyond the outer wall, they could see a huge Saracen army, just out of arrow range.

Every man woman and child that had worked on the castle had either taken refuge inside its monumental walls or had dispersed into the nearby forests. Every soldier able to stand had taken their positions on the outer and inner walls, ready to defend them at all costs, Men used to riding into battle astride warhorses now bore their lances on the battlements, their mounts safely tethered back in the stables. The lessons of Marj Ayyun had been learned and there would be no suicidal cavalry charge against such a strong enemy force.

The Saracens had been there for an hour, just standing and staring at the imposing fortress while their commanders rode back and fore, issuing their commands. Gradually the reason became clear as hundreds of archers came to the fore. Behind them came more men, each unarmed but weighed down with baskets full of arrows.

'I don't understand what they intend to do,' said the castellan. 'They cannot bring these walls down with arrows alone. They need siege engines.'

'Yet I see none,' said Rénier. 'What are your orders?'

'We will not waste any more men than we need to,' said Simon. 'These walls have already proved their worth and now they are twice as strong. We will fight back as long as we can from the outer wall but cede the outer bailey as soon as it becomes clear it will be lost. Like last time, I will give covering fire from up here while you bring the outer cordon back through the gates. Let them pound away at Chastellet's walls if that is their intention, we can just pick them off one by one until Baldwin arrives with his army, and when he does, we will pour through the gates like water from a breached dam. Saladin is not going to get it all his own way, my friend, not this time.'

He has hardly finished speaking when the relative quiet of the castle was shattered by a cacophony of noise. The air resounded with the sound of battle drums and horns, designed to strike fear into the heart of every living person in the castle, and as they watched, the enormous Saracen army started to advance.'

'Stand to the walls,' roared the castellan, 'here they come.'

Seven leagues away, Cronin and Hunter rode their horses right up to the castle gates in Tiberius.

'Hold there,' shouted the guard, 'what's the rush?'

'We need to see the king,' gasped Cronin, 'Chastellet is under attack.'

The guard stared in shock before turning and pushing open the gate.

'Let them through.'

Cronin and Hunter spurred their horses again before coming to a halt and dismounting to run up the steps towards the inner bailey. Again, they were challenged and though they were let through, this time they were accompanied by two guards who led them to the keep.

'Wait here,' said one and headed inside. Minutes later he emerged again and beckoned them in with his head. 'Come with me,' he said and led them through a maze of corridors until they reached a room containing William of Tyre.

'Brother Cronin,' said the prelate as they entered, 'and James Hunter. It seems you are here more than at Chastellet these days. Perhaps we should station you here permanently. The kitchens perhaps.'

'Father William,' said Cronin, ignoring the prelate's jibe, 'I have grave news and need to see the king.'

'The king is indisposed,' said a voice and both men turned to see Raynald of Chatillon walking into the room carrying a goblet of wine.

'Sir Raynald,' said Cronin, 'I thought you were in Jerusalem.'

'I was but when the king got ill, Father William here saw fit to summon me to take charge of the army. Apparently, the Templars have let him down and we need a change of direction.'

'I'm not sure that is a true reflection of the situation,' said Cronin. 'The brotherhood has been true to the king without fault and many have died in his name.'

'That may be true,' said Raynald, 'but perhaps those deaths could have been avoided with better leadership.'

Cronin glanced at Hunter, not sure how to respond.

'So,' continued Raymond, dropping into Baldwin's chair and sipping from his goblet. 'What is this urgent news that demands the attention of our sick king?'

'My lord,' said Cronin, 'Chastellet is under attack by Saladin.'

Raynald turned to stare at the two messengers, and slowly placed the goblet on the table at the side of the chair.

'What did you say?' he asked.

'The castle at Jacob's Ford,' said Hunter, 'it is under siege.'

'Are you sure about this?'

'Yes, my lord,' said Cronin. 'The castellan sent us here to request the king musters the army and sends reinforcements as soon as possible.'

'Did he now?' said Raynald. 'And this castellan, would he be the Templar knight, Sir Simon of Syracuse, given the role my Grand Master Amand himself?'

'I am not privy to who appointed him,' said Cronin,' but yes, the castellan is Sir Simon of Syracuse.'

The regent paused and looked between the other three men in the room.

'The thing is,' he said eventually, 'if I recall correctly, it was to the Templars this project was entrusted. The financing, the construction and even the garrison, all was to be provided by Amand's precious order. In fact, in order to enable this project, my campaign against Saladin in Egypt was put on hold just because of this precious castle, a delay that has now come back to haunt us.'

'My lord,' said Cronin, 'the politics of this situation is beyond me, all I know is Chastellet needs your help.'

'How big is the garrison in Chastellet?' asked Raymond.

'About fifteen hundred men at arms and another five hundred civilians.'

And how big is this Saracen army?'

'I don't know, my lord,' said Cronin. 'We left before it arrived, but the scout said it was less than half a day away.'

'The scout?'

'The one who had seen their approach.'

'So, the castle was not actually under attack when you left?' said William walking over, 'you just think it is.'

'My lord,' said Cronin, continuing to adress the regent, 'our scouts are the best and not one would report such a thing if he was not sure. Saladin is headed for Chastellet with an enormous force at his back and intends to lay siege.'

'You don't know that for sure,' said William.

'Why would the scout lie?' shouted Hunter turning to face the prelate. 'Why would any man report an enormous army if there was none?'

'I don't doubt he saw something,' said William, 'perhaps a Saracen patrol, even a small army perhaps, but even so, men are prone to exaggeration and the fact that his tale has not been backed up by someone else gives me cause for concern. Do you scouts not ride in pairs at all times?'

'Usually but...'

'Then where is his partner.'

'I don't know,' said Hunter. 'Perhaps he was a distance behind him.'

'And did you recognise him?'

'Why should I?'

'You too are a scout. Do you not mingle with men of the same calling?'

'In the name of God,' shouted Cronin, 'Chastellet is at risk and the castellan has asked for your help. Why won't you believe us?'

'His caution is well-founded,' interrupted Raynald. 'At Marj Ayyun the king lost many men through reckless decisions and it is a mistake I do not want to repeat. I fully believe that your man saw a Saracen army but is it possible they could be headed elsewhere?'

'Possibly,' said Cronin, 'I do not know the detail.'

'Exactly,' said the regent, 'none of us do and until the time that the facts are revealed, we should proceed with caution. After all, we do not want to ride into another trap.'

'But my lord,' said Hunter, 'we are wasting valuable time.'

'I am told Chastellet is a fortress like no other,' said the regent, 'and I'm sure that even if you are correct, an extra day or so will make no difference. I am told the castle is well stocked with food and I understand the well is now fully functioning. You have just told me yourself that the garrison is at full strength and I see no reason to rush into a situation that could leave us vulnerable. Nevertheless, it is a situation that needs addressing so this is what we are going to do. Tonight, you will stay here and rest your horses. Get some sleep and in the morning, you will return to Chastellet with an armed patrol to see for yourself what is happening. If you are correct and it is under siege, I will speak to the king and if he is agreeable, summon every man available to arms and march on Chastellet. In addition, I have been told that Henry of Champagne is on his way from Acre and together we will deal with Saladin once and for all. Now, get yourselves over to the guard room and get something to eat.' waved his hand in dismissal and watched as the two messengers left the room.

'What do you think,' asked Raynald when they had left.

'I don't know,' said William, 'I am just wary of anything that comes out of Chastellet. With the traitor still at large, it could be a trick to lure the king from Tiberius.'

'My thoughts exactly,' said Raynald, 'but we will find out soon enough.'

Back in Jacob's Ford, the Christian garrison was reeling under one of the most aggressive and unrelenting attacks any of them had ever experienced. Within moments of their first advance, the Saracen archers had filled the evening air with volley after volley of iron-tipped arrows, a solid wall of death that hailed down upon them without pause. The relentless pressure prevented the defenders from offering any effective response and the outer wall had already been abandoned under the onslaught.

The wooden palisades, once defended by Christian foot soldiers, now swarmed with Saracen warriors setting up their own positions to lay siege to the castle proper. As the archers kept up the relentless barrage against the Christians high on the battlements, others brought bails of pitch-soaked hay through the captured palisades, piling them up against the castle walls and throughout the outer bailey. Others brought piled of firewood or dragged dead trees behind them while others set about cutting down trees in the forest to their rear, much needed fuel for what they were about to attempt.

'I don't know what they think they are doing,' said Rénier, peering over the battlements. 'Any fires are going to be useless against these walls and the gates are iron-clad. They are wasting their time.'

'Saladin is too clever to do anything without purpose,' said Simon of Syracuse at his side, 'he has a plan, you can count on it.' An arrow bounced off the battlements, inches from Rénier's head and he dropped down behind the safety of the parapet wall.

'The light's almost gone,' he said, 'I'll double the sentries in case he tries something after dark.'

'You do that,' said Simon, 'I'll check the rest of the wall. The last thing we need now is for men to fail in their duty.' He got to his feet and crouching to stay out of sight of the enemy archers, ran along the battlements.

Down at the abandoned wooden palisades, Salah ad-Din himself stood amongst his generals having come forward to see the assault for himself.

'It is even more impressive close-up,' he said to Shirkuh ad-Din at his side, 'the infidels certainly know how to build a fortress.'

'It is just stone upon stone,' said Shirkuh ad-Din, 'and will fall like the humblest of huts.'

'Are the Sappers ready?'

'They are, my lord.'

'Then use the cover of darkness to start the tunnel. Work them day and night if needs be, we have little time so cannot afford to stop. Once Baldwin learns of our presence, he will ride here and fall upon our rear.'

'As you wish, my lord,' said Shirkuh ad-Din and the sultan turned away to head for his horse.

An hour later, as night finally fell, the noise from the Saracen drums and horns increased and under cover of darkness, the first of several dozen sappers climbed over the palisade and made their way to the centre of the bailey, completely unseen by those on the castle walls above. After a few moments searching around for the best place to start, they found the gap in the bedrock.

'This is it,' said one and without further ado, they removed their picks and shovels from their backs and started to dig. The tunnelling had begun.

Chapter Thirty-Five

August – AD 1179

The Siege of Jacob's Ford – Day two.

The following morning, just as the sun started to rise, archers sent flaming arrows across the outer bailey, setting light to the many piles of fuel they had put in place the previous evening. Immediately black plumes of smoke filled the air, swirling in the breeze to create a choking curtain cutting off any clear lines of sight from those on the battlements above. Some of the exhausted sappers who had been tunnelling throughout the night emerged and were immediately replaced with fresh men. Others dragged baskets of spoil away from the entrance while even more waited their turn to carry wooden props inside to support the ceiling. The whole operation was organised and efficient and despite the looming walls of the castle above, the continued throughout the day, the detail hidden from sight by the smoke.

To take the pressure off those defending the tunnel entrance and to keep the defenders' attention focused elsewhere, Saladin organised assaults on the other walls, even though they were doomed to failure. A small Mangonel hurled stones over the walls and a constant rain of fire arrows fell within the inner baileys.

Despite this, Christian casualties were few and the men on the ramparts returned fire whenever their own archers had the chance. Other missiles were hurled from the castle walls including rocks, spears and burning pitch, forcing the attackers back at every attempt and though the occupants of Chastellet knew they were under siege, their confidence in the castle walls was high.

Late in the evening, Hunter and Cronin left their horses hidden amongst the undergrowth and crawled up to a ridge a league or so from Chastellet. Alongside them were several of the king's men, sent with them to witness the truth of the matter.

Reaching the top, they peered towards the distant castle, realising that the scout had been correct. The castle was surrounded by Saracens and plumes of black smoke filled the air.

'Did we not tell you?' said Cronin to the officer at his side, 'yet nobody would believe us.'

'The king had to make sure,' said the officer. 'Now we have seen it with our own eyes, he will muster his army with all haste. Come, I have seen enough. We should get back to Tiberius.'

Cronin hesitated for a while still staring at the castle.

'What are you waiting for?' said the officer. 'Come on, let's go.'

'I should be in there,' said Cronin, 'alongside my brothers in arms.'

'And how do you intend to do that?' asked Hunter at his side.

'I don't know, there must be a way.'

'Look at them,' hissed Hunter, pointing to the huge besieging army,' they are like ants upon a dead bird. You will never get back into Chastellet until the king's army brings relief and the castellan opens the gates. The only thing we can do now is to get back to Baldwin and ride with his army. With any luck, we will be back here within days.'

Cronin realised his comrade was right and crawled back to the reverse slope of the hill. Within moments they were galloping hard back to Tiberius.

Nearer the castle, in one of the Saracen campaign tents, one of the sappers knelt before Saladin, his face smeared with dirt as he reported on the progress.

'My Lord,' he said, 'the digging has gone better than expected and we are already halfway. The ground is firm but digs easily. In addition, the cleft in the bedrock seems to run all the way beneath the inner walls.

'When do you reckon you will get to them?' asked Salah ad-Din.

'We should be in place sometime tonight,' said the sapper, 'and expose the foundations by noon tomorrow. My men will support them with timber and fill the void with brushwood. Once lit, the support beams will burn away, and the castle walls will collapse under their own weight.'

'You have done well,' said Salah ad-Din, 'and you will be well rewarded. But I urge you to double your efforts for there is no doubt that the Christian king will be aware of our assault and I suspect he is already issuing a call to arms. This castle must fall within three days if we are to avoid fighting another army to our rear. Can you do that?'

'I will do everything in my power,' said the sapper and bowed his head to the floor in subjugation.

At the far end of the upper bailey in one of the tents used by the squires, Hassan sat up in his cot, needing to empty his bladder. He left the tent and walked over to the nearest wall to relieve himself in the darkness. After he finished, he was about to return when he saw someone move in the shadows. Hassan stopped for a moment, wondering who would be amongst the piles of unused stones at such an hour but thinking it was probably someone doing the same as himself turned to walk away.

He was about to return to the tent out when a second man stepped out from behind a wall and dragged the first man down, pinning him to the ground. The boy quickly stepped back and hid amongst the rocks.

'I told you not to contact me again,' hissed the second man, holding the first by the throat. 'What do you want?'

'Nothing,' said the first, 'this time I have something of value to you.'

Hassan swallowed hard, recognising the voice. It was Ramaz, the overseer.

'What could you possibly have that would interest me?' said the taller man.

'The most valuable thing you could possess,' said Ramaz, 'your life.'

The hooded man paused before standing up and allowing his victim to get to his feet. Hassan strained to see who he was, but the cloak and the darkness concealed his identity.

'What do you mean?' asked the cloaked man.

'The walls will soon fall,' said Ramaz, 'of that there is no doubt, but I have a proposition for you. For a price, when the time comes, I can get you out of here.'

'Saladin has promised me my life,' said the hooded man.

'In the heat of battle there will be little time to decide who lives or dies,' said Ramaz, 'you of all people should know this. All I am saying that for a fair price, I can get you out of here, with or without Saladin's blessing.'

'How?'

'Because, my lord, there is a passageway.'

'What passageway?' asked the man. 'I know of no such thing.'

'Nevertheless, it exists. I know because I worked on it myself alongside others.'

'What others?'

'Worry not, they are all now dead, so it is only I who knows where it is. For a hundred golden Bezants, when the time comes, I will lead you through myself.'

'A hundred Bezants?'

'Aye, a tiny sum in exchange for your life.'

'I hold no such amount.'

'Not yet, but when you leave this place, you will pick up your payment from Salah ad-Din and be a rich man.'

'And you will wait for payment?'

'I trust you,' said Ramaz, 'and besides, as lowly as I am, nobody betrays Ramaz without consequences.'

The hooded man paused before taking a deep breath.

'We have a deal,' he said eventually. 'Where is the tunnel?'

'For the moment, that will remain my business,' said Ramaz. 'If the castle falls, as it will, meet me here and I will lead the way. Bring no other for the path is narrow and steep.'

'So be it,' said the hooded man, 'but if this is a trick, I swear I will kill you myself.'

'It is no trick,' said Ramaz. 'Just be ready when the time is right.'

The hooded man nodded and walked away leaving the overseer behind him.

Hassan waited amongst the rocks before creeping from his hiding place. For a moment he just stood there but as the moon appeared from behind a cloud, he saw something on the ground. He picked it up and recognising it immediately, hid it within his jerkin before heading back to his tent. His heart raced with fear and excitement for although he didn't know who the second man was, it was obvious the two were the spies he had been warned about. The night was still long before him and he knew that no matter how hard he tried; he would get no sleep.

The following morning, Sumeira walked amongst the wounded in the hospital tent, offering comfort and treatment to those that had been hurt in the assault so far. Luckily the numbers were few and there were still plenty of empty cots in case they were needed. Other women carried water gourds and platters of food and though they knew the castle was under siege, the mood was calm and quiet.

At the end of the tent, Hassan ducked his head inside and waited until he caught Sumeira's attention. She handed the water jug she was carrying to another woman and walked over to Hassan, wiping her hands on the cloth tucked in her rope belt as she went.

'Hassan,' she said, 'it's good to see you. How are you?'

'I'm much better,' said Hassan, 'but I need to talk to you.'

'About what?' asked Sumeira.

'Not here,' said Hassan. 'Can you come away?'

'I'm busy,' said Sumeira, 'but we could talk after our meal at nightfall. What's all this about?'

'I'll talk to you then,' said Hassan, looking around. 'Meet me by the stables.'

'Hassan,' said Sumeira but it was too late, the boy was already walking away back to his duties.

Later that night, Sumeira sat amongst her fellow workers outside the hospital tent, eating a bowl of potage from one of the many campfires around the inner bailey. When she had finished, she turned to her daughter sitting beside her.

'You stay here, Emani,' she said, getting to her feet, 'I'll be back soon.'

'Where are you going?' asked the girl.

'I just need to speak to someone,' said Sumeira, kissing the girl on the head. 'I won't be long.'

She placed her empty bowl on the trestle table and walked further up into the upper bailey towards where the main stables were only half-built. As she neared, Hassan stepped out of the shadows and beckoned her to step behind one of the walls.

'Hassan,' she said once they were both out of sight, 'what's all this about?'

'My lady,' said Hassan, looking around, 'you are in great danger, we all are.'

'From who?' asked Sumeira.

'The Saracens,' said Hassan, 'if they get in here, they will kill us all, including Emani.'

'Hassan,' said Sumeira, 'what are you talking about? I know we are under siege, but this castle is impregnable, and it is said the king is already on his way with a great army. Saladin will never breach these walls so all we have to do is wait.'

'No, my lady,' said Hassan, 'that's not true. By the time the king gets here the walls will be breached and we will all be dead. We have to escape.'

'Hassan,' said Sumeira, 'you are worrying me. What are you talking about?'

Hassan took the woman's arm and pulled her deeper into the shadows.

'My lady, last night I overheard two men talking. They knew the walls would soon fall and they were planning their escape.'

'Who were these men?'

'I only recognised one,' said Hassan, 'his name is Ramaz, an overseer from amongst the masons. The other's face was hidden amongst the shadows. I'm not mistaken, my lady, both men are the traitors that we have been warned about.'

'What do you mean traitors, Hassan, and if that is true, how do you know such a thing?'

'Master Cronin told me,' said Hassan, 'and he learned of it from Sir Jakelin. All the Templars know but were sworn to secrecy. Brother Cronin asked me to report anything unusual directly to him, but he is not here, and I don't know what to do.'

'And you think you saw something last night?'

'I know I did,' said Hassan, 'for I heard them talk.'

'What else did they say?'

''They discussed a hidden passageway built into the castle walls,' said Hassan, 'and agreed they would both use it when the castle fell.'

'The postern gate?'

'No, another door, hidden in the base of the wall above the cliff. It seems it was placed there for exactly this sort of thing and known only to a few. Ramaz was one of those who built it.'

'And you learned all this last night?'

'I did, my lady. Ramaz was explaining everything. It was if the second man was hearing it for the first time.'

'Hassan,' said Sumeira, 'have you reported this to the castellan?'

'I have not for I am afraid to do so.'

'Why,' asked Sumeira, 'we have to tell someone?'

'We cannot,' said Hassan, 'because when the man in the shadows left, he tripped in the darkness and left something behind.'

'What?' asked Sumeira.

'This,' said Hassan and held out a piece of black fabric.

'What is it?' asked Sumeira taking it from the boy's hands.

'It is a felt cap, my lady, the sort that knights wear beneath their helms.'

'The other man is a knight?' She gasped.

'He is,' said Hassan, 'but there is more. Look at the emblem on the back of the cap.'

Sumeira turned the cap around to see a small cross embroidered from red thread. For a few moments, she stared, not sure what to make of it but suddenly her eyes widened as she realised the significance.

'In the name of God,' she said, looking back up at Hassan's face with fear in her eyes, *'it belongs to a Templar.'*

Chapter Thirty-Six

August – AD 1179

The Siege of Jacob's Ford – Day three.

The following morning, Sumeira sat on her bed, the skull cap rolled up in her hand. A passing guard patrol had forced her and Hassan to abandon their conversation the previous night and they had returned to their tents, each as worried as the other. If what Hassan had said was true, and the castle had been betrayed at the highest level, then they were indeed in terrible danger.

'Are you unwell, my lady?' asked a voice and she looked over to see one of the young slave girls looking at her with concern.

'I'm fine,' said Sumeira with a forced smile as she placed the skull cap in her pocket. 'Just hoping this siege will soon end.'

'My friends are saying the king is only hours away,' said the girl, 'is that true?'

'Who knows the truth anymore?' said Sumeira getting to her feet.' Now come, we should be getting to the hospital tent.'

'I'm just glad those fire arrows can't reach all the way up here,' said the girl as they went.

'Me too, Akifah,' said Sumeira, her thoughts still far away, 'me too.'

Outside the castle, men stumbled through the sickening smoke, carrying more buckets of spoil from the tunnel. Amongst them was the overseer who ran over to the palisade to report on the progress to Shirkuh ad-Din.

'My Lord,' he said as he climbed the ladder, 'we have done it. This morning we hit the foundations and are currently excavating beneath them to create the cavern.'

'Great news indeed,' said Shirkuh. 'How long until we can set the fires?'

'If you can give me until midday, my lord, the cavern should be big enough for the fuel. If Allah is with us, the walls could be down by nightfall.'

'I will convey this back to the sultan,' said Shirkuh ad-Din, 'you get back to work. In the meantime, I will have the men bring up brush and timber for the fires.'

'As you wish, my lord,' said the sapper and turned to return to the tunnel.

Despite having been awake all night, Hassan was not tired in the slightest. Indeed, he was alert and determined to make the best of a bad situation. Having been allocated to the masons working on the towers in the upper bailey, he knew where the traitorous overseer worked and was determined to get as close as he could.

Throughout the morning he gradually worked his way nearer until eventually, he was within a few paces and able to watch his every move. As time passed, he started to doubt his own suspicions but as the mealtime came, the man disappeared.

'Where's the overseer?' asked Hassan sitting on a grassy bank to eat his bread and cheese.

'Who knows?' said the worker at his side. 'I expect he is sleeping in some corner.'

'Really?' said Hassan.

'Aye. Somewhere near the northern wall, 'we are better off without him.'

Hassan nodded and finished his food before taking the bowl back to the table. He looked around and seeing no other overseers in the area, quickly walked over to where he and Sumeira had talked the previous evening. Seeing nothing untoward he headed between the partly finished walls, creeping as silently as he could to avoid detection. Finding nothing of interest he turned to walk away but a muffled cough made him stop in his tracks. Quickly he hid amongst a pile of dressed stone and waited to see if the overseer would reveal his location.

A few minutes later, Ramaz emerged from one of the few buildings already finished, a cold store designed for the hanging of meat.

Hassan watched him close the door and hurry back down into the lower bailey. Once he had gone, the boy emerged from his own hiding place and opened the door to the food store.

Inside was dark but a small shaft of light from an unfinished window allowed him to just about see what he was doing. At first, he could see nothing out of the ordinary but as he reached the rear wall, he could see a pile of old sacks piled up in the corner. He pulled them away and gasped as he saw a hole at the base of the wall no higher than his knees.

He dropped to his knees and crawled through the hole, emerging into a narrow tunnel heading down into the mountain. The rock on either side meant the passage was a natural formation and must have been known about before a single stone had been laid.

After fifty paces or so, Hassan came to a wooden gate set into the end of the tunnel. He pulled back the tree heavy bolts and pushed the door outward. Outside, several bushed hid the doorway from any prying eyes below it and beyond them, the ground fell away almost vertically to the valley far below. Hassan looked along the tiny ledge and could see it was an old goat's path, just big enough for one person to traverse without falling over the cliff. He hurried back the way he had come, locking the door behind him. Back in the food store, he replaced the sacks over the hole and returned to work. His suspicions had been right, the overseer was one of the traitors and he was planning his escape for when the Saracens arrived.

Later that evening, Hassan once more met with Sumeira, though this time well away from the kitchen area in case they were discovered.

'How far does the tunnel extend?' asked Sumeira.

'A few hundred paces,' said Hassan, 'no more than that.'

'What I don't understand,' said Sumeira, 'is if this castle is so impregnable, why would they build a secret escape route?'

'Most castles have some way of escape,' said Hassan, 'usually by way of the postern but some have secret ways, like this one. The passage is natural and heads down through the mountain below the castle walls. It emerges in the cliff but is still high above the valley. Whatever the reason, it is our way out. All we have to do is collect some supplies, wait until dark and we can go.'

'No,' said Sumeira, 'we have to stay, at least until we know there is no other option.'

'But why?' asked Hassan. 'To wait only invites death.'

'These people need me,' said Sumeira. 'I am a healer and my place is amongst them.'

'There are few in the hospital tents, my lady and they are well cared for by Loxley and the rest of the women. You will not be missed.'

'You forget,' said Sumeira, 'we are still under siege. Hardly a day goes by without someone getting hurt by a Saracen arrow and that doesn't include the illnesses amongst the civilians. This is only going to get worse and I have to do everything within my power to help. Besides, who's to say they will succeed? This may all be over before they get anywhere near.'

'But if I am right and the Saracens break through the walls?'

'Then we will go,' said Sumeira, 'but until then, my place is here. In the meantime, perhaps we can collect a little food and water and hide it away just in case.' She stopped talking and stared at Hassan's worried face. 'I'm sorry, Hassan,' she said, taking his arm, 'but this is the way it has to be. However, if you are concerned, then you must go on without us.'

'I will not leave you, my lady,' said Hassan. 'If the worst happens, I will seek you out and guide the way but if I fall, then you must take Emani and go alone. The passage is at the end of the food store in the unfinished kitchens.'

'Thank you, Hassan,' said Sumeira. 'It's just a shame we don't know who the Templar spy is so we could tell the others.'

'They would never believe us anyway,' said Hassan, 'they are brothers unto death and would see our accusations as nothing more than rumours.'

'We have to tell someone, Hassan,' she said, 'this is too big a secret to keep to ourselves.'

'If only Master Cronin was here,' said Hassan, 'he would know what to do.'

Outside the castle walls, Salah ad-Din and his Mamluk bodyguards rode towards the wooden palisade surrounding the castle. Everywhere they looked they could see men running with arms full of hay and bracken, heading towards the mine entrance.

As they neared, Farrukh-Shah saw his approach and walked over to greet the Sultan.

'Allah Akbar, my lord,' he said touching his hand to his forehead and chest and bowing his head in greeting.

'Allah Akbar, nephew,' said Salah ad-Din. 'I see there has been progress.'

'There has,' said Farrukh-Shah, 'the tunnelling is complete and the filling has begun. Soon we will set the flames and if the calculations are correct, we should see a breach in the wall by nightfall.'

'Excellent,' said Salah ad-Din, 'I will inform my generals and prepare the men. As soon as the wall falls, we need to attack immediately while the surprise is still ours. If we wait, they could prepare temporary defences and hold us out until Baldwin's army arrives.'

'So, it will be done, my lord,' said Farrukh-Shah.

Up on the walls, Sir Rénier peered between the battlements, squinting to get a clearer view between the swirling veil of smoke. The constant rain of arrows falling within the castle was nothing more than an irritation and few men fell to their impact. The fire arrows were of more concern and several tents and wooden buildings had been affected though the quick response of the many civilians in the lower bailey meant that the damage was limited. As he watched, the castellan approached along the ramparts, checking each man was on station and fully alert.

'My Lord,' said Rénier as Simon neared, 'you should see this.'

'What?' said Simon, joining the Under-Marshal up on one of the firing steps.

'There,' said Rénier pointing down into the outer bailey, 'there has been a lot of activity these past few hours. I think they are up to something.'

The castellan stared down and as the smoke swirled, saw groups of men hurrying forward from the palisade with more fuel for the fires.

'They have been doing that for days,' said Simon. 'To what end I do not know but it harms us not.'

'No,' said Rénier, 'this is different, look there.'

Again, he pointed and this time, the smoke cleared long enough for the castellan to see the men disappearing into a fold in the ground.

'What are they doing?' he asked when several emerged empty-handed.

'There is only one thing they can be doing, my lord,' said Rénier, 'taking fuel into a tunnel.'

The castellan stared at the Under-Marshal with growing concern on his face. '

'Do you think they have tunnelled under the walls?' he asked.

'It is the only thing that makes sense,' said Rénier. 'For days they have kept our heads down with arrows and blinded us with smoke. I think that was so their sappers could get close enough to dig.'

'But the castle is built on rock,' said Simon. 'There is no way they could tunnel that far in a few days.'

'Unless there was a fault,' said Rénier. 'Now it seems they have already reached the foundations else why would they be filling the tunnels with firewood.'

'They mean to collapse the wall,' said Simon as realisation dawned, 'in the name of God, Rénier, *call the men to arms.*'

Less than ten minutes later, every man capable of holding a weapon stood on the battlements or in the lower bailey, facing the outer walls. None could be sure which, if any wall would collapse but they stood ready to repel any Saracens coming through the breach with everything they had. All the women and children stayed in the upper bailey out of the way, but they knew that if their men were bettered, then they too would become victims to Saracen steel.

As the foot soldiers waited, the Templars rode down from the upper bailey, fully adorned in their battle armour. Their destriers were draped with their heavy caparisons, designed to deflect all but the heaviest of blows and they lined up in front of the foot soldiers, ready to be the first into battle. At their head rode Simon of Syracuse for though he was the castellan, he was still the senior Templar officer present and by default, the garrison commander.

'Listen to me,' he roared, riding back and forth along the lines, 'we have no idea if this wall will fall, but if it does, we will have no time to consider our options. Even as the last stone falls, we will attack the breach, forcing the Saracens back. As soon as we advance, you will follow us in and fight like your lives depended on it, which they surely do. Are you ready?'

'Aye,' roared the men and each turned their attention to the wall, fully expecting it to fall at any moment.

For the next few hours they waited and though the activity outside the castle had increased, there was no sign of any collapse. The walls had held.

Outside the castle wall, darkness fell and behind the timber palisade, several sappers knelt, their heads resting on the ground as they waited for the arrival of the Sultan. Each knew full well that in the next few moments, they could all die as the price for failure.

Salah ad-Din rode into the camp alongside the ever-present Mamluk guards and jumped from his horse to walk amongst the terrified men.

'Tell me what happened,' he shouted, 'why is that castle still standing?'

'My Lord,' said one of the men on his knees, 'the strength of the walls is greater than any that I have seen.'

'Stand up,' snapped Salah ad-Din, 'address me directly.'

'My Lord,' said the sapper, getting to his feet, 'we did what we needed to do and even as we speak the fires are raging in the tunnels, but the walls are like none I have ever seen and hold even without support.'

'Nothing can stay up without support,' said Saladin. 'The tunnels must not be big enough. Make them larger and the walls will fall. Excavate further beneath the foundations so there is a greater load above.'

'I agree,' said the Sapper, 'but we cannot get back in there until the fires have died down. The place is a furnace.'

'How long will it take to cool?' asked the Sultan.

'Two days, my lord, maybe three.'

'And the time to expand the tunnel?'

'Another day on top, my lord. You are looking at four days in all before we can reset the fires.'

'We don't have four days,' said Salah ad-Din, 'I need those walls down now.'

'My Lord,' said the sapper, 'with respect, it is just too hot.'

Salah ad-Din thought furiously, knowing this was his last chance. Eventually, he had an idea and turned to address the men who had gathered around.

'Listen to me,' he shouted, 'Allah is testing our resolve and he wants us to prove our devotion. This castle must fall in his name or our people risk being cut off from the great sea for generations. I ask you, my friends, help me defeat these infidels. Join together to put out these fires and I swear that I will pay a golden dinar to every man who throws a bucket of water into the flames. This I swear in Allah's name.' He paused and looked around the shocked faces. 'Well?' he said eventually, pulling a golden dinar from within his cloak and holding it up high. 'Who will be the first?'

For a few seconds, nobody moved until suddenly an archer cast aside his bow and ran forward to kneel before the Sultan.

'I will take the first bucket, my lord,' he said, 'let it be me to lead the way.'

Saladin looked at the archer and then back up to the other men.

'This is a true believer,' he said before raising his voice to echo through the darkness, '*Allah Akbar.*'

'*Allah Akbar,*' roared the men before him and everyone rushed forward to reach the Sultan, each committed to extinguishing the fires.

Salah ad-Din looked down from the cart.

'I have no more coins about me this night,' he shouted, 'but I swear in the name of Allah himself, I will honour my pledge. Extinguish those flames and you will all be rich men before this night is done.'

The men turned away to seek whatever vessels they could to carry water, each caught up in the fervour and as they streamed away, Salah ad-Din climbed down from the cart to address the sappers still kneeling in the dirt.

'Stand up,' he said, staring at their terrified faces. 'Your heads should be on spikes, but all is not lost. As soon as the fires are out, restart the dig and increase the tunnels in size. You have one night and one day, no more. Succeed and you will be rich beyond your dreams, fail and your heads will find a new place to sit. Is that clear?'

'Yes, my lord,' they said in unison.

'Good, now begone and ensure you do what has to be done.'

Chapter Thirty-Seven

August – AD 1179

The Siege of Jacob's Ford – Day four.

The following morning dawned with the walls of Chastellet still intact and hundreds of men still stationed within the lower bailey. Many lay upon the ground, fast asleep after the long and uneventful night but others stayed awake, still afraid that the walls may come tumbling down at any moment. The Templars stood to one side, talking quietly amongst each other as the grooms and squires took care of the horses. The feeling of relief was tangible, and the talk was of what to do next.

'I say we open the gates and ride out,' said one of the knights. 'In here we are nothing but prisoners within our own walls.'

'No,' said Simon of Syracuse, 'they outnumber us fivefold and have archers surrounding the castle ten men deep. As soon as we rode out, we would be cut down like hay.'

'Better to die a martyr than live a thousand lives a slave,' said the knight.

'Slaves we are certainly not, brother,' said Simon, 'but it is pointless dying for no reason. If we fall, who will protect these people should Saladin breach the walls?'

'My Lord,' shouted a voice and Simon looked up to see Sir Rénier peering down from the battlements.

'What is it?'

'You should come,' said Rénier, 'I think something is happening.'

'What's the problem?' asked the castellan when he reached Rénier's position.

'Look,' said the Under-Marshal, 'there is hardly any activity around the tunnel entrance.'

'Perhaps they have given up?'

'Possibly but it was a hive of activity throughout the night with men coming and going without rest. Now there is quiet but look over by the palisade.'

Simon turned to gaze outward and saw piles upon piles of brushwood surrounded by men waiting to carry it to the mine.

'I thought they had already set the fires,' he said.

'As did I, my lord, but it looks like they failed so there is going to be a second attempt. I suspect the fires were extinguished overnight and Saladin's sappers are currently increasing the size of the tunnels.'

'Is there anything we can do?' asked Simon.

'The bedrock inside the bailey is too thick,' said Rénier, 'else we could dig our own tunnels and confront them beneath the ground. Other than that, all we can do is prepare for the worst and pray Baldwin is on his way with his army.'

'Then may he ride with Angel's wings,' said Simon.

In Tiberius, Hunter and Cronin were once more standing before Sir Raynald in the king's audience chamber, as they had done for the past four days.

'My lord,' said Cronin, 'with the greatest of respect, why can we not ride this very morn?'

'Because,' said Raynald, 'like I told you yesterday, and the day before that, the king's army is not yet ready. The archers are short of arrows and many of the new recruits are short of weapons and chainmail. I have every blacksmith and fletcher in Tiberius addressing the issue but until their needs are met, we will remain here.'

'My lord,' said Hunter, 'you have a strong cavalry and a thousand well-equipped men at arms ready to go. Even if we just send those alone, Saladin will see them and know he has run out of time.'

'Or,' said William stepping forward, 'he will see they are a weakened force and attack them before they can make any difference, and if that happens, there will be no relief column until Henry of Champagne arrives from Acre.'

'So, we just stay here and do nothing?'

'Like I said,' replied Raynald, 'the garrison are safe within the walls of Chastellet for the time being. I would even go as far as to say, they are probably at less risk out there than many of our own people in Tiberius. I appreciate your concerns, my friends but we have to prepare properly.'

'Do you have any idea when the army will be ready?' asked Cronin.

'The king's armourers tell me that everything should be in place by dawn tomorrow and I have no reason to disbelieve them.

Sharpen your blades, brother Cronin, for by tomorrow night I suspect they will be stained with Saracen blood.'

Back in the castle, Hassan sat on a cot alongside Sumeira in one of the empty tents. They talked quietly so nobody could hear them through the fabric walls.

'My lady,' said Hassan, 'I am begging you. At least get into the tunnel just in case. If the walls remain intact then you can emerge to carry on as before but if they fall, you will have a head start.'

'We've been over this,' said Sumeira, 'even if the walls fall, the garrison is full of men used to the trials of war. The Saracens can only send a few at a time through any breach and they can be cut down by our archers.'

'Who told you this?' asked Hassan.

'There is talk amongst the women,' said Sumeira. 'Many of them are married to those tasked with defending Chastellet. They say the mood is high that even if a breach occurs, it will be easily repelled.'

'I hope you are right,' said Hassan, 'for all our sakes.'

The day dragged on with little activity. Archers on the wall did what they could to hit the Saracen workers near the mine entrance, but it was at the edge of their range and most arrows fell short without effect. The women and children distributed food and water but the fear had dissipated, and the occupants believed once again that their hopes had been confirmed, the castle was impregnable.

'It can't be long now,' said one of the sergeants, 'King Baldwin must be on his way and we will be able to open the gates at last.'

'I don't think it matters either way,' said another, swigging beer from his flask, 'it would need a thunderbolt from God himself to even scratch these walls. Let the Saracens play their silly games as far as I'm concerned, as long as there is food and ale, I'm happy to stay here until Christ's mass.'

By the evening, most of the men had been stood down with only a hundred or so still on duty in the lower bailey. The battlements were still fully manned but Saracen activity outside had significantly dropped, though many of their warriors now lined the wooden palisades, watching as the fires that had smoked so heavily over the past few days, slowly died out.

Beyond the timber wall, Saracen cavalry and foot soldiers manoeuvred into place, thousands of men, each heavily armed and ready for war. Carpenters and slaves started to remove large sections of the palisade and by the time nightfall came, the ground between the castle and the Saracen army was completely clear.

'I don't like this,' said Rénier to a knight to his side, 'send for the castellan.'

To the rear of the Saracen army, Salah ad-Din once again stood on a hill overlooking Jacob's Ford. Alongside him stood the overseer of his sappers.

'Look before you, my friend,' said Salah ad-Din, 'glory in the strength of our army.'

'It is truly magnificent, my lord,' said the sapper.

'It is,' said the Sultan, 'and each man is prepared to fight and die to remove the Christian castle that threatens our way of life. That was my task, my friend, to rally the tribes in the name of Allah. To you fell the task of collapsing the walls.' He turned and stared menacingly at the sapper. 'I have fulfilled my duty; now tell me you have done yours.'

'I have my lord,' said the sapper, 'the cavern beneath the foundations is now three times the size of what it was and the wall above only stays up because of the wooden supports we have put in place. The tunnels are already packed full of firewood.'

'And when these fires are lit?'

'The wall will collapse, my lord.'

'How long will it take?'

'A few hours, no more.'

'Are you sure?'

'I am, my lord, there is no way they can stay up when the supports have burned away. The walls will fall, I swear it upon my life.'

'Yes,' said Salah ad-Din quietly, 'you do.' He turned away and looked towards Shirkuh ad-Din, waiting on his horse to one side. 'Muster your men, nephew,' he said, 'and stand to your horses for tomorrow we take Chastellet.'

Chapter Thirty-Eight

August – AD 1179

The Siege of Jacob's Ford – Day five

The sun was just about rising when the first sign of trouble appeared on the southern wall. A movement on the battlements made the sentries stare at each other with worry.

'Did you feel that?' asked one.

'I did,' said his comrade, 'the wall lurched.'

The other soldier did not answer but stared at the wall behind his friend.

'Look at that,' he said and walked over to insert his finger into a crack that had appeared down part of the outer wall. 'That wasn't there last night.'

Both men peered over the parapet and though there were no Saracens anywhere near the wall, they could just about make out a vast army beyond the timber palisades, all formed up and ready for battle.

'Sweet Jesus,' said the first sentry, spotting a few more cracks in the wall, 'I think we should call the guard commander; he should see this.'

Within minutes, several officers were up on the battlements staring out at the Saracen army. The garrison had already been called to arms and the men who had spent the best part of two days waiting in the lower bailey, reassembled, wondering what was going on.

'When did this happen?' asked the castellan, seeing the cracks in the wall.

'This morning, my lord,' said the guard. 'There was a shake and the hole just appeared.'

'My Lord,' shouted a voice from below where a group of men had gathered at the base of the wall, 'the stones are hot to the touch.'

The castellan's face grimaced with worry. He looked over the battlements at the waiting Saracen army before turning back to the Under-Marshal.

'Grab every man who can wield a blade, Sir Rénier,' he said, 'drag them from their hospital beds if needs be. Despite our hopes, I think Chastellet is about to let us down.'

Hassan and Sumeira stood in the upper bailey, looking over the much smaller wall into the bailey below. Already they could see the mood was entirely different as the nervous defenders hustled into position, over a thousand men at arms spreading out throughout the castle as they waited for the inevitable. Again, the Templars sat astride their horses, waiting to charge into the face of the enemy if they came through any breach. The mood was desperate, the fear tangible.

'My lady,' said Hassan, 'surely you can see there is no point in waiting longer. We should go.'

Sumeira watched as the Templar officers walked amongst the foot soldiers, reminding them of their duty and stirring them to aggression. It was obvious now that they fully expected the walls to fall and the size of the enemy army gathered outside meant it would be a battle like no other.

'I still think they can do it,' said Sumeira, 'there's no way Saladin can get enough warriors through any breach to break our lines, there are just too many.'

'My lady,' said Hassan, 'please, you must make ready.'

'Hassan,' said Sumeira, 'I'll tell you what we will do. You collect Emani and gather the stores we have hidden away. Take her to the tunnel and wait for me there. If our men prevail then we will meet again when the fighting is done. If we are defeated, then I will come as soon as I can.'

'Are you sure, my lady?' asked Hassan.

'Yes, Hassan. Do as I say but know this. If the lower bailey is taken and I am not with you by the time they assault the upper level, you should leave. Take my daughter to Jerusalem and place her in the hands of the Christian church. Will you do that?'

'I cannot leave without you, my lady,' he said.

'You have to. swear this upon your life, Hassan, for the sake of my daughter.'

'Of course, my lady,' said Hassan, 'as you wish.'

'One more thing, Hassan,' said Sumeira, 'we have kept this secret to ourselves too long. If there is indeed a tunnel as you say, then we should tell someone. At the very least it may enable others to escape if the worst happens.'

'Leave it to me, my lady,' said Hassan. 'I know just the man.'

Hassan headed down into the lower bailey, seeking the Under-Marshal. Sir Rénier was known as an honourable man and as he wasn't a Templar, could not be the traitor. The boy hurried along, pushing his way amongst the throng when suddenly an arm shot out and dragged him into a small room at the base of the gate tower.

'Slow down there, boy,' said his captor, pushing him against a wall, 'what's the hurry?'

Hassan's heart dropped. It was Bullard, the officer who had threatened him after the battle of Marj Ayyun.

'Well look who it is,' said Bullard, his breath stinking of ale, 'if it isn't our own pet Saracen.'

'Let me go,' said Hassan, 'I need to see the Under-Marshal.'

'And why would he want to see the likes of you?' asked Bullard. 'I think he's a bit busy right now, don't you?'

'This is important,' said Hassan, 'I have something he needs to know.'

'Well why don't you tell me?' said Bullard. 'I'm an officer after all.'

'This is for his ears only,' said Hassan, 'now let me go.'

Bullard stared at Hassan before suddenly throwing him to the floor and slamming the door shut.

'What are you doing?' gasped Hassan, getting to his feet. 'This is folly. I need to see Sir Rénier.'

Bullard leaned closer; his face full of menace

'You listen to me,' he growled, 'I reckon this place could be swarming with Saracens within hours and if that happens, you could be my only chance to survive.'

'How?' gasped Hassan in disbelief.

'Because you are one of them and you can speak for me.'

'I've already told you,' said Hassan, 'I'm not of the Ayyubid, I'm a Bedouin.'

'I don't care if you are the king of England himself,' said Bullard, 'you look like them, sound like them and can speak their language. In my eyes that makes you a Saracen and the best chance I've got of surviving this mess.'

'Then you are a bigger fool than I thought.' said Hassan.

Bullard lunged forward and pushed Hassan back against the wall, pressing a blade against the boy's throat.

'Now you listen to me,' Saracen, he snarled, his spittle spraying onto the boy's face, 'you and me are going to stay in here until the fighting is done. If the castle falls, then you are going to go outside, with me close behind you and you are going to beg your friends for mercy, understand?'

'I told you, they are not my friends,' gasped Hassan.

'You had better hope they are,' said Bullard, 'or this knife will end up hilt deep into your back. Now, what's this important information you have for Rénier?'

Hassan thought furiously. If he refused to say anything, he would likely be beaten half to death and forced to stay in the room until the assault ended. If the Christians prevailed, Bullard would have to kill him anyway so his own cowardice would remain hidden and if the Saracens won the fight, they were both as good as dead anyway. His overall fear was for the safety of Sumeira and Emani and no matter what the cost, he was determined to get them to safety. If that meant Bullard went along with them, it was a price worth paying.

'Well,' said Bullard, 'I'm waiting.'

'If I tell you,' said Hassan, 'I want your word that you let me go immediately.'

'And why would I do that?'

'Because I have a way out of here. There's no need for any of us to die.'

Bullard stared at Hassan in silence, blinking heavily as he digested the information. Eventually, he lowered his blade and replaced it in his belt before stepping back.

'I hope for your sake this is true,' he said, 'because if you are lying then I will stick you like a pig.'

'It is true,' said Hassan. 'I know of a way out and have been sent by the healer to inform the Under-Marshal.'

'Why?'

'Because if it looks like the castle will fall, we need to save as many people as we can.'

Bullard stared in surprise, hardly believing his luck.

'Even if you are telling the truth,' he said, 'what's to stop Saladin's men just rounding them up again when they get out?'

'Because the track is narrow and hidden amongst the trees on the cliff. No Saracens cover that approach because they would never get up undetected. All we have to do is head down the path and wait until darkness before making our way to the hills.'

Again Bullard stared, his mind racing. If the boy was telling the truth it was the miracle he had been hoping for.

'Who else knows about this tunnel?'

'Just me, the healer and the two traitors.'

'And who may they be?'

'I only know one. He is an overseer amongst the Masons.'

'But you want to tell the Under-Marshal?'

'I do. That way he can arrange as many as possible to escape with their lives.'

'Where is the tunnel entrance?' asked Bullard.

'I'm not telling you that,' said Hassan, 'you could leave right now and give away its location to anyone waiting outside. If you want to escape this place, you'll let me go and you can come the same time as the rest of us.'

'That's not going to work,' said Bullard.

'Why not?'

'If we allow too many people to go, they will be noticed. It has to be just a select few. Just you, me and the wench.'

'No,' said Hassan, 'we can't just leave all these women and children to die or be sold into slavery.'

'You'll never get them all out.'

'Perhaps not but they deserve the chance.'

'You say the tunnel emerges on the cliff.'

'Aye.'

'In that case, it must be on the north wall.'

Hassan didn't answer but the look on his face confirmed the officer had guessed correctly.

'I knew it,' said Bullard, and turned towards the door.

'Where are you going?' asked Hassan.

'To get my stuff,' said Bullard, 'and to get the hell out of here before it's too late.'

'But you promised you would set me free,' shouted at Hassan and ran towards the officer.

Bullard turned and knocked Hassan to the floor before lifting him up again by the neck of his jerkin.

'You just be thankful I'm letting you live,' he hissed, 'when the castle falls you can beg your countrymen for your life.' Before Hassan could answer, Bullard punched him again, knocking the boy out cold.

Simon of Syracuse and Sir Rénier de Maron sat upon their horses at the top of the slope leading up to the inner bailey. Both were fully armoured, as were all of the men around them. The sounds of solid rock splitting apart echoed through the castle and they waited for the inevitable. Already one of the enormous walls was listing and they knew it was just a matter of time until the collapse.

'Prepare to advance,' shouted Simon, 'as soon as the first of the enemy come through, we will cut them down with a flanking charge. If the numbers are too great, abandon the horses and fight on foot. Is that clear?'

'Aye, my lord,' shouted the men and many drew their swords ready for the advance.

Again, a number of loud cracks rang out around the lower bailey and a large portion of the wall dropped a few inches as the supports beneath the foundations started to give way.

'Archers ready,' roared the castellan.

Every man prepared themselves, expecting the wall to collapse down into a huge mound of rubble, but what happened next took everyone by surprise.

'Here it goes,' roared the castellan as the wall finally started to move, 'prepare to charge,' but no sooner than the words had come out of his mouth when all thoughts of attack or even defence were quickly forgotten.

To everyone's surprise, the entire area below the wall, collapsed in on itself, forming an enormous hollow where the fires raged in the caverns below. For a few seconds, the wall remained standing, defying the laws of gravity but suddenly, with an enormous roar, the rest of the giant structure followed, collapsing into the furnace and sending a maelstrom of rubble and flames into the castle bailey.

The wall of fire and rubble smashed into the massed Christian ranks, deadly to man and beast alike, and as the Templars looked on in horror, the waiting foot soldiers were engulfed in the inferno.

Men screamed in pain as the flames burned the flesh from their bones but blinded by fire and unable to get free from their own massed ranks, the panicking lines descended into chaos, a pandemonium of screaming, dying men.

The force of the blast reached past the desperate defenders, engulfing the many tents and wooden huts situated throughout the bailey, setting fire to anything that would burn. Horses to the rear whinnied in fear and broke from their harnesses to rampage through the castle, their caparisons in flame. Women screamed from the upper bailey and fell to the floor covering their babies with their bodies in desperation. The chaos was overwhelming and as the lucky few watched on, hundreds of men and horses died without a blow being struck in anger, burned alive in a hurricane of stone and fire.

The sky immediately turned dark, filled with smoke and dust but even as the castellan looked up, hundreds of tiny lights illuminated the darkness as if a thousand distant stars were falling to earth. For a second, Simon was transfixed but as the first of the lights slammed into the chest of a Templar sergeant next to him, he realised what they were. Fire Arrows.

'Take cover,' he roared but it was too late and volley after volley of fire arrows rained down into the castle. New fires raged everywhere throughout the fortress, engulfing anything that would burn.

'My Lord,' shouted Sir Rénier, 'what are your orders?'

Simon didn't reply, he just gazed around the castle as if in a trance, transfixed at the sight of so much death and destruction.

'My Lord,' shouted Rénier again, 'the lines have fallen. Shall we dismount and defend the breach?'

Again, there was no response and Rénier turned to take matters into his own hands.

'Templars dismount,' he roared, *'every man to the breach before it's too late.'*

All the remaining knights raced down the bank and as they, and the last of the defenders rushed to defend the castle, Simon of Syracuse slowly turned his horse to ride up into the upper bailey.

'Where are you going?' roared Rénier, but it was no use, the castellan either couldn't or wouldn't hear him.

Inside the guard tower, Hassan groaned as he gradually returned to consciousness. Blood flowed from the wound on the side of his head where Bullard's chain mailed fist had split open his skin and his breathing was shallow from the broken ribs caused by the officer's kicks.

Slowly he got to his feet and leaned against the wall to catch his breath. Outside he could hear the screams of fear and pain as people panicked amongst the devastation. He opened the door and peered out, seeing only destruction and carnage. Bodies lay everywhere and he could see that the main wall had disappeared, replaced by a fiery hell of flames and rubble. He gasped in horror, holding his hand against the burning pain in his side. He had known the walls may fall but seeing the reality was a horror he had not expected.

Knowing there was no more he could do, his mind turned to Sumeira. The castle had fallen but there was still a chance he could get her to safety. He staggered from the tower and headed towards the upper bailey; his body wracked with pain.

Outside the castle, Shirkuh ad-Din couldn't believe what he was seeing. Never in his wildest dreams could he have expected such a devastating result and even from his position several hundred paces beyond the timber palisade, he could hear the screams of men and beasts as they were burned alive.

To his front, a thousand archers filled the air with a permanent blanket of arrows, stopping the defenders from mounting any sort of counterattack. Volley after volley flew through the sky, adding to the devastation but even as he watched, he could see the movement of armed men within the smoke and he knew he had to act.

'Archers,' he roared, 'prepare to change your aim.' He turned to face the army lined up behind him, holding his scimitar high above his head. *'To the death,'* he roared *Allah Akbar!'*

As one, thousands of Saracen warriors raced across the open ground to attack the breach. Archers that had loosed their arrows into the middle of the castle moments earlier changed their aim towards the defenders still up on the remaining castle walls, their sheer firepower stopping even the bravest of Christian archers from lifting their heads above the parapet.

Women ran throughout the castle, desperately looking for their menfolk amongst the devastation. More collapses followed as the last of the supports burnt through in the tunnels below and as they stared in fear, one of the gate towers collapsed sideways, killing dozens more men and women alike.

Others raced to help whoever they could, guiding the burned and the blinded up into the lesser affected upper bailey, but even as the few survivors scrambled away from the devastation, they knew there was no place to run.

Amongst them all rode the castellan, silent and calm, as if he hadn't a care in the world, his white cloak hanging regally from his shoulders. Those running to escape the flames stared in astonishment as the Templar dismounted and headed towards the rear of the castle. As he walked, he saw the body of a young girl laying in the dirt, bloody and seemingly lifeless. He stopped and stared down, watching the blood run smoothly down her forehead where she had been struck by a flying piece of rubble. Suddenly the moaned and her small hand clenched in pain as she started to cry.

For a moment, the castellan emerged from his daze, his deeper consciousness recognising the girl needed help and he leant down to scoop her up into his arms.

'Worry not, child,' he said quietly, 'you'll be safe with me.' He continued walking towards the far end of the upper bailey, oblivious to the disaster happening behind him.

'My Lord,' shouted a voice and he turned to see Sumeira standing next to a burning tent. She too was filthy and bled from dozens of tiny scratches on her face and arms where the dust cloud had hit her but there was no serious damage.

'My Lord,' she said again, 'what are you doing?'

The Templar looked up at healer staring into her eyes with a gaze as blank as the darkest sky.

'This girl is hurt,' he said, 'I'm going to find help.'

'I am her mother,' said Sumeira. 'You can give her to me.'

'No,' said Simon, shaking his head. 'You are going to die. All of you. The only chance she has is with me.'

Sumeira swallowed hard. It was obvious by the man's tone and manner that he had lost his mind and she had to be careful.

'My lord,' she said, 'if you put her down, I can tend her wound and then we can all leave this place. I am a healer and can make her well again.'

'There is nothing here for her except death,' said Simon. 'With me, she will live, and I can beg God for forgiveness in her name.'

'But she is my child,' gasped Sumeira, her eyes welling with tears, 'she belongs to me.'

'She belongs to God,' said Simon and turned to walk away.

'Nooo,' screamed Sumeira and ran at the knight, desperate to retrieve her daughter.

The castellan turned and with one swipe of his mailed fist, knocked her to the floor before drawing his sword with his free hand and pressing it against the woman's throat.

'Stay away from me,' he shouted.

'Hold,' roared a voice and Simon turned to see Sir Rénier walking towards him through the smoke.

'My Lord,' said the Under-Marshal, 'we need you at the breach. What's going on?'

'Nothing that concerns you,' said Simon. 'Just walk away.'

'I don't understand,' said Rénier, 'your place is with the men, not up here with the women. What are you doing?'

'I told you,' growled the castellan, 'this is none of your business.'

Before Rénier could answer, Ramaz ran through the smoke, stopping in his tracks as he saw the standoff between the two knights.

'What's happening,' he asked to the castellan. 'My Lord, we have to go.'

'Go where?' shouted Rénier, his hand creeping to the hilt of his sword.

'Nowhere that concerns you,' said Simon turning to face Rénier, 'now back off.'

'My lord,' gasped Ramaz, 'please, we really have to go.'

'I know where they are going,' gasped Sumeira from the ground at the knight's feet. 'He's trying to escape the castle, the two of them are.'

'Escape,' said Rénier, 'what do you mean?'

'These are the traitors you have been seeking,' cried Sumeira. 'They caused all these people to die are now fleeing like the cowards that they are.'

'What are you talking about?' shouted the Under-Marshal. 'Sir Simon is no traitor.'

'Oh no?' said a voice behind him, 'why don't you just ask him?'

They all turned to see Hassan limping heavily through the smoke. His clothes were filthy, and his face covered with blood from his wounds.

'Who are you?' asked Rénier.

'I work with the Brotherhood,' said Hassan weakly, 'and was coming to inform you about a tunnel that escapes this place.'

'A tunnel?'

'Aye. One built by that man,' he pointed at Ramaz, 'a traitor who even now urges his comrade to leave alongside him.'

Rénier turned to Simon.

'What is he saying, my lord?' he said. 'Tell me he is lying.'

The castellan withdrew the sword from Sumeira's throat and took a step back. The healer got to her feet and turned to face him.

'My Lord Knight,' she said, her voice shaking in desperation, 'I don't know what is going on here and I don't care, all I ask is you return my little girl to me.'

Simon stared at Sumeira without responding.

'Please,' she said, 'I implore you. We may not have much time left and she needs to be with me.'

'She needs to be in a place of safety,' said the castellan, 'I can provide that. She is my penance and my forgiveness.'

'She needs to be with her mother,' said Sumeira and took a step forward, holding out her arms. 'Please, she is all I have.'

Instead of answering, Simon turned to look into the frightened girl's eyes.

'I would have looked after you, little girl,' he said eventually, 'I am a good man and promise you would have been safe,' He lowered Emani to the ground and as the girl ran back into her mother's arms, turned to face Sir Rénier.

'I do not want to hurt you, Sir Rénier,' he said, 'now do what is best and return whence you came.'

'Tell me what's going on,' growled the Under-Marshal, 'tell me these people are lying.'

Simon looked at Hassan before turning to face the Under-Marshal again. Behind Rénier, in the lower bailey, they could hear the roar of the Saracen warriors as they poured through the breach.

'Your men need you, Sir Rénier,' he said calmly, 'now be on your way.'

'*No,*' roared Rénier, drawing his sword, 'not until I know what is going on.'

'The Outremer is doomed, my friend,' said Simon. 'Jerusalem will fall, of that, there is no doubt. It may be this year or in a hundred years, but the end result is the same so why get killed for defending the indefensible?'

'*What are you talking about?*' gasped Rénier, 'Jerusalem won't fall, it belongs in Christian hands. *It is God's will.*'

'We don't belong here,' said Simon. 'These people walked these hills long before our ancestors ever set foot upon these shores. This land belongs to them, not us. All I have done is bring forward the inevitable.'

'And you took Saracen gold for this?'

'A man has to live,' said Simon. 'We all do what we have to do.'

'*You sold us out,*' gasped Rénier, 'like the boy said. You are a traitor, not just to your brothers or to the king but to Christianity itself.'

'Call it what you will,' said the knight. 'My conscience is clear.'

'*How can your conscience be clear?*' roared Rénier. 'Hundreds, if not thousands of men are dead or soon will be because of your treachery. Look to the fires, Templar, see how many men suffer the torments of hell in your name. Listen to their screams and tell me that Saracen gold was worth it because from here, I only hear pain and terror.'

Simon of Syracuse lifted his gaze and stared past Rénier. High up on the battlements, he could see dozens of men fighting and dying against the swarming Saracens while down in the bailey, the few men left fought a futile last stand. It was obvious they were doomed to failure and as he watched, he swallowed hard, the cries of fear and pain echoing in his brain.

'Oh, sweet Jesus,' he whispered eventually, '*what have I done?*'

'My Lord,' cried Ramaz, 'forget them. There are horses waiting at the foot of the cliff. Come now while we have the chance.'

Sir Simon stared at the overseer and then down at the sword still held loosely in his hand.

'I'm not going,' he said simply.

'What?' gasped Ramaz. 'There is nothing you can do now, the castle is lost, we have to leave.'

'I said, I'm not going,' said the castellan, 'and neither are you.'

Before Ramaz could respond, the knight spun around and struck the overseer's head from his shoulders, sending it bouncing across the dirt to rest against Hassan's feet.

Sumeira screamed and pulled Emani closer to her, hiding her daughter's head in the folds of her dress as Sir Rénier ran across to place the point of his own blade against the Templar's throat.

'Tell me why I shouldn't kill you right here,' he shouted, 'give me one good reason.'

Sir Simon stared at the Under-Marshal; confident he could easily disarm the man. Instead, he dropped his sword in the dust and lifted his head.

'I cannot,' he said, 'do what you have to do.'

Rénier gritted his teeth but despite the point of his blade drawing blood, he could not bring himself to press it home.

'No,' he said finally, stepping back from the Templar, 'I will not release you from your shame. You do not deserve it.'

'My Lord,' gasped a voice and they turned to see a wounded knight staggering through the smoke. 'The Saracens have taken the lower bailey; the castle is lost.' As the last of the words left his mouth, he fell forward into the dust with three arrows sticking out of his back.

Sir Simon turned to Rénier.

'The day is done,' he said, 'take these people and get out while you can.'

'And what of you,' snarled Rénier, 'where are you going, back into the arms of your true master?'

'In a way, yes,' said Simon, 'now be gone before it is too late.' Without waiting for an answer, he walked over to his horse and climbed back into the saddle.

'What are you doing?' shouted Rénier.

'To do what I should have done months ago,' said the castellan and turned away to ride through the smoke towards the lower bailey.

When he had gone, Sir Rénier looked around the partly built walls in desperation. In amongst the rubble and smoke, dozens of terrified people stared back, desperate for his help.

'You,' he said, pointing at Hassan, 'you said something about a way out.'

'Aye my lord,' said Hassan. 'It's over there in the far wall.'

'Then take these people through,' he said, 'I'll see how many more I can round up.'

Sir Rénier followed the disgraced castellan, through the smoke, emerging near the small wall that separated the upper and lower baileys. Coughing violently, he wiped the burning smoke from his eyes and stared into the carnage below. The Saracens had already taken the lower bailey and were now attacking the slope leading to the upper half of the castle. Men lay dead in their hundreds, scattered across the ground like autumn leaves while those that remained fought furiously, no longer for the castle, but to retain their lives. The Under-Marshal looked over to the right, seeking the castellan and saw him astride his horse looking over the furnace still roaring in the giant pit. Even from his position, Rénier could feel the heat and he knew it would be days before the inferno died out.

As he watched, the castellan turned his horse and rode several yards away before turning again to face the firestorm. He made the sign of the cross on his head and chest before looking over to face Rénier.

'I will not ask your forgiveness, my friend,' he shouted, 'I just hope that you realise, that in my moments of weakness, I did what I thought was right.'

'I will never forgive you, Simon of Syracuse,' shouted Rénier, 'and neither will God.'

'We will find out soon enough,' replied the castellan and with an almighty roar, dug his spurs deep into his horse's flanks, sending it galloping forward to soar over the flames, and deep into the fires of hell itself.

Sir Rénier stared in horror down into the fire pit. There was no way the castellan could ever have hoped to escape the inferno and he knew that in his madness, Sir Simon of Syracuse, devoid of honour, had paid for his treachery with the only thing he had left. His own life.

In the upper bailey, Sumeira hustled the people past, urging them towards the food store where Hassan leant against the door, guiding them through.

'Quicker,' he said, 'do not stop. As soon as you are on the other side, hide amongst the bushes on the cliff.'

More and more terrified people came through the rubble. Amongst them were the sick and the wounded, all desperate to escape the awful battle behind them. Eventually, Sir Rénier appeared through the smoke carrying an injured child.

'That's about it,' he said, handing over the child, 'the rest are beyond help. Get yourselves out of here.'

'What about you?' asked Sumeira.

'My place is here with my men. There is yet a chance we can defend the upper bailey, but you have to go. Lock the door from the other side, that way you will gain more time.'

'If we do that, you cannot follow.'

'Either way, we will not follow,' said Rénier, 'now go.'

The Under-Marshal turned and walked back through the smoke towards the fighting leaving Sumeira, Emani and Hassan alone amongst the rubble.

'Are you alright?' asked Sumeira.

Hassan looked up. Every inch of his body ached, and dried blood mingled with the dust across his face. His expression was one of exhaustion and he looked at the end of his strength.

'I will be fine,' he said, 'now take Emani through. I will follow.'

'Are you sure?' said Sumeira, 'for I will not leave without you. Your work is done here, Hassan, do not think you can make any difference by staying.'

'I'll be right behind you,' said Hassan, 'I swear.'

Sumeira gave a tight-lipped smile and turned to enter the food store, ushering Emani before her.

Hassan's head dropped again, and he grimaced as waves of pain shot through his chest. He pushed himself upright and turned towards the doorway when a voice called out behind him.

'Wait.'

Hassan turned around to see Bullard standing a few paces away holding a leather satchel and a food bag.

'Well, well,' said the officer, 'if it isn't our own pet Saracen. You escaped.'

'What do you want, Bullard?' said Hassan.

'Isn't it obvious? Now that little drama has been concluded, I can get out of here. I saw it all from amongst the rubble. Who'd have thought the castellan was a traitor.'

'Shouldn't you be fighting alongside your command?'

'And die for no reason? Nah, I think I'll take my chances out there.' He nodded towards the food store. 'Besides, I've taken a liking to your healer friend. She'll keep my bed warm for a few nights I'd wager.'

'She would never go with you,' growled Hassan, 'she is too much of a lady.'

'Who said she would have a say in the matter?' said Bullard. 'Now get out of my way.'

Hassan stared at the officer, anger burning in his soul. There was no way he could better the man in a fight and there would be not enough time to run into the tunnel and bolt the door. All he could do was delay him as long as possible.

'Stay back,' said Hassan.

'Or what?' said Bullard.

'Or I swear I'll kill you.'

'Really,' laughed Bullard, discarding the satchel and food bag, 'with what, your bare hands?'

Hassan reached for his knife, but the sheath was empty, lost amongst the mayhem of the last few hours.

'I'm warning you, boy,' said Bullard, drawing his sword, 'this time I will finish the job.'

'Do what you have to do,' said Hassan, 'I am going nowhere.'

With a roar of rage, Bullard charged forward, swinging his sword to cut Hassan in half. Despite his injuries, Hassan threw himself downwards, crashing into the officer's knees, driving one of them backwards.

Bullard cried out in pain as something snapped inside and he fell against the wall in agony. He turned quickly and glared at Hassan, laying in the dust.

'You'll pay for that,' he snarled, 'and before you die, know this. I'm gonna have that woman and her pretty daughter. And when I've finished, I'm going to kill them both real slow. That's down to you, Saracen, their fate will be your fault.'

Hassan scrambled across the ground, gasping for breath as his ribs sent waves of agony through his body. He tried to stand but fell again, rolling onto his back as Bullard limped across to finish the job. Hassan's arms stretched out, trying to find leverage to get up but his hand found something else, something far more useful.

Bullard loomed above him but half-blinded by the pain from his damaged knee, failed to see the threat and as he raised his sword to deal the killing blow, Hassan drove the castellan's discarded sword up through Bullard's groin.

The officer fell backwards, screaming in agony and Hassan scrambled to his feet. Quickly he grabbed Bullard's own knife from the wounded man's belt and dropped to straddle his victim's chest.

'I told you I would kill you,' he hissed as blood ran from the officer's mouth, 'this is for every woman you ever raped.'

With tears of rage pouring down his face, Hassan plunged the knife down through one of Bullard's eyes.

The following day, Hassan and Sumeira sat amongst a group of people hiding in the hills. Behind them in the distance, clouds of black smoke still billowed skyward above Chastellet, now occupied entirely by the Saracen forces. Exhausted from their sleepless night, the escapees rested amongst in a copse, praying that no one would find them before nightfall. Everyone talked in whispers and shared what little they had, knowing that discovery meant living the rest of their lives in slavery, or worse.

Hassan sat against a tree, exhausted after his ordeal. His face and clothing were still splattered with Bullard's blood and his breathing was laboured.

'How are you doing?' asked Sumeira, pouring some water on a rag to wash the blood from his face.

'I'll live,' said Hassan.

'We owe you our lives, Hassan, all of us do.'

'I did what anyone else would have done,' said Hassan.

'Nevertheless, it was you and I will never forget it.'

'We are not safe yet,' said Hassan. 'We still need to get to Tiberius.'

'God will look after us,' said Sumeira, 'now see if you can get some rest. There is a long walk ahead of us tonight.'

Hassan closed his eyes but as tired as he was, all he could think about was Bullard's dead face.

Sumeira walked amongst the rest of the escapees offering whatever aid she could. Finally, she came to a group of four people and knelt down to help comfort a crying baby.

'I'm sorry, my lady,' said the mother, 'I'm trying to keep her quiet, honest I am.'

'Just do your best,' said Sumeira with an encouraging smile.

'What's that?' asked another woman at her side, 'I heard something.'

'Where?' asked Sumeira.

'In the trees,' said the woman getting to her feet, 'someone's coming.'

Everyone stood up and stared into the undergrowth. The sound of several people approaching was now obvious but there was nothing they could do. All the survivors grouped together, frightened at what was about to happen.

Hassan forced himself through the group to stand at the front, bearing his knife and the castellan's sword, a last forlorn hope of defence.

'Get ready to run, my lady,' he said, 'I'll do what I can.'

Everyone stared, their hearts in their mouths but as the first man burst from the trees, Hassan dropped to his knees in relief, tears rolling down his face. It was Thomas Cronin.

'*Cronin,*' gasped Sumeira and ran forward to embrace him.

'*Sumeira,*' said Cronin, shocked and looked over her shoulder at the rest of the survivors. 'What happened?'

'We escaped,' said Sumeira, 'but thought you were Saracens.'

'There are no Saracens around here,' said Cronin, 'in fact, I am here with the army led by Baldwin himself. We heard the baby crying and came to investigate.'

Everyone stared at the sergeant in disbelief.

'The king is here?' asked Sumeira eventually.

'Aye, at the bottom of this hill along with five thousand men at arms. We've come to relieve the castle.'

'You're too late, master Cronin,' said Hassan without looking up.

'What do you mean, Hassan,' said Cronin, 'what's happened?'

'What I mean,' said Hassan, looking up from his place in the dirt, 'is that there is nothing any of you can do. The Saracens have won, Cronin. Chastellet has fallen.'

Chapter Thirty-Nine

October – AD 1179

Two Months Later

Hassan stood alongside his horse, looking down at the caravan heading for the port of Acre. Beside him were Hunter and Cronin, all finally reunited after the fall of Chastellet eight weeks earlier. The carts below carried many of the survivors that Hassan had helped escape from the doomed castle, amongst them, John Loxley, Sumeira and her daughter Emani.

The fall of Chastellet had been an unprecedented disaster for the Christians in the Outremer. The Saracens had overrun the castle killing hundreds in the battle and slaughtering hundreds more in the aftermath. Any survivors had been taken into slavery and the castle torn down stone by stone.

'She'll be safe now,' said Hunter at Hassan's side. 'The road to Acre is protected by Henry of Champagne's men and when she gets there, she can buy safe passage.'

'Where did she get the money?' asked Hunter.

'It was in Bullard's satchel,' said Hassan, 'along with several other trinkets he had stolen from his victims.'

'So, what are you going to do now?' asked Cronin, turning to Hunter. 'Are you going to stay with Arturas?'

'Aye, I think so,' said Hunter. 'We work well together, and the king has given him a year's contract. What about you?'

'I've been posted to Karak along with the rest of the Templars who survived.'

'Sir Raynald's castle?'

'Aye.'

'Well one thing is certain,' said Hunter, 'you will not be easily bored out there. Raynald will see to that.'

'I signed up to serve the order,' said Cronin, 'so will take whatever comes my way.'

'What about you, Hassan,' said Hunter, 'I hear you are heading east?'

'Aye,' said Hassan, 'I am. I thought my future was with the Templars, but many things have happened since first I saw master Cronin on the dock at Acre. Now I know my path lies eastward, back to my own people.'

'I hear you have a pretty little thing waiting for you there,' said Hunter with a wink.

'I hope so,' said Hassan, 'her name is Kareena and she is more beautiful than the stars in the sky.'

'I wish you well, Hassan,' said Hunter, 'I really do and hope our paths meet again someday.' He turned to Cronin, 'Until next time, my friend,' he said, reaching out his arm, 'take care.'

'Something tells me we will meet again, brother,' said Cronin taking the scout's wrist in friendship.

'Aye,' said Hunter, 'of that I have no doubt.' He turned away and with a kick of his heels, headed back the way he had come to rejoin the mercenaries waiting for him at the base of the hill. When he had gone, Hassan turned to Cronin.

'So, what really happened?' he asked. 'We suffered the siege for five days, yet the king was only half a day's ride away. Why did he not come, Cronin, what held him back?'

'To be honest, I still don't know,' sighed Cronin. 'Sir Raynald claimed his army wasn't ready, but I think the king was still suffering after Banias and Marj Ayyun and didn't want to risk a third defeat. By the time we found you in the hills, there was nothing we could do to aid Chastellet, so the king just turned his army around and headed back to Tiberius.' He looked over at the boy. 'What you did in Chastellet was very courageous, Hassan,' he said, 'you do know that don't you? Many of the people down in that caravan are only alive because of you.'

'All I did was lead them out,' said Hassan. 'The path was already there.'

'Nevertheless, you were the one to find it and lead them to safety. I reckon if I told the order of your bravery, they would immediately fulfil your dream of becoming a squire.'

'It is a tempting offer, master,' said Hassan, 'but the desert is pulling at my heart. If you release me from my bond, I will return to my people.'

'I am not your master, Hassan,' said Cronin, 'and the only bond between us is one of brotherhood.'

'How many of those you called brother survived?'

'Twelve knights and ten sergeants.'

'And the rest?'

'All dead.'

'Did you hear anything about Sir Jakelin?'

'Nothing. I'll say a prayer for him in the chapel at Karak.' He reached out and grabbed Hassan's shoulder. 'It's time to be going my friend, but you be careful out there, it's still a dangerous path for a man alone.'

'I won't be alone,' said Hassan, 'there is a Bedouin scout named Abdal-Wahhab who will ride alongside me.'

'Is he that one-eared Bedouin I have seen you talking to?'

'Aye, it is. He is from the same village as Kareena. We were supposed to ride back yesterday but he said he had things to attend, something about paying a debt. We leave in the morning.'

'Then fare ye well, Hassan,' said Cronin. 'Until the next time.'

'Travel well, Thomas Cronin,' said Hassan and watched the Templar sergeant ride his horse down the track to return to Tiberius.

Later that night, in the forests of Banias, the last of the Saracen tribes sat around their fires, talking about the great battle and how they had torn the Christian castle down stone by stone. Even now, weeks later, the mood was high and the celebrations went on late into the night.

Finally, the men went back to their tents, exhausted and looking forward to the long ride to Egypt the following day. The Mamluks had fought hard over many campaigns and were at last heading home.

Bakir-Shah stayed alone by one of the fires, happy to stay beneath the stars, and as the forest gradually fell quiet, he dropped into a deep sleep with nothing but a thin blanket to keep himself warm.

In the depths of the night, when the fires had reduced to embers, Bakir-Shah's eyes shot open and he held his breath in fear, recognising the feel of cold steel resting lightly upon his throat.

'Don't move.' whispered a voice, 'or it will be the last move you ever make.'

'Who are you?' whispered Bakir-Shah, his voice calm despite the threat.

'An old friend,' said the voice, 'and I have come for payment.'

'Payment for what?' asked the Mamluk officer.

'For this.' said the voice and a hand dangled a necklace in front of the Mamluk's eyes.

'What is it?' asked Bakir-Shah, not recognising the withered lump at the end of the cord.

'It's an ear,' said the voice, my ear.'

Bakir-Shah thought furiously and finally recognised the voice.

'Abdal-Wahhab,' he said, 'I remember. What do you want?'

'Revenge,' said the man and before the Mamluk commander could answer, he thrust his blade deep down into the Mamluk's throat, cutting off any cries for help. Bakir-Shah shuddered and gasped at the pain, his hands clawing at his throat as the blood pumped out of the wound to splatter on the Bedouin's face.

'That's not just for me, my friend,' he said, forcing the blade through to sever the spine, 'but for the death of every man that fell to your blade. Now, they are even.'

Epilogue

May – AD 1180

Damascus

Eudes de St. Amand sat on a stone slab beneath one of the buildings in Damascus. His body was emaciated and weak from the many beatings he had received at the hands of his captors. The cell was hardly five paces square with no blanket or light, and he had only an overflowing bucket for waste.

In the distance, he heard the jingle of keys and he got to his feet, expecting the twice-weekly flask of water and a stale loaf of bread. The keys rattled in the lock and as the door flew open, two guards walked in and pushed him back down onto the slab. A third stood just inside the doorway, his profile illuminated by the lights of the torches burning in the corridor behind him.

Amand squinted, trying to see the man's face but it was too dark.

Outside, the jailer continued to open doors and the sound of prisoners being dragged from their cells echoed through the prison.

'Grand Master Amand,' said the half-hidden man, drawing Amand's attention back to his own predicament, 'I hear you are being obstructive.'

'I am a man controlling my own will,' said Amand, 'nothing more.'

'You certainly are stubborn,' said the voice, 'and if truth be told, it surprises me not, though it may yet be your undoing.'

'You know nothing about me,' said Amand.

'On the contrary,' came the reply, 'I know far more than you think for we have met several times, across the field of battle.'

'Who are you?' growled Amand.

'I am known as Farrukh-Shah, loyal servant to Allah and nephew to Salah ad-Din, Sultan of all Syria and Egypt.'

'Saladin's henchman,' spat Amand.

'Name-calling is for the children of the street,' said Farrukh-Shah. 'I have come here to represent the Sultan himself.'

'To slit my throat?'

'No, to offer you your freedom.'

'So, you have finally agreed on a price.'

'We have.'

'And how much blood money am I worth?'

'Not a single dinar,' said Farrukh-Shah. 'All we want is the return of one man in return.'

'And who is this man?'

'It doesn't matter,' said Farrukh-Shah, 'all we asked is for the lowest of all their prisoners to be returned, whether he be a foot soldier or one of our slaves. Anyone will do.'

'And in return, you will set me free?'

'We will. '

Amand got slowly to his feet and stared at the Saracen General.

'I don't understand,' he said, 'I am worth a fortune to the king. Why do you not ask for gold?'

'Because to us, you are a man, nothing more.' He tilted his head, listening to the sound of the others being dragged from their cells. 'Do you hear that?' he asked. 'That is the sound of your fellow prisoners being taken to their freedom. Templar knights, Jerusalem knights, even some foot soldiers, all freed in return for a ransom. Hugh of Ibelin and Hugh of Galilee both commanded more than their weight in gold for their release, but for you, Grand Master, we will accept the life of the lowest of the low.'

Amand stared at Farrukh Shah, his ire rising.

'And you think that I will accept,' he growled, 'that I, Eudes de St. Amand, Eighth Grand Master of the Knights Templar, will walk out of here knowing you have valued my life as equal to the lowest of your unbelievers?'

'Are all men not equal under the eyes of your God?' asked Farrukh-Shah.

'All Christian men,' said Amand, 'your people are just filth, fit for nothing more than dying beneath the blades of those doing God's work.'

'I will give you one more chance,' said Farrukh-Shah. 'Just accept the exchange and you can join your comrades. You will be back in Jerusalem within days.'

Amand stared into the unflinching eyes of Farrukh Shah before stepping back.

'Never,' he said, 'I would rather die than accept the comparison.'

'So be it,' said Farrukh Shah with a sigh and stepped back out of the cell while the guards secured the lock. As he turned to walk away, the Grand Master flew against the inside of the cell door, beating his fists against the thick timber.

'*I am Eudes de St. Amand,*' he roared, '*Eighth Grand Master of the Knights Templar*. Do you hear me, Farrukh-Shah? I am worth a thousand of your men, ten thousand. Are you listening? Tell your master that I am a Christian to my soul, but I would rather rot in hell than accept that there is any Muslim, alive or dead that is my equal. *Do you hear me, Farrukh Shah? Are you listening?*'

The Saracen general kept walking, not acknowledging the desperate cries of the knight as they faded in the distance. Salah ad-Din had offered him his life, but he had chosen differently.

Outside he waited as the chained prisoners were dragged into the sunlight. Each had commanded a fine ransom, especially the Templars and were to be freed immediately, their lives having been bought by the King of Jerusalem. He watched as they filed out, each chained to the other as they stumbled into the sunlight. Most lifted their hands against the sun and crouched in fear at the sight of the guards who had made their lives hell in the cells. All except the last man in the chain, a tall man who despite his injuries, stood tall and proud.

One of the guards walked over, drawing a cudgel from his waistband but Farrukh-Shah called out, stopping him in his tracks. He approached the prisoner and stared into his eyes.

'You,' he said slowly, 'I have seen you before. What is your name?'

'Me?' said the prisoner, returning the stare. 'My name is Jakelin de-Mailly, Brother of the Knights Templar. Remember it well, Farrukh-Shah, *for I swear you will hear it again.*'

The End

Author's Notes

As usual in these sorts of books, historical facts have been intertwined with fiction, enabling a much easier read around the reality of the battles and the events leading up to them. Wherever possible I have stuck to the facts but allowance must be made for artistic license. In the notes below I have tried to highlight the more important information, separating fact from fiction.

Terminology

The term *'Saracen,'* was a general derogatory name often used for any Arab person at the time. It did not refer to any one tribe or religion and was considered offensive by many of the indigenous cultures of the Holy Land.

Similarly, the term *'Crusader,'* was never used in the twelfth century as a reference to the Christian forces. They were usually referred to as the *'Franks* or *Kafirs'* by the Saracens.

The *'Outremer,'* was a general name used for the Crusader states, especially the County of Edessa, the Principality of Antioch, the County of Tripoli, and the kingdom of Jerusalem.

The Knights Templar

The Order of the Poor Fellow-Soldiers of Christ and of the Temple of Solomon was formed in or around AD 1119 in Jerusalem by a French knight, Hugues de Payens. They were granted a headquarters in a captured Mosque on the Temple Mount in Jerusalem by King Baldwin II.

At first, they were impoverished, focussing only on protecting the weak on the road to Jerusalem but after being supported by a powerful French Abbot, Bernard of Clairvaux, the order was officially recognised by the church at the Council of Troyes in AD 1129. From there they went from strength to strength and soon became the main monastic order of knights in the Holy Land. Their influence grew across the known world, not just for their deeds of bravery but because of their business acumen and the order went on to become very wealthy and very powerful.

The Emblems of the Templars

The Templar seal was a picture of two men riding a single horse. This is thought to depict the order's initial poverty when it was first formed though conversely, one of the rules of the order was that two knights could not ride one horse. When travelling or going to war, they rode under a white flag emblazoned with a red cross. Some historians believe it was in honour of St George, who's spirit many soldiers believed was seen at the battle of Antioch in AD 1098 during the first crusade.

The image of the cross was also used on other items of clothing and equipment by the Templars, and indeed other orders of warrior monks (though not in red.) However, research shows that the red cross was not officially adopted until it was awarded by Pope Eugene III in AD 1147. Before this time the knights wore only a plain white coat.

Templar Ranks Used in This Book

The Grand Master was head of the Templars and was in charge of the entire order, worldwide. Odo de St. Amand (often known as Eudes) was the Grand Master of the Templars between AD 1171 and AD 1179. He was a powerful leader and fought in several campaigns but was most prominent in the Battle of Montgisard where he and a relatively small number of Templar knights led the charge that ultimately defeated a far superior Saracen army led by Saladin himself.

During times of war, the Seneschal organised the movement of the men, the pack trains, the food procurement, and other issues involved in moving an army.

The Marshal, on the other hand, was very much a military man, and the Master would usually consult with him, as well as the Seneschal before making any final decisions on tactics.

King Baldwin IV

Baldwin IV ruled the kingdom of Jerusalem at the time, and though others claimed otherwise, he was also the king of the Oultrejordain, the lands to the east of the river Jordan and the dead sea. He suffered terribly from Leprosy and though was often debilitated by the disease, often led his forces into battle, even if it meant being carried on a stretcher. Despite his young age, he was considered a strong and capable leader.

Eudes de St. Amand

The Templar Forces at the time were led by the Grand Master, Eudes de St. Amand. It was he who was instrumental in persuading the king to build the castle in the first place. Amand was a formidable character, well versed in the practices of warfare and politics. He was unrelenting in his drive to further the order's interests and resolute in defence of its existence and reputation. During the battle of Marj Ayum, he was captured by the Ayyubid and held in a prison in Damascus for over a year. Apparently, Saladin tried to exchange a Muslim prisoner for the Grand Master's life but Amand himself refused the exchange, preferring death over having his own life valued equal to that of a Muslim.

William of Tyre

William is reputed to have been the king's teacher when Baldwin was a boy and went on to become his advisor and chronicler. Whether he had the level of influence he enjoys in our story is unknown but there is no doubt that his chronicles have become the best record about life in Jerusalem at that time.

William was not a fan of Grand Master Eudes de St. Amand and held him solely responsible for the catastrophic loss at Jacob's Ford. He recorded the following:

'He was dictated by the spirit of pride, of which he had an excess' and referred to him as *'a worthless man, proud and arrogant, having the spirit of wrath in his nostrils, neither fearing God nor having reverence for men.'*

Raynald of Châtillon

Raynald was the son of a French noble who joined the third crusade in AD 1146. He served as a mercenary in Jerusalem before marrying the princess of Antioch, Constance of Hauteville in AD 1153. This made him the prince of Antioch and he soon became known for his brutality and warlike tendencies. Always in need of funds, his reign was cut short in AD 1161 when he was captured by the Muslim governor of Aleppo after a raid in the Euphrates valley against the local peasants. He spent the next fifteen years in jail before finally being ransomed and set free.

King Baldwin made him *'Regent of the kingdom and of the armies,'* in AD 1177 and he was one of the leaders at the famous battle of Montgisard.

Jakelin De Mailly

Although his role in this book is fictional, Jakelin De Mailly was a famous French Templar Knight who became renowned for his ability in warfare. I found no accounts that he fought at Jacob's Ford, but he came to prominence a few years later at the infamous battle of Hattin, more of which can be read in the next book, Templar Blood.

Humphrey II of Toron

Humphrey was the Lord of Toron at this time. It was indeed his intervention at the battle of Banias that saved the king from being captured. Humphrey later died of his wounds.

Raymond III of Galilee

Raymond was the Lord of Galilee at the time and answered Baldwin's call to arms after the battle of Banias. He succeeded in defeating Farrukh-Shah but was subsequently defeated by Saladin who had been watching from the nearby hills. It was at this battle that Eudes de St. Amand was captured, later to die in captivity at the hands of the Ayyubid.

Henry II – Lord of Champagne

Henry arrived at Acre around this time along with his army, having taken the cross earlier that year. Saladin would certainly have been aware of this sudden strengthening of the Christian forces which probably explains why he did not press home his military advantage by attacking the city of Jerusalem.

Simon of Syracuse

In this story, Simon was the traitorous Templar who betrayed the Christians to Saladin. Though there is no hard evidence that this actually took place, there is certainly evidence that a Templar Knight of the same name betrayed the order around that time. It is also true that a Templar knight, probably the castellan of Chastellet, rode his horse into the heart of the pit of fire when defeat was inevitable.

Jacob's Ford

Jacob's Ford, also known as Vadum Iacob, was an important crossing point over the River Jordan just north of the sea of Galilee, laying directly on the traders' route between the cities of Acre and Damascus. Due to the marshy ground to the north and the unstable nature of the River Jordan to the south, it was also the safest crossing point for many miles in either direction.

Technically within the kingdom of Jerusalem, the ford was under Christian control though people of all races used it freely on a daily basis. The inhabitants of the area were mixed with some owing allegiance to Damascus while others were ruled by Jerusalem. For years, despite its strategic importance, there was no military fortress constructed on the site, with the nominal border between the lands of the Christians and the lands of the Muslims being represented by a lone Oaktree.

With the rise of Salah ad-Din, the Leper King, Baldwin IV, became increasingly concerned about the growing threat from Damascus. The vulnerability of the crossing at Jacob's Ford meant the fertile lands of Galilee to the west were at increased risk from attack and with the responsibility of defending the kingdom of Jerusalem falling more and more on the shoulders of the Knights Templar, it soon became clear that something had to be done.

The Construction of Chastellet

In AD 1178, the Order of the Knights Templar, commanded by its Grand Master, Eudes de St. Amand, persuaded the reluctant king, Baldwin IV, to undertake the construction of a huge fortress near the crossing. This castle, when complete, would not only provide complete control over Jacob's Ford but also provide a base from which they, (The Templars,) could launch military campaigns into Saracen territory with probably Damascus as the ultimate prize. Despite his misgivings, the king eventually relented and in October AD 1178, construction began in earnest.

The castle was intended to be one of the greatest in the Outremer with some reports suggesting it would have been as big, if not greater than Crac de l'Ospital, (known today as Krak de Chevaliers) the majestic crusader fortress occupied by the Knight's Hospitaller. It was built on top of a hill overlooking the ford and reports suggest that the imposing walls sat atop glacis buttresses, the steep sloping walls at the base of a castle designed to slow down any attackers' advance to the main wall, while still exposing them to the weapons of the defenders above.

Research suggests that the walls were at least ten metres tall and upon completion, would have been defended with several towers situated at the corners and along the walls themselves. The space inside would have easily held a garrison of over a thousand men and horses along with all the necessary support mechanisms needed for such a huge castle to operate.

Upon completion, it would have been a majestic fortress, ideally situated to control all traffic between the eastern region and the west, as well as a base from which Baldwin could despatch his forces to raid the lands of the Ayyubid. But more than this, it would have been a statement to all his enemies, highlighting his military strength, his dominance of the region, and his unfailing dedication to defending Jerusalem.

Saladin's Response

After the devastating rout of his forces at the battle of Montgisard where over twenty-five thousand of his men were defeated by an army of ten thousand Christians led by eighty-eight Templar knights, *(The Brotherhood - Book One, Templar Steel,)* Saladin fled to Egypt on a racing camel.

For the next year or so he consolidated his strength in Egypt before turning his attention on the troublesome tribes to the east. Towards the end of this period he became aware of the construction of Chastellet, and, realising the devastating effect it would have over the control of the region, tried diplomacy to persuade King Baldwin to abandon his plans. When this failed, he offered the king the sum of sixty thousand golden Dinars, increasing it to a hundred thousand when the first offer was refused. When this was also declined, he knew he would have to deal with the threat by different means.

The First Battle

In the spring of 1179, while Chastellet was still only half-built, Saladin sent his nephew Farrukh-Shah out to monitor the king's army to the south of Damascus. Seeing an opportunity, Farrukh-Shah ambushed the king's party with devastating force and only the heroic actions of Humphrey of Toron stopped the king himself from being captured.

Seizing the initiative, Saladin immediately attacked Jacob's Ford, hoping to take advantage of the confusion. However, despite being only half-built, the fortress was already more than strong enough to withstand the assault and when one of the Sultan's leading Emirs was killed by a well-aimed arrow from a knight named Rénier de Maron, Saladin called off the siege and retreated to set up a camp at a place called Banias.

Farrukh-Shah on the other hand, continued his rampage into the Christian lands west of the Galilee, raiding the harvest before heading back east of the Jordan. A furious Baldwin called upon Raymond III to assemble an army and set out in pursuit of Saladin's nephew.

The Battle of Marj Ayyun

Eventually catching up with Farrukh-Shah at the Litani River, Raymond, along with other Christian forces, inflicted a terrible defeat on the Muslim army. However, unbeknownst to Raymond, the whole battle had been observed by Saladin from some nearby hills and the Sultan counter-attacked with the full strength of his own forces.

The Christian army fled back across the river Litani to take shelter in the fortress of Beaufort, but those left behind on the other side of the river were slaughtered without mercy.

It was at this battle where Eudes de St. Amand was captured along with many other Christian knights, some eventually being ransomed back to the king.

Baldwin returned to Tiberius to rebuild his forces, thinking that Saladin would also retreat eastward but within a few months, the Sultan once again attacked, but this time, his sole focus was the castle at Jacob's Ford.

The Siege of Jacob's Ford.

On the 24th August AD 1179, Saladin attacked the castle at Jacob's Ford for the second time. This time his army was far bigger and though the outer walls of Chastellet had now been completed, he laid siege, fully aware that the main Christian army was only a few days ride away in Tiberius. In addition, the imminent arrival of Henry II of Champagne meant that time was limited and he had to act quickly or be at risk of defeat from the combined Christian armies.

Inside the castle, the Templar defenders, along with many others, numbered well in excess of a thousand and though the inner buildings and many of the towers had not yet been completed, they were more than confident they had the defences and manpower to repel the Ayyubid army.

Saladin, however, was not interested in breaking through the walls, instead, he sent sappers under the castle to set huge fires, weakening the defensive structures above. At first, the attempt failed as the fires, although fierce, were not big enough. Saladin paid his men a Dinar for every bucket of water taken in to extinguish the fires so the miners could widen the passage. On the fifth day, one of the walls collapsed, affording the Ayyubid army complete access into the castle.

The following battle was brutal and research suggests approximately seven hundred Christians were killed, many more executed and over eight hundred others taken prisoner.

The castellan of Chastellet, upon realising his fortress was lost, is reported to have ridden his horse directly into the furnace of the giant pit formed by the collapse of the walls.

Having received a plea for reinforcements from Chastellet days earlier, King Baldwin was already leading his army from Tiberius but he was too late. By the time he was within striking distance, he could see the castle was in flames and completely destroyed.

Saladin's army piled the dead into the water cisterns, but their corpses soon spread disease and his army was heavily infected. By the time the Sultan left, the castle at Jacob's Ford was no more than a ruin and the surrounding area ravaged by his men. The following year of drought devastated the region further and any hope of building a fortress at Jacob's Ford was abandoned.

The Aftermath

To celebrate their victory, the Ayyubid eventually built a Mosque on the hill as a reminder of their great victory. In the following centuries, most of the stones from the fortress were reused in other nearby building projects including a bridge over the River Jordan called The Daughters of Jacob, a bridge that remains to this day.

The terrible defeat of the Christian forces at Jacob's Ford was a turning point in the crusader wars and Saladin's success encouraged him to hugely increase his effort against those he saw as invaders of the Holy Land. His control of Syria and Egypt became total and he was successful in uniting most of the warring eastern tribes against the Christians.

Skirmishes and minor conflicts continued over the next few years with the Ayyubid usually coming out on top until eventually, the two sides met once more in a great battle beneath the peaks of two mountains called the Horns of Hattin, a battle that would probably decide the ownership of the Holy Land once and for all.

Continue the Journey in

The Brotherhood – Book III

TEMPLAR BLOOD

More books by K M Ashman

The India Sommers Mysteries
The Dead Virgins
The Treasures of Suleiman
The Mummies of the Reich
The Tomb Builders

The Roman Chronicles
The Fall of Britannia
The Rise of Caratacus
The Wrath of Boudicca

The Medieval Sagas
Blood of the Cross
In Shadows of Kings
Sword of Liberty
Ring of Steel

The Blood of Kings
A Land Divided
A Wounded Realm
Rebellion's Forge
Warrior Princess
The Blade Bearer

The Brotherhood
Templar Steel – The Battle of Montgisard
Templar Stone – The Siege of Jacob's Ford

(Coming Soon)
Templar Blood – The Battle of Hattin
Templar Fury – The Siege of Acre
Templar Glory – The Road to Jerusalem

Standalone Novels
Savage Eden
The Last Citadel
Vampire

Audio Books
Blood of the Cross
The Last Citadel
A Land Divided
A Wounded Realm
Rebellion's Forge
The Warrior Princess

Printed in Great Britain
by Amazon